"May very well give J. K. Rowling a run for her money."
—*School Library Journal*

✦➼○⇐✦

"If you have kids who love Harry Potter and are constantly casting about for similar books to read, Gideon might be just the ticket."
—EntertainmentWeekly.com

✦➼○⇐✦

"Buckley-Archer spins a rip-roaring tale replete with the raw details of life in the eighteenth century . . . Nonstop action, appealing secondary characters, and healthy dollops of humor, all of which will have readers panting for the sequel."
—*Kirkus Reviews*

Also by Linda Buckley-Archer

The Gideon Trilogy, Book One: THE TIME TRAVELERS
(previously titled GIDEON THE CUTPURSE)

LINDA BUCKLEY-ARCHER

THE
TIME
THIEF

BEING THE SECOND PART OF
THE GIDEON TRILOGY

ALADDIN PAPERBACKS
NEW YORK   LONDON   TORONTO   SYDNEY

ALADDIN PAPERBACKS
An imprint of Simon & Schuster Children's Publishing Division
1230 Avenue of the Americas, New York, NY 10020
Copyright © 2007 by Linda Buckley-Archer
First published in Great Britain in 2007 as *The Tar Man* by Simon & Schuster UK Ltd
First U.S. edition, 2007
All rights reserved, including the right of reproduction in whole or in part in any form.
ALADDIN PAPERBACKS and related logo are registered trademarks of Simon & Schuster, Inc.
Also available in a Simon & Schuster Books for Young Readers hardcover edition.
Designed by Al Cetta
The text of this book was set in Caslon Old Face BT.
Manufactured in the United States of America
First Aladdin Paperbacks edition November 2008
2 4 6 8 10 9 7 5 3 1
The Library of Congress has cataloged the hardcover edition as follows:
Buckley-Archer, Linda.
[Tar man]
The time thief / by Linda Buckley-Archer.—1st American ed.
p. cm.
Summary: When an attempt to bring Peter and Kate back to their own time is bungled, Peter finds himself stranded in 1763 while the Tar Man, a villainous eighteenth-century criminal, returns with Kate to twenty-first-century London.
ISBN-13: 978-1-4169-1527-0 (hc)
ISBN-10: 1-4169-1527-3 (hc)
[1. Time travel—Fiction. 2. Robbers and outlaws—Fiction. 3. Great Britain—History—
George III, 1760–1820—Fiction. 4. London (England)—Fiction.] I. Title.
PZ7.B882338Tim 2007
[Fic]—dc22
2007017859
ISBN-13: 978-1-4169-1528-7 (pbk)
ISBN-10: 1-4169-1528-1 (pbk)

For
Catherine Pappo-Musard

Contents

CONTENTS

CONTENTS

TO THE READER

The accidental discovery of time travel in a laboratory in Derbyshire sent two twelve-year-old children hurtling through the centuries, and once set in motion, the train of events triggered by the unlikely encounter of a golden Labrador, a Van de Graaff generator, and an antigravity machine seemed unstoppable.

It is said that a person's nature is only revealed in adversity. If that is so, then the events described in this volume will put the characters of Peter Schock and Kate Dyer into sharp relief. For, as I have previously described, it was at the instant these children believed they were leaving the eighteenth century never to return, that they were plunged into a new set of circumstances which would test their courage to the limit. Kate and her father, Dr. Dyer, managed to return to their own time, but Peter was left stranded in 1763, his place taken by the Tar Man, a villain whose path, it seemed, they were fated to cross.

Dr. Dyer blamed himself for the escape into our century of the Tar Man, henchman to the corrupt Lord Luxon, and one of the most gifted and feared criminals in the London underworld of 1763. Here was a man who, at a tender age, was hanged for a crime he did not commit, and when, miraculously, he managed to cheat death at the gallows, it left him angry at the world that had dealt him such a cruel blow. Yet Dr. Dyer should not have been so quick to blame himself—after all, who can shut Pandora's Box once it has been opened?

It was of much comfort that Gideon Seymour would be at Peter's side, trapped as he was in 1763. Formerly in the employ of Lord Luxon, along with the Tar Man, Gideon had befriended the children at great risk to himself. Despite his brief career as a cutpurse, Gideon was an honorable young man who, as Parson Ledbury said on more than one occasion, had a more finely tuned conscience than any man of the cloth of his acquaintance. As in the first volume of this tale, it is to Gideon's unique testimony, *The Life and Times of Gideon Seymour, Cutpurse and Gentleman*, 1792, that I sometimes turn.

The crucial role that Gideon Seymour played in the disastrous aftermath of the discovery of time travel is yet to be related. However, this present volume must focus on the stories of two characters above all—the Tar Man, also known as Blueskin, and Kate Dyer. It chronicles the former's dramatic entrance into the twenty-first century and the latter's brave and determined search through time for her young friend, Peter Schock.

This is not a story about hopeful beginnings and easy endings; this is a story about characters who find themselves in a harsh place, not knowing—which is true for us all—how it will all end, and always conscious that only hope and determination stand between them and disaster. The Marquis de Montfaron, who always displayed such steadfast faith in science and truth, was very fond, as you will see, of philosophy. Kate noted down some of his ideas because they gave her comfort when her own grip on time was failing. Kate asked me if I could reproduce them here and this I am very happy to do.

Time is not our master, despite the relentless swing of the pendulum. Through the power of memory and of imagination, do we not swim through the rivers of time at will, diving both into our past and our future? Equally, the notion that time is constant is mere illusion. The passage of time, which is irrelevant in our dreams, is ignored in activity and is only truly experienced in a state of extreme boredom. Therefore, do not let time be your master, rather, seek to master time.

—*Citoyen Montfaron, ci-devant Marquis de Montfaron* (Citizen Montfaron, formerly Marquis of Montfaron), 1792

THE TIME THIEF

I DID NOT SLEEP THE NIGHT I FEARED WOULD BE MY LAST ON EARTH. INSTEAD, MY MIND'S EYE SURVEYED THE FAMILIAR LANDSCAPE OF MY LIFE'S JOURNEY AND I TRIED TO MAKE WHAT SENSE OF IT I COULD. MY FEVERED MIND SWUNG BETWEEN TERROR OF THE NOOSE THAT WAS TO SQUEEZE THE LAST BREATH OUT OF ME; ANGER AT THE INJUSTICE OF MY PLIGHT; AND BLIND, THREADBARE HOPE THAT MY OWN STORY WOULD NOT END—JUST YET.

I DID NOT SLEEP. HOW COULD I WASTE ONE SECOND OF THE LIFE THAT REMAINED TO ME? TO BE ALIVE! JUST TO BE ALIVE! TO THINK AND FEEL AND SEE AND TOUCH! YET I BELIEVE THAT BY THE TIME DAWN BROKE OVER NEWGATE GAOL, I HAD MADE MY PEACE WITH GOD AND I PRAYED, NOT ONLY FOR MYSELF, BUT ALSO FOR HE WHO HAD FALSELY CONDEMNED ME: LORD LUXON.

OFTTIMES IN THE INTERVENING YEARS, I HAVE DESIRED TO RECALL THOSE DARK HOURS IN MY CONDEMNED CELL—NOT FOR THE HORROR OF IT BUT FOR THE CLARITY IT BROUGHT TO MY SOUL. FOR NOTHING IS MORE PRECIOUS THAN LIFE ITSELF—AND NOTHING IS EASIER TO TAKE FOR GRANTED. I NEVER FORGET THE DEBT I OWE TO MY RESCUERS WHO RISKED SO MUCH TO PLUCK ME FROM THE JAWS OF DEATH AT TYBURN: TO THE LATE SIR RICHARD, AND PARSON LEDBURY, BUT, MOST OF ALL, TO KATE AND TO PETER.

A SMALL FLICKER OF HOPE LIVES ON THAT PETER AND HIS CHILDHOOD FRIEND MIGHT ONE DAY, BY THE GRACE OF GOD, BE REUNITED, BUT WE NO LONGER SPEAK OF IT. THERE IS ONE EXCEPTION, HOWEVER. ON THE ANNIVERSARY OF THE DAY MY LIFE WAS SAVED AND PETER'S BIRTHRIGHT WAS LOST, PARSON LEDBURY HAS LONG BEEN IN THE HABIT OF CALLING AT HAWTHORN COTTAGE, BEARING BOTTLES OF HIS BEST CLARET. WE SIT UNDER THE SPREADING BOUGHS OF THE OAK, AND AS WE WATCH THE SUN SET OVER THE VALLEY WHICH WELCOMED PETER INTO OUR CENTURY SO MANY YEARS AGO, THE THREE OF US RAISE OUR GLASSES TO LIFE, TO ABSENT FAMILIES, AND TO THE HEALTH AND HAPPINESS OF MISTRESS KATE DYER.

IT WAS, OF COURSE, ON THAT SAME DAY, AUGUST 1, 1763, THAT THE TAR MAN, IN TAKING HIS PLACE AT THE MAGIC MACHINE, STOLE THE LIFE THAT RIGHTFULLY BELONGED TO PETER. HAVING CHEATED DEATH AT THE GALLOWS, WE SHARE MORE THAN ONE BOND, BLUESKIN AND I. I PITY HIM NOW ALL THE MORE, AS I TRULY UNDERSTAND HOW HIS BITTERNESS TOOK AWAY ANY CHANCE OF HAPPINESS ON THIS EARTH. MANY IS THE TIME I HAVE WONDERED WHAT PETER'S CENTURY HELD IN STORE FOR THE TAR MAN AND WHAT HE DID WITH THE LIFE THAT HE STOLE.

—*THE LIFE AND TIMES OF GIDEON SEYMOUR,*
CUTPURSE AND GENTLEMAN, 1792

ONE

OXFORD STREET

*In which the Tar Man has his first encounter
with the twenty-first century, and Kate and Dr. Dyer
agree to conceal the truth from the police*

It was late afternoon on December 30, the last Saturday of the Christmas holidays, and freezing fog had settled, shroudlike, over London. It had been dark since four o'clock and wherever street lamps cast their orange glow, droplets of moisture could be seen dancing in the icy air.

In Trafalgar Square, seagulls, drawn inland by the severe weather, perched on top of Nelson's head. In St. James's Park, pelicans skidded on frozen ponds. Harrods, its immense contours outlined by a million twinkling lights, appeared to float down Knightsbridge like a luxury liner. To the east of the city, dwarfing St. Paul's Cathedral, gigantic skyscrapers disappeared into the fog, their position betrayed only by warning lights blinking like ghostly spaceships from within the mists.

Meanwhile, in a dank, dark alley off Oxford Street—a road that in centuries past led to a place of execution at Tyburn—a homeless man was stuffing newspapers down his jacket and covering himself with layers of blankets. His black and white dog, who had more than a touch of sheepdog in him, lay at his side, shivering. The echoing noise of the street and the *drip*, *drip*, *drip* of a leaking gutter swiftly lulled the man to sleep and he did not even stir when his dog got to its feet and gave a long, low growl. If the man had looked up he would have seen, looming over him at some yards distant, silhouetted black on black, and perfectly still, an alert figure in a three-cornered hat who sat astride a powerfully built horse. His head was cocked to one side as if straining to hear something. Satisfied that he was alone, the dark figure slumped forward and laid his cheek against the horse's neck, expelling the breath that he had been holding in.

"What manner of place is this," he complained into the animal's ear, "to unleash all the hounds of hell for making off with a single prancer? Though 'tis true you wouldn't look amiss even in the stables at Tempest House. You have spirit—I shall keep you if I can."

The Tar Man patted the horse's neck and wiped the sweat from his brow, though every nerve and sinew was ready for flight or combat. In his years as Lord Luxon's henchman he had earned a fearsome reputation. Few dared say no to him, and if they did they soon changed their mind. He had his hooks caught into enough rogues across London, and beyond, that with one twitch of his line he could reel in anything and anyone. Nothing happened without the Tar Man hearing of it first. But here, wherever "here" was, he was alone and unknown and understood nothing. It suddenly struck him that his journey here had stripped him of everything—except himself. He clutched instinctively at the scar where the noose had seared into his flesh so long ago. *What I need*, he thought, *is sanctuary. And a guide in this new world* . . .

The Tar Man knew precisely where he was and yet he was lost. The roads were the same but everything in them was different. . . . This seemed to be London yet it was a London alive with infernal carriages that moved of their own accord at breathtaking speed. The noises and the smells and the sights of this familiar, yet foreign, city tore his senses apart. He had hoped that the magic machine would take him to some enchanted land where the pavements would be lined with gold. Not this . . .

He became suddenly aware of a faint scraping of heels on gravel behind him. Then a flicker of torchlight illuminated the deeply etched scar that cut a track down the blue-black stubble from his jaw to his forehead. He wheeled around.

"Stop! Police!" came the cry.

The Tar Man did not answer but dug his heels into the sides of the horse he had stolen two hours earlier from the mounted policeman on Hampstead Heath. Without a second's hesitation, horse and rider jumped clear over the vagrant and his dog and plunged headlong into the crowds. The frenzied barks that followed him were lost in the blast of noise that emanated from the busiest street in the world.

Wild-eyed, the Tar Man stared frantically around him. It was the time of the Christmas sales and half of London, after a week of seasonal overindulgence, was out in search of bargains. Oxford Street was heaving with shoppers, packed so densely that it took determination to walk a few feet. Never-ending streams of red double-decker buses and black cabs, their exhausts steaming in the cold, moved at a snail's pace down the wide thoroughfare.

The Tar Man drove his horse on, vainly trying to breach the solid wall of shouting pedestrians that hemmed him in. His heart was racing. He had stepped into a trap of his own making. He berated himself furiously. *Numbskull! Have I left my head behind as well as my nerve? Do I not have sense enough to look before I leap?*

If he could have, the Tar Man would have mown down these people like a cavalry officer charging into enemy infantry. But he could scarcely move an inch. He was trapped. Glancing around, he saw a group of men in dark blue uniforms emerging from the alley, pushing their way violently toward him, as menacing as any band of footpads of his acquaintance. Curiously, one of them was shouting into a small object he held to his lips.

Everyone was jostling and pressing up against him and screaming at him to get out of the way. All save a little girl who reached up to stroke the horse's moist nose. Her mother snatched her hand away. The Tar Man's eyes blazed. *I have not come this far to fall at the first post! They shall not have me! They shall not!* And he leaned down into the mass of pedestrians that pushed against him, and when he reappeared he was gripping a large black umbrella as if it were a sword. He thrust it at the crowd, jabbing at people's chests and threatening to thwack them around the head to make them move away. Their piercing screams reached the policemen, who renewed their efforts to reach him through the crowds. Soon, though, the Tar Man had won a small circle of space in which to maneuver. He reversed the horse as far as it could go and whispered something into its ear. The policemen, now only five yards away, watched open-mouthed as they beheld a display of horsemanship the likes of which they were unlikely ever to see again.

The Tar Man held the horse still for an instant and then urged his mount into a majestic leap. Four horse hooves exploded like a thunderclap onto the top of a black cab. The impact was deafening. All heads turned to discover the source of the commotion. Skidding and sliding on the shiny metal, the horse could not keep its footing for long and the Tar Man, his great black coat flying behind him, guided it onto the next cab and then the next and the next. . . . Hysterical passengers scrambled to get out onto the street. Pedestrians stopped dead in their tracks. And, looking down from their ringside seats on the upper decks of buses, people gawked in disbelief at the spectacle of the Tar Man and his horse playing leapfrog with the black cabs from Selfridges to beyond John Lewis. Soon screams were replaced by laughter and whoops and cheers and the furious shouts of a long line of outraged cabbies. The merest hint of a smile appeared on the Tar Man's face, but just as the thought flashed through his mind to snatch off his three-cornered hat and take a bow, he became aware of an unworldly wind and a rhythmic thrumming that caused the ground beneath him to vibrate. He looked up.

The police helicopter slowly descended. It hovered directly above the Tar Man, its blades rotating in a sickening blur. When a booming voice, like the voice of God, spoke, he held up an arm to his face and paled visibly, paralyzed with fear.

"Get off your horse. Get off your horse and lie on the ground!"

A pencil beam of blinding, blue-white light moved over the Tar Man. He was center stage, spotlit for all to see. The visitor from 1763 could not have orchestrated a more public entrance into the twenty-first century if he had hired the best publicist in London.

The pilot's magnified and distorted voice bounced off the high buildings into the foggy air:

"GET OFF YOUR HORSE! NOW!"

The Tar Man did not—could not—move. The helicopter descended even lower. In a reflex action to stop his three-cornered hat from blowing away, he clasped it to his head and, somehow, this simple action seemed to break the spell. He managed to tear his gaze away from the giant, flying beast and quickly scanned his surroundings for an escape route. Out of the corner of his eye he thought he recognized an alley from the Oxford Road he knew. Praying it would not be a dead end, he tugged sharply on the reins and urged his horse on. The crowd was less dense here and the Tar Man broke out, unchallenged, from the circle of light and vanished into black shadows. The helicopter pilot, anxious not to lose his prey, instantly flew higher and headed to the south of Oxford Street, training his searchlight onto half-lit sidewalks and picking out bewildered shoppers in its powerful beam, but the fugitive horseman was lost to sight.

The Tar Man emerged from the alley and rode at breakneck speed through the network of quieter streets toward Piccadilly. Onward the Tar Man galloped, never stopping nor slowing down. He encountered few of these outlandish carriages that moved without horses, and whenever he did see one, the Tar Man charged directly at it, wielding his umbrella fearlessly and daring it to attack him. In every case the strategy worked—the carriages squealed to an immediate halt. But how little bottom their passengers displayed, cowering behind those queer, curved windows! *Faith, they are meeker than milkmaids! Why do they not challenge me?*

"Does no one ride in this city?" he yelled at a young man in a black MINI Cooper. "Where are the horses? Where is the dirt?"

The bewildered man shook his head slowly from side to side.

The Tar Man took off again. Onward he galloped, but always above and behind him he sensed the thudding of the flying beast getting nearer. He backtracked and hid in doorways and still managed to outwit his airborne pursuer. As he rode, window displays of impossible refinement flashed by—extraordinary costumes and shimmering jewels, all illuminated by lights that seemed as bright as the sun. *With candles or lamps as powerful as these,* he thought, *the city need never sleep.* Moon-cursers and cutthroats and assassins would be at pains to find a dark enough spot in which to do their business.

Sirens still wailed all around, but like the insistent whirring sound of the helicopter, the fearful noise was beginning to recede into the distance. The Tar Man allowed himself to slow down and he scrutinized the sky above. To the west of him, he could just make out the fuzzy white line of the helicopter's searchlight piercing through the swirling fog. He let out a sigh of relief.

The horse was tiring. Steam rose from its flanks and its breath came out in short bursts. When the Tar Man turned a corner into a grand square and saw that there was an enclosed garden at its center, he decided to rest there awhile. He whispered into his horse's ear, clicked his tongue, and galloped toward the iron railings. The horse sailed over them and came to a halt under the cover of trees. The square was deserted except for a few couples strolling around its perimeter. The Tar Man slid off the horse and patted its neck.

"You have done well, my friend," he said. The horse blew noisily through its velvet nostrils and reached down to tear what blades of grass it could from the clipped turf. The Tar Man walked over to one of the wooden benches that lined the gravel path and slumped down. He put his head in his hands. He was trembling—whether on account of the cold or the danger he did not know.

Unnoticed by the Tar Man, a police car glided into Berkeley Square, and when its driver spotted the horse, he turned off his engine and spoke into his radio. Slowly and quietly, two police officers got out of the patrol car and scrambled over the iron railings, landing noiselessly on damp earth.

A gray squirrel, ferreting about among plastic wrappers in the litter bin next to the Tar Man, disturbed him. He looked up. As he did so, he caught sight of the row of fine, tall buildings on the east side of the square. Distressed, he jumped up and looked at the west side and then looked to the south. His heart skipped a beat. Did he find himself in Berkeley Square? Could that huge edifice be Landsdowne House? He tipped back his head and peered up at the topmost branches of plane trees. These trees must be nearly two hundred years old!

"How in heaven can this be?" he exclaimed aloud. "This *is* Berkeley Square!"

He had accompanied Lord Luxon here only last month on a trip to see Mr. Adams, the architect, who was trying to persuade his master to sell his house on Bird Cage Walk and build a five-story house here in Berkeley Square instead. Yet there had not been a single plane tree in sight on that day and the front facade of Landsdowne House was barely started! The thought struck him that he had understood right from the start why this London was at the same time friend and stranger to him—yet he could not admit it to himself until now.

"I am undone!" he exclaimed aloud. "The machine has brought me to the future! How am I to return home?"

"Would this be your horse, sir?" asked a flat, deep voice behind him.

The Tar Man swung around. He had been surprised in attack too often in his time to hesitate. As soon as he saw the two men, dressed in the same uniform as his pursuers on Oxford

Street, he dived straight at their legs and grabbed a knee each, so that they toppled over one on top of the other. Before they were back on their feet, the Tar Man had already leaped onto his horse and was galloping away up the gravel path beneath the plane trees. The policemen ran back to their patrol car, radioing for assistance as they went.

The Tar Man's heart was pounding. These soldiers, with their ugly dark blue uniforms and cropped hair, were clearly not about to give up the chase. He was the fox and the pack of hounds was baying for his blood. Sirens blared from all directions. Then he heard the helicopter alter its course and move nearer. It was beyond his understanding how they did it, yet he was convinced that the soldiers could signal to each other from great distances. . . .

He had to find his way back to his old haunts, seek sanctuary at St. Paul's Church in Covent Garden. At all costs he must avoid the main thoroughfares where he would be easy game for the flying beast. Instead, he would head south toward Green Park and then east toward Leicester Square, taking care to avoid Piccadilly.

When the Tar Man turned into Dover Street, however, he was confronted by another horseless carriage, this time with blue lights blazing on its roof and a wailing siren so piercing it hurt his ears. It accelerated straight at him at tremendous speed. The Tar Man pulled on the reins so sharply that the horse reared up into the air on its back legs. He retreated backward and turned around, only to see two more police cars coming

toward him from the direction of Berkeley Square. Now he
fled toward Albermarle Street, but fearing that he would be
trapped into riding into Piccadilly itself where he would be too
exposed, he pulled up sharply and turned right into New Bond
Street instead. London was clad in different, garish clothes and
yet, here, its bone structure was still the same. He knew these
streets. He galloped recklessly on, but a moment later he knew,
without even needing to turn around, that his pursuers were
upon him.

"So," he cried to the horse, "it seems that you are the last
prancer in London and I am to be hunted down by persons
determined to offer me hospitality of a kind I should prefer to
refuse. . . . Ha! Damn their eyes, I say! If they're bent on nab-
bing us, let us not give them an easy ride!"

He swerved right into the Burlington Arcade and even as
he rode for his life through the glass tunnel of luxury shops,
all crystal and silver and jewels and silks, his jaw dropped at
the sight of such rich pickings. It was near closing time and
there were only half a dozen people left in the arcade. The
air rang with the deafening sound of horse hooves striking
polished stone.

"Hold, there!" he cried and pulled hard on the reins. His
mount reared briefly onto its hind legs and horse and rider came
to a skidding halt outside the window of a jeweler's shop. The
Tar Man's eyes devoured the king's ransom of precious stones
and gold that nestled in dove-gray velvet before him. A woman
in a pearl necklace and cashmere coat stood cowering next to

the same display. If the Tar Man was transfixed by the sight of a sapphire as big as a chestnut, sparkling under a spotlight, the woman was equally transfixed by the dark figure towering above her. She could feel the heat coming off his horse's steaming sides. The explosive roar of police motorcycles flying into Burlington Arcade broke the sapphire's spell, but the Tar Man was not going to flee without some reward. He switched his attention from the shop window to the woman's necklace in the blink of an eye. He snatched hold of her pearls and gave them a sharp tug. The clasp broke, leaving her neck bare and her face frozen in shock. Two powerful motorbikes screeched past her as, opening and closing her mouth like a fish out of water, she watched the Tar Man—and her pearl necklace—vanish out of sight into Piccadilly.

A few hundred yards away lay Piccadilly Circus. London was coming to life for the evening. Giant neon signs blinked on and off above the bustle of the street, black cabs deposited theatergoers close to Shaftsbury Avenue, and couples stood hand in hand outside restaurants, examining the menus. A large group of young tourists sat on the edge of the fountain under the statue of Eros. They were drinking from cans and were dressed in T-shirts despite the bitter cold. One of them filmed his friends as they stood, laughing and posing outrageously, on the steps beneath the fountain. When they suddenly stopped playing around, their attention drawn by something behind him, the boy turned and focused his lens on a sight that had not been advertised in the travel brochures.

A lone figure on horseback was galloping toward them, picking his way through the crowds on the sidewalk and the traffic in the street. In front of him, people scrabbled desperately to get out of his way. When a stunned driver braked right in front of him, the horseman simply jumped onto the roof of the car before continuing on his way toward Piccadilly Circus.

"Wow!" exclaimed the boy and zoomed in on the Tar Man's pursuers. A wall of police cars and motorcyles, headlights blazing and sirens screaming, stretched fully from one side of the street to the other. Above them all, a helicopter hovered angrily, like a wasp that has been brushed aside once too often and is getting ready to strike.

The boy trained his camera on the rider. He was wearing a bizarre black hat as well as a look of intense concentration, and the boy recognized an unmistakeable glint of enjoyment cross his face. A surfer on the crest of a wave of police cars! This guy was actually having fun! The boy gave a whoop of appreciation. Whatever he'd done, he sure had gotten under the skin of the police—they looked mad!

When the rider drew close to Piccadilly Circus tube station, and he saw the steady flow of people descending beneath the sidewalk, he slowed down briefly. Giving a cursory glance over his shoulder at the stream of patrol cars sweeping up behind him, he suddenly turned one hundred and eighty degrees and disappeared down the steep stairs into the London Underground. The horse had such confidence in his new master that he trotted down willingly, for all the world as if he caught the tube every day. Up above, police cars and motorcycles screeched to a halt. Passengers started to flee up the stairs in panic but immediately had to press themselves against the walls as a small army of uniformed officers converged on the ticket hall in hot pursuit of the desperado on horseback who had left a trail of destruction halfway across London.

A few minutes later, shortly after the horse had trotted calmly back up the steps, a man emerged from a different exit, wearing a tweed jacket several sizes too big for him. He had long black hair which settled in rats' tails on his collar and fell forward across his face, concealing the rather nasty scar on one cheek. The man set off, head down and hands in his pockets, in the direction of Covent Garden.

Kate woke up screaming, "Peter!"

Dr. Pirretti, who was driving the hired estate car up the M1 through dense fog, swerved involuntarily with the shock of it.

"Whoa!" she exclaimed. "That was a close call!"

Kate's Labrador, Molly, who was sitting in the trunk, started to whimper and put her golden head over the rear seat so that she could lick her face. Kate's father, Dr. Dyer, pushed the dog away.

"Everything's all right, Kate," he reassured her. "You're safe. I thought you were never going to wake up—you've missed all the fun. . . ."

"Where am I, Dad? What's happening?"

Kate was not quite awake and felt sick and confused and disoriented.

"You're going home. Anita is driving us back up to Derbyshire."

"Anita?"

"Dr. Anita Pirretti—from NASA. I told you—she and Ed Jacob came over from the States when they heard that you and Peter had disappeared from the lab. She's been team-leading the antigravity project. . . ."

"Too much detail!" protested Dr. Pirretti. "The poor kid's scarcely conscious!"

"Anita and Ed managed to get us out of Hampstead Heath without attracting too much attention."

"If we'd been spotted," laughed Dr. Pirretti, "we'd be in police custody by now! Your dad and I must have looked a tad suspicious bundling an unconscious girl and a dog into a car in the dark. . . ."

"Ed was no better. He certainly looked as if he was up to no good sliding the antigravity machine into the back of that massive van. . . ."

"Better too big than too small! . . . Kate, you don't know how glad I am to meet you at last. . . ."

But Kate was not listening.

"Dad!" she exclaimed, ignoring Dr. Pirretti. "What happened to Peter? Where is he? Did he make it?"

There was a pause. "No. Peter was left behind. The Tar Man took his place. . . . There was nothing I could do. . . ."

"But we've got to go back! We can't leave him there on his own!"

"I'm taking you back to your mother before we decide what to do next. . . ."

"What's to decide? We have to go back and get him!"

"Ssshh . . . Kate. Calm down. Everything will be fine. . . ."

"We *are* going back to get him, aren't we? I promised I'd never leave the eighteenth century without him!"

"Of course we are, love, but I'm not going to keep you from your mum a second longer than I have to. . . . She's been through enough. Not to mention your brothers and sisters. Sam was there when your mum took the phone call. He was beside himself—I couldn't tell if he was laughing or crying."

"Poor Sam."

Kate sighed deeply and let her tired eyelids close, but immediately the vivid memory of Peter being hurled backward from the antigravity machine came at her again, and for a split second she relived the horror of that moment. The dismay in Peter's dark eyes as he faded from view . . . She shuddered involuntarily and put her hand to her forehead.

"Does your head hurt?"

Kate nodded.

"Mine too. I'll give you some something for it."

"Do you think Molly's got a headache, too?"

"Probably."

Kate twisted round and stroked Molly's soft ears.

"Good girl."

Dr. Dyer poured some hot, sweet tea from a vacuum flask and passed it to Kate. She swallowed the painkillers her father held out for her, and then gobbled down the chocolate he proffered to take the taste away.

"Mmmm . . . I've missed chocolate."

Her father laughed. "So *are* you going to say hello to Anita?"

"Oh, I'm sorry. Hello, Anita."

"Good to meet you, Kate," said Dr. Pirretti. She spoke in a mellow Californian accent. "You've been on an amazing and unique journey—but I sure hope there won't be anyone following in your footsteps!"

"But we've got to go back for Peter!" exclaimed Kate, looking alarmed.

"Of course, we will," said Dr. Dyer quickly. "But for the time being, at least, we can be grateful that he's with friends. Gideon will look out for him until we can rescue him. . . ."

"But, Dad, Gideon will be on the run!"

"Well, if Peter *is* with Gideon, they'll just both have to be on the run for a while, won't they? And Gideon, of all people, knows how to handle himself when he's up against it. If he needs to get lost and stay lost in 1763, he'll do it. It's not like today, when you can't take a step without a security camera pointing at you."

"I *swore* I wouldn't come back without him. I feel so guilty that he's still there and I'm here. . . ."

"It was hardly your fault! Kate, I really think you should get some rest while you can. You look even worse than I feel and we won't be at the farm for a couple of hours at least."

"But—"

"No buts. You'll just have to be patient until we can sort this mess out. . . . Okay?"

Kate nodded reluctantly. She snuggled up to her father's shoulder and closed her eyes. She felt terrible, as if recovering from a bad illness. She fell in and out of sleep, vaguely aware of the hum of the car engine and the spasmodic conversation between her father and the woman with the American accent. Once she woke up and heard herself ask, still half-asleep: "Where's the Tar Man?"

"I don't know, love. When I woke up he was already gone."

When he was sure that Kate was finally asleep, Dr. Dyer discussed with Dr. Pirretti what they, or rather Kate, should say to the police—not to mention Peter's parents. They agreed that the only course of action open to them was to insist that Kate was suffering from amnesia. She would have to say that she could remember nothing that happened to her after running down the corridor after Molly in the laboratory.

"Will Kate be able to pull it off, do you think?" asked Dr. Pirretti.

"She understands how vital this is. I know she'll do her best. And although Inspector Wheeler won't give her an easy ride whatever she tells him, it'll be much easier for her to deny remembering anything than coming up with some far-fetched story which Inspector Wheeler will take great pleasure in demolishing. If he catches even the vaguest scent of the truth, we've had it. We'll never be able to kick over the traces."

They fell silent as the car sped through the foggy night toward

Derbyshire. After a while Dr. Dyer said: "I wish I'd managed to tell Peter that his father had tried to telephone him just as he and Kate were being catapulted across time. . . . They'd had a serious falling-out apparently. It occurred to me a couple of times to say something, but people were around and it just wasn't the right moment. I don't know what Peter's last memory of his dad was, but it certainly wasn't a good one. It's too late now. . . ."

"Don't beat yourself up about it, Andrew. How were you expected to know that the boy was going to leap off the machine and that an eighteenth-century villain was going to hitch a lift to the twenty-first century?"

"I feel bad about it all the same. . . . So what are you planning to do with the antigravity machine?"

"I've told Ed Jacob to keep it locked up in the van until he can find a safe hiding place. Then I want him to go back to the States to see Russ Merrick at MIT. I told you that one of the main reasons we came over to see you after Kate and Peter's disappearance was because Russ's antigravity machine vanished without trace the same night as his office cleaner. . . ."

Dr. Dyer nodded. "And you were speculating that the same thing had happened on both sides of the Atlantic. . . ."

"Except that now it transpires it was all a red herring. The cleaner wasn't lost in the mists of time, after all—he turned up in North Carolina."

"And the machine?"

Dr. Pirretti shrugged her shoulders. "It's a mystery. I feel uneasy about not even knowing whether it was stolen or not. I sincerely hope we won't live to regret being unable to trace it. Russ called me last night to say that he has nearly completed a prototype of an antigravity machine which incorporates elements of your friend Tim Williamson's design with his own."

"Did you tell him the real reason you commissioned him to build it so quickly?"

"No . . . and he's not going to be happy when Ed tells him that now that we have Tim's machine I want him to stop work on it. I don't think I'll mention that we intend to destroy it. . . ."

"Destroy it! But surely we should wait until we've got Peter back—what happens if Tim's machine has been damaged?"

"It's because of Tim Williamson that I'm in such a hurry to destroy both antigravity machines."

"What do you mean?" asked Dr. Dyer, alarmed at the mention of his colleague. "What's he done?"

"It's more a question of what he *will* do. He came to see me a couple of days ago. He said that if we've discovered time travel, before long someone else will, too. You can't un-discover something. You can't turn back the clock. Ha! Except now, it seems, you *can*. He said that it was absurd and illogical to walk away from something so momentous as the discovery of time travel."

"And, of course, if you say it quickly enough, that sounds perfectly reasonable," said Dr. Dyer.

"He was talking about patenting 'his' invention and approaching the Ministry of Defence to ensure that it didn't fall into the wrong hands . . ."

"How can it *not*, sooner or later, get into the wrong hands? People would kill for such a secret—surely Tim can see that!"

"I have this sinking feeling," continued Dr. Pirretti, "that there will never be an end to this. . . . We're doomed to failure. A bunch of King Canutes ordering the waves to stop."

"I'll go and see Tim and try and talk some sense into him. I can't say I'm surprised, though. A bit tough to know you've made a world-shattering discovery only to be told that you have to deny all knowledge of it. . . ."

Dr. Pirretti did not respond and Dr. Dyer saw a frown appear on her face in the rearview mirror. She looked exhausted.

"I keep thinking about the first nuclear explosion," she said. "And what Oppenheimer said when he saw that deadly cloud rise up into the sky, knowing that it was his own creation—'I am become Shiva, destroyer of worlds.'"

"Is that how you feel about time travel?" asked Dr. Dyer.

"Don't you? The more I think about it, the more terrified I am by what we've done."

Kate groaned in her sleep and her father tried to make her more comfortable, tucking in the blue tartan blanket that covered her knees and smoothing back the strands of red hair that tumbled over her face.

"Is she okay?" asked Dr. Pirretti.

"Yes. She's fast asleep. By the way," continued Dr. Dyer. "I meant to ask how *you* are doing. Did the hospital sort out your headaches?"

"No. Plus I'm now having problems with my hearing. Not

that I can't hear . . . sort of the reverse. It's difficult to describe. . . . Sometimes I think I'm . . ."

"What?"

"No . . . I mustn't make too much of it. My overactive imagination sometimes plays tricks on me." She changed the subject abruptly. "What are we going to do about our uninvited guest from the past? I guess it's our duty to track him down and send him back to his own time—though I suspect that he'll disappear out of sight never to be heard of again. After all, who's going to believe he's from the eighteenth century? What did you call him?"

"The Tar Man. It's on account of him being hanged for a crime which he probably didn't commit. Unfortunately for him, they didn't find out he was still alive until after he'd been covered in tar and strung up from a gibbet on the village green for the crows."

Dr. Pirretti shuddered. "Great . . . so you didn't just bring back anyone, you brought back an eighteenth-century villain with a grudge against the world!"

"It's not the Tar Man who's worrying me—it's Peter. You're . . . you're not actively *against* trying to rescue him, are you?"

Dr. Pirretti did not answer right away and then replied: "If you knew, for sure, that going back in time again could potentially damage the universe in some catastrophic way we can't yet envisage, would it be right to risk the safety of the rest of humanity for the sake of one innocent boy? That's the question I've been asking myself—and I don't know the answer."

The evening air in Covent Garden was full of applause and laughter. Large circles of people had formed around one of the street entertainers who are always ready to perform for the crowds near the market halls. This particular entertainer was riding on a unicycle as tall as a bus. He was inviting members of the audience to throw up a variety of objects, all of which he would endeavor to catch on his head, balancing all the while by pedaling backward and forward and holding his arms stretched out wide. Someone had thrown up an empty beer can and he had managed to balance it on his forehead while whistling "Oh my darling Clementine." This earned him a big round of applause. The Tar Man marveled at the bizarre contraption which the entertainer rode with such skill, and idly wondered about the beer can, which looked as if it were made of metal and yet appeared to weigh so little.

He stood, half-hidden behind a pillar, under the portico of St. Paul's Church, which rose up like a small Roman temple on the west side of Covent Garden Piazza. The Tar Man had stood in this selfsame spot so many times in his life—either sheltering from the rain or, more likely, on the lookout for fresh talent, as he watched the spectacle of London's villains plying their trade. He would admire the skill of a cutpurse filching a snuffbox, or perhaps a lace handkerchief, from a gentleman on his way to see Mr. Garrick in his latest role at the Covent Garden Theatre—and if he was any good his victim would be none the wiser. Or, on a moonless night, he would watch a gang of footpads lurking at the entrance to an alley, waiting for the linkboy to reappear, panting, into the Piazza. The linkboy, paid to escort a party through an unlit passage with his high lantern, would abandon his terrified victims in the darkness, helpless and ripe for the picking. . . .

The main entrance to St. Paul's Church was not in the Piazza but at the opposite end of the building through a pleasant churchyard to be reached via Bedford Street. The Tar Man had just come from there and he was not well pleased with the elderly church official who had refused him entry.

The church was hosting a concert that evening and a soprano's voice trilled and soared up into the night. It was fortunate for the Tar Man that the police had lost his trail because the sanctuary that he had claimed at St. Paul's was not going to be granted to him on this evening. The old man had even gone so far as to try and sell him a ticket.

"I ask for sanctuary and you demand ten pounds!"

"Or five for concessions. Are you a student or unemployed?" asked the old man, but his outraged interlocutor had already left in disgust.

Now, as the Tar Man stood looking out over Covent Garden Piazza, refused sanctuary in this world as he had been in his own, his mind turned to how he was going to make his way in this strange, modern world. It would be a new beginning. Powerful though he had been, the Tar Man was tired of being Lord Luxon's henchman. In this London he would bow to no one. . . . Fate had led him to the magic machine in Derbyshire and nothing would stop him from making his mark.

The crowd in front of him burst into peals of laughter. The Tar Man looked over and saw the cause of the merriment. A little girl, perhaps five years old, who announced that her name was La-La, had been invited to throw up some plastic rings for the entertainer to catch in his teeth. She found that she got more applause if she missed, and started to throw them randomly into the crowd instead. Sensing the entertainer's thinly disguised anger, the crowd was in fits of laughter. Soon, the entertainer had had enough of a child stealing his thunder and wound up the show. He took his final bow and passed around a top hat. The spectators reached into their pockets and coins rained into its silk interior. Those who drifted off without contributing, he shamed by shouting after them. Most of them sloped back guiltily and dropped fat pound coins onto the pile with a clink. When the entertainer thrust his hat at the Tar Man, he glanced up at him and coolly shook his head.

The street entertainer insisted and poked his hat, jingling with coins, at the Tar Man once more.

"So you expect me to provide you with free entertainment, do you?"

The Tar Man laughed in his face in such a way that the entertainer felt obliged to join in even though he felt the hackles rise on the back of his neck.

"Upon my word, sir, you do entertain me vastly!"

The Tar Man grabbed hold of the entertainer's arm with an iron grip and forcibly wrenched the hat from his grasp. He had stopped laughing and was fixing the entertainer with a stare that made his blood go cold. Without breaking eye contact the Tar Man flung the hat and all its contents onto the Piazza so that dozens of coins rolled all over the cobblestones.

"Oi!" squawked the entertainer and raised an arm in a fist as if to thump him. But the Tar Man easily deflected the half-hearted blow, and taking hold of the entertainer's ear, he twisted it mercilessly until the man sank to his knees, crying out with the pain of it.

"Where I come from, beggars have better manners," the Tar Man commented with an expression on his face that discouraged any thought of retaliation. "Pray that our paths do not cross again."

It pleased the Tar Man that his old haunts were as busy and lively as ever. And so respectable now that it made him want to laugh—what sights he had witnessed in these streets! No doubt the men in the dark blue uniforms had put a stop to that sort of thing. . . .

It is astonishing how quickly novelty wears off. After half an evening strolling around Covent Garden, the Tar Man was no longer shocked at the sight of women in trousers and with their hair cut short. In fact, he even appreciated it, in a way. But how the cloth merchants must suffer, he thought, on account of this fashion. Why, the material needed for one dress in his time would surely clothe three or four women now. He was no longer taken aback by girls revealing their ankles—and knees and thighs, for that matter. And he was already accustomed to seeing the large number of foreign faces. It took him longer, however, to get over the lack of poverty and malnourished faces on every street corner. . . . Gone were the armies of barefoot children and beggars in rags, skin stretched tight over bone. Instead he saw plump, clear complexions and shining hair and such white teeth! This truly was a land of plenty. He drank it all in and reveled in it. Was the whole of London like this? He loved the shop windows bright as a sunny day and the neon signs and the orange streetlights. The Tar Man quickly learned to keep to the sidewalk and noticed that if people wanted to cross to the other side of the street, they tended to walk over black and white stripes painted on the hard, dark surface. The Tar Man preferred to take his chances and darted through traffic, causing waves of drivers to screech to a halt or sound their horns. But as he played tag with the streams of horseless carriages, he began to take some interest in them. He admired the way they glided along and how the passengers looked so at ease inside. A low, silver carriage, parked on a quiet back street, caught his eye and the desire swept over him to sit inside it. He struggled in vain to open the door and ended up kicking it in frustration. When the vehicle came to life, screaming at him with an unworldly, pulsing, deafening howl and with lights flashing, the Tar Man fled as fast as his legs would carry him. But at the end of the street he turned back to look and saw an elderly man walking past the protesting vehicle, quite unconcerned. Intrigued, the Tar Man walked up to another carriage, this time a large, shiny green one, and waited until no one was looking. This time he did not jump quite as much when his kick provoked a stream of high-pitched staccato beeping. Again, no one seemed to take any notice. The Tar Man smiled to himself. *If these carriages could talk,* he thought, *they would be shouting "Stop, thief!" Save their plea falls on stony ground, for the good citizens do not care a fig for their predicament....*

Back in the main thoroughfares, the Tar Man observed that when people raised their hands, large black carriages would swoop to the pavement, whereupon the passenger would climb into the back and recline on a spacious seat and be transported away. Soon he, too, would command a carriage and ride in style through the streets of the city—but not yet. First, he needed to learn the rules of the game . . . and above all he needed a guide.

As the evening wore on, he became increasingly tired and hungry and thirsty. He stopped for a moment in front of a French restaurant and peered through an abundant display of flowers at elegant couples who sat at circular tables bathed in pools of gentle light and at attentive waiters in black waistcoats who proffered menus and brushed crumbs off white linen tablecloths. The Tar Man licked his lips. This was a tempting chop house; he could smell meat.

He made a note of the entrance where waiters periodically appeared laden with plates of steaming food. Then he waited for the right moment and walked confidently into the restaurant, weaving between the tables and making directly for the kitchens.

London is a tolerant city that welcomes eccentrics and the Tar Man's dress—overlarge tweed jacket over knee britches and buckled shoes, with a hairstyle resembling dreadlocks—provoked little comment and at least one complimentary remark. A girl indicated his knee britches, smiled, and gave him the thumbs-up sign. Unsure of the meaning of her gesture, the Tar Man nevertheless bowed his head in acknowledgment and continued into the bright, white kitchen.

A young chef was pouring brandy over a pan of sizzling steak. He paused for a moment when he saw the Tar Man.

"Ze toilets is to ze right, *monsieur*," he said in a strong French accent, indicating the direction with a wooden spoon.

The Tar Man nodded and smiled and glanced around the cluttered surfaces. There, near the door, he spotted a row of freshly arranged plates ready to go. The chef tipped the sauté pan so that the gas ignited the warmed brandy. Blue flames shot high into the air. When the chef turned back, the Tar Man had gone.

Back outside, on Floral Street, the two roast breasts of duck burned into the Tar Man's hip through his pocket lining. He took one out, blowing on it and passing it from one hand to the other while tearing at its piping hot flesh with his teeth. He discovered that there was some loose change jingling at the bottom of his pocket. He took out the greasy coins and examined them. *What I fancy now,* he thought, *is some decent ale,* and he wondered if the tavern he used to frequent nearby was still there. He doubted it but headed, in any case, toward Rose

Street. To his delight, there it was, almost the same except, like everything else now, or so it seemed to him, cleaner and more respectable.

"By the devil!" he exclaimed. "The Bucket of Blood! Though I'll warrant they've put a stop to the fistfighting!"

The pub was smoky and crowded, with low beams and an open fire burning at the back, and there were far too many people trying to get served at the bar. The Tar Man instantly felt at home. He took up a position at one end of the polished wooden bar and threw down the coins on the counter.

"A tankard of ale, if you please, mistress."

The barmaid, who was used to tourists shouting their orders in Olde Worlde English, reeled off the names of the different beers she could offer him. Confused, he pointed to the glass of pale amber liquid that his drunken neighbor was nursing in his hands. The barmaid nodded patiently and deposited a pint of lager in front of him. It was only when he pushed all his coins at her and was still ninety pence short of the price that she began to show signs of irritation. She was on the verge of calling the manager when the drunken man slumped over the bar offered to buy him a pint.

"Are you sure?" said the barmaid, unwilling to let this character take advantage of one of her regulars.

"A friend indeed is a friend in need," he slurred, and pulled a five-pound note out of his wallet.

The Tar Man looked at it with interest. "You can pay with that?" he asked.

The drunk screwed up his eyes and turned to look at him. "You foreign or somethink?"

"I am from far away."

"Well, welcome to London, mate. Cheers!"

"Thank you, my friend," said the Tar Man, and they clinked glasses.

He took a large mouthful of lager and all but spat it out in shock.

"Oh!" he exclaimed, then cautiously took another sip and shook his head in delighted surprise. He drank again and smiled broadly.

"What's up? You all right?"

"It's cold," breathed the Tar Man. "It's as cold as a mountain stream!"

"Don't they serve beer cold where you come from?"

"No."

"Where do you come from?"

"1763."

"Course you do, mate! Nice scar you've got. A real beauty. How did that happen, then?"

It amused the Tar Man to tell him his life story, knowing that the drunk would remember nothing in the morning. Indeed, soon afterward, his generous drinking partner collapsed onto the bar.

The Tar Man looked down at him and shook his head. "People haven't changed for the better," he said to himself, gulping down more lager, "but some things definitely have!"

⊶∞○∞⊷

When the barmaid called "Time, gentlemen, please!" at closing time, the Tar Man slapped the drunk man's face to rouse him. When this had no effect he heaved him up and supported him into the street. He propped him up against the nearest wall and removed his wallet. He slid out the wadge of paper money and slipped the wallet back into the man's pocket.

"Never let drink get the upper hand, my friend," the Tar Man whispered into his ear. "And never let sentiment rule your actions."

THAT FIRST NIGHT, IGNORANT OF THE KING'S PARDON AND FEARFUL OF BEING APPREHENDED, PETER AND I SLEPT UNDER THE STARS. WE HAD SPOKEN LITTLE SINCE OUR ESCAPE FROM HAMPSTEAD HEATH AND PETER SEEMED TO ME LIKE A SLEEPWALKER, PRESENT AND YET ELSEWHERE, UNABLE TO COMPREHEND WHAT HAD BEFALLEN HIM. WE HAD ALREADY WISHED EACH OTHER A GOOD NIGHT WHEN I CALLED OUT TO PETER IN THE DARKNESS AND ASKED HIM THE QUESTION I HAVE NEVER DARED PUT TO HIM SINCE: DID YOU CHOOSE TO STAY IN 1763?

"NO!" HE EXCLAIMED WITH GREAT VIOLENCE, AND THEN, "I HAD TO SAY GOOD-BYE—DIDN'T I?"

IN THOSE EARLY DAYS I NEVER DOUBTED THAT MISTRESS KATE AND HER FATHER WOULD SOON RETURN FOR THEIR FRIEND. AFTER MANY WEEKS AND THEN MONTHS PASSED, HOPE SLOWLY STARTED TO FADE. I WONDER IF, IN THE END, IT WOULD HAVE BEEN BETTER FOR PETER IF HE HAD DESPAIRED OF EVER RETURNING HOME.

—*THE LIFE AND TIMES OF GIDEON SEYMOUR, CUTPURSE AND GENTLEMAN, 1792*

TWO

THE FALL OF SNOWFLAKES

*In which Mrs. Dyer sees something alarming,
the Tar Man finds what he is looking for,
and Kate contacts Peter's father*

When Kate walked into the kitchen at the farm, exhausted and utterly overwhelmed by her conflicting emotions, she was immediately enfolded in a forest of arms that refused to let her go. Her brothers and sisters stood on the threshold, huddled around her. Only Sam, the next eldest, held back a little, his eyes too brimful of emotions to risk anything more. The twins, Issy and Alice, covered her with kisses, as she knew they would, while the two youngest, Sean and little Milly, crawled up her legs as if she were a tree trunk. She tried to speak, but couldn't. When she looked at her mother she saw, etched into her features, despite her current joy, the pain and fear of the preceding weeks.

But now it was Monday morning, barely a day and a half since her return, and Kate was helping her mother with the milking. She wanted to feel that everything was back to normal even though it was far from it. The calm patience of the cows and the smell of the milking parlor were so familiar and comforting it made her want to cry. Where was she going to find the courage to leave her mother and her brothers and sisters and return once more to 1763? And what if something went wrong? She might never see them again. She almost wished that her father had not brought her home—surely it would have been better to go back and search for Peter straightaway.

In the blinking fluorescent light, beads of moisture shone on Erasmus Darwin's broad pink nose as she waited her turn to be milked. Kate stroked the cow's soft, black ears and admired, as she always did, the length of her eyelashes. The memory of her meeting with the cow's namesake, the real Erasmus Darwin, suddenly flooded into her head—she recalled how excited she had been to meet the great man in Lichfield after the party had been attacked by the highwayman, and how she had let slip that Darwin's grandson, Charles, would discover evolution. Peter had been so cross with her afterward! . . . She smiled at the thought but then, unbidden, another memory rushed in. She pictured the tiny attic room in Lincoln's Inn Fields where she and Peter had sat sweltering in the heat of a sunny summer afternoon. It was the day of the blood pact and she could hear herself making Peter repeat after her, "I swear on my life that I shall never return to the twenty-first century without you." Except it was she who had broken that sacred promise. A wave of grief and guilt passed through her but she did not allow herself the release of tears.

"There," said her mother, standing up and pushing back a

dark curl from her face. "All done. Let's go and get some break-fast inside you. Megan's mum sent over some Cumberland sausages; she knows how much you like them."

"Can Megan come over later?"

"Yes, of course she can. Inspector Wheeler promised he'd be finished with you by noon."

Kate's face dropped.

"I hate having to lie. I don't think he believes me."

"Oh, Katie . . . I wish we didn't have to put you through this."

"I know."

Kate put her arms around her mother's waist and buried her head in her shoulder.

While Mrs. Dyer finished up, Kate opened the barn door and stood against it watching the line of peaceable animals pass through. The cows ambled across the muddy yard in their roll-ing, ungainly way, following the exact diagonal path they always trod. They trooped into the field and she clanged shut the metal five-bar gate behind them.

Dawn had just broken and a few fluffy flakes of snow floated down from a lead-gray sky. The wind had dropped and the valley seemed eerily still. Kate's spirits rose a little, for she loved snow. If it settled, she and Sam could make a snowman—at least once Inspector Wheeler and his entourage had finished asking her their interminable questions. With any luck his police car might get stuck in a snowdrift! She twirled round and round, head back, mouth open, hoping that a snowflake would land on her tongue. As she looked up, she had the strangest sensation that the laws of gravity had been temporarily suspended and that the snowflakes were hanging, immobile, in the column of cold air above her. It must be a trick of the light, she thought.

"Look, Mum!" she shouted. "It's snowing!"

Mrs. Dyer did not answer her but stood, motionless, an anxious expression forming on her face, at the other side of the farmyard.

"Mum! Look, it's starting to snow! Mum? . . . Is anything wrong?"

Her mother neither moved nor spoke and then Kate heard an unearthly sound behind her, horribly loud and deep, an unrelenting, throbbing noise which she felt in the pit of her stomach. Fearful of what she might see, she pressed the palms of her hands over her ears and whipped around. Yet there was nothing unusual as far as she could make out—apart, perhaps, from the cows, which would normally have reached the other side of the field by now. Instead, they were still all clustered around the gate and every single one of them was looking directly at her. Then she noticed that none of them was moving at all—not even a twitch of a tail. The huddle of black and white cows fixed their unblinking gaze on her, and all the while this awful, piercing sound drilled into her.

But when Kate looked back at Mrs. Dyer for reassurance, she saw that her mother was, just like the cows, motionless, seemingly frozen, and, in a deeply distressing way, elsewhere.

"Mum!"

Horrified, Kate ran over to Mrs. Dyer. Something was very wrong indeed—she was not responding.

"Mum, please! What's happening?"

Kate reached out to shake her, but the instant she touched her mother everything was transformed. She experienced a sensation similar to opening the door of a quiet, air-conditioned train and stepping out onto a bustling station platform: one moment you are cocooned and safe, the next you are buffeted by waves of noise and activity. All at once the volume was turned up: The cows were mooing, her mother was speaking, the cold wind was blowing, and the snow was falling. She was a part of the world again, and she brushed aside the small voice in the back of her mind that asked why, if there was something wrong with her mother, did *she* suddenly feel so different?

Kate scrutinized her mother. She did not look ill.

"Are you all right? What happened to you?" asked Kate. "You were acting really weird!"

"*I* was!" exclaimed Mrs. Dyer. Kate watched her mother pass her hands over her eyes and shake her head as if to clear her mind. Then she said: "I'm all right—low blood sugar or something. . . . For a minute, I thought . . . Oh, never mind, let's go in and get some breakfast inside us."

Kate kissed her mother's cheek. "You've been working too hard what with me and Dad being away. I think you were about to faint. It was really strange—almost like you were moving in slow motion."

The cows were still mooing and pressing up against each other, their hooves churning up the mud next to the gate.

"Look," said Kate, pointing at them, "you've even spooked the cows."

As they were walking back to the house, the newspaper boy arrived. He was a couple of years ahead of Kate at school.

"It's you!" he grinned. "We all thought you was a goner!"

"That's nice!" laughed Kate.

"Look," he said, opening up the front page of their newspaper and pointing to a photograph. "You're famous! Here, you can have that one, too, I've got a spare. Bye! Don't go getting lost again!"

Kate and her mother spread out the newspapers on the table. They looked at the first. The news of her return had not made the front page, owing to an England soccer star's divorce, but there, on page two, was Kate in her old school photograph. Kate was appalled.

"Oh no! You let them use *that* photo?" she exclaimed.

Then she noticed the puzzling and bizarre headline above it and quickly scanned the article. The news reporter had asked Inspector Wheeler if he would like to speculate on what could have happened to Kate Dyer to have made her lose her memory. A traumatic event of some kind? An attempt to conceal the truth? . . . The Inspector had replied that, despite extensive investigations, all their lines of inquiry had turned up one blank after another; he therefore could not afford to leave any stone unturned. The reporter had clearly taken him at his word.

"Oh no," said her mother as she saw the headline. "Your father and Dr. Pirretti are going to go mad when they see this. . . ."

It read: POLICE STUMPED: WAS MISSING GIRL ABDUCTED BY ALIENS?

It was early afternoon and a wintry sun shone down on London from a cloudless sky. There had been a hard frost that night and the puddles were still iced over and the wind was bitter. The Tar Man, however, sat warm and at his ease, his long legs stretched out beneath a window table at The George, a former coaching inn, a stone's throw from London Bridge. His fingers were draped over the fascinating black radiator beneath the window ledge and were periodically withdrawn when they grew too hot.

The Tar Man found that he preferred to sup his ale in taverns he had frequented in his previous existence. The George Inn was one such, and it had changed surprisingly little. All the stage-coaches between London and Canterbury used to stop here, and there were rich pickings for any highwaymen prepared to tackle the guard and his blunderbuss. The George Inn still had its pretty, galleried balconies that overlooked the large cobbled yard, but gone were the noise and bustle, the passengers clamoring for food and the drivers shouting at the stable lads to bring water for their horses. It was here that the Tar Man liked to meet the highwayman, Doctor Adams, so called on account of his habit of dislocating the shoulder of any victim who proved uncooperative.

He would, however, generously push back the arm into its socket before taking his leave for, as he freely admitted, once he had deprived his victims of their valuables, they would be hard-pressed to pay for a doctor afterward.

"Enjoy your meal, Sir."

One of the bar staff placed a large plate of fish and chips in front of him, golden brown and crunchy. There was a steaming mound of green peas on the side. The Tar Man devoured it with his eyes first. At that time of day, the low winter sun hit the windows of the modern office block opposite and its rays were reflected back through the casement windows into the dark, wood-paneled room. A narrow beam of sunshine passed through his glass of ice-cold beer and cast a pleasing amber glow on his succulent meal. The Tar Man licked his lips. And fresh peas, too! How the devil did they manage to grow garden peas in the middle of winter! He was beginning to warm to the twenty-first century.

While he ate, the Tar Man's gaze fell onto the cleanly swept yard with its rows of wooden tables and benches and curious outdoor heaters like giant mushrooms. He took another gulp of beer and looked at the scene outside. It amused him that all these people would choose to eat under the open sky when they could be sitting here in the bar. Something made him look twice at a girl of perhaps fifteen or sixteen who was walking past his window. She settled herself at a bench underneath one of the heaters. He watched her pull open a packet of what he had only that morning discovered were crisps. He did not care for them.

They hurt his gums. The girl took a swig from a red-labeled bottle. What was it about her? She *was* very pretty—she had olive skin and large, expressive, dark eyes, and her silky black hair was cut short like a boy's—but it was more than that. Her clothes, which the Tar Man found ugly in the extreme, like most of the fashions paraded on London's streets, were deliberately ripped and baggy and drab, yet her outfit could not disguise her natural grace. But what caught the Tar Man's attention above all was the professional way in which she scanned the yard before she sat down, as if she were making a careful mental note of who sat where, who was worth a second look, and where the nearest exit was to be found. He recognized a kindred spirit. They belonged to the same tribe, he and this girl; he was certain of it.

The Tar Man ate the last morsel of fish and pushed away his plate contentedly, although his gaze kept wandering back to the yard. Four youths walked by carrying pints of beer and chose to sit at the table adjacent to the girl. She had taken out a paperback book from her pocket and was poring over it, popping crisps mechanically into her mouth as she read. The youths were all loud and intent on having a good time, but one of them, the leader of this little gang, was more full of himself than the rest. He was tall and blond and kept looking over at the girl and after a while started to imitate her, hunched up over a book, in order to win her attention. His mates laughed; the girl did not react. Then the youth reached over and tried to grab her book. Before he could touch it, she swung her arm up sharply, without even raising her head, and knocked his wrist out of the way. He could not stop himself from crying out—she was wearing a chunky metal bracelet, and she had hurt him. She continued to read. His mates, on the point of laughing, stopped themselves when they saw the thunderous expression on his face. He shouted something at the girl. The Tar Man could not make out the words he used, but by the reaction of the people seated at tables around them, they were ugly. At first the girl did not move but then she coolly raised her head and looked up at the boy. Whatever it was that she said to him, all his mates burst into spontaneous laughter, spluttering their beer into the air. The blond youth kicked out petulantly at the girl's table, causing her bottle of Coca-Cola to wobble from side to side. The girl's hand shot out to steady it and calmly went back to her book. The Tar Man smiled appreciatively. She had spirit and knew how to handle herself. A thought came to him: Could this girl be the guide he was seeking?

After a few minutes, he observed her gather her things together and walk toward the inn, squeezing through the rows of benches. She slid past a large, burly man whose generous rear was jutting out over his bench. He was staring deep into the eyes of an attractive woman opposite him as if the rest of the world had ceased to exist for him. The Tar Man did not have a clear view, yet he was certain that the girl had taken something from his back pocket. She had chosen well—of all the customers in the yard he was the easiest target. Then he saw her tap the big man on the shoulder, whisper something in his ear, and point at the table of youths. The big man immediately got up, felt in his trouser pocket, and, finding it empty, tore across the yard like a charging bull elephant.

Her pretty face alight with a delighted smile, the girl entered the low-ceilinged bar where the Tar Man sat. She ordered a cup of decaffeinated coffee at the bar, and while the barman had his back to her she removed several ten-pound notes from the big man's wallet and shoved the evidence between a potted plant and its holder. The Tar Man called over to her from his table.

"That was neatly done."

The girl whipped round. She was angry with herself that she had not noticed him sitting there.

"What you talking about? I never did nothing!"

The Tar Man smiled broadly. "Never try to hoodwink a hoodwinker. I say it as one who has an appreciation for such things."

The girl looked the stranger up and down, took in his scar and his unusual taste in clothes.

"Well, I can see you ain't the law. . . ."

She walked toward his table, ignoring the Tar Man, so that she could see what was going on outside. She grinned broadly. The burly man was dragging the youth, shouting and kicking, out of the yard into Borough High Street.

The barman came over to the table with the girl's coffee, thinking they were together.

"No—" she started to say.

"Yes," interrupted the Tar Man, "let us drink a glass together."

"You don't half speak funny. . . ."

"I see that it pleases you to read."

The girl looked askance. "Yeah, and . . . ?"

"Would you do me the kindness of reading this for me?"

The Tar Man pointed to a small framed poem hung on the wall next to the window. It was a surprising request and the girl found herself reading it before she could think of a reason to refuse.

"Weep on, weep on, my pouting vine!

Heav'n grant no tears but tears of wine!"

She reads well! thought the Tar Man. *Even better* . . .

"Forgotten your specs, have you?" asked the girl.

"Specs? I do not understand you."

"Spectacles! You know . . ."

"Ah. No. It is not for that reason that I cannot read."

"You're dyslexic, then?"

"Upon my word your speech is hard to follow!"

"You get your letters confused?"

"As I never knew my letters, I could hardly confuse them. In my time, natural good sense was more than sufficient and I never felt the lack. I fear that things have changed."

The girl looked at the Tar Man. He read suspicion and curiosity in her features.

"I have a fancy we could be of use to each other, you and I."

He had unsettled the girl. Usually she was good at sizing people up, but she did not know what to make of this character.

"I gotta be going."

"Tell me your name first."

"My name ain't none of your business!"

The Tar Man stood up and bowed his head. "Then until we meet again . . ."

"I doubt it."

The girl swallowed down her coffee and made for the door. The Tar Man made sure that he was looking away when she sneaked a final glance at him, as he knew she would.

It was the first day of the spring term for Kate's younger siblings. Sam, who never usually gave his sister hugs, ran back from the Land Rover to give her one before he left. She had tousled his hair roughly and told him that he had gone soft while she had been away, but he could see that she was pleased. Kate was half-expecting her parents to say that she had to go to school too, as her mum was always so strict about taking days off. Instead, her mother had encouraged her to take it easy and catch up on her sleep if she could. Mrs. Dyer had then gone even further and, to Kate's astonishment, had telephoned Inspector Wheeler to insist—forcibly—that her daughter was exhausted and needed rest and calm and could not possibly be questioned again today. So Kate found herself at a loose end: She had eaten lunch, taken Molly for a walk, and read the two little ones a story before their afternoon nap. She decided to go downstairs and watch television. Sean and Milly were both light sleepers, so she crept carefully down the creaky stairs so as not to disturb them. The kitchen door was shut and she thought she could hear voices.

Her dad had gone out mid-morning so she presumed it was the radio, but as she was about to turn the handle she recognized both her parents' voices. They were speaking in a desperate tone and, fearful, she stood for a moment to listen. What she heard convinced her to remain outside the door unannounced. She pressed her cheek against the heavy oak door.

Her mother was speaking. She sounded agitated.

"Dr. Pirretti can't be serious about destroying the antigravity machine *tonight*! Even if it's true that Tim Williamson intends to get it back, it doesn't follow that he is going to spill the beans to NASA or to the press."

"I think he will," replied her father. "I think he wants to go down in history as the inventor of time travel. Anyway, he lied to me about where he was going. It was only because his flatmate happened to be there that I found out that he wasn't going to be around over the next couple of days because, quote, 'he's picking up a large bit of equipment.'"

"Where is the antigravity machine, anyway?" asked Mrs. Dyer.

"In a lock-up garage behind a post office in a village in Hertfordshire. Middle Harpenden or something."

"But how can Anita even think of destroying it now?" said Mrs. Dyer. "It's monstrous!"

Dr. Dyer did not answer.

"Please don't tell me that you would be prepared to leave Peter stranded in 1763!" shouted his wife.

Kate bit her lip. This was awful. She could tell her mother was close to tears. It was bad enough eavesdropping and hearing her parents argue—which was something they never did—but she could not believe what she was hearing.

"Listen," said Dr. Dyer. "I am trying very hard to keep my head and to do the right thing. I didn't say that I was happy about leaving Peter in the eighteenth century! And I'm quite sure that Anita isn't either—but can't you see that she is justified in fearing the consequences of going back even one more time? And she's worried that Inspector Wheeler may wheedle the truth out of Kate, that Tim Williamson may go public, and that the antigravity machine will be impounded. . . . If the tabloid press get their hands on this story, we'll have more to worry about than headlines about alien abductions."

"But a boy's life is at stake!"

"You don't need to tell *me* that!" roared Dr. Dyer. "And who knows how many lives will be at stake if we *do* go after him!"

"Ssh . . . ," said Mrs. Dyer. "Kate might hear us."

With difficulty, Dr. Dyer made himself speak slowly and calmly.

"Can't you see what a nightmare time travel could be? The future of history would be up for grabs. . . . Just imagine what it could be like—the person you're talking to could suddenly disappear because someone went back in time and changed something that wiped out his entire bloodline. We're old enough to have learned that life is a game of chutes and ladders at the best of times. I, for one, don't want to live in a world where you are forced to play it in several dimensions."

"And Anita Pirretti thinks it's okay to sacrifice Peter to her doomsday theory?" asked Mrs. Dyer.

"Of course she doesn't think it's okay! But she does think it might be the most responsible course of action. . . ."

Mrs. Dyer let out a desperate little cry.

"And does the same go for you? Are you going to stand by and let her do it?"

"I . . . I don't know yet. My heart and my head are saying different things."

"Peter's father is coming over this evening," Mrs. Dyer cried. "Tell me, what are we supposed to say to him?"

"As little as possible. . . ."

Behind the door Kate clenched her fists. She turned white with anger.

"And remember," continued Dr. Dyer, "that we have no guarantee that we *can* return to 1763 a third time or, if we manage it, that we could then return to the present."

"But we've got to try, surely! Peter is an innocent victim in all of this. He didn't ask to be sent back in time!"

"True—but how many innocent victims will there be if we let the world know that time travel is possible?"

Kate had heard enough—was this really her Dad talking? What kind of a monster had he turned into? She took a deep breath, composed her face into a smile, and burst into the kitchen. Her parents were standing at opposite sides of the room, and her mother's complexion was blotchy. Both immediately clammed up and stood looking awkwardly at their daughter.

49

"Is it still okay for me to invite Megan over?" asked Kate brightly.

"Yes, of course it is, love, if you feel up to it," answered her mother. "But you . . . you will be careful what you say to her, won't you?"

"Of course," replied Kate. "I'll give her a ring, then. She'll probably be back from school by now. Can she stay for a sleepover?"

An hour later Mrs. Dyer stood at the window holding little Milly. They watched Kate run out into the yard to greet Megan. The valley was already in dark shadow, and the hilltops with their light dusting of snow glistened red. Banks of ominous gray clouds were building up to the north. "I shouldn't like to be out tonight," she said. "Aren't you glad we'll all be warm and cozy inside. . . ." Milly did not reply, preoccupied as she was with puckering up her lips against the pane of glass like a fish in an aquarium. Through the window they heard squeals of delight as the two friends ran toward each other arms outstretched, so happy to be reunited. Kate and Megan had talked endlessly on the telephone but this was their first meeting. The girls' breath came out in great clouds of steam. They hugged and talked and hugged each other again. Then they disappeared into the cowshed for some privacy, as they often did. Mrs. Dyer smiled to see them.

"Do you know," she said to Milly, "your big sister and Megan have been friends since they weren't much older than you? It seems like only yesterday since I saw them walking hand in hand into nursery school on their first day, eyes wide as saucers at this big new world. You've got that coming, my love. . . ."

Milly blew bubbles on the glass. "Your big sister is going to want to go back and rescue Peter. I know she is. . . ."

"Pe-ta," repeated Milly.

"But I shan't let her—not again. I almost hope that the anti-gravity machine will be destroyed tonight! Why should our family suffer anymore? It wasn't our fault! Perhaps it is right that one boy's happiness be sacrificed for the greater good. . . . And he has a difficult relationship with his father, according to Margrit. Why, he might even *prefer* it in the eighteenth century. . . ."

The toddler started to wriggle and Mrs. Dyer put her down. "You're getting heavy, Milly, my love."

As she stood up again, her hand pressing against the small of her back, shame pricked at her. She thought of Peter's mother and what she must be going through, and then turned her mind to what on earth she was going to say to Peter's father when he arrived in a couple of hours' time.

Kate was telling Megan about her parents' argument. "It's like they'd had a personality change! I couldn't believe it!"

They were sitting side by side on a bale of hay, their backs against the cold brick wall. Kate's long, red hair made Megan's blond ponytail seem even paler. Megan knew her friend well enough not to argue.

"Stress does funny things to grown-ups."

"You will help me, won't you, Meggie?"

"Yes, of course I will. . . . Not that *I* want you to go back in time again either."

"I don't have a choice! If I don't try to save him, I'll have to live with it for the rest of my life. It was a blood pact."

"You *are* going to tell Sam, aren't you? You don't realize what a terrible state he's been in. I don't know how he'd cope if he woke up and found you'd disappeared again."

"Wouldn't it be better if I just went? He'll only get upset anyway and then he might give the game away."

"That's not fair, Kate—we didn't know if you were alive or dead! It's torture not knowing. . . . If you explain it to him, he won't like it but at least he'll understand."

"Okay, okay. I'll tell him."

Megan's big Christmas present was a state-of-the-art mobile phone which had barely left her hand since she had pulled it excitedly out of its box. Now she used it to track down Mr. Schock's office number. She was convincing enough to per-suade the receptionist to reveal her "uncle's" mobile number. She put her own mobile to her ear and waited.

"He's not answering—it's gone into voicemail," she said. "Now what do we do?"

"Leave a message, of course! Here, give it to me!" exclaimed Kate.

She gulped and took a deep breath, suddenly unsure what to say.

"Hello, Mr. Schock. You don't know me but I know your

son very well. My name is Kate Dyer. Will you please ring this number urgently. I need to talk to you before you come to the farm. Before you speak to my parents. Please. This is a matter of life or death for your son."

"Well, if that doesn't get a response, nothing will!" said Megan.

There was a knock on the barn door. It was Sam.

"Come on in, Sam," called Megan. And then, with a pointed look at Kate, "We need you to help us with something. Kate's got something to tell you. Kate, you'd better keep hold of the phone in case Peter's dad calls."

The poor boy looked alarmed as Kate patted the haystack next to her. He sat down next to his big sister and Megan discreetly retreated to the house.

"You can start packing," Kate called after her. "Look under my pillow. . . ."

Sam looked even more alarmed.

Megan waited in Kate's room. She picked up the pillow and saw, neatly arranged underneath, all those items which Kate had deemed essential for a stay in the eighteenth century. Megan picked them up one by one and stashed them in Kate's canvas backpack. It was strangely like packing for a vacation. There was a wide-toothed comb and shampoo; toothbrush and toothpaste; perfumed soap; plasters and antiseptic wipes, plus a small brown bottle labeled PENICILLIN: TAKE ONE CAPSULE THREE TIMES A DAY. COMPLETE THE COURSE which she'd filched from the medicine cabinet; a large bar of chocolate (Kate's belated Christmas present from the twins); three cans of Coca-Cola; a small flashlight with spare batteries; two old watches (presumably to sell); lace doilies (ditto); spare sneakers; enough underwear for a week; and her Swiss Army knife.

After twenty minutes, Kate and Sam reappeared. Both their noses were red and Kate sniffed between sentences.

"It's on. Peter's dad called. He's meeting me in the lane at eight o'clock. And I've told Sam. You're going to help us—aren't you?"

Sam was going on ten and in looks took after his mother. He was skinny with thick dark hair which went curly when it was damp. He nodded but looked close to tears.

Megan gave him a hug. "She'll come back. You know your big sister—no one gets the better of Kate Dyer. . . ."

"You better," said Sam gruffly.

At ten to eight, Kate stood at the kitchen door. Her mum was preparing the grown-ups' supper in time for Mr. Schock's imminent arrival. Issy and Alice were on the floor in front of the Aga cooker stroking Molly, who was almost asleep, lulled by the heat and all the attention. Kate walked over and crouched down next to the little group. She rested her head on Molly's fat belly for a moment.

"I'm cold. I'm going to have a hot bath," she announced. "Then I think I'll read in bed; I'm really tired."

"Okay, love, I'll come up and kiss you good night later," said her mum, giving her an anxious look. "Your dad's gone out. . . . I wish he hadn't. Mr. Schock will be here any minute. . . . If you're too tired to say hello to Peter's dad tonight, can I tell him that you'll speak to him in the morning? I know it'll be hard, but . . ."

"Yes. I don't mind. . . ."

Kate walked over and put her arms round her mother's waist.

"I love you, Mum."

Her mother put down the tea towel she was holding and took hold of Kate's face. She kissed her forehead.

"And I love you."

Kate retreated from the kitchen before her courage failed her.

"Good night, Issy. Good night, Alice. . . ."

True to his word, Sam stayed in the bathroom and turned the water on and off and splashed and even hummed his sister's favorite song. Kate turned up the music in her room and then she and Megan crept down to her dad's study downstairs. Dr. Dyer reluctantly allowed Kate's mother to store Bramley cooking apples wrapped in newspaper on his corner bookshelves—and it was the familiar smell of books and waxy fruit and leather that caused a lump in Kate's throat. It was in this room, sitting on her father's knee, that she had learned to read, and he had told her so many wonderful stories. . . . Suddenly, the urge to leave it all for the grown-ups to sort out nearly overwhelmed her—but she forced herself to run to the window and push it open. A blast of icy air slapped her face and brought her to her senses.

Suddenly the wind caught hold of the window and she only just managed to grab hold of the frame before it smashed against the shutters. Snowflakes blew into the room and immediately melted on the worn Oriental rug. Kate climbed out, her feet leaving short-lived evidence of her escape on the snow-covered lawn. Megan leaned out to pass her the backpack.

"Here, catch!" said Megan, throwing a small object to her friend.

"Not your mobile! I can't! You've waited all year for this!"

"It's fully charged. If you keep it switched off most of the time it ought to be okay for a couple of weeks. I've already downloaded lots of my favorite songs. . . ."

"Oh, Meggie . . . I can't. What if I lose it?"

"Don't! Just take me some good pictures of 1763 and shut up!"

"Thanks, Meggie. . . . You'll like Peter."

"He'd better be worth it. I'll see you soon. Okay?"

"Yeah. Very soon."

When Mr. Schock saw Kate walking toward him he started up the engine and turned on the headlights of his long silver car. The blue-white beams illuminated dense flurries of snow. He leaned over to the passenger seat and pushed open the door. Kate got in and brushed wet tendrils of hair from her face. Mr. Schock took hold of the backpack and threw it onto the cream leather backseat. Then he turned round to look at her. His blue eyes blazed.

"You must be Kate Dyer."

"Yes."

"Then you'd better stop playing games and tell me what's going on! Where's my son?"

"I'll do better than that. I'll take you to him."

THREE

ANJALI

*In which the Tar Man shows what he
is made of, and Kate and Mr. Schock
break the law in Middle Harpenden*

The Tar Man stopped to pull his wide-brimmed, black hat
down over his forehead. He never removed his gaze for a
moment from the four youths. They had been tailing the girl
since the George Inn. The Tar Man had spotted the leader
of the gang, sporting a thunderous expression and a fresh
bruise on his cheek, sloping past the window of the bar as
the girl left the cobblestone yard and stepped onto Borough
High Street. Now they stood, awkward and self-conscious,
in a grimy shop doorway while they observed the girl slowly
descending the narrow stairs to the underground station. It
was a dry-cleaner's shop and the dusty-looking man behind
the counter was surprised to see lads like these taking such
a keen interest in his dry-cleaning tariff. It had been a quiet
day and he got up hopefully and walked toward the door to
ask if he could be of any assistance, but the moment the girl
had vanished from sight, the youths bounded toward the

underground station and darted after her. The man sat down again, a little sadly, on his high stool behind the counter.

The Tar Man was unimpressed, not only by the youths' pitiful attempt at blending into the background, but also by the girl's lack of awareness. She had not looked behind her once since he had been following her, and for someone who seemed to court difficult situations, this was careless and stupid. He felt a twinge of disappointment. The Tar Man considered what to do next. His hesitation was in part due to his recent experience of standing on an underground platform at Piccadilly Circus, a hand's breadth from a snakelike carriage of immense proportions, all wind, lights, and beeping doors, that tore out of the gaping black tunnel like a rampaging dragon. He had fled back to the surface and doubted that he could ever get used to such a thing. There was a distinctive smell down in these tunnels too, which he mistrusted. Besides, was the girl worth the effort? Yet he liked her spirit. While he had taught the tricks of the trade to a fair few rogues, even dim-witted ones, it seemed to him that you were either born with spirit or you were not. Spirit was not a quality you could acquire at a later date. Very well, he decided, he would give the girl this one chance. He stooped down and picked up a handful of decorative pebbles from a trough planted with evergreen shrubs, and dropped them into his pocket. Then he strode toward the stairway, placed one foot on the first step and looked all about him twice, before vanishing into the bowels of the earth below Southwark.

Mid-afternoon in this corner of London is not a busy time and so, on this cold January weekday, the underground was almost deserted. The girl walked smartly through the interminable tunnel to catch the tube home. She never cared for this part of her journey. Bare, yellow lightbulbs illuminated curved walls that were painted a shiny, sickly green. Her footsteps echoed annoyingly, announcing her presence and making her feel vulnerable. Suddenly she became aware of other footfall behind her. The girl was relieved; there was safety in numbers. She hated to be the only person on the platform with only the blackened mice that foraged, precariously, on the live track for company. She noticed, however, that no conversation accompanied these other footsteps. And they were all speeding up. The gap between her and the strangers was closing.

She reached a sharp bend in the tunnel. High on the wall was a convex observation mirror which allowed her to see what lay behind and before her. The tunnel ahead was empty. To her rear, the blond youth she had played a trick on and his three sidekicks were approaching fast. She recognized them instantly and swore under her breath. Her heart started to pound and it was with difficulty that she prevented herself from running a race she knew she could not win. Better to use her head. . . .

The girl turned the corner. Her eyes searched the tunnel for a security camera, finally spotting one directly above her head. She jumped up and down, waving her arms in front of it, gesturing silently and desperately for help. With any luck, a guard would soon be on his way. The girl felt a fraction calmer: Now it was a case of playing for time and she was good at that. She was not to know that high above, in his dark little office, the security guard was having a good, long stretch, his back to the bank of monitors, oblivious to her plight.

She strode on ahead and was a third of the way down the tunnel when an ominous clatter of feet signaled the arrival of her pursuers. The girl permitted herself to look back at them. She pointed at the security camera and cried: "Oi! Watch the birdie!"

A black-haired youth with a tattoo on his neck immediately spat out the gum he was chewing and reached up to smear it all over the lens at the same time that the leader of the gang hurled himself at the girl, arm already outstretched to catch hold of her. The girl had made an unforgivable mistake: She had caused him to lose face in front of his mates, and he would make sure that she would live to regret it.

"I'll teach you!" he shouted.

The girl started to run and fled from them as fast as she could. She broke out in a cold sweat—they weren't playing around. They meant to hurt her. All her instincts told her to be defiant, not to cave in. . . .

"You!" she replied, calling back over her shoulder. "What could a zero like you teach *me*?"

A second later the blond gang leader caught up with the girl and pinned her against the wall. She spat at him. He wiped away the spittle with the back of his hand, looked her straight in the eyes, and delivered a stinging blow to the side of her head. She did not give him the satisfaction of hearing her cry out in pain.

"Lowlife bully . . . ," she said.

The girl took in his freshly bruised cheek and the sleeve of his denim jacket which was ripped at the shoulder.

"I can see you didn't give that bloke no trouble," she taunted, while trying to work out her chances if she made a run for it. "And 'im twice your size and a belly like an expectin' hippo."

The other youths smirked, but the blond youth glowered at them, his skin glistening in the harsh light. He grabbed hold of the girl's arm and pulled it behind her back until she whimpered.

Meanwhile, the Tar Man had arrived at the bend in the tunnel. He stared curiously for a moment at the observation mirror and made a mental note of it. It could be a useful device for someone in his profession, he thought, but when he heard the girl's cries and saw the reflected image of the gang leader twisting her arm up behind her, he delved into his pocket and plucked out a couple of pebbles. He stepped into view and, with impeccable aim, hit the leader of the gang on the temple and the black-haired youth on the back of the head. Both of them yelped with pain and clutched at their scalps, swiveling around to see their attacker. The Tar Man stood, poised, in the center of the tunnel.

He lifted his hat off and inclined his head in a slight bow. All eyes were irresistibly drawn to the silvery-white scar that was etched so deeply into his cheek. He replaced his hat.

"Well, gentlemen, I take it you have business with this lady, though 'tis an unseemly spot for a rendezvous."

The girl's eyes lit up. She did not understand what was going on, but she was going to press her advantage. She turned her face toward her tormentor.

"You didn't know I had a minder, did you?"

A sharp *click* drew everyone's attention to the black-haired youth. He had taken out a switchblade and had released the blade. He started to walk toward the Tar Man, breathing heavily. The leader of the gang lost concentration momentarily, and with a massive effort, the girl escaped his grasp and sprinted away from him. The gang leader shot after her. The other two youths held back, waiting to see what would happen. The black-haired youth was becoming increasingly agitated. Normally, all he had to do was unsheathe his knife and his victim would instantly back off. But this guy! He was showing no sign of being afraid. Either he was mad, or stupid, or he could handle himself better than anyone the youth had ever come across. To look at his expression you'd think *he* was the one with the knife.

The gang leader soon caught up with the girl again and dragged her back, holding her tightly, arms pinned to her sides. She stamped repeatedly on his heavy boots, but he would not loosen his hold.

Trembling with a surfeit of adrenalin, the black-haired youth took a swipe at the Tar Man. The latter ducked, easily missing the blade, and stood tall once more.

"Upon my word, a poorly executed move! When you wield a blade, lad, you need to be light on your feet. Come, try your luck again, for it is plain for all the world to see that you would not be the first to cut me!"

The youth gawked at him. What nerve he had was draining slowly away, for there was a look in this man's eyes that terrified him. This man was a hunter and he himself was the hunted. He might be holding the knife, but he felt as if the stranger were playing with him, like a cat plays with a mouse.

"What are you waiting for?" cried the leader of the gang. "Look at 'im! He's well past his sell-by date."

The Tar Man raised his eyebrows. He would discover the meaning of that particular insult later. Instead of responding, he yawned ostentatiously and tapped his foot. This was enough to provoke a reaction and his adversary lunged at him. With a deft flick of the wrist, the Tar Man disarmed him, kicked the knife behind him, out of reach, and grabbed hold of the youth's arm. He forced it behind his back and simultaneously pulled his neck backward with his elbow. The youth let out a strangulated cry.

"Let her go," ordered the Tar Man calmly.

"Go hang yourself!" replied the leader of the gang.

Dark eyes blazing, the Tar Man turned on him in fury.

"You are insolent. Release her now if you do not want me to break your friend's neck."

"Don't make me laugh! Who do you think you are?"

"Someone who has more important things to do than trouble myself with maggots like you. I am waiting. . . ."

When the Tar Man detected no response, he suddenly heaved

the black-haired youth up, bearing his full weight on his chest so that his sneaker-clad feet kicked pathetically above the floor. Straining and shuddering with the effort, the Tar Man slowly squeezed, never releasing his formidable grip. Now the youth's feet dangled limply and a second later a mighty *CRACK!* echoed around the tunnel. The Tar Man exhaled his pent-up breath in a loud burst and allowed the dead weight of the youth to collapse to the floor.

The girl let out a shrill scream and clapped both hands to her face. The three remaining youths stood immobile and slack-jawed. The Tar Man stepped over the body at his feet and took a long stride toward the others.

"Who's next?" he asked in a low, gentle voice.

The leader of the gang, white-faced, turned to the girl and hissed, "This isn't the end of it. . . ."

The three youths vanished back up the tunnel at high speed without looking back. The girl stood rooted to the spot, too shocked to move. She watched, bewildered, as the Tar Man laid out the young man's body, as if to make him more comfortable. Then she saw him manipulating his arm. Slowly she became aware that there was something horribly wrong with it, and she watched as the Tar Man heaved and pushed as if he were trying to force the arm back into the shoulder socket. Beads of sweat appeared on his brow with the exertion and suddenly the youth started to come round, shaking his head from side to side, groaning and crying out.

"Doctor Adams always says that dislocating an arm is easy; it's putting it back again that needs skill . . . ," panted the Tar Man.

"I thought you'd killed him!" the girl practically shouted, relief written all over her face.

"I have not. . . . A killing mostly gives rise to an adder's nest of consequences. I take pains to avoid it except in cases of the utmost need."

The girl gulped. Alert, the Tar Man looked over his shoulder at the observation mirror. There was no one yet in sight but he could hear footsteps in the distance. He leaped up and started to walk away. The girl followed him, struggling to keep up with his long legs.

"Thanks," she said awkwardly. "Er . . . Why did you . . . ?"

The Tar Man bowed his head in acknowledgment. "I am a stranger here. I need a guide."

"You want *me* to be your guide?"

"Yes. I will reward you handsomely—anything you wish. . . ."

"I . . ."

"Meet me on the steps of St. Paul's Cathedral tomorrow at sunset and we will talk terms."

"But I don't know if I want to . . ."

The Tar Man ignored her hesitation. "But be warned: Once you have accepted my trust, if you cross me, you will live to regret it. . . . So, will you at least tell me your name now?"

"Anjali. My name's Anjali."

"Your car is really nice," said Kate, dabbing at the pale beige leather with the sleeve of her sweater and remembering how particular Peter had said his father was. "I'm sorry, I'm dripping melting snow all over the seat."

"I don't care about that!" exclaimed Mr. Schock. "All I want to know is why *you* have come back and not Peter? And how come Inspector Wheeler said that you'd lost your memory when, instead, you're leaving me messages about Peter being in a life-or-death situation? What's going on, for heaven's sake?"

Mr. Schock was shouting.

"There's no need to get so angry! Peter said you have a bad temper!"

Mr. Schock took a deep breath and gripped the wheel hard. "I apologize . . . but we've been half out of our minds with worry. And I suspect that your father knows far more than he's letting on. In fact, I'm certain of it. . . ."

"He does," replied Kate simply. "But he's keeping quiet for a very good reason. At least, he thinks he is. Look, I *will* tell you. I promise. But we've got no time to lose. Can you *please* just drive and I'll explain everything on the way?"

Mr. Schock was on the point of objecting, but stopped himself and stared at her intensely instead, searching her face for something—she did not know what. Then he started up the engine.

"Where to?"

"Middle Harpenden in Hertfordshire. To a lock-up garage behind the post office."

Kate refused to tell him anything until they reached the motorway, because, she said, what she was about to tell him would come as a bit of a shock and he would need to concentrate while driving over icy, single-lane roads in a snowstorm. So they picked their way out of the valley in silence. The headlights, on full beam, illuminated great, swirling eddies of fluffy snowflakes that clung to the bare branches of solitary trees and blew into drifts at the base of the drystone walling. It took twice as long as normal to reach Bakewell. The snowstorm had begun to abate, and as the roads leading into the market town had been well salted, the tires now splattered noisily through the mud and slush. Without warning, Kate dived down, hiding her head under her hands behind the dashboard.

"What's wrong?" cried Mr. Schock.

"That was my dad's Land Rover—do you think he saw me?"

Mr. Schock looked in his rearview mirror at the grimy white Land Rover that had just passed them. Its lights blinked away into the darkness without slowing down.

"No. He can't have. He would have stopped. I think there was a woman in the car, as well. . . ."

"I bet that was Dr. Pirretti."

"Who?"

"I'll tell you in a minute."

It had stopped snowing altogether by the time they reached the motorway and the southbound carriageway was almost clear of traffic. Mr. Schock's car coasted down the fast lane, easily overtaking what few vehicles they came upon. *Dad never drives anywhere near this fast*, thought Kate, *but then, our car is a bit different from this one. . . .*

"You're the spitting image of your father," said Mr. Schock, taking a sidelong look at her.

"I know. Everyone says I take after him. But Peter doesn't look anything like you—I thought you'd be dark, like him."

"No. I'm a throwback to my grandparents who came from Ulm in Germany. They were blond, too. Peter takes after his mother. . . . Now, Miss Kate Dyer, it's easy driving from now on. Are you ready to tell me what this is all about?"

As the dark, featureless landscape sped by, Kate told Peter's father everything. It poured out of her, and she could not stop until she had finished her story, her mouth dry, her throat sore, and her voice croaky. She left out nothing: She told him about the accident with Molly, the Van de Graaff generator and the antigravity machine; Peter's encounter with the Tar Man; the kindness of the Byng family and Parson Ledbury. She told him how Gideon Seymour—who used to be a cut-purse for Lord Luxon until he decided to turn his back on his old life—had saved them from a highwayman and a gang of footpads. She told him how, in an effort to win back the anti-gravity machine by racing against the Tar Man, Gideon had ended up in Newgate Gaol and had narrowly missed being hanged. She explained that when they were on the point of returning to their own time, right at the very last second, the Tar Man had taken Peter's place at the antigravity machine. She told him that there was nothing anyone could have done to stop him. Finally, she described how terrified her father and the NASA scientists were that time travel would become public knowledge and that the future of history could soon be at risk.

Mr. Schock's mind was reeling. It was too much to take in, let alone believe.

"So that office girl in Lincoln's Inn Fields wasn't kidding when she said that you were stuck in 1763!"

"No."

"And you're telling me that Peter is still in 1763 while there's an eighteenth-century henchman on the loose in London?"

"Yes."

Mr. Schock shook his head incredulously.

"It's too incredible. . . ."

"Well, it's true. It is incredible but it's also true. And if you don't get me to the antigravity machine tonight, I shan't be able to go back and rescue Peter, because either Tim Williamson will have stolen it or Dr. Pirretti will have destroyed it."

"But you can't be expected to rescue him! You're a child! I'm his father! It should be me who goes after him!"

It should have been obvious to her, Kate thought, that Mr. Schock would want to come too, but she had not thought beyond getting to the antigravity machine.

"I *want* to go back!" she cried. "We made a pact not to leave without each other. I *have* to go back. . . . And anyway, you don't know about the antigravity machine and you wouldn't know what Gideon looks like, or where Sir Richard's house is, or anything! So, I'm going too, whether you like it or not!"

Mr. Schock looked thoughtful for a moment and suddenly laughed. "You're quite bossy for a twelve-year-old girl. I bet you kept Peter in his place."

Kate's face fell.

"Don't call me that! My dad says that I know my own mind and I stick up for myself, and there's nothing wrong with that. And if I wasn't 'bossy,' you wouldn't be here now on your way to rescue Peter."

"I'm sorry, Kate," said Mr. Schock, surprised and contrite. "You're quite right. I was out of order. . . ."

They fell silent for a while, and Kate calmed herself down by busying herself with the map, trying to work out which exit they should take for Middle Harpenden.

Mr. Schock tried to break the ice: "It must be quite something to have a dad who invented a time machine. . . ."

"It wasn't Dad. It was his colleague, Tim Williamson. And it's an antigravity machine."

"I stand corrected."

"The time thing is an unexpected side effect and my dad reckons that something accelerated it—like oxygen making a fire burn stronger. Only he can't figure out what it might be—yet . . ."

"I see. . . . I think . . . I never was much good at science—but if you want to know about the rise of the French novel, I'm your man!"

Kate wondered what earthly use that would be to anybody but smiled politely all the same.

Then Mr. Schock asked, a little hesitantly: "Did Peter get along with this . . . cutpurse character, then?"

"Yes—he really liked him. Well, he did save our lives. And he put his own life in danger to help us get back. . . . He taught Peter to ride and everything."

"Did you know that Peter and I had a terrible argument the day you both disappeared?"

"He might have mentioned it," answered Kate, tactfully.

"The last thing he said to me was 'I hate you.' You don't think Peter *meant* to stay behind in 1763, do you?"

"Oh, you mustn't think that," said Kate hurriedly. "Anyway, you'll be able to ask him yourself soon. . . ."

She changed the subject. "How is Mrs. Schock? Is she back in California? Peter said she was making a film."

"No, no—of course she didn't go back to the States with Peter missing! They've replaced her. To be truthful, Kate, I didn't tell her I was coming. Inspector Wheeler telephoned us to say that you had amnesia and could not give us any useful information. My wife felt that we should give you some breathing space. She said you must have been through enough without us badgering you."

Kate couldn't help smiling. "But you came anyway. . . ."

"I couldn't *not* come. I had to know. . . . I tend to think with my feet—I'm not always an easy person, I know that."

Mr. Schock did not seem to want to talk after that, and he put on some classical music, all cellos and harpsichords. Kate soon nodded off, moaning fitfully in her sleep as she lived through a series of vivid dreams in which she would find herself in different locations with her parents, but always at some kind of crossroads. They would want to go one way but she would pull against them in the opposite direction, and she always ended up falling, falling, falling into nothing. . . .

"Pick up! Pick up!" Mr. Schock muttered. He sounded exasperated.

Kate woke up with a start to the sound of a ringtone on Mr. Schock's car speakerphone.

"Is everything okay?" asked Kate.

"I think my wife must have switched the phone off—I'll try her later. I'm sorry to wake you up. . . ."

Mr. Schock rubbed his eyes.

"I wish I could get rid of that van. I swear he's been behind me since we left Derbyshire. Some people do that at night. They'd rather follow right on someone's tail than drive into the darkness. Its headlights need adjusting too; they're dazzling."

"Van?" Kate turned around to look but immediately ducked down again. "It's Tim Williamson!" she cried.

"Are you sure?"

"Positive. How are we going to get to the antigravity machine before he does?"

"That," said Mr. Schock, "shouldn't prove to be a problem."

He jammed his foot on the accelerator and they rocketed down the outside line with Kate gripping the seat and squeezing her eyelids shut. The van was soon left far behind, but Peter's father did not slow down. The car flew underneath a bridge with a camera trained on the carriageway.

"I'm sure the police will be understanding when I explain . . . ," he said with a grin.

Tiredness soon overcame Kate again and she started to nod off. Mr. Schock leaned over and pressed a button at the side of her leather seat. It started to glide into a reclining position. This car was *so* comfortable. . . .

Someone was prodding her arm. She stretched and sat up, stiff and cold and a little dazed. She felt the chair moving into an upright position again. They were no longer on the motorway but driving along a narrow country lane with tall hedges on both sides. There was no snow here. The headlights lit up an old black and white signpost.

"Look," said Mr. Schock.

"*Middle Harpenden, two miles!*" read Kate, amazed.

Soon they reached a village green and overlooking it they saw the small, red-brick terraced house, half-covered with the gnarled branches of an ancient wisteria, that served as Middle Harpenden's post office. Mr. Schock pulled over under a willow tree at the edge of a duck pond and parked in such a way that the car could not be seen by passing traffic. It was misty here. It was half past ten and lights glowed behind red floral curtains on the upper floor.

"This must be it," said Mr. Schock, turning off the engine and grabbing Kate's bundle. "Hurry—I don't think there's much more than ten minutes between us and that van."

They ran across the road and down a driveway at the side of the house. A security light clicked on, revealing a shabby-looking yard pitted with gravelly puddles, and a concrete garage. Mr. Schock caught hold of Kate's hand and dragged her out of the pool of light and into the dark shadows at the side of the garage. When Kate found she was standing on a discarded TO LET sign she tugged at Mr. Schock's sleeve and pointed—he nodded but put his finger to his lips.

The air was freezing and damp and they could see their breath. They kept very still until the security light clicked off once more and then crept out to examine the garage door. Mr. Schock tugged at the handle. Unsurprisingly, it was locked. They heard a vehicle approaching and glanced toward the road anxiously. A car sailed past into the night. Mr. Schock rattled the handle furiously while Kate looked behind her, hoping that no one could hear him.

"I fear there's only one solution to our little dilemma: I'm going to have to ram the garage door."

"You're going to *what?*" exclaimed Kate, horrified.

But Mr. Schock was already running toward his car, and moments later Kate found herself caught in the blinding glare of headlights. An electric window swooshed slowly down and Mr. Schock's head appeared.

"Er . . . you'd better move out of the way, Kate."

"But your car!"

Mr. Schock revved the engine and Kate jumped out of the

way. Peter's father put the car into gear, adjusted his safety belt, then paused momentarily, it seemed to Kate, like an athlete preparing himself mentally before starting his run-up for the long jump. When he was ready, he stamped hard on the accelerator and aimed his car squarely at the up-and-over door. Kate winced and clapped her hands to her ears as the thunderous, metallic impact caused half the windows in Middle Harpenden to vibrate. Mr. Schock reversed to inspect the damage: The door now gaped open, having become detached from the frame on the left-hand side. He got out of the car, a large grin on his face.

"That was fun. . . ."

Kate gawked at the damage. Behind him, the hood of his sleek, executive car had caved in; the license plate swung by a single screw. Lights appeared and curtains twitched in windows. The back door of the post office opened, a timid face peeped out, and it closed again. They heard the sound of keys in locks and bolts being drawn. Kate looked at Peter's father. For a grown-up he was surprisingly reckless. . . .

"I wonder how long it will take the police to get here," she said.

"Just tell me that this *is* the right garage," said Mr. Schock, "and I haven't just written off my car for nothing."

Kate slipped through the gap in the door. A light went on inside and Mr. Schock heard her shout:

"It's here! It's the antigravity machine!"

Mr. Schock dived into the garage after Kate.

"Oh no!" exclaimed Kate at the sound of a car engine. "It can't be Tim Williamson already!"

They heard a door slamming and fast-approaching footsteps. Mr. Schock pushed against the door to close the opening. It clanged shut but it was now impossible to lock it. An eye appeared in the crack.

"Kate! It's you! What do you think you're doing? Open up!" Tim Williamson shouted and banged his fist on the door.

"Temper, temper," shouted Mr. Schock from within the garage.

"And who exactly are you?" cried Tim.

"Oh, just the father of the boy your machine sent skidding into another century, that's all. We're going to fetch him back if that's all right with you."

"Ah. I'm sorry about your son. . . . But, you see, I *can't* let you take it. . . ."

"You can make another machine—you can't make me another son!"

"Just think about what you're doing for a moment! If anything happens to the machine, you can kiss good-bye to any hope of bringing your son back."

"Each of us has his own priorities, Dr. Williamson. . . . I'm going to get Peter back, with or without your help!"

Tim Williamson kicked at the garage door. "Well, you asked for it. . . ."

Then came a barrage of blows as the scientist threw himself repeatedly at the door. Mr. Schock braced his back against the cold metal, bent his knees, and pushed as hard as he could with his feet in an attempt to keep the gap between door and frame as narrow as possible. *Bam!* He looked over at Kate, who was on her hands and knees in front of the antigravity machine peering at a couple of digital readouts, a frown etched onto her freckled forehead.

"You're going to have to start it up by yourself, Kate. I wouldn't know how to help you even if our friend here would stop bugging me. . . ."

Bam! Bam!

Mr. Schock looked over at the antigravity machine. It stood a little less than six feet high and was composed of a giant metal bulb, contained in a Perspex case, which rested on a dull gray metal box. There was a disappointing lack of flashing lights and shiny chrome fittings. "So this is it," he panted. "It doesn't look like it could make a cup of tea, let alone transport us back in time. . . ."

"It's what's underneath that counts," said Kate.

Bam! Bam!

Increasingly giddy with all the awful banging, Kate looked in dismay at the antigravity machine. She realized that she had not paid enough attention to how her father had started it up on Hampstead Heath. *What if I'm supposed to adjust the settings?* she thought. *Or do I just switch it on? What if we don't go back to 1763 . . . ? What if . . . ?* She had a vague recollection of her father changing the settings back in the laboratory before the accident. Would they have to be the same for the machine to

78

work? All at once she was in a blind panic—it had all gone wrong! She hadn't used her head, she had not been careful enough, and now Peter was going to be a refugee in another time forever!

"I'm sorry! I can't remember how to do it . . . ," she wept.

Bam! Spread-eagled against the back of the garage door as Tim's violent blows juddered right through him, Mr. Schock met Kate's desperate gaze. She watched him make an effort to smile encouragingly at her, but sensed his feeling of utter helplessness. It suddenly struck her that his family's future happiness now lay on a knife edge—and it was all up to her.

Bam! I will *remember,* she told herself. *I* can *work out how to do it.*

"It'll be okay, Kate," Mr. Schock shouted. "I'm sure it will come back to you. . . ."

Kate rested her forehead on the cold metal and the machine shifted slightly.

"Careful!" warned Mr. Schock. "Look, it's caught on half a brick at the back—it's not level."

Kate moved away to look but suddenly the banging stopped and in its place they heard the sounds of a scuffle. Mr. Schock peeped through the door.

"It's your dad! And a woman."

Kate's heart leaped. She wanted to call out to him, but she bit her lip instead.

"Let me talk to my daughter!"

"Why should I let you talk to your daughter when you are prepared to let my son rot in 1763?"

"It's not like that . . . ," started Dr. Dyer, but before he could finish, Kate peered through the gap between the frame and the door.

"Dad, don't try to stop us. If you're not going to go after Peter, we are. It's not like the universe is going to vanish in a puff of smoke because a few people have gone backward and forward in time."

"Kate, please, *please*, don't do this! Your mother will be heartbroken! Not to mention Sam. I just don't know how he would take it!"

"Sam already knows. He helped me."

"Sam knows?"

"Look, it's not like I'm never coming back! Mum will understand. I thought you would, too. . . . And, anyway, if you're worried about Tim going public about time travel, the machine will be a lot safer with us in the eighteenth century where no one can get their hands on it."

Dr. Dyer laughed despite the situation. Kate always had an answer for everything.

Kate disappeared back inside the garage while Tim shoved Dr. Dyer out of the way in order to resume throwing himself at the garage door.

"They are *not* going off with my machine!"

"I think you'll find that, strictly speaking, it's NASA's machine," commented Dr. Pirretti.

"We'll have to agree to differ on that one," said Tim, launching himself furiously at the door. Mr. Schock was taken by surprise and lost his balance, giving Tim enough time to force his head through the gap. Mr. Schock quickly recovered and threw himself at his opponent, shoving his face backward with the flat of his hand so that the scientist's nose was squashed to one side. Crying out in pain, Tim momentarily withdrew, allowing Mr. Schock to take up his defensive position again.

"The brick!" exclaimed Kate all of a sudden. "It's because of the fail-safe device—the antigravity machine won't work unless it's on the level. All I've got to do is kick the brick away!"

Bam! Bam!

"Whatever you're going to do, it'd be great if you'd do it quickly!" panted Mr. Schock.

"Dad!" shouted Kate. "I'm starting up the machine now. If I need to adjust anything you'd better tell me now before it's too late. . . ."

"No! Kate! . . . Don't do it!"

There was a pause. Kate waited for perhaps five seconds.

"Okay, I'm going anyway," she said, and kicked the brick away. "Good-bye, Dad!"

Without her even having to switch it on, she immediately heard a low humming noise, rather like the sound of a fridge.

"Wait!" shouted Mr. Schock, leaping toward her. He threw his arms around the base of the machine.

With a final, violent blow, Tim smashed open the door and erupted into the garage. Dr. Dyer, with a father's protective instinct, threw himself at his colleague's legs, pinning him down. He looked up at his daughter. There was nothing he could do to stop her now; the machine was already liquefying around its edges. His eyes filled with tears. Tim's jaw dropped in wonder.

"Oh my . . . ," murmured Dr. Pirretti.

"Kate," said Dr. Dyer as calmly as he could manage, "don't alter anything. The bottom readout should be six point seven seven, but no one will have touched it. . . ."

Mr. Schock turned his head toward Dr. Dyer. "Tell my wife!"

"I will."

"Make sure you do!"

"And you—keep my daughter safe!"

"I had to do it, Dad! Say you understand. . . ."

But before her father could answer, an ever-strengthening force began to repel the three scientists and they found themselves leaning forward as if walking into a strong wind. Kate looked down on them as if from a great distance. The edges of her vision became clothed in darkness, and the now-familiar spirals began to form somewhere above her, rising up into the never-ending reaches of space and time. And then, consciousness clicked off like a light switch and she knew no more.

Doctors Pirretti, Williamson, and Dyer found themselves alone in the cold, damp garage. There was a stunned silence. Dr. Pirretti was trembling.

"Did you feel it?" she said. "It was as if an infinitely small crack just appeared in the universe. . . . What have we done? What *have* we done?"

No one replied.

Then Tim asked very reasonably: "Would you mind getting off me now, Andrew?"

"Oh, I'm sorry, Tim," said Dr. Dyer, getting to his feet. "Nothing personal."

"Likewise."

"I suggest," said Dr. Dyer, "that unless we're all in the mood for a tête-à-tête with Inspector Wheeler, we get out of here as fast as we can."

As the scientists retreated hurriedly back to their vehicles, a middle-aged couple in dressing gowns and slippers peered at them through the back door of the post office. When they heard them roar away into the night, they tiptoed over to the garage to inspect the damage.

"It's gone!" said the woman, as a police siren grew ever nearer.

"I told you letting the garage to strangers would be a mistake. . . ."

"Fancy wrecking a beautiful car like that! What do you think was in there?"

"I told you, I thought it was a jukebox or something at first, but when I went to have a closer look, I couldn't tell what it was. . . . I pressed a few buttons but nothing happened. . . ."

"You don't think they were terrorists, do you? It wasn't ticking, or anything?"

"Don't make me laugh! In Middle Harpenden? Who in their right minds would want to plant a bomb here?"

FOUR

THE OBSERVER

*In which a gentleman takes a keen
interest in an article on cricket*

He was a good half a head taller than most of the folk making their way down Cheapside, and he strode along, carrying a pile of papers under one arm and swinging a silver-topped ebony cane with the other. Clear-eyed and rosy-cheeked, he wore a yellow waistcoat and, to set it off, a handsome blue jacket which was well-cut and had deep cuffs and gold braid buttons. His back was straight and he held his chin high. He was neither young nor old; he was, in short, an English gentleman in the prime of his life.

The gentleman had walked from the Baltic Exchange, in the city, where he had business, and as he drew closer to St. Paul's, the intermittent, southwesterly breeze carried to his nostrils the stench of the great river. Although he loved the Thames, he was happy, he reflected, particularly during the summer, that he was not obliged to live too close to its banks.

Cheapside was less frenetic than usual, which meant that

it was still noisy and full of Londoners about their business. Church bells chimed, a Scotsman in a kilt played a mournful air on his bagpipes, and, thundering over the granite sets, there was the regular stream of heavy wagons laden with goods from the port of London. Unusually, however, there was room enough on the sidewalks to saunter and admire the window displays at one's ease. There were only a couple of street hawkers today: a flower girl and an old crone selling oysters. The gentleman had heard rumors of a bad outbreak of measles in the east of the city and wondered if this was the cause of the comparatively empty streets. It was a warm and humid day and the mellow, late summer sun had persuaded the portly fellow walking in front of him to slip off his wig and stuff it into his pocket. In its place he had put a large pocket handkerchief. The breeze blew it off his head, and the handkerchief landed at the gentleman's feet. The latter swooped down to pick it up and returned it to its owner. The man, who was puffing and panting on account of the heat, immediately mopped his perspiring brow and then thanked the gentleman most kindly.

The gentleman inclined his head in acknowledgment, and said: "Mark my words, sir, there will soon come a day when a fellow can walk from one side of the city to the other without spotting a single wig."

"I fear it is only the very young who can avoid the wearing of hairpieces without appearing ridiculous," replied the portly man. "The new fashion for natural hair is too late for me. It is only this confounded heat and my lack of vanity that drives me to show my naked scalp to the world!"

The gentleman wished him a good day and moved on. The twenty-five shillings a year the gentleman paid his barber for styling his hair were well worth it, he thought, to avoid the torture of melting under a foul-smelling wig all summer. He always had his dark brown hair dressed in exactly the same style—four tightly rolled curls at each side and the rest pulled back into a neat ponytail secured with a black taffeta ribbon. He had never been happy with the idea of putting a wig on a perfectly good head of hair. The best use to which he had ever put a wig was to place a kitten underneath it and push it into the candlelit study of his old tutor at Cambridge. Like a miniature, hairy turtle, the kitten had scuttled and skidded along the polished wood floor, dispersing clouds of white powder as it went. The gentleman laughed at the memory of it; his tutor had shrieked like an old woman who had seen a ghost . . . but that was long ago.

Soon the gentleman reached the Chapter Coffeehouse in Paul's Alley. The coffeehouses around the Bank of England and Guildhall were best if one wanted to catch up on trading and shipping news or talk politics, but it was altogether more agreeable at the Chapter Coffeehouse. Here, booksellers and publishers and writers and thinkers gathered at all hours of the day and night and it was rare if some sharp-tongued wit did not reduce the customers to helpless laughter, or if a serious debate did not deteriorate into a heated fight—which was always more entertaining than philosophy. The coffee, it was true, left something to be desired, but it was here, in this rickety building in a quiet alley near St. Paul's Cathedral, that the gentleman came for good company and to discover what was going on in the world, and where, if conversation flagged, there was always the well-stocked library to divert him.

He pushed open the door of the coffeehouse and entered the low-ceilinged room, the first in a series of small rooms which each accommodated their own regulars. The air was thick with swirls of blue tobacco smoke. He walked past the dark staircase in the center of the ancient building and through to the cozy room at the back where he headed for a window seat beneath tall, diamond-paned windows.

The gentleman flicked out the tails of his jacket before lowering himself, straight-backed, onto the wooden settle. Then he placed his papers on the table in front of him and pulled out today's copy of *The Observer* from the bottom of the pile. It was dated Monday, 3rd September, 1792. He also took out a beautiful pipe, carved from a walrus tusk, which had been left to him in Colonel Byng's will—a memento from a voyage to America some twenty years past, when it was still a British colony.

The gentleman stuffed the ivory pipe with tobacco from a small leather pouch and lit it with a taper. Then he picked up *The Observer* and began to read, puffing at his pipe and taking pleasure in blowing smoke rings toward the ceiling. It was a habit he relished, not least because it reminded him of a particular wizard in a book he had loved as a child and longed to hold in his hands once more. As he read, his face took on a more serious expression and he put down his pipe. A waiter brought him a steaming cup of strong coffee, and a jovial old gentleman, a bookseller by trade, leaned over and asked him if he would do him the honor of telling him the latest news as he had just returned from a month in the country and felt singularly ill-informed.

"Is the talk still all of France, sir?" he asked.

The French Revolution was now in its third year and much of the news that filtered across the Channel made for grim reading whichever side you were on. Many aristocrats had already fled the country, and since the spring, France had been at war with Austria and Prussia. It seemed that it would not be much longer before England became involved too.

"The talk is, indeed, still all of France," replied the gentleman. "But then, the Revolution continues to occupy all our attention, does it not? So you have not heard tell of the August atrocities?"

His neighbor shook his head. "No, sir, I have not."

"The Prussians did King Louis no service when they swore to destroy Paris if he was hurt. His people now see him as their enemy. A rampant mob stormed the Tuileries Palace these two or three weeks past. It was nothing less than a massacre. The King's Swiss Guard were butchered."

"No! The Swiss Guard?"

"They were not properly armed, it seemed. Hundreds of the mob perished, too. They say that the gutters were awash with blood. Queen Marie-Antoinette and King Louis and his children are now under arrest."

"What is to become of the French King and his family? Will they let them live?"

"That remains to be seen. They may not have killed the King but it seems they have already killed the monarchy."

The gentleman flicked through the pages of *The Observer*, searching for other news.

He paused and pulled a face. "A priest escaped his prison cell in Paris, only to be eaten by wolves in the Bois de Boulogne as he tried to make his way toward England and safety."

"Poor fellow. Just when he thought he was home and dry."

"Yes," agreed the gentleman with feeling, thinking that he, too, knew what *that* felt like. He took another puff of his pipe.

A foppish young man threw himself down on the other end of the wooden seat.

"Good morning, gentlemen!" he said and helped himself to some of the gentleman's tobacco. "Don't mind, do you, my dear fellow? Your baccy has so much more flavor than my poor stuff."

"Good morning, Mr. Fitzpatrick, and, as I have told you before, you may purchase the same blend of tobacco from Fribourg & Treyer in the Haymarket whenever you please. . . ."

The gentleman continued to scan the newspaper. Suddenly he froze, all his concentration focused on a small article on the second-to-last page. His companions looked at each other, amused and intrigued by the expression on his face.

"You seem shocked, Mr. Schock!" said the young man, peering over the gentleman's shoulder at what appeared to be a story about cricket. "Pray don't keep us in suspense! What fascinating tidbit have you discovered? What is so amazingly shocking to so shock Mr. Schock?"

Without bothering to react or even to say good-bye, Peter Schock, for it was he, leaped up, gathered his papers and rushed out into the street, where he hailed a hackney coach and instructed the driver to take him to the Blue Boar, the coaching inn at Holborn, from whence he caught the first stagecoach to St. Albans.

PETER NEVER BLURRED AGAIN AS FAR AS I AM AWARE. IT WAS AS IF, WITHOUT MISTRESS KATE, HE DID NOT HAVE THE NECESSARY FORCE. IT WAS ONLY AFTER WE SETTLED INTO HAWTHORN COTTAGE AND LIFE HAD TAKEN ON A QUIETER RHYTHM THAT THE PANGS OF HOMESICKNESS STARTED TO ASSAIL HIM. HE ALSO FELT THE ABSENCE OF MISTRESS KATE MOST KEENLY. ANYTHING WHICH REMINDED HIM OF HIS FORMER LIFE WAS APT TO TRANSPORT HIM TO AN INNER, SOLITARY WORLD WHERE I COULD NOT FOLLOW. HE DESPAIRED OF EVER SEEING HIS FAMILY AND FRIENDS AGAIN, AND FOR MANY WEEKS HE SOUGHT ONLY HIS OWN COMPANY. ON SOME DAYS SCARCELY A MORSEL OF FOOD PASSED HIS LIPS. PARSON LEDBURY AND YOUNG MASTER JACK WERE OF GREAT SUPPORT TO HIM AT THIS TIME AND DID MUCH TO LIFT HIS SPIRITS AND COAX HIM TOWARD A SUNNIER FRAME OF MIND. BY DAFFODIL-TIME, THE FOLLOWING SPRING, THE WORST WAS OVER. PETER BEGAN TO TAKE PLEASURE IN LIFE ONCE MORE, AND I WAS GLAD.

—*THE LIFE AND TIMES OF GIDEON SEYMOUR,*
CUTPURSE AND GENTLEMAN, 1792

FIVE

ALTERED SKYLINES

In which Kate and Mr. Schock make a surprising entrance into the eighteenth century, Peter steals a can of Coca-Cola, and the Tar Man makes a useful discovery

The coach arrived at its destination at half past seven. Peter Schock then hired a horse and galloped the eight miles of dirt roads between St. Albans and the tiny hamlet of Middle Harpenden. The setting sun cast long shadows over mile after mile of harvested fields where wiry-stemmed poppies pushed their way through stubble and earth baked hard by summer heat. An excellent rider, as was only to be expected from a gentleman, and one schooled so attentively in his youth by Gideon Seymour, Peter sat easy and straight-backed on his mount, whose hooves kicked up clouds of dust with every stride. His eyes were fixed on the horizon, searching for the first sign of that place where his life would, he believed, be changed forever. . . .

He was in a fever of anticipation, scarcely daring to hope that after twenty-nine years, his heart's desire was about to come true. He had thought of a thousand reasons why no one from his century had come to rescue him, but mostly he feared that his companions had not survived their journey home and that the antigravity machine had been damaged or destroyed. Sometimes Peter worried that Kate and her father had, like him, become lost in time and were stranded in a foreign century. He never doubted, however, that they would come to find him if they could. But now, oh joyful day, Kate and his own father had contrived to travel back in time and he would soon learn the reason for the long delay. It seemed to him that he had been waiting for this moment his entire life. Exiled in a different time, now, God willing, Peter Schock, child of the twenty-first century, was about to return home as a grown man. His heart raced and his mouth was dry. It had been decades since he had thought about the M1 motorway but now he did—and how he resented the long hours he had spent traveling barely thirty-five miles. When, at long last, he reached Middle Harpenden, he asked for directions to the vicarage where, *The Observer* had reported, the two strangers were staying until it was decided how best to proceed.

The long gravel path that led to the vicarage was lined with apple trees, and their branches were weighed down with an abundant crop of russet fruit.

Peter Schock pulled hard on the reins and he sat immobile on his weary horse, staring at the red-brick house that he hoped sheltered his own father and his long-lost childhood friend. Had they been looking for him all these years? Would he even recognize them? His father must be seventy now, at least, and Kate, too, would be in her middle years. She could never have married, for *The Observer* referred to her as Miss Dyer. . . . He wondered why. She had been so bright and pretty and there would surely have been no shortage of willing suitors. . . .

When, with an effort, Peter tried to picture his father's face, a fleeting image came and vanished as soon as it appeared. Memory is a disobedient servant, he thought. And then, would *they* recognize *him*? Was he the same person? The boy that he had been when they last saw him must still be a part of him, for the adult does not just discard the child that he was. Surely when you behold the child, the promise of the man is plain for all to see? They would recognize him, at least, would they not? He could not bear it if he were as a stranger to them—or, worse, if they did not like what they saw. . . . Peter frowned and pushed back his hair distractedly. But then again, he had finished his growing up and lived his entire adult life away from them—in another time, in another world.

The horse whinnied, bored with having to stand still for so long, and took a step nearer to the garden. It lowered its long neck over the half-open gate into the flower borders and started to eat a clump of orange marigolds. Peter wondered if he would have been a different man if the Tar Man had not taken his place on Hampstead Heath and he had, instead, grown up in the twenty-first century. *Is your identity formed,* he asked himself, *by the basic nature you are born with or by what happens to you in life?* He found the thought strangely distressing that, in different circumstances, he could have become a different person.

He stroked the horse's neck absentmindedly, too deep in

thought to notice it munching noisily, and unaware that the animal was demolishing a fine display of late summer flowers. He realized that over the years he had thought less and less about his own time—to the extent that the twenty-first century now seemed like a dream to him, or a far-off foreign country that he had visited long ages ago. In most ways, double-decker buses or space probes seemed as improbable as dragons or unicorns. Now he looked, behaved, and sounded like an eighteenth-century gentleman. In all respects save one he *was* an eighteenth-century gentleman. Could his father and Kate accept him for who he had become? Suddenly, Peter lost all his courage and was seized by the overwhelming desire to turn back, to return to London and pretend that he had never clapped eyes on today's newspaper.

Just as he was about to pull on the reins and dig his knees into the horse's sides, the sound of footsteps crunching in the gravel prompted him to recover himself. And although he felt things as keenly as ever he did, the intervening twenty-nine years had certainly taught Peter Schock, if not how to master his feelings, at least how to conceal them when he needed to. He jumped down off his horse, put on an easy smile, and strode confidently forward to greet the gentle-looking soul who walked toward him.

"Good evening," replied a wispy-haired man a foot shorter than Peter Schock. He wore a white dog collar and a hessian apron tied around his middle. He held a pair of garden shears in one hand and a gardening basket overflowing with dead rose heads in the other. "As you can see, sir, I am cultivating my garden . . . and what more pleasurable task could there be on such an evening? It seems that your horse, too, is enjoying the fruit of my labors. . . ."

Peter turned around, aghast, as he realized that his horse had already demolished half of the good vicar's ornamental display.

"I am so sorry!" he exclaimed, yanking the horse's head out of some nasturtiums. "How can I make amends . . . ? I . . ."

The Reverend held up his hand and smiled.

"Do not trouble yourself, my dear sir; the Lord giveth and the Lord taketh away. I saw you arrive. . . . You seemed more than a little preoccupied and uncertain whether to stay or go. May I be of any assistance? I am Mr. Austen, the vicar of this parish."

"How do you do, Reverend," replied Peter Schock. "In truth, I hope that *I* might be of some assistance to *you*. I understand that a certain Mr. Schock and a Miss Dyer are currently lodging with you in somewhat unusual circumstances. I hope that I may be able to shed some light on the matter."

"In which case you are most welcome, sir!"

Peter Schock was led into a comfortable, airy drawing room, painted a delicate shade of duck-egg blue. A generous picture window looked out over the gardens. The vicar's roses, in a jug on the windowsill, shed their petals onto the cream damask sofa which stood beneath them. Peter brushed away the petals and perched on the edge of the lumpy sofa while he listened to the story Reverend Austen had to tell him. His nerves tingled as he wondered whether the sound of creaking floorboards directly above was due to the footsteps of his own father. It was all he could do to swallow a few sips of tea while the slab of Madeira cake, brought in by the vicar's buck-toothed teenage daughter, remained untouched on its pretty china plate.

The previous Thursday, Reverend Austen told him, there had been a cricket match between Middle Harpenden and a neighboring village. It was an annual event, and as there was much rivalry between the teams, practically the whole village had turned out on the green to watch. At a critical moment Middle Harpenden's best batsman hit a six over the heads of the spectators who sat near the pond. All eyes followed the fielder who charged after it, pushing through the spectators and into the field on the other side of the high street. Just as the young fellow bent over to pick up the ball, at least two dozen witnesses swore they saw a curious device, as tall as a man, materialize out of thin air and topple over into the long grass. The game of cricket was instantly forgotten and everyone rushed over to take a look. They did not dare get too close, however, for the machine shimmered as if it were made of molten liquid and, which was worse, there appeared to be two human figures attached to it in a most disturbing way.

"Oh, you should have seen it, sir!" said the teenage girl who had been hovering in the doorway. "It was horrid! The most horrid thing I ever saw. You could see through it as if it were made of glass, and the man's leg was trapped underneath it. It made my flesh crawl!"

"Thank you, Augusta," said her father and wafted her away with his napkin so that he could finish his tale. "I had arrived on the scene by this time and I can assure you that what happened next will revisit me in my dreams for many a long year. The bodies of Miss Dyer and Mr. Schock, which were attached to the machine much as flies are stuck to a spiderweb, were suddenly blown away from the machine and landed—happily in soft grass—several yards away. You would have said that an invisible giant had picked them up and tossed them as far as he could."

"Were they hurt?" asked Peter Schock anxiously, and found himself clutching at his forehead where he had been injured in that selfsame way all those years ago in Derbyshire.

"Miss Dyer was unconscious but did not sustain any injury that she complained of. Mr. Schock, however, whose leg had been trapped under the device until that unworldly force expelled him, was injured and is, I am sad to relate, still in a great deal of pain. His leg is badly swollen and bruised. Thankfully it is not broken."

"I am relieved to hear it!"

"Mr. Schock," interjected Augusta, "has been demanding anti . . . anti . . . insipid . . . Oh, I cannot recall the word—to put on his leg. . . ."

"Antiseptic?"

"Yes! You know what it is?"

"Ah . . . I recognized the word, that is all. I cannot tell you what it is," replied Peter Schock.

Antiseptic. He had dredged the word from the bottom of

his memory but instantly he caught a whiff of the antiseptic his mother would use after he had scraped his knees. Doubtless antiseptic would not be invented for decades yet. All at once his heart melted. In his mind's eye he saw his mother. She was smoothing down a plaster as he sat on the kitchen sink. He saw her so clearly. She was young, probably ten years younger than he was now. He bent down hurriedly to adjust the buckle of his shoe so that he could recover himself.

"Anyway," continued Augusta, "I offered him tincture of wormwood, but in the end he used half a bottle of Papa's malt whisky to clean his leg, which we thought very queer indeed, do you not agree, Mr. . . . er . . ."

"Ah, yes, sir," said the vicar. "Pray tell us whom we have the pleasure of addressing."

"I apologize . . . how remiss of me not to introduce myself. My name is . . . Seymour. Joshua Seymour." Peter Schock colored slightly, which did not go unnoticed, but the vicar was a courteous and discreet man and made no further inquiry.

"Perhaps you could tell me," he continued, to cover his embarrassment, "why Mr. Schock and Miss Dyer are lodging with you? They remain here under your roof as guests, I take it? They are not detained here by force?"

"Upon my word, no! Dr. Wolsey, who examined Mr. Schock's injury, Colonel Brownlie—recently returned from India—and myself met here on the evening of the incident, in this very drawing room, while our visitors lay unconscious upstairs. While we agreed that they had not broken any law, we thought it best, in these dangerous times, to err on the side of caution until we could confirm that they were neither spies nor mad. There was talk in the village of sorcery which, being rational men, we naturally disregarded. However, we did request that they remain here until certain questions arising from the manner of their arrival and the purpose of their . . . machine . . . could be explained to our satisfaction."

"And have you reached any conclusions?"

"Both our guests have the demeanor of educated gentlefolk despite the unseemly—not to say exotic—attire they arrived in. Thankfully, Colonel Brownlie's wife has been able to provide more seemly apparel. Miss Dyer is charming as, indeed, is Mr. Schock, although he is forthright and not slow to express his opinions forcibly. . . ."

Peter could barely suppress his laughter.

The vicar smiled. "I see you are acquainted with our guest. . . ."

That's my dad, all right! Peter thought to himself. And it suddenly struck him that no one born in the eighteenth century would have come up with such a sentence. He said the phrase under his breath: "That's my dad, all right!" That simple remark contained some of the rhythm of another century's language. *How strange,* he thought, *that a part of the future is buried deep in my memory and now comes out in this present. . . .* A slow smile came to his face and then he realized that the vicar was looking at him in some consternation.

"In fact, it was at Mr. Schock's suggestion, nay insistence, that an account of the extraordinary incident be sent to the newspapers and that he and Miss Dyer should remain here in the hope that a member of the public might recognize their plight. . . . *The Observer* did not publish the entire story—I have not yet seen the article, but Dr. Wolsey tells me that its author omitted to include the reason for Mr. Schock's journey here. . . ."

"Which is?"

"His search for his lost son."

Peter's heart missed a beat. His *son*. After all these years, at long last he was someone's *son* again. He was this man's own flesh and blood. The vicar scrutinized Peter as one emotion after another scurried across his face like clouds across a wind-swept sky.

"I hope it would not be impertinent, Mr. Seymour," continued the vicar, "to enquire what relationship, if any, there exists between yourself and my guests."

"It is possible," Peter replied, "that they are former acquaintances, but I cannot say for certain as yet."

"Well, my dear sir, there is but one way to get to the truth of the matter—pray allow me to inquire on your behalf if they are prepared to receive you."

Peter's heart suddenly started to race. The moment could be put off no longer.

"By all means," he said weakly.

"I hope you will forgive me for remarking on it, Mr. Seymour," said the good vicar considerately, "but you seem a trifle pale. Would you care for a glass of water or something stronger to fortify the blood? A glass of port, perhaps? Or we still have some of the Madeira wine Colonel Brownlie brought for us, do we not, Augusta?"

"Yes, Papa."

"Thank you, Reverend. A glass of Madeira wine would be very welcome."

The vicar sent off his daughter to the kitchen and then excused himself, walking up the creaking stairs to announce Mr. Joshua Seymour's arrival to Mr. Schock and Miss Dyer. He paused briefly, one foot on the bottom step, and turned to look at Peter.

"It is a curious thing, but many years ago, when I was still a young man and embarking on my ministry here, three strangers came to the village in search of a gentleman and a girl with red hair who would be dressed in unusual attire. If they had arrived today, I would be able to help them."

"That *is* most curious, as you say. . . ."

Augusta soon returned and offered Peter a small crystal glass and a decanter of amber Madeira wine. Peter poured himself out a glass and downed it in one gulp. He closed his eyes and felt the warmth travel down to his stomach. The sound of a muffled conversation reached his ears from the floor above. When he reopened his eyes he saw that Augusta's gaze was fixed on the glass which he held in his trembling fingers. He immediately placed the glass on a small table and put his arms behind his back. He noticed that the girl appeared almost as agitated as he felt. Suddenly she stepped toward him and put her face very close to his.

"I do not wish to speak out of turn," she whispered, "but beware of the girl, Mr. Seymour. She is strange. I feel sure that she is possessed or that she is a witch. I dare not say as much to my father who prides himself on being a man of reason. You will not say anything to my father?"

"You can count on my discretion, of course, but what moves you to believe that Miss Dyer is a witch?"

"I saw her in the garden yesterday at dusk. She was flitting about like a bat! Too fast for the eye to easily follow . . . I swear it to be true! The sooner they are gone from this house the happier I shall be."

Peter stared back at her, alarmed and confused. The vicar chose that instant to descend the staircase and he eyed his daughter suspiciously.

"I hope you have not been troubling Mr. Seymour, my dear."

"No, Papa!"

The vicar turned to Peter. "Mr. Schock and Miss Dyer will be delighted to receive you and have requested—for a reason best known to themselves—that you go up unaccompanied. It is the door at the far end of the hall."

The vicar seemed put out. Peter took a deep breath and started to climb the steep stairs, his heart pounding in his ears. Soon he caught sight of a generous-sized landing. Bare floorboards were covered with a royal blue runner. Several doors led off from the landing, all of which were closed except for the far door, which was partly ajar. The remains of the soft evening light poured through the doorway onto the blue carpet highlighting an intricate pattern traced in scarlet and gold. Through an open window, swallows called as they swooped and dived beneath the eaves. Peter heard someone pacing impatiently around the room.

Holding his breath, Peter stepped forward across the narrow carpet, so nervous he could have been walking the plank. Halfway across the landing he halted and rested his hand on a console table to steady himself. He looked down and what he saw made him gasp out loud. There, laid out neatly on the polished wood, Peter saw a canvas backpack, two cans of Coca-Cola, and a key ring made of brushed stainless steel. Without even needing to look at it, he knew that the key ring—which his mum had given to his dad after her first success at a film festival—was engraved with a picture of a camera on a tripod and the words: FESTIVAL DE CANNES. . . . Peter reached out to stroke the canvas of Kate's backpack and then laid his hand on the key ring as if it were a sacred relic. With his index finger, he gently traced the contour of a small brass key. He recognized it instantly. Two centuries into the future it would open the front door of the Schock family's home on Richmond Green. His spine tingled with the thrill of it. Then he picked up one of the cans of Coca-Cola and pressed it against his cheek. It was cold, though somehow not as cold as he was expecting. . . .

"What's keeping him?" said a man's voice. Mr. Schock suddenly appeared in the doorway, clearly illuminated in golden sunshine. He was squinting, for Peter was standing in deep shadow.

"Hello there?" Mr. Schock said uncertainly.

Peter was so stunned he could not help taking a step backward. He felt winded. Just as if someone had punched him in the stomach. His father was *exactly* as he remembered. *Exactly*. He had not aged a day. His well-cut blond hair flopped over his forehead. He was tanned and lean and, apart from one bandaged leg, in the peak of health. Why, they must be the same age! How could this be? Then a young girl with long, bright red hair appeared in the doorway next to his father.

"What is it?" she asked, peering into the dark landing.

It was Kate! It was his Kate, but she was still twelve years old! Peter's mind reeled. He was dumbstruck. I have grown old and they have stayed the same! It cannot be!

"Forgive me!" he muttered incoherently. "I cannot stay. . . . I must leave at once. . . . Forgive me . . . ."

Peter fled down the stairs. The vicar and Augusta stood waiting for him.

"How old is the son they are looking for?" he almost shouted at them, although he already knew the answer.

"Why, twelve years old, I believe. . . ."

"Then I cannot help you. I am sorry. . . ."

And with that Peter ran out of the house and leaped onto the horse, who was drinking from a pail of water by the front door. Two bewildered faces looked down at him from the upstairs window as he galloped down the gravel drive.

"Did you recognize him?" Mr. Schock asked Kate.

"No. I've never seen him before. . . . And the cheek of it—whoever it was, he pinched one of my cans of Coca-Cola!"

❖❖○❖❖

Called back to NASA headquarters by her boss, Dr. Pirretti was determined to fit in at least one pleasurable afternoon before catching her plane for the States. Apart from the fiasco with the antigravity machine, she was becoming increasingly worried about her constant headaches and the disturbing sounds she could often hear inside her head which would stop as suddenly as they started. The doctors said it was tinnitus, a condition probably brought on by an ear infection, and that it would settle down in time. She was not convinced.

After catching a cab to Tate Modern, she walked over the Millennium Bridge for the unique view of London it afforded, took far too many photographs, and then strode toward the building she had wanted to visit ever since her first trip to England as a teenager. She knew little about architecture but she loved big buildings, big enough so that, if she looked up, they would make her feel light-headed. If they were old, too, that was even better. While skyscrapers were good, what she liked more than anything else was domes. She found them magical. Over the years she had been drawn to visit domes all over the world. This one had been at the top of her list for a very long time. And in spite of her scientific training, she always felt the urge to stand directly below the center of the dome she was visiting, as if some benevolent force might wash over her if she found the exact spot, or, rather like dogs being able to hear higher frequencies than humans, she felt that if she could just manage to tune in her mind, she might discover a secret world. . . . Although she would not dream of admitting it to her colleagues, it was a little how she felt about her research into dark energy.

She walked around the perimeter of St. Paul's Cathedral, craning her neck to get a good view of the famous dome, and then, finding herself facing the West Front, she admired the carved stone and the symmetry of its form. Soon her neck started to ache, and she climbed up the deep flight of stone steps toward the entrance. She stopped for a moment in front of the massive doors, about thirty feet high. As she turned around, she tried to picture cheering crowds stretching back down Ludgate Hill, and the thought of the long line of kings and queens in whose footsteps she was currently standing made her spine tingle with the thrill of it.

She entered the cathedral. The dimensions of the building when viewed from the inside were breathtaking. How many lives must have been lost building St. Paul's? How much money must have been poured into its construction? You would not undertake such a gargantuan project with thought only for your own time—St. Paul's was built for those who came after. . . . What faith in the future!

She walked slowly up the aisle, feeling a surge of electric excitement as she approached the symbol, set into the stone floor, that indicated she was at the true center of the dome. Only then did she allow herself to look upward, and she let out an involuntary gasp. Its diameter was staggering. It towered over her head, supported by eight pillars and adorned with sumptuous mosaics and murals, while far, far above, shafts of pale sunlight streamed through vast space into the inner dome, so distant it appeared misty. The dome made her feel at once tiny yet proud to belong to a race who could design and construct and protect such a stupendous building for future generations.

Reborn from the ashes of the Great Fire of London, St. Paul's Cathedral had witnessed a nation's history: weddings and funerals of the great and the good, the outbreak of wars and the return of peace. Suddenly Dr. Pirretti felt a tremendous sense of time passing, of history, of mankind's slow and hard-won progress. She sent up a silent prayer that all of this would not be about to crumble into dust. *The future can only be built on the past,* she thought—she would oppose the arrival of time travel with every last bone in her body.

It so happened that while Dr. Pirretti was staring up at the dome of St. Paul's, the Tar Man was also approaching the cathedral, picking his way through the crowds on Ludgate Hill. His thoughts were focused on less high-minded topics. His dark hair was slicked back in a ponytail and he wore jeans and a suede jacket. Only his shoes could give cause for comment—they were black and buckled and of the eighteenth-century variety. He had come early for his meeting with Anjali, not because he thought she was likely to be punctual—on the contrary he would take a bet that she would be late—but because he was running out of cash, or rhino, as he thought of it, and he needed to acquire some more.

It offended the Tar Man's sense of morality that he should have to *pay* to see St. Paul's, particularly since theft and not tourism was the purpose of his visit, and so he walked past the ticket desk with a party of young Dutch schoolchildren, a solemn and respectful look on his face, pretending to be one of their teachers. A small boy at the edge of the group stared up at him, eyes glued to the scar running down his cheek. Seeing him about to tug at his teacher's sleeve, the Tar Man put a finger to his lips, winked at him, and slipped a one-pence coin into the boy's hot little hand. When he still seemed uncertain, the Tar Man, continuing to smile at the boy, mimed slitting someone's throat. The poor boy's gaze dropped to the floor and when he looked up again, fearful and eyes brimming with tears, the hateful figure had disappeared.

As the Tar Man strolled around the nave, a white marble statue caught his eye. *I swear I know that man,* he thought, but he could not recall where he had seen him. He glanced at the inscription underneath, but as he could barely read, and as the inscription was in Latin, the Tar Man was none the wiser. It was a statue of an elderly man in a toga and it was carved in the classical manner. He had a broad, noble brow and chiseled muscles, clearly a prince among men. . . . An American couple walked past, clutching guidebooks.

"Hey, what do you know!" exclaimed the woman. "It's Samuel Johnson!"

"Cute toga!" commented her husband, and they walked on.

The Tar Man started to laugh heartily.

"Why, I scarcely recognized you, good Dr. Johnson! The last time I caught sight of you rolling out of the Cheshire Cheese on Fleet Street, you did not cut such a fine figure as this! Ha! I say 'tis well they remembered your way with words and not your way with fashion and deportment, else they should not dare display you in such fine company!"

The Tar Man moved away, his attention focused on the wealthy tourists milling around the cathedral rather than on Sir Christopher Wren's masterpiece. A queue of people had formed in front of the stairs that led to the viewing galleries high above. At the end of the queue stood an elderly lady, in a well-cut coat and elegant shoes. As she pulled off a leather glove in order to extract her ticket from her purse, something glittered. The Tar Man drew nearer and stood behind her in the queue. He saw two rings: one emerald, the other diamond. Both were set in gold. When she pushed a strand of hair behind her ear, a fine pearl earring was revealed and a waft of expensive perfume met the Tar Man's nostrils. He had found his victim and, satisfied, stood back and watched the old lady step into the stairwell and start the long climb up inside the dome. . . .

One among many, Dr. Pirretti was climbing the broad spiral staircase. It was made of wood and the steps were curiously shallow. People climbing up walked next to the center of the spiral; people coming down kept to the outer edges. Dr. Pirretti was a fit woman and started off at a brisk pace, eager to get to the top, but before long her heart started to pound in her chest and she was forced to slow down. She felt a touch giddy from walking around in circles, and when a group of children flew past her, charging down four steps at a time, shouting, "It's quicker on the way down!", she came to a halt, putting the flat of both hands on the inner wall to steady herself. After a few more steps she arrived at a kind of alcove with a stone bench carved into the wall. An elderly lady, her bejewelled fingers massaging her aching knees, sat at one side of the bench. She invited the breathless Dr. Pirretti to join her.

"This better be worth it!" panted Dr. Pirretti with a smile.

The elderly lady spoke with a strong Italian accent. "Believe me, it is! I always come here. So beautiful. And you must listen to the whispers—it is astonishing!"

"I will," Dr. Pirretti replied, "if my heart doesn't give out first!"

"You're still a child! Enjoy!"

Dr. Pirretti continued up the wooden stairs and a few minutes later stepped through a narrow door into the Whispering Gallery. She walked across the narrow, uneven walkway, worn down by centuries of visitors, and held on to the stone balustrade. A hundred feet below lay the cathedral floor, while seventy feet above, the curve of the immense dome began and completely filled her vision like the sky. A full two hundred and fifty feet above where Dr. Pirretti stood, the golden ball and cross at the summit of the cathedral pushed upward toward the heavens as they had done for three centuries.

She sat down on the stone bench that encircled the Whispering

Gallery and watched the dozens of visitors walking around its circumference. She rested her head against the wall and when she closed her eyes for a moment she became suddenly conscious of the strange, unearthly quality of the sounds she could hear.

"Can't you hear me?" she heard. It was a man's voice, deep and echoey.

Overlapping this voice, there was another, a tired mother's voice. "Why must you always do that?" she scolded. She sounded a long way away but the sound was too loud—it was as if she was eavesdropping.

Then an Australian voice: "Well, that would explain a lot! Her father owned the airline!"

It was, she realized, the structure of the dome itself which was acting as a mysterious conduit for all these sounds. She let them wash over her. Whispers and calls and fragments of sentences rose and fell and disappeared into the vibrating air. It was an intriguing yet soothing soundscape. How could she be hearing all these conversations? "Joyce! Look at me!" a voice called, near and yet far away. "I'm waving! Can you hear me?"

"Yes! Yes, I can!" a woman's voice responded right next to her. Dr. Pirretti's eyes snapped open and far away, on the opposite side of the gallery, she saw a man waving at her neighbor.

Wow! This is *amazing!* said Dr. Pirretti to herself. *His voice has traveled halfway around the circumference of the dome and yet it's as clear as a bell!*

She tuned into the soundscape, letting the voices go in and out of focus. One second she could recognize intelligible words,

the next she heard sounds whose significance escaped her. . . .
Abruptly she sat up, a euphoric expression on her face.

The sounds in my head, she thought, *they're voices! I haven't got
tinnitus! Someone is trying to speak to me! I just haven't been listening!* A second later the smile disappeared from her lips as the
thought came to her that this could, instead, be the first sign of
madness. . . .

All at once a scream reached the Whispering Gallery, traces
of the terrified cry traveling over the surface of its walls like
a pebble skims the surface of a pond. Dr. Pirretti was torn
abruptly from her reverie and, along with the rest of the visitors, looked wildly around her, searching for the cause of such
distress. It was impossible to determine with any certainty the
source of the scream.

All eyes latched on to the Tar Man as he strode nonchalantly
into the Whispering Gallery and started to move along the
walkway, leaning over the balustrade and admiring the view one
could get of the cathedral floor. He seemed relaxed and easy and
after a few seconds no one paid him any more notice. Dr. Pirretti,
however, found herself staring at him, and a pinprick of emotion
stirred inside her. She could not have explained it, nor could she
have identified the precise emotion she was experiencing. It was
just that there was something about this man which made her
want to . . . pay attention. As he walked toward her she fancied
that he was breathing slow and deep, as if trying to get his breath
back. A bead of sweat trickled down his cheek. There was nothing unusual in this, she thought, remembering how she had felt

after the long climb up. Then she noticed his buckled shoes, dusty and hand-sewn from soft leather. They were strange, they looked almost antique. When she looked up, their eyes met and the Tar Man smiled at her. His gaze was steady and confident. Forgetting momentarily that he was no longer wearing his three-cornered hat—indeed, he felt naked without it—he lifted his hand to raise it. Realizing his mistake at the last minute, he inclined his head instead. Unsettled, Dr. Pirretti looked down, unsure how to react, but not before she had noticed the snakelike scar. The stranger disappeared through the doorway that led to the Stone Gallery and, after that, to the Golden Gallery at the top of the dome. Nothing had passed between them, and yet this brief encounter stayed with her for many days afterward.

Concerned voices rose up from the spiral staircase that led to the gallery. Dr. Pirretti hurried down it, partly out of curiosity and partly to see if there was anything she could do to help. She hoped someone had not lost their footing and taken a fall. About a third of the way down she came across a cluster of people gathered around the stone bench where she had rested for a while. An agitated guard was speaking hurriedly into his walkie-talkie. As she drew nearer she could discern, through the huddle of bodies, a female guard comforting the elderly Italian lady whom she had spoken to not ten minutes before. The poor woman was hysterical, her soft, carefully arranged hair all awry. She stared at the back of her hands, which were now devoid of all jewelry. The joints of her fingers were bleeding where the rings had been torn roughly off. The guard dabbed at them with a tissue.

"My rings! My rings!" she wailed, inconsolable. "Even my wedding ring!"

"Did you get a look at him?" asked the guard.

"No . . . it happened so quickly . . . he pushed me over. . . ."

"Did he go up or down?"

"I think he went up . . . yes, up . . . *Dio mio!* What monster would do such a thing in this holy place?"

Dr. Pirretti passed a hand over her face. She felt sick. *How horrible!* she thought. She felt deeply sorry for the Italian lady, but could not also help thinking that she had had a narrow escape. It could have been her. She wondered if the man she had encountered in the Whispering Gallery could have had anything to do with it but decided that having a scar and wearing strange shoes was not reason enough to accuse someone of robbery.

The Tar Man ran up the steep and narrow spiral staircase toward the Stone Gallery. By the time he was nearing the top his lungs were close to bursting—even with his exceptional stamina he could run no more. He was heading for a secret chamber, barely big enough to accommodate two standing men. He had used it on several occasions and it had been shown to him, as repayment for a favor, by the grandson of the mason who had worked on it. But he could go no farther and the Tar Man stopped, slumped against the cold wall, and rested his forehead on clenched fists while his rib cage rose and fell and he took in huge gulps of air. Through half-closed eyes he saw a date cut deeply into the stone wall. He was slow to decipher letters but figures were easier for him. There was a name, T. MOHUN, which he spelled out painfully, one letter at a time.

"Greetings, Master Mohun," he said out loud. "I'll warrant you were not in such a predicament as I when you took a fancy to carving your name and announcing your presence to the future. . . ."

Underneath was a date: 1724. The Tar Man smiled to himself. I must be the oldest man in London, but you were born before me—and you are long gone now.

The sound of raised voices and people running up the stairs drew him back to his senses with a jolt, and the fear of capture gave him the strength to move his legs, still trembling with overexertion. He flew up the last few steps and dived to the right where he knew the chamber was located. To his horror he was confronted with a kind of office, with windows and an ugly modern door. At least it was empty, but the secret chamber was no more, converted into a bare guard's room with a desk and a chair. Fear clutched at his heart: fear of capture, fear of incarceration. It had only happened once in his life, all those years ago at the age of fourteen, and they had not shown him an ounce of mercy. He hated the men who had unjustly put him away with a black hatred, and he still picked at the wound which the experience had inflicted upon him, refusing to let it heal, so that it would keep him strong. Being innocent was no protection, so you might as well be bad, as bad as you dared. . . .

So the Tar Man sprang across the corridor, past the stairwell, where he could hear his pursuers close on his heels, and on through a small door that opened out onto the Stone Gallery. The gallery was open to the skies and encircled the base of the dome. It was here that visitors would poke their heads through the stone balustrades and marvel at the magnificent views of the capital. The gallery was almost deserted. Dusk was approaching and an icy blast of wind struck the Tar Man as he hastened around the gallery in search of the stairs which led down to the lower levels. When he found them, he flung open the door and charged down the stairs several steps at a time until, heading toward him, he heard voices and feet thundering up the stairs. He froze. How had they managed to go down and across and up again so quickly? *Confound these talking devices!* he thought. Now he was trapped. He had but one choice: to go up. Up to the Golden Gallery at the top of the dome. This was not good. . . .

The Tar Man retraced his steps and pulled open a door leading to a series of steep spiral staircases, this time made of iron. Grabbing hold of the thin handrails, he used his arms as well as his legs to climb to the top, alternately pulling himself up and taking giant strides, covering several steps at once. With each step the freestanding metal staircase clanged and vibrated; the noise he was making would instantly give him away as soon as his pursuers entered the stairwell. But better this than to move slowly. He was beginning to feel giddy climbing round and round and round, and started to see spiral shapes in his mind's eye, nauseating, luminous spirals. Just as he was beginning to fear that his legs would no longer support him, he arrived at a narrow stone corridor. He squeezed through and stepped out through a small doorway onto the Golden Gallery.

He was alone. A strong, glacial wind slapped his cheeks, and through eyes that watered with the intense cold he was fleetingly aware of London stretching to the horizon on all sides. Wasting no time, he unbuckled his belt and tied it firmly around the bottom of one of the metal railings that encircled the gallery. Then he climbed over, hanging on to the railings with one hand and grabbing hold of the belt with the other. His feet were wedged painfully between the metal bars. Screwing up all his courage, he dislodged his feet, let go of the rail, and caught hold of the leather belt with his other hand as gravity caused him to drop sickeningly toward the ground. He clung on. As he dangled there, buffeted by the wind and swinging this way and that, like a carcass on butcher's hook, he could just make out the sound of approaching voices. His hands were so numb with cold he could scarcely feel them. He was beginning to lose his grip. The Tar Man closed his eyes and gritted his teeth and willed his fingers to hold firm.

For a moment his head swam and strange shapes floated before his eyes. And then he realized that the wind had suddenly dropped and that it was much lighter; in fact, hot sunshine was pouring down on him. He opened his eyes and squinted in the glare. This was not the same London. What miracle had transported him here? Before his last ounce of strength failed him, he heaved himself up and onto the handrail, and threw one leg over so that he was balanced half on and half off, three hundred and fifty feet above the ground. He looked to see if he was alone and saw that there was a kind of dark border on the edges of his vision and that he could make out three or four guards walking around the Golden Gallery who soon gave up their search for him. He heard a shout as if from a great distance:

"He's not here, mate!"

Then the guards disappeared.

The Tar Man dropped down from the rail, leaned against the wall of the cathedral and fell to his knees in thanks. He looked out over an altered landscape. It was summer. He saw green hills in the distance and a river with sailing boats and a thicket of church spires and wood smoke rising up from chimneys. He did not need to be told the date. This was August 1763. He tipped back his head and laughed.

"I have faded!" he cried. "I have the secret!"

And as abruptly as he had returned to his own time, he was catapulted back to the twenty-first century and he stood, alone, above the dark and windswept city. The Tar Man looked down at Fleet Street, running like a steep ravine through the buildings that lined it; he looked to the west and glimpsed the Millennium Wheel and the Houses of Parliament; he looked to the east and saw great skyscrapers rising up in front of him, and further east still, he saw the towers of Canary Wharf winking in the twilight.

He shouted into the wind:

"Never will I be brought low again! Now shall I make my mark on the world and no man will know how to stop me!"

Six

VEGA RIAZA

*In which Hannah speaks her mind,
the Tar Man gets a new name, and
Kate gives Augusta a fright*

They did not come back for me. *They came back for my twelve-year-old self.*

Exhausted and overwrought, this one thought went around and around the adult Peter Schock's head. That morning, in the coffeehouse, all he had wanted to do was to get to Middle Harpenden as quickly as humanly possible. Now his sole desire was to be at home in Lincoln's Inn Fields with the sheets thrown over his head, dead to the world and all conscious thought.

Little light remained. Nevertheless, Peter still urged the tired horse to gallop through the warm, still night. He stopped when St. Albans came into view. The moon was three-quarters full and he could see moonlight reflected off slate rooftops. He decided to walk the last hundred yards to the coaching inn, dragging the weary and complaining horse behind him. He was thirsty, and the knowledge that the can of Coca-Cola was in the saddlebag played on his mind like an itch he could not scratch. This precious object was the only concrete evidence he possessed which confirmed the existence of his future—or was it his past? He came to a halt and reached into the saddlebag. He grasped the can and drew it out. It was cold to the touch, smooth and heavy. Nothing in the eighteenth century felt precisely like this. *I shall keep it forever,* he thought. He peered at it by the light of the moon. How strange that a fizzy drink, which his mother used to strictly ration for fear of tooth decay, had suddenly been transformed into a symbol of a whole civilization that had been lost to him. . . . *I cannot drink it! I must not drink it!*

The horse grew impatient and Peter, wondering how his mother would have reacted to some of the sets of teeth he had seen, pulled on the reins more roughly than he had intended. The horse trod on his big toe and Peter yelped in pain, hopping on one leg. And then, despite his best intentions, and without quite understanding why he did it, Peter found himself tearing at the ring pull. The Coca-Cola had been shaken up in the saddlebag and frothy sweet liquid spattered over his waistcoat. It was too late now. He drank. And as that long-forgotten flavor exploded on his taste buds, the night and his loneliness and his sadness all disappeared, and instead he was back in Richmond, at his childhood home, surrounded by his friends singing "Happy Birthday"; and then the picture changed and he was sitting outside the pub on Richmond Green on a sunny afternoon while his dad watched the cricket; and then he was in the cinema, sitting between his parents, eating popcorn and watching an animated film on the big screen, eyes wide with pleasure, and he was laughing, laughing fit to burst. . . . When Peter consciously tried to remember his past life, somehow the images his mind dredged up were fleeting and two-dimensional, and more often than not the memories he selected were of difficult moments—missing his mother and arguing with his father. But now, vivid and wonderful and alive, it was as if all his long-lost childhood and the century that had given him birth rose up, like a genie, out of that cheap aluminum can, and the grown-up Peter Schock allowed himself to sit in the dirt of the road and weep tears of sadness and of joy.

Early next morning Peter's housekeeper, Hannah, was in full flow in the basement kitchen in Lincoln's Inn Fields.

"I was told by the grocer, who makes it his business to know such things," said Hannah, "that the Earl of Sefton has employed Louis XVI's chef for three hundred guineas a year! He would not have offered such a princely sum for a plain English cook. Upon my word, it makes my blood boil!"

Hannah had come to work for Gideon and Peter when they moved to London away from Derbyshire. Now that Gideon was back in Hawthorn Cottage running the estate and finishing off that book of his, he had asked her to stay on with Master Peter. Her plump cheeks were flushed and her blond curls were falling out from under her bonnet. She was now in her middle years but was still a fine-looking woman and her cheerful nature kept her young.

"Oh, I know you have a liking for France, sir, but it maddens me that good English cooks are thrown to one side on account of this vogue for continental cooking. London is full to bursting nowadays with French chefs! This one pushed right in front of me and bought ten pounds of butter! Ten! There wasn't a scrap of butter to be had in the whole of Holborn and here I am with a supper to cook when I have scarce half a pound of butter and no decent dripping."

Peter sat preoccupied at the kitchen table, drinking tea and paying little heed to Hannah, despite his great affection for her. He often sat down here, even though he was a gentleman.

"'Tis a terrible pity that some of the poor souls have had to flee for their lives over the Channel with naught save the clothes they stood up in—but the *extravagance* of their cooking!" Hannah put on a heavy French accent: "'*Ma chère madame*,' he says, 'I 'ave three dozen eggs to cook—how can I manage with less? It eez impossible!' 'Monsieur, ' says I, 'I could cook your eggs with a fraction of such an amount.' 'Yes, madame,' says he, 'but they would not be the same eggs.'"

"Well, my dear Hannah, you never could abide French sauce." Peter laughed but he soon turned serious again.

Hannah observed her employer as she busied herself putting her purchases away. He had not shaved and there were dark circles under his eyes, and she realized that he was wearing the same clothes as yesterday. He clearly had not slept.

"You need not vex yourself about supper," he said after a while. "I have urgent business to attend to in town."

"If I might be so bold, sir, is there anything amiss?"

Peter looked at her. "My father and Mistress Kate have arrived from the future in search of me."

Hannah pulled out one of the kitchen chairs and sat down with a thump.

"Oh, Master Peter!" She could not get out of the habit of addressing him in this manner even though it had been inappropriate for at least two decades. She was so shocked she hardly knew what to say. "My heartiest congratulations, sir! Your dream has come true!"

Peter looked at her and nodded. Hannah wondered why he did not seem more pleased.

"Yes, it is wondrous news, is it not?" he said. "After all this time . . ."

A cloud passed over Hannah's face. "When will you be leaving, sir? Have you written to Mr. Seymour?"

Hannah was certain she saw tears in Peter's eyes.

"I shall not be leaving, Hannah. It is too late. They have come in search of a twelve-year-old boy, not a grown man who has made a life in a different age. . . ."

"A twelve-year-old boy? I do not understand. . . ."

"Nor do I."

"But you have waited all your life to be rescued!" burst out Hannah. "You would have married and had children of your own if you had not held yourself in readiness for this very moment!"

"I know . . . I know . . . ," Peter said sadly. "But now that they are come I see that it cannot be. A father has come in search of his child. Kate has come in search of her young friend. They are come twenty-nine years too late. Their search is not over."

Hannah burst into floods of tears and Peter found himself having to comfort his faithful servant. He recounted everything that had happened at Middle Harpenden—everything, that is, except for Augusta's description of Kate flitting around the garden like a bat. Hannah tutted when he told her that he intended to pretend he was Gideon's missing half brother.

"The truth will out," she commented. "It always does. Poor Mr. Joshua—he went off to America with such hope in his heart and the Lord only knows what became of him."

When Peter told her that he and his father were the same age and that Mistress Kate was still twelve years old, she gasped in astonishment.

"It is a mystery beyond my understanding! How can time have stopped still for them and not for us? But surely you intend to tell your father that you are, in truth, his son?"

"It is better that I do not."

"Oh, Master Peter, I have never heard a crueler thing!"

"It would be more cruel, indeed, Hannah, if I were to tell him I am his son and then refuse to return. Better I persuade him to go back to 1763 to find the child that he remembers."

"I can scarce believe what I am hearing!"

"I intend bringing them to this house and when I do, I expect you to refer to me as Mr. Joshua Seymour. I shall tell them it was Peter Schock and not Joshua Seymour who has been missing believed dead these last twenty years."

Hannah did not respond.

"Hannah, I need you to agree to do this."

"Very well, Master Peter, but I think it a wrongheaded notion and the saddest thing I ever heard."

"On your honor, Hannah?"

"On my honor, sir, but I should like to know what happens if your father *does* rescue you aged twelve years old. I have cared for you man and boy—if you never lived with us, I shall have a great, gaping hole in my life!"

Peter looked at her in surprise as the logic of Hannah's question slowly permeated his unsettled mind.

The Tar Man emerged from the shadows to see Anjali, some little distance away, standing with her hands in her pockets on the steps of St. Paul's Cathedral. He did not know what to make of what he saw and stepped back again. Three people appeared to be threatening her. It was surprising to the Tar Man that they should risk doing so in such a public place. They must be very well armed. He stood and watched.

Half on the lookout for the Tar Man, Anjali was trying to appear unperturbed by the microphone thrust into her face and by the large camera, labeled BBC LONDON, which was trained on her. It had been difficult to say no to their request for a quick interview and, anyway, she liked the idea of being on the television.

The sound engineer who was holding the microphone took

off his headset and said: "That's fine now, the sound levels are good."

"Are we okay to go?" asked the woman interviewer.

The cameraman nodded.

"Okay. London Youth, take two . . . Action!"

As the Tar Man stared at Anjali being accosted by these three villains, he noticed that all around him other people too had stopped in their tracks and were gawking at the scene. Not one person was trying to help her! The Londoners of the twenty-first century had so little bottom! At least Anjali was looking defiant— but why was she not trying to run away? The Tar Man reasoned that the baton held so aggressively to her face was more deadly than it looked . . . and as for the device which the big man supported on his shoulder, it seemed very heavy and was doubtless full of gunpowder. This girl certainly had an instinct for trouble! He started to edge nearer.

"In his election manifesto the mayor of London pledged to do more for young people in London. Can I ask you if you are a Londoner?"

"Yeah, you can ask."

A flash of irritation at Anjali's cheek crossed the interviewer's features but she tried to laugh appreciatively.

"So, are you a Londoner?"

"Yeah."

The Tar Man drew even closer and the film crew, well used to curious members of the public wanting to smile and mouth "Hello, Mum!" over their interviewees' shoulders, did nothing to stop him. The Tar Man was perplexed; no one was behaving quite as he would have expected. He kept his eye trained on these unknown weapons.

"And what do you think the mayor could most usefully do for young people in the capital?"

Anjali looked thoughtful as she gave serious consideration to the question:

"Ban grown-ups?"

The interviewer raised her eyes to heaven and shouted, "Cut!"

The Tar Man leaped into the center of the group, crying: "You'll cut no one or you'll have me to reckon with!"

Then he chopped the microphone out of the sound man's grasp, hurled himself on top of the cameraman and wrestled him to the ground. The stunned interviewer managed to grab hold of the camera before it smashed against the stone steps.

"Stop it, you idiot!" screamed Anjali. "I never wanted to be filmed anyway!"

The Tar Man paused, a knee in the cameraman's chest. He took one look at the expression on Anjali's face and realized he had misunderstood the situation.

"Get this nutter off me!" shouted the cameraman.

The Tar Man, who hated to look a fool above all things, jumped up and walked off without saying a word.

"He's my uncle," said Anjali by way of explanation. "He's been through a lot and he's a bit . . ."—she made a circular movement with her finger—". . . mental. It's the stress of modern life—the mayor should be doing something about people like him. . . . Gotta go. . . . Bye. . . ."

The film crew picked themselves up and watched Anjali skip after the dark figure striding down Ludgate Hill.

"Oi!" shouted Anjali. "Slow down!"

Furious, the Tar Man continued walking so fast that Anjali had to jog to keep up. Eventually he came to a halt and looked back at her.

"You got something against film crews?" Anjali panted, and seeing the blank look on the Tar Man's face, she burst into peals of laughter. His expression was thunderous and he raised a hand to strike her. He changed his mind at the last instant but his hand hovered in mid-air, so close to her cheek that she could feel the warmth of his skin. Anjali no longer felt any desire to laugh.

"Learn some respect, girl. I shall not ask you a second time. As you can see, there is much I have to learn and I need a guide."

Anjali looked back at him. "Who *are* you?"

"Come, I need to eat. Take me to a chop house of quality."

A quarter of an hour later, Anjali and the Tar Man were sitting at a corner table in a café she'd occasionally been taken to when she was younger. It was all check tablecloths and red paper napkins and candles pushed in old wine bottles. Anjali had gone through the entire menu twice but the Tar Man had recognized nothing.

"Have the Bolognese—it's a meat sauce. . . . I can't believe you've never had it. It's good. Where *do* you come from?"

"London has been my home since I was fourteen years old."

"Then you should get out more!"

The Tar Man flashed her a warning look.

"Sorry . . ."

"I was born in 1729."

About to laugh, Anjali stopped herself. He was serious!

"I am not a madman, Anjali. The world is a far more mysterious place than you think. Many people sleepwalk through life, but if you keep your eyes open you will learn much. Mine is a long story. However, all you need to know is that an unworldly device came to 1763 from your time and transported me here. I do not yet know if I can return home, yet it is in my mind that I shall stay. I foresee a life here ripe with possibilities."

Anjali was speechless. She looked around for a hidden camera. "You're putting me on, right?"

"If you think I would waste my time in idle jests, you are impertinent."

Anjali looked at him and tried not to look too incredulous. The waiter arrived with two steaming dishes of pasta and refilled the Tar Man's glass with red wine. The Tar Man poked at the pasta with his fork.

"What is this? Is this supposed to feed a man? Where is the meat?"

The waiter looked alarmed.

"The meat is in the sauce, sir."

The Tar Man picked out a grain of minced beef from the

tomato sauce and held it between thumb and forefinger in front of the waiter's eyes as if it were an affront to humanity.

"*This* is meat?" he growled. "Damn your eyes, do you take me for a fool? Bring me some meat."

"Perhaps you could bring my friend a couple of lamb chops?" Anjali asked brightly.

The waiter scurried off.

"This is a nice place," said Anjali quietly. "You're not supposed to be rude to the waiters in restaurants—unless you're a food critic, that is. . . ."

"A food critic?"

"Never mind . . . just . . . you know . . . be polite. Otherwise you'll draw attention to yourself. Unless that's what you want."

The Tar Man smiled for the first time. "Thank you. This is why I need a guide. I need to slip into your time like an egg-thief into a bird's nest. Tell me, what are these?"

The Tar Man dug into his pocket and dropped a pile of credit cards with a clatter onto the tabletop. The couple at the next table glanced around. Anjali swiftly dropped her napkin onto them. Then he placed two rings, one diamond and one emerald, into her hand.

"And I need to find a fence for these. . . ."

"Best put those away if you know what's good for you," said Anjali, gathering together the pile of credit cards underneath the napkin. "You've been busy since you got 'ere, ain't you?"

He may be a nutcase, thought Anjali, but he was certainly not strapped for cash—however he got hold of it. Best to play along with him and see what she could get out of this situation. She took a pen from her bag and started to make a list on the back of her menu: credit cards, pawn shops—she glanced at the Tar Man's shoes—clothes . . .

"What are you writing?" asked the Tar Man.

"If—and I'm not saying I will—but *if* I'm going to be your guide, I'll need to think of topics for your twenty-first-century lessons. I'd better put film crew down 'n' all if we don't want a spate of cameraman killings. . . ."

The Tar Man looked at her. She was not fooling him: He knew full well she did not believe him. It did not matter—she would in time . . . and in the meantime the rings would hopefully secure her services.

The waiter arrived with two grilled lamb chops. The Tar Man looked at these pitifully small chunks of meat with disdain and removed the sprig of watercress that had been laid artfully over them. Then, glancing at Anjali, he composed his face into a benign smile.

"Thank you kindly. A tastier morsel of flesh I cannot imagine."

Anjali smirked. He reached into his jacket pocket and pressed some coins into the waiter's hand.

The waiter examined his tip coolly. "Seven pence! Why, thank you, sir! I'll treat myself tonight!"

"And fetch me another bottle of wine!"

The waiter sloped off and Anjali wrote down "the value of money" on her list.

"What's your name?" asked Anjali. "We've gotta get you some ID."

"ID?"

"Identification! You know . . . Trust me, you need ID. You can't get nothing in the twenty-first century without ID. What's your name?"

"I have left my old name behind. I need a new name here."

"Okay. So what do you want to be called?"

The waiter returned and deposited the wine bottle on the table.

"One bottle of Vega Riaza. Anything else, sir?" he asked with no enthusiasm.

The Tar Man waved him away impatiently.

"No, thank you very much," said Anjali pointedly.

"Vega Riaza," repeated the Tar Man, rolling the r. "I like the sound of that. Vega Riaza . . . I do not want an English name, for it strikes me that London is thick with people arrived from foreign shores."

"You can't go calling yourself after a bottle of wine!"

"And why not? It has a pleasing ring—Vega Riaza."

The Tar Man picked up one of the lamb chops and tore off all the meat in one mouthful.

"If this is how much the rich eat, on how little must the poor survive?"

"It's the other way round—the rich eat designer salads and get thin and the poor eat junk food and get fat."

The Tar Man leaned back in his chair and looked Anjali in the eye for a long moment. The girl wanted to look away but forced herself not to.

"The world has changed in two hundred years—that much is plain to see—and in ways which ofttimes confound me. Anjali, will you be my guide until I no longer have the need of one?"

Anjali took a deep breath. What was she getting herself into? She could walk away right now. She only had to say "no." . . . But he did save her from the gang. Maybe she owed him something.

"All right. Until the wind changes . . ."

"I do not understand you."

"Sorry, I guess Mary Poppins wasn't around in seventeen hundred and whatever. . . . What's the going rate for twenty-first-century lessons?"

"Going rate?"

"What's in it for me?"

"Anything you want."

"Anything?"

"Yes. Here, take this as a token of my good intent."

Round-eyed, Anjali stared at the emerald ring which he held out to her beneath the table. Quickly looking around to make sure no one was watching, Anjali took the ring and thrust it into her purse. She snapped it shut.

The Tar Man watched a pulse beating strongly in her neck. *It is true that many things have changed since my time,* he thought, *but human nature is not one of them.*

⋆═○═⋆

A strong southwesterly wind had blown up during the night and the branches of an old pear tree grated and scraped at the window of Kate's room in the vicarage at Middle Harpenden. Somehow the scratching of branches against glass transformed itself during the course of Kate's fitful sleep into the crackling and spitting of a bonfire, and she dreamed she was back under the great oak near Shenstone under attack by the Carrick Gang. Joe Carrick was gripping tight hold of her and she could feel the beating of his heart against her back and smell his foul stink. . . . She tossed and turned and thrashed about in her sleep as she vainly tried to get away. All at once he let go of her and she dropped, flat on her back, onto the hard, unforgiving ground, and when she looked up it was young Tom, the youngest and most reluctant member of the Carrick Gang, that she saw, lodged in the branches of the oak tree above her. There was an expression of deep anxiety on his face and he held his beloved white mouse to his cheek. Then a deafening shot rang out and Kate sat up with a start.

"It's Ned Porter!" she cried. "They've killed Ned Porter!" Her forehead was damp and she was breathing hard, but gradually the vivid images of the dead highwayman faded away, and she became aware of the calmness and coolness of the room, of the fresh dawn light beginning to drown out the darkness, and of the first blackbird to greet the day with its joyful song.

She dressed and crept out into the garden, walking barefoot over dewy turf and through showers of pink and white rose petals dislodged by the wind. The sun shone, the birds were singing and all seemed well with the world. Yet Kate was more troubled than she cared to admit. How she longed to leave this place and set off in search of Peter and Gideon—but how could they even think of leaving until Mr. Schock could at least put his weight on his injured leg? And then, there was their mysterious visitor who had fled in such a puzzling fashion and whose name, it appeared, was Joshua Seymour. Gideon had a half brother called Joshua who was barely out of his teens, so it could not be him. It was perhaps nothing more than a coincidence, but all Kate's instincts told her that it was not. The crippling lack of any decent means of communication in this century was beginning to drive her wild. How frustrating that all she could do with Megan's mobile was listen to music and take pictures (not that she had dared take any yet). In the twenty-first century they would probably be able to track down Peter in an afternoon with a telephone and access to the Internet! But in *this* century, if Gideon and Peter were still in hiding, scouring the English countryside in search of her friends would be worse than looking for a needle in a haystack. And, in the meantime, what were they going to do with the antigravity machine? They could hardly trust the vicar of Middle Harpenden not to tamper with it.

While resisting a growing sense of panic, Kate did give in to a sudden urge to check up on their one means of getting back to their own century. The precious machine had been stored in one of the outbuildings at the back of the vicarage. She had spotted the vicar hiding the key under a curtain of ivy which draped itself over a small, high window. She had stood on tiptoe, resting her chin on the window ledge, and had furtively peeped in at the Reverend Austen, who stood before the antigravity machine, frowning and smoothing down his wispy hair, deep in thought. Kate's and Mr. Schock's inability to remember or explain how they had arrived had been largely accepted by the vicar and all the other village worthies who now came up, on a daily basis, with increasingly far-fetched theories about the intriguing device. How long before their curiosity got the better of them and they either damaged the machine or set it off?

Kate slipped her hand behind the ivy, felt for the key, and unlocked the door. The barn was dark and musty and where a long ray of sunlight cut through the gloom, she could see clouds of dust dancing in the still air. The sight of the domed machine made her remember the distraught expression on her father's face as he poked his head through the gap in the garage door. She bit her lip. It was then that his last words suddenly came to her, at the very moment that the antigravity machine was beginning to liquefy, when it was too late to do anything about it. Don't alter anything, he had said. The bottom readout should be six point seven seven, but no one will have touched it. . . . Now Kate crouched in the straw at the bottom of the machine and scrutinized the tiny figures. She read: seven point six seven megawatts. Her blood froze. It was the wrong figure. *Could* her father have said seven point six seven and not six point seven seven? Could the Reverend Austen have tampered with it? She racked her brains but she just could not be sure. She peered at the setting for the tenth time but it still read seven point six seven. Perhaps it did not matter. After all, they must surely have come back to 1763. Hadn't they? She had asked the vicar what date it was, shortly after their arrival, but he had only informed her that it was the first of September and she had not dared risk giving herself away by asking what year it was. She had not been overly concerned, however, because King George and Queen Charlotte had come up in conversation, and while no one was wearing court dress in Middle Harpenden, the fashions looked similar—even though ladies' skirts here did not seem so wide and the waistlines were higher, and perhaps fewer of the men wore wigs. . . . But Kate had put this down to living in the middle of the countryside. At any rate, the food was as dodgy as ever. She had scarcely been able to look at her portion of the jellied ox tongue which had been placed on the table so proudly the first night, let alone swallow it. All the same, a sinking feeling started to come over Kate, and doubts about the accuracy of the setting started to gnaw away at her. She resolved to discover the exact date as soon as possible.

A tiny, high-pitched squeaking nearby distracted her from her worries and she tiptoed toward the source of the sound. In a dark corner of the barn, in a hollow in some straw, lay a tabby cat and seven newborn kittens. Their eyes were still closed and they were crawling blindly over each other, struggling to stake their claim, their one purpose in life to suckle at their exhausted mother. Kate watched, smiling, for a long while and then stepped back out into the bright morning sunshine.

Kate noticed Augusta from some distance away. She was

emerging from the front door, holding something that looked like a newspaper. She was standing as still as a statue and when Kate shouted out "Good morning!" she did not even move, let alone respond. That girl is weird, said Kate to herself and continued walking toward the house. As she did so, Kate became aware of an annoying buzzing in her ears, yet when she put her hands to both sides of the head in order to work out what it was, the buzzing immediately stopped. Kate looked around her in alarm and then realized that the dawn chorus had stopped. Her eyes focused first on Augusta, still immobile and the beginnings of an expression of pure terror on her face, and then on the rose petals which were suspended in midair just like the snowflakes the day that her mother appeared to go into slow motion. Kate gasped and a sensation of utter dread gripped her so that she could hardly breathe.

"No, no, no! This can't be happening!" she cried.

She ran to a rose tree and plucked a white petal out of the air and let go of it. It did not drop but rested there as if lying on the palm of an invisible hand. Either the laws of gravity had temporarily ceased to work, or she was moving through time so quickly the pull of the earth was too slow for her to notice. She ran toward Augusta and screamed uselessly into her face:

"What's going on? How can this be? Make it stop! Somebody make it stop!"

Augusta's eyes were still trained to the spot where Kate had come into view in the garden. The half-formed expression on her face would normally have made Kate laugh, but she was far too frightened. Tears started to stream down her cheeks. Suddenly she grabbed hold of Augusta's shoulders and tried to shake the poor girl. Her body did not respond how Kate had expected—her flesh seemed hard as a rock and her body remained inert.

Blinded by her tears, Kate ran back into the barn and flung herself onto the straw. She lay absolutely still and closed her eyes tight. Something was terribly wrong! It was as if she had lost her grip on time; it was slipping away from her. She had been fast-forwarding and she had not even noticed! How she wanted her dad right now. He would understand what was making this happen. Just thinking about her dad made her calm down a little. She made herself breathe very slowly, in, out, in, out, in, out, and gradually her pulse quietened down and she felt, if not calm, at least less agitated. After a long while, she realized that the buzzing, which was, in any case, less noticeable in the barn, had receded and soon after that she heard the tiny meowing of the kittens. Kate stood up slowly, hardly daring to look, but there they were, the seven kittens still desperately seeking their mother's milk. The tabby cat opened one eye, regarded Kate for a moment and then closed it again. Kate scratched the cat behind her ear and she curved her neck into the palm of Kate's hand and purred.

"You don't care if I fast-forward, do you, pretty cat?"

Kate returned to the house. The birds had resumed their singing, gravity was drawing the rose petals to the ground at a more familiar rate and Augusta was reanimated. When she spotted

Kate she gave a little shriek, crossed herself, and fled into the house. *What a scaredy-cat that girl is,* thought Kate, *she must be at least three or four years older than me—and it wasn't even happening to her!*

As Kate approached the front door, she heard raised voices and the sound of someone clumping up the stairs. Then Mr. Schock appeared in the doorway. He was limping, but at least he was managing to walk unaided this morning. He blinked in the bright morning sunshine.

"What on earth have you been doing to poor Augusta?" he asked, trying not to laugh. "I know you have your faults but you're not that bad. . . . Only joking!" he added quickly when he saw Kate's face. "Is anything wrong?"

Kate stared back at him, suddenly speechless. What *could* she say about this to him? She realized that she was not ready to say anything to him—yet.

"Why don't you come in and have some breakfast . . . and look, have you noticed? I'm on my own two feet at last! No stick!"

"That's great," said Kate flatly.

Mr. Schock looked at her. He was positive something was amiss and was about to press her, but changed his mind and held up Augusta's newspaper instead.

"Look," he said, "Dr. Wolsey has sent over his copy of *The Observer*. We can read the article about us over breakfast."

When the cook brought in dishes of scrambled eggs and freshly baked bread and butter, she told them that Miss Augusta

141

was feeling indisposed and begged to be excused from joining her guests for breakfast much as she would have liked to.

"Oh, dear," said Kate innocently. "Please tell her I hope she feels better soon."

As the Reverend Austen had already left on parish business, Mr. Schock and Kate found themselves alone in the sunny dining room. Kate picked at her food. Mr. Schock had second helpings of everything.

"They sure know about cooking eggs in the eighteenth century! Here, have some, Kate, before I scoff the lot."

"No, thanks."

"Is there something wrong?"

"No . . ."

"I know you're anxious to get going," Mr. Schock persisted, "and, as my leg is so much better, perhaps today is the day to decide what to do next. What do you think?"

Kate nodded. She could not answer as she was holding back the tears with some difficulty. While she wanted to share her fears about what had happened to her, she did not, in truth, want anyone to know. She felt like a freak. Blurring was bad enough, but this was worse. At least with blurring she felt, to some extent, in control. This was *really* scary. It was as if she were alone in a different world. Not only that, she was beginning to suspect that she had already had another episode of fast-forwarding a couple of days ago but had managed to explain it away to herself. And what if it kept happening? What if she ended up fast-forwarding all the time?

Mr. Schock sighed, stood up, and sweeping away Augusta's place setting, laid out the newspaper on the polished wooden table. He tried to change the subject.

"I don't know why reading eighteenth-century headlines in an eighteenth-century newspaper should be any more thrilling than spotting genuine eighteenth-century weevils in oatcakes, but it is. . . . I've got genuine shivers going up and down my spine just holding this copy of *The Observer.* . . . To think I still buy the same newspaper every Sunday. . . ."

Kate made an effort to snap out of it, as her mother would have said.

"Can you manage to make out what it says?" she asked, glancing sideways at it. "The print is really difficult to read. . . ."

"Just about . . . All the news is about France! How strange . . . There's a story about an aristocrat eaten by wolves while escaping from Paris!"

"Ugh . . . ," said Kate, "I didn't know there were wolves in France. . . . I hope there aren't still wolves in England. . . ." and then, hearing Mr. Schock's sharp intake of breath, she asked in alarm: "What is it?"

Mr. Schock did not answer but feverishly flipped over the pages, forward and backward, scanning all the articles, and then he turned back to the front page again, sank back into his chair, and covered his face with his hands.

"The paper is full of stories about the French Revolution," he said through his fingers. "This isn't 1763!"

Kate shot up and grabbed hold of the newspaper. She read

the date on the front page: MONDAY, 3RD SEPTEMBER 1792. She let out a little cry of anguish.

"It's all my fault! I should have checked the setting *before* I kicked the brick away!"

"What do you mean?"

"The number on the digital readout—it should have been six point seven seven. I'm an idiot!"

"So the setting affects how far back in time we go?"

"That's what Dad and Dr. Pirretti think—not that they've had time to prove it. . . . Oh, I've messed up everything! I'm so sorry!"

Mr. Schock sat up and rested a hand on Kate's arm. They sat in silence as the awful truth sank in.

"What shall we do?" asked Kate, finally.

"Well, where do you think it would take us if we just switched the machine on? Home?"

"I guess so. I hope so. It's happened twice so far."

"Then let's do that. I hate to say it, but we need your dad's help. . . . I can't see we've got any alternative unless we're prepared to risk traveling randomly through time."

A quarter of an hour later, Kate found herself in the barn once more, her canvas backpack on her shoulder.

"Ready?" asked Mr. Schock, before dislodging the log that had been placed under it at one side.

"Don't you think we should at least say good-bye to Augusta?"

"No," said Mr. Schock with a wry grin, "you can send her a thank-you note when you get back home!"

They both put their hands on the machine and braced themselves. Mr. Schock kicked the log out of the way. Nothing happened. Kate opened her eyes and waited. Then they both had the same idea and started to shift the machine around in the straw, trying to make sure that it was on the level. Both could see the rising panic on the other's face. Still nothing happened. They tried again but already they both knew. . . . Mr. Schock suddenly kicked out at the machine in frustration, which he regretted as soon as he had done it. Kate looked at him in alarm.

"Don't!" she exclaimed.

"Well, that's it," Mr. Schock exclaimed bitterly. "We're stranded and there's nothing we can do about it."

Kate felt numb. First the fast-forwarding, then the discovery that it was 1792, and now *this*! They were stranded in a different century and this time it could be forever! She could scarcely take it all in. And then a thought struck her like a thunderbolt.

"You don't think Peter could still be here, do you? Waiting to be rescued after all this time . . . ?"

SEVEN

KANGAROOS AT KEW

*In which Queen Charlotte offers her friendship
to Peter, and Kate and Mr. Schock hear some distressing news*

Far away from the pomp and ceremony of court life, King George and Queen Charlotte kept a private residence, in large grounds, near the river at Kew. The family soon became so numerous that all fifteen princes and princesses and their servants spilled out of the White House, as it was called, into the handsome Dutch House, opposite, with its rounded gables and distinctive red bricks.

While the grand red and white houses looked out at one another at one end of the gardens, less than half an hour's stroll away, past trees and shrubs collected from all four corners of the globe and past a giant, Chinese-style pagoda one hundred and sixty feet high, there lay a pretty cottage with a thatched roof. The cottage had been given to Queen Charlotte as a present, and she used it as a summerhouse. It was in a green and peaceful place, surrounded by trees and birdsong, and it was here that she would often enjoy summer picnics and sip drinks cooled by ice gathered from the lake in winter and stored under straw for many months in the cavernous ice house.

Queen Charlotte had invited Peter Schock to visit her at the cottage many times over the years, but today it was at his own request that he was here. The front door was opened by none other than the Viscountess Cremorne, close friend and lady-in-waiting to the Queen. She was an upright figure in a dark dress, whose copious white curls were barely restrained under a white lace cap. Her face was lively and intelligent. Peter bowed low.

"Good day to you, Lady Cremorne."

"And a good day to you, Mr. Schock! And to what do we owe this urgent desire to visit us at Kew?"

Peter hesitated. "I have some news for Her Majesty . . . of a personal nature."

The Viscountess was too tactful to press him further and continued: "Her Majesty is at present receiving Sir Joseph Banks in the Picnic Room upstairs. I will announce your arrival directly. The Queen was delighted to hear of your visit and although she is excessively fond of dear Sir Joseph, you can depend upon it that her appetite for all things botanical will have been sated by now."

The Viscountess invited Peter to wait in the Print Room and she disappeared up the curved staircase. He sat down on a chair made of bamboo and admired the many fine engravings by William Hogarth on the walls. Peter recalled that when he first set eyes on Joshua Seymour, he was apprenticed to Mr. Hogarth at Covent Garden. Joshua became a fine craftsman and artist.

He remembered the celebratory supper Gideon had arranged for Joshua the night before he left for America with such high hopes of starting his own engraving business. Peter felt a pang of guilt about taking on the identity of Gideon's missing half brother but could think of no better alternative—with luck, all this would be over before Gideon needed to hear of it. Joshua had been the last remaining member of his family and Gideon had taken the news of his disappearance very hard.

"Out of all my brothers and sisters I am the only one left. Why should I have been spared?"

And then he had said to Peter, laughing because that was his way, "Yet we are brothers in all but name, are we not, my friend? Brothers and orphans at the same time."

And Gideon did seem destined, thought Peter, to survive the ones he loved. And Joshua's disappearance in America, was, alas, neither the last nor the worst loss which Gideon had endured. But Peter did not want to recall such sad memories now. Presently he heard voices and people descending the staircase. He stood up and hurried to the entrance hall.

First to appear was Queen Charlotte, a good-looking woman, now in her fiftieth year. She wore a dove-gray gown with a cream lace corsage. Her hair had turned a silvery gray. Peter heard the rustle of silk as she negotiated the steep wooden stairs. Queen Charlotte's bearing was formal and graceful, but when she saw Peter her face lit up and she walked toward him with outstretched hand and a spring in her step.

"Peter!" she said. "It is good to see you again."

Peter gave a deep bow, took hold of her hand and kissed it. They spoke in German at first, a habit they had fallen into long ago when Queen Charlotte was still teaching him her native language.

"Good afternoon, Your Majesty! I am grateful to you for receiving me at such short notice."

"I read your letter at breakfast, Peter, and I immediately sent my own landau and a company of guards to collect your father and Miss Dyer and their machine. I have every expectation that they will arrive within the hour."

Peter grinned at the thought of the Queen's carriage arriving in the sleepy little village. "Thank you, Ma'am. Middle Harpenden will be buzzing with the news for a decade at least!"

The Queen laughed, then, taking pity on her other guests, who spoke little or no German, Queen Charlotte resumed the conversation in English.

"Peter, I do not believe you have met Sir Joseph Banks, distinguished scientist and President of the Royal Society, who continually adds to our growing collection of plants and trees. Sir Joseph, may I present Mr. Peter Schock, a good friend whose fortunes and affairs I have followed with keen interest these thirty years."

The two men shook hands warmly. Sir Joseph wore a dark, curled wig and clutched a clay pot against his bottle-green velvet jacket. The pot contained a tall, purple-leafed plant with a large, spherical flower head made up of numerous tiny umbels.

"I have read accounts of your voyages around the world with great interest, Sir Joseph. . . . How I envy you the sights you must have seen with Captain Cooke on *The Endeavour*!"

"Thank you, Mr. Schock. It is true that one lifetime is not enough to appreciate Nature's infinite bounty. I hope that those who come after me will continue my work, for there is so much to do!"

"I am certain of it," replied Peter.

"And it is a pleasure indeed to make *your* acquaintance, Mr. Schock," remarked Sir Joseph. "I have long heard tell of a certain favorite of the Queen whom few of her courtiers are permitted to meet."

Queen Charlotte laughed. "Mr. Schock is an old family friend. I fear he would find life at court exceedingly dull. It has pleased me to teach him a little German, from selfish motives, I admit, and in return he amuses me with stories of his, let us say, *unusual* past. But come, Sir Joseph, we must not detain you any longer with that heavy pot!"

"Ah, yes!" said Sir Joseph, his eyes lighting up with enthusiasm. He held up the plant for everyone to admire. "*Angelica atropurpurea*—a beauty, would you not agree, Sir?"

"Indeed," said Peter, nodding vigorously, although the straggly-looking plant aroused little emotion in him. "It is a . . . most splendid . . . er . . . specimen."

"I shall plant it in boggy soil near the lake, if it pleases Your Majesty."

"By all means, Sir Joseph, by all means. And I shall be sure to point out your latest gift to us to Mr. Schock. The rangakoos are a fine addition to His Majesty's menagerie."

"Forgive me, Ma'am," said Sir Joseph, "but they are *kangaroos*."

"Kangaroos," repeated Queen Charlotte. "Kangaroos!"

Peter tried not to laugh. Kangaroos at Queen Charlotte's cottage! How wonderful! The last time he had seen one he was at London Zoo with his mother on a birthday treat.

"I first tasted kangaroo meat in Australia in 1770," explained Sir Joseph to Peter, "and it has been my intention ever since to introduce the kangaroo to this country. At long last I have acquired a pair for Their Majesties. I hope that they shall breed."

"And if the beasts decide to oblige," commented Queen Charlotte wryly, "it will certainly make family picnics all the more diverting. . . ."

Sir Joseph took his leave and Viscountess Cremorne withdrew. Peter inquired after King George's health.

"The King continues to do well. With every month that passes I am more confident that his madness will not return. However, I have learned not to look beyond tomorrow."

Queen Charlotte suggested they take a stroll in the grounds before taking afternoon tea. When they were out of sight of the cottage she rested her hand on his arm and said: "I received your message yesterday evening, Peter, and it gave me great pain to read it. To have awaited rescue for so long only to decide that it would be wrong for you to leave!"

"For a long time I have thought that Kate and her father never reached the twenty-first century. I imagined that the machine had been damaged and that they had been killed or—worse—trapped in some nightmarish place and caught forever between the past and the future. Little did I imagine that they would reappear, twenty-nine years later, wholly unaltered."

"I lay awake in the small hours pondering your dilemma. I cannot advise you but I shall support you in any way that I can."

They walked awhile without speaking. The call of some exotic bird from King George's menagerie nearby echoed through the trees.

"It is true, Peter," she continued, "that after a lifetime of exile, were you to return now you could discover that you were a foreigner in your own land. When first we met, I remember that we both longed to see our homes again. Yet now, were I to be offered the chance to live forevermore in the land of my youth, only as an adult, and with no guarantee of happiness, I doubt that I should take it. To be wrenched from the life to which I have become so accustomed would be difficult to bear."

"My decision was not so hard in the end. My father seeks his twelve-year-old son, Ma'am. It is best for all concerned that he continues his journey through time to find him. Were I to return with him, my parents would lose their child forever. I should be the same age as my father and older in years than my mother! Nature would be turned on its head. It is not how things should be. Nor am I sure that I could find it in my heart to leave Gideon Seymour to whom I owe such a great debt. We are family. Not by blood, but family nonetheless. Here, I have made my place in the world. I have friends. In the twenty-first century who would I be? 'Upon my word,' they would say, 'isn't that the man who is older than his mother? He was lost in time. What he cannot tell you about the eighteenth century isn't worth knowing! A fascinating fellow!'"

"Yes," said Queen Charlotte. "It is true that you would be sought out by the curious. You would tour the country and make speeches. Books would be written about you. As likely as not they would make a film about your adventures—and perhaps I should be portrayed too! Would it not please you to be the center of attention?"

"For a week or two, perhaps. Not for a lifetime."

"You are wise. Most who crave notoriety live to regret it."

"To return home has always been my heart's desire—how ironic that now it comes to it, I find that the price is too high."

The Queen stopped walking and turned to face Peter.

"Words are easy, Peter. Are you *certain* that you mean them? Will you not regret this decision for the rest of your life? Do you not desire to see your mother again in this life? For such a chance will surely not come again."

At the mention of his mother Peter was suddenly overcome with conflicting emotions, and Queen Charlotte kindly turned her gaze instead to the skies and watched a flock of geese flying noisily overhead in the form of a *V* until Peter had recovered himself and the birds had disappeared from sight.

"Stay or go, Ma'am, I shall have profound regrets—but I am compelled to make a decision."

"What would Gideon advise you to do, would you say?"

"To return with my father—which is why I shall not ask him."

A frown grew on Queen Charlotte's face.

"And yet, if you send your father back to find your younger self, and he succeeds in his quest, will the Peter I see before me still exist? Will he have grown into a man in *this* century, found a guardian and friend in Gideon Seymour, and visited his Queen? And if not, *how* will his existence be teased out of the interweaving webs of our lives? Forgive me, Peter, but it is beyond my understanding."

"Hannah voiced the same fears. She said that were my father to succeed, she would have a great gaping hole in her life."

"And what say you?"

"I say that I cannot envisage how the man that I have become, how the life that I have lived—and earned—could be swept away. I say that I cannot accept that the traces of my existence could vanish from the world like breath dispersing from a mirror. It is against all reason. I *cannot* believe it."

"No, indeed, my mind cannot comprehend such a thing. How could all the marks you have made on the world be suddenly removed? To uproot a plant in such a manner that it seemed it never existed—*that* I can imagine. But to remove all signs, all vestiges of a man's life—his actions, his relationships, his imprint on the world—how could that be achieved?"

"I recall that a few days before I was stranded in this century

Dr. Dyer spoke of the possibility of time travel causing parallel worlds to come into existence. There is a pleasing logic to the theory, although it is curious to imagine duplicates of oneself playing out different versions of one's life. But how am I to know? I doubt that there is a man alive who could advise me, so I must decide and accept the consequences of that decision. All I *do* know is that I do not wish to leave this century and those I have grown to love in order—at the age of forty-one years—to take the place of the twelve-year-old whom my parents seek. History has already been changed—of that I am the proof— and yet, still the world turns."

Queen Charlotte nodded. "Then what would you have me do, Peter?"

"As I ask in my letter, Ma'am, could you find it in your heart to help me in my deception? I wish to help my father and Kate but I do not wish them to know who I am."

"With a heavy heart, Peter, I will. Remind me of the means of your deception."

"I shall become for a short time the half brother of my friend and guardian. I shall assume the identity of Joshua Seymour, Ma'am."

"Joshua Seymour," repeated the Queen. "Well, Mr. Joshua Seymour, while I most earnestly hope that you are not about to commit a grave error, I cannot deny to be glad that I shall not be deprived of your company."

"You have my eternal gratitude, Ma'am. I owe you a debt I strive ever to repay. It is on account of your generosity that I am an educated man and enjoy some standing in the world. And you have kept your promise to me all of these years and have never given me away."

Queen Charlotte smiled and shook her head. "I was touched by your plight. Yet I, at least, have benefited from your exile in this century. Over the years you have described the wonders of your age so vividly I almost believe that I have seen them in person. . . ."

Out of nowhere a kangaroo bounded in front of them. Peter stepped instinctively between the animal and his monarch. The Queen peeped her head over his shoulder and started to laugh.

"I do not know who seems the more startled—you, Peter, or this . . . kangaroo!"

The kangaroo's mate poked its anxious face from behind a laurel bush and hopped uncertainly toward the little group, its long ears twitching. Balanced on their elongated feet, their thick, strong tails trailing behind them, both kangaroos frowned deeply at the two humans and stared at them with large, dark eyes fringed with long lashes. Their short forelegs dangled awkwardly in front of them. Now it was Peter's turn to burst out laughing. The kangaroo nearest them lost interest and hopped slowly away.

"I have a whim to ask George to ennoble them. They would make a welcome addition to the court of St. James." Queen Charlotte laughed. "Although it would do little to restore His Majesty's reputation."

The kangaroos moved away and the Queen turned to face Peter.

"I believe it will be more than you could bear to tell your father of your own death. If this is truly your wish, I shall receive your father and Miss Dyer alone. They will not doubt the word of the Queen of England. If you will not return with him, this deception will ease your father's path. Afterward, perhaps, in the guise of a family friend, you could pass on some cheerful memories of your childhood which might give some comfort to your father. It is right that he at least knows that you wanted for nothing and have known happiness even in another time and even away from your own family. I am certain that he will then choose to resume his search through time as quickly as he is able."

The late-morning arrival at the vicarage of the Queen's black-lacquered landau, together with a company of guards, did indeed cause a sensation in Middle Harpenden. The entire population turned out to wave and doff their hats and tug their forelocks. They admired the four magnificent black horses, groomed to perfection, and the royal crest emblazoned in gold on its doors. The antigravity machine was carefully wrapped in oilcloth, packed around with hay and loaded onto a cart brought especially for the purpose. The bewildered Kate and Mr. Schock were able to say a formal thank-you and farewell to the equally bewildered vicar and Augusta in front of a small but enthusiastic crowd. They left the village to the cries of "Huzzah! Huzzah!" and for nearly a half a mile barefoot boys and girls ran alongside them, trying to keep up with the Queen's carriage. Kate felt that she ought to wave, as Mr. Schock was busy examining the luxurious interior of the landau with its chestnut leather seats and ivory damask lining.

"What on earth is going on?" asked Mr. Schock. "I'm not sure how much more I can take today!"

"Queen Charlotte has invited us to tea!"

"Yes, but why? Why us? Why now?"

"I guess we'll soon find out! Of course, Queen Charlotte and I already know each other . . . ," said Kate grandly. "And at least traveling with this massive escort, we don't have to worry about highwaymen or footpads."

"Footpads?"

"Highwaymen minus the horses. Not even the Carrick gang would have enough bottom to attack the Queen's carriage."

"Bottom?"

"Don't you know what bottom is?"

"No, but I suspect you're going to tell me."

"In which case I'll let you find out for yourself and we'll see if you've got any. . . ."

"You're very cheerful for someone who's just found out they are stranded in the eighteenth century."

"We'll find a way. There's always a way. The important thing is to believe that there is—otherwise you don't stand a chance."

Mr. Schock looked at her in grudging admiration. *She's a remarkably resilient girl,* he thought, *tougher than me if the truth were known—and a match for Peter.*

The journey over heavily pitted roads was, as Kate knew it would be, interminable.

For the first two hours Mr. Schock hung out of the window, drinking in the eighteenth-century English countryside, in raptures over the rural idyll that for mile after long mile passed before his eyes. Thatched cottages and mighty elms and hedgerows bursting with flowers and berries. He could not stop remarking on the lack of tarmac and road signs and out-of-town supermarkets and on the abundance of insect life and in consequence of birds. . . . And the butterflies! Oh, and the old-fashioned breeds of sheep and cows!

For the following two hours Mr. Schock hung out of the window for a different reason. Riding in a well-sprung carriage over uneven and poorly maintained roads is surprisingly like sailing in a ship. The joys of the countryside lost their attraction and instead he felt queasy and giddy. With the sound of a dozen horses thundering in his ears, what Mr. Schock desired more than anything else was to be absolutely still and totally quiet.

"You'll get used to it," pointed out Kate helpfully. "Peter and I did."

Kate was expecting to be taken to Buckingham House, so when the landau pulled up in front of a sweet little cottage in what seemed like the middle of nowhere, and when two kangaroos proceeded to hop in front of her line of vision not twenty feet away, she felt more than a little confused.

They followed a footman into the cottage and up a curved staircase. His skinny form was clothed in a uniform trimmed with gold braid and he wore a stiff white wig complete with ponytail or *queue*, as they were called, tied with taffeta ribbon. The white stockings that covered the footman's dispropor-tionately muscular calves were spotless; the effect was spoiled, however, by the dark curly hair that showed through the fine silk of the hosiery. Kate paused for a moment to put a little more distance between herself and the footman and wrinkled her nose. She wondered how many more days without a shower it would take for her to smell as bad. .... As she climbed the stairs she smoothed down her dress and tried to tidy her hair which, although she had pinned it up this morning, was now tumbling down in untidy strands over her forehead. Mr. Schock, whose face was pale gray, still had the sensation that he was swaying and clung on to the banisters to steady himself. He was creased and crumpled but felt too awful to care what he looked like, even if he was about to meet the Queen of England.

At the top of the stairs the footman opened a door with white-gloved hands, bowed deeply, and invited Kate and Mr. Schock to enter. He closed the door and stood stiffly to attention next to it. They found themselves in a modest-sized room, painted pale peppermint green, with bare oak floorboards and a high vaulted ceiling. Daylight from a huge picture window poured onto an oriental-style table set for tea in the center of the room. Seated in a bamboo chair was a silver-haired woman in a gray silk dress. She scraped back her chair and stood up, smiling, in anticipation of her guests' imminent curtsy and bow. Instead Kate stared. She did not mean to but she could not help herself. Then, involuntarily, she put her hand to her mouth in shock. Could this really be the young Queen of England she had seen at Buckingham House only two or three weeks ago? She had grown old! Her hair had turned gray! Her face was no longer firm and deep wrinkles were etched into her forehead. She scarcely recognized her. She understood, of course, that twenty-nine years had passed for her but, all the same, from Kate's point of view this abrupt decrepitude was hard to accept.

The Queen, too, was taken aback. Her gaze was fixed on Kate and she, too, gasped and held on to the back of one of the chairs.

"It *is* you. . . . It is scarcely to be believed. . . . You are *exactly* the same! I remember that day as if it were yesterday . . . you held my little George's hand . . . he could barely walk. We strolled in the gardens. . . . It was the day that Peter Schock entered my life. . . ."

At the sound of his son's name Mr. Schock immediately forgot all about his travel-sickness and looked from Kate to the Queen and back again. Kate finally remembered her manners and curtsied.

"Bow!" she whispered to Mr. Schock.

The Queen composed herself and motioned for them to join her at the table. The footman poured Earl Gray tea from an exquisite teapot and the Queen instructed him to withdraw. No one felt like drinking anything.

"Mr. Schock, it is a privilege to welcome a visitor from the future. Miss Dyer, it is good, if unsettling, to be able to renew our acquaintance after such a long period of time. I understand, Mr. Schock, that you have come here in search of your twelve-year-old son."

"Yes, I have—except we've ended up in 1792 instead of 1763 which was our intention . . . Your Majesty."

"So, if I understand you correctly, it was an error that brought you here?"

"Yes."

"And you intend returning to 1763?"

"In principle, yes, but—"

"I am glad to hear it for I have grave news which I am obliged to break to you."

The Queen bowed her head, and Kate and Mr. Schock exchanged worried glances.

"Peter Schock set sail for America nearly twenty years ago in order to start a new life in a new country. It is my sad duty to inform you he has not been heard of since. If you wish to be reunited with your son, it is through time which you must travel."

"Oh no," gasped Kate. "Not Peter . . ."

Mr. Schock stared blankly in front of him and the muscles of his face began to contort in anguish.

"Excuse me, Your Majesty," he said and walked unsteadily to the door. He opened it, and after a swift, desperate glance at Kate, he fled down the stairs and out into the grounds as fast as his injured leg would allow him. In the Picnic Room upstairs, Kate burst into tears. So her friend, whom she had promised never to abandon, was never to see his home, nor his family, nor his own time again. And without the machine she and his father would end their days here too. The Queen looked at Kate, distraught.

"What a truly terrible thing I have told you," she exclaimed bitterly. "But you can travel back to a time when Peter was safe, can you not? To a time when he was still a child and the possibility of going to America had not even entered his head. . . . Then you can return home with the young Peter Schock and all will be as it should be?"

Kate wiped away her tears with the back of her hand.

"The antigravity machine is broken, Ma'am. We can't go back to 1763 and we can't go home either."

"Broken!" The Queen looked horrified.

"Yes."

"But, it can be mended? Surely it can be mended?"

"I don't know. . . . It's a complicated piece of machinery. Who would understand how to mend it?"

"We must mend it!" exclaimed Queen Charlotte. "We *shall* mend it! Sir Joseph will be able to advise. He is a man of science, the President of the Royal Society no less! Come, let us seek him out at once!"

The Queen's faith in Sir Joseph kindled a spark of hope in Kate's heart against her better judgment and she thought, *Well, if we don't try we certainly won't get back.* The Queen took Kate's arm and they hurried down the stairs, out into the grounds and toward the lake. Mr. Schock, too, though he did not know it, was headed toward the lake. He came to a halt close to the water and rested his forehead against the rough bark of a Scot's pine.

As Kate struggled to keep up with Queen Charlotte's frantic pace she tried to imagine what Peter's father must be feeling. He had seemed so cheerful when she saw him before breakfast because, at long last, his leg had improved enough for them to contemplate beginning their search for Peter and Gideon. But scarcely ten hours later, here they both were, reeling from a series of blows, each worse than the last: they had arrived twenty-nine years too late; the antigravity machine, their only means of returning to the twenty-first century, was broken; and, most terrible of all, Peter had been missing believed dead for the best part of twenty years. . . . Poor Mr. Schock, she thought. Poor Kate, too. It was like some awful game of chess in which, one by one, all their pieces had fallen, and now, it seemed, they faced checkmate.

Meanwhile, deaf to the birdsong all around him, Mr. Schock sank to his knees against the tree trunk, utterly defeated. Had he but known it, the son whom he mourned stood, in point of fact, only a stone's throw away, deep in conversation with Sir Joseph, and wielding a muddy spade. They were clearing away some reeds in order to give the *Angelica atropurpurea* a chance to get established. Sir Joseph was telling him about the dreadful problems Captain Bligh had encountered with his crew on the *Bounty* on the way to Tahiti to gather breadfruit. Normally Peter would have been fascinated by Sir Joseph's stories, but he was currently listening with only half an ear. He had heard the landau approach the cottage and knew that the Queen must at this very instant be telling his father that he was missing presumed dead. Peter's mind had wandered and all at once he realized that Sir Joseph was no longer talking to him but was marching off toward a large pine tree. Then Peter noticed the blond-haired figure crouching at the base of its broad trunk. Sir Joseph placed a hand on the man's shoulder, leaving a muddy imprint.

"What ails thee, sir?"

Mr. Schock shot up, in fright, and turned to face Sir Joseph.

"Dad!" Peter cried.

His cry was drowned out by Queen Charlotte herself.

"Sir Joseph! Mr. Schock!" she called. "Where are you?"

Queen Charlotte and Kate appeared on the scene, flushed and a little out of breath.

"Ah," said the Queen to Peter's father, "Mr. Schock. I am happy to have found you. Miss Dyer has explained to me that your machine is broken and I am come to tell you not to despair. Sir Joseph, here, is a man of great learning and the President of the Royal Society. You can count on him being able to come to your aid."

"The machine is broken?" exclaimed Peter, his expression, as he approached them, betraying the horror that he felt.

Kate eyed Peter suspiciously. Why should this stranger care?

"Yes, it *is* broken. Was it you who came to the vicarage a couple of days ago? I think you took my can of Coca-Cola. . . ."

Peter did not answer, for his father had turned to look at him. His mouth went dry and his stomach lurched. He clenched his hands to stop them trembling. Would his father recognize him? He fervently hoped that he would not. But, then again, a part of him fervently hoped that he would. Peter waited for his father to react. His heart thumped wildly in his chest. For a moment Mr. Schock's eyes bore deep into his own and Peter discerned in them a flicker of doubt, the stirring of recognition in the far reaches of his mind. But then, all of a sudden, like a light being switched off, the intensity of his father's gaze diminished, contact was broken, and Peter had to suffer the agony of knowing that his wish had been granted: His father took him for a stranger.

"Are you Mr. Seymour who came to Middle Harpenden in search of us?"

Peter would have cried out if he could. As it was, he only trusted himself to remain silent. Queen Charlotte gave a sharp look in the direction of Sir Joseph, indicating that he should remain silent. Kate and Mr. Schock exchanged glances—who was this person? Then the grown-up Peter Schock shot a desperate look at his Queen and she immediately understood that his courage was failing and that he needed her help.

"This is indeed Mr. Joshua Seymour, Gideon Seymour's half brother who always treated Peter with such kindness."

Mr. Schock stepped forward and shook him warmly by the hand.

"So you knew my son?"

Peter gulped and somehow the right words came out. "I did, sir, very well indeed."

Kate, too, stepped forward and offered him her hand. She had met Joshua briefly at Tyburn at Gideon's hanging but she did not recognize him now. And yet, there *was* something familiar about this handsome man although she couldn't quite put her finger on what it was.

"Do you remember me, Joshua? I know we only met for a short time. . . ."

When Peter saw how young she was, and when he thought of how long he had waited for her to come to rescue him, he had to blink back a tear. "I do remember you," he said. "How could I forget?"

They shook hands, her skin smooth and pale, his rugged and already showing the early signs of age. But when they touched both of them stepped backward in shock. It was as if a strong electric current had passed from one to the other. *How bizarre,* thought Kate. *Where did all that static come from?*

"My dear Sir Jos," Queen Charlotte whispered to Sir Joseph on the way back to the cottage, "I would ask of you that you inquire neither about the reason for the collective deception of which you have unwillingly been a part, nor about the provenance of this device. All you need know is that it is broken and that it is *vital*—I do assure you, *vital*—that it be mended. I am counting on you as a man of science to find a solution to this problem and I trust that I can rely on your discretion."

The machine had been placed behind a Chinese screen in one corner of the Picnic Room. Torn away from his *Angelica atropurpurea*, the bemused Sir Joseph had been crouched behind the screen for some ten minutes while the rest of the party paced about downstairs like anxious relatives waiting for the doctor to give his diagnosis.

"Your son would tell me such wonderful things about the twenty-first century," the Queen said to Mr. Schock in an effort to lighten the atmosphere. "I have vivid pictures in my head of cars and planes and hospitals and telephones . . . and police cars. I have often found it difficult to keep this knowledge to myself. Peter taught me to imitate a police . . . er . . ."

"Siren," interrupted Peter. "A police siren."

Kate flashed a look in his direction.

"Peter . . . taught me, too," he added hastily. "*Nee-noo, nee-noo . . .*"

Mr. Schock laughed heartily at the thought of his son teaching the Queen of England how to sound like a police siren.

"But what I loved to hear about most of all," continued Queen Charlotte, "was the movies. He often talked about cinemas—he frequented one near Richmond Bridge, I believe . . ."

"Yes," laughed Mr. Schock. "He did! We used to argue about the price of popcorn!"

"Yes! I know of popcorn. How fascinating. He would throw it at people's heads in the dark."

"I didn't know that!"

"Ah," continued Queen Charlotte, "I should love to see the big screen and hear the music. To see a face as big as a house! He told me the stories of all his favorite films and would act out the parts. I recall there was one about a creature from . . ."—she gestured vaguely toward the sky—". . . space? Who was stranded on Earth . . ."

Queen Charlotte did not notice Peter desperately indicating with his facial expression that she should go no further with this anecdote.

"Yes, this creature longed to be reunited with his own kind. He was an *extraterrestrial*. What was it that he said? Ah yes . . ." Queen Charlotte mimed putting a telephone to her ear. "E.T. phone home . . . E.T. phone ho-o-o-me . . ."

Queen Charlotte laughed in delight but Kate had to turn away and tears came into Peter's father's eyes. Unlike E.T., his son had never made it.

Dismayed at their reaction, Queen Charlotte said sadly: "Ah, I see that you know of it. . . ." She looked up at Peter. "I am sorry, the connection had not struck me before now."

Sir Joseph finally emerged wiping his hands on a large handkerchief.

"I have never seen the like of this machine! A truly astonishing device! Extraordinary! I should dearly like to investigate its workings yet I dare not dismantle it lest I damage it further. What expertise I have is in botany and zoology—this device is beyond my understanding. Do you have a notion, in broad terms, of the areas of knowledge one might need to comprehend the workings of this machine?"

Kate and Mr. Schock shook their heads sadly.

"Not really," said Kate. "Antigravity?"

"Electrical circuits?" said Mr. Schock, looking at Kate.

She shrugged her shoulders.

"It is depressing to be quite so ignorant about science," said Mr. Schock. "Suddenly I regret all those times I skipped physics class. . . ."

"No matter, my dear sir, we will do what we can. . . . 'Tis a pity good Benjamin Franklin is no longer with us! With his inventive turn of mind and his knowledge of electricity and interest in all things mechanical, I fancy he could have given you a helping hand. There's Volta, of course. He is sound. He has recently published a work on the storage of electricity. But he is far away in Italy, and, besides, I think we have need of a generalist, a person with a broad knowledge and with a practical bent. Someone, above all, who is prepared to take a risk and will not easily be discouraged."

Viscountess Cremorne arrived to inquire if there was any service she could perform for the Queen before taking her leave for the evening.

"Ha! I have it!" exclaimed Sir Joseph. "The Marquis de Montfaron! A true scientist and a philosopher. I invited him to speak to us at the Society two, or perhaps three, years ago—an immensely tall fellow, and a more fertile and impressive intellect I have yet to encounter. He is a fine mathematician and has published well-received papers on electricity and gravity. He has, moreover, a particular interest in all things mechanical, and, being a prolific correspondent, he keeps abreast of all the latest developments. Yes, I am certain you could not find a better man than Montfaron in the whole of Europe."

A smile came to Sir Joseph's lips. "Although I should warn you that his belief in the healing powers of garlic makes it preferable to speak to him in a well-ventilated room. . . ."

All at once Sir Joseph's face fell. "Alas there is a problem there, too. Montfaron has a large estate in France and heaven knows what fate he has suffered since the Revolution began."

"I believe you are mistaken," Viscountess Cremorne interjected. "The Montfarons are currently living in Golden Square. I encountered his wife, la Marquise de Montfaron, only last week at a *soirée*—a frightful woman but utterly exquisite. . . ."

"Ah, that is welcome news!" said Peter, stepping forward toward Kate and his father. "I hope you will permit me," he said earnestly, "to offer you my hospitality in the house in Lincoln's Inn Fields which is already familiar to Miss Dyer. I should then be happy to accompany you to Golden Square tomorrow as early as good manners permit. I can assure you, sir, that for the sake of father and son I shall do everything in my power to enable you to return to 1763. We shall seek out this Marquis de Montfaron and we *shall* repair the machine."

Touched and bemused at the same time, Mr. Schock took Peter's hand and shook it again. "Thank you, Joshua, we appear to have had the good fortune to find a friend."

EIGHT

INSPECTOR WHEELER'S CHINESE TAKEOUT

In which Inspector Wheeler congratulates himself on a successful hunch and enjoys a celebratory meal

Detective Inspector Wheeler was treating himself to Chinese takeout. The telephone receiver was lodged between shoulder and ear as he ordered his favorite dishes. He moved around the room in time to the *Blue Danube Waltz* which crackled at high volume from his old-fashioned record player.

"One chicken in black bean sauce, one sizzling king prawns, one crispy beef, and some egg fried rice. Yes, that's it. And— why not?—a couple of wee spring rolls, as well. No, no, I'll be collecting it myself. I'll be seeing you shortly, then."

The Inspector opened his front door onto an untended garden and walked into the drizzly night with a big grin on his face. He had not felt this cheerful in weeks. Today had taken ten years off him. He walked to the car with a spring in his step and slammed the door shut. He brushed the sweet wrappers and the pile of crumbs off the passenger seat onto the floor, switched the seat heater on to high, and rubbed his cold hands together gleefully.

Ninety-nine times out of a hundred you had to be so patient to see your hunches come to fruition but today, he told himself, he had been in outstanding, no *stupendous*, form, and the result had been spectacular! Spec-tac-u-lar! Even Sergeant Chadwick had forgotten not to look impressed.

It had been sheer coincidence that he was in New Scotland Yard when a colleague was showing his team a video recording of a daring and baffling robbery in one of London's most exclusive jewelers. The Inspector stood in the doorway sipping a cup of strong, sweet coffee as the video was played over and over again in slow motion.

The thief had walked calmly into the shop with a sledge-hammer, forced all the staff out into the street at knifepoint, and locked the door behind them. Then, as they all stood there, open-mouthed with horror, they watched the thief, who wore a mask and a knitted hat, smash every glass display cabinet in the shop and drop countless pieces of priceless jewelry into a large carrier bag. By now every alarm in the shop was going off and the first police car to respond to the staff's frantic telephone calls for help had arrived. Unperturbed, the thief merely stood stock-still in the middle of the shop and—there was no other word for it—*vanished* in front of everyone's eyes.

All sorts of theories were put forward, from mass hallucination to developments in nanotechnology (one of the policeman had read an article about a chameleon-like material designed to take on the appearance of whatever it was put next to). Inspector Wheeler, however, was less interested in the "how" than the "who." He was surprised, though pleased, that no one else had spotted the similarity between the thief's inexplicable disappearance and the ghostly shenanigans in the Schock/Dyer missing children case. True, the thief was not wearing eighteenth-century dress as the children had been in the other incidents, but the *way* that he had disappeared was identical. He presumed that this was because most people seemed to have categorized these previous incidents as manifestations of the supernatural—something which Inspector Wheeler had never been prepared to do. It was not instantaneous. The thief faded over a period of several seconds so that at one point he became transparent and slightly out of focus. The Inspector would never forget seeing the ghostly vision of Kate Dyer lying between the goalposts at her school near Bakewell. She had disappeared before he could get to her. He was now convinced that he had witnessed the first example of this mysterious fading phenomenon. And where had Miss Kate Dyer disappeared to now? Could it be that her second disappearance was linked to this thief in any way? He had always had his doubts about the motives of the Dyer family and that Dr. Pirretti woman for that matter. He was convinced that she had feigned that highly convenient fainting fit when he had questioned her about the children's disappearance before Christmas. The hospital had been unable to find anything wrong with her—which came as no surprise to him, for she was the picture of health. He knew her type. Organic bean sprouts and jogging. You wouldn't catch someone like Dr. Pirretti indulging in Chinese takeout. He shrugged. Why was he letting that woman get to him? Besides, what did he care? He had just engineered the first clue in the most baffling case he'd dealt with in three decades.

Another possible connection to the thief intrigued him. He had seen footage from surveillance cameras of the notorious mad horseman denting the roofs of twenty black cabs down Oxford Street over the New Year. Now that character *was* in fancy dress. When he saw the thief moving about in the shop it occurred to him that these two men could be one and the same person. It was something about the way he held himself. He had a certain economy of movement, a certain physical poise—and he had a stiff neck. Eyewitness accounts from terrified shoppers on Oxford Street indicated that the horseman had a bad scar down one cheek. It was dark, of course, and he wore a large hat; none-theless, three independent witnesses were sure they saw a scar.

The robbery was not, of course, his case and he was reluctant to make a formal request for cooperation—at least not yet. So he had called in a few favors and arranged, discreetly, for six officers, in plain clothes, to patrol the top half-dozen jewelers in central London. If they saw a man with a scar and a suspected neck injury they were to arrest him on suspicion of attempted theft and inform Wheeler immediately.

At five o'clock that afternoon, less than twenty-four hours since the beginning of the operation, one of his men, at a Knightsbridge jeweler's, spotted and detained a man with a scar. The arresting officer called the Inspector from the police van en route to West Kensington police station. "You should have seen him, sir," he said. "He's either totally reckless or stupid.

He walked right up to one of the cameras and tapped it with his fingernail. Which was black by all accounts . . ."

Inspector Wheeler gave instructions for the suspect to be put in a holding cell for the night and said that he would drive back down to London to interview him first thing in the morning.

Inspector Wheeler collected his celebratory takeout and bought a couple of bottles of beer on the way home. As he stood at the front door, juggling the takeout, the bottles, and his door key, a voice startled him so much he nearly dropped his beer.

"Can I hold something, sir?"

"Sergeant Chadwick! Do you want to give me a heart attack?"

"Sorry, sir. I wanted to break the news to you in person."

"What news?"

"The guy with the scar. He vanished again. The van doors were locked. They were stuck in traffic at Hyde Park Corner, and one minute he was there and the next he was gone. . . . They've got no idea how he got out."

"Are you telling me they've lost him?"

"'Fraid so, sir. They're calling him the new Houdini."

Inspector Wheeler thrust the bag of Chinese food at Sergeant Chadwick's chest.

"You have it. I've suddenly lost my appetite."

NINE

DR. PIRRETTI'S BOTTOM LINE

*In which Mr. Schock gets on Kate's nerves
and Dr. Pirretti surprises Dr. Dyer*

Sleeping under the same roof as his father for the first time in twenty-nine years, Peter tossed and turned all night. Having come to a decision about concealing his identity, the news that the antigravity machine was broken had planted a fresh crop of doubts into his tired brain. Should he now tell his father and Kate who he was? He heard every hour strike. Finally, at six o'clock, exhausted but wide awake, Peter flung back the bedclothes and stood up. Drawing back the heavy curtain, he surveyed the streaked dawn sky over Lincoln's Inn Fields. It was a view he had grown to love. Beyond the neatly kept green square with its shrubberies and straight gravel paths, there was a broad swathe of mature trees. Behind them a dense cluster of church spires rose up, perhaps fifteen or twenty, all of them dwarfed by the towering, benevolent presence of St. Paul's Cathedral. Suddenly a break appeared in a cloud, and sunshine pierced the morning from behind the great dome. Peter felt the urge to wake up his father and share this panorama with him. He was proud of his adopted century, he wanted to tell him of the amazing things he had seen and done and experienced. He was a man of the world now, respected, well-educated, and a wealthy man in his own right; he wanted his father to approve of who he was and what he had become. . . . Peter shook his head violently. "No, enough!" he said out loud and then, more gently, as if speaking to a small child, "Enough." He and his father were the same age. In everyone's eyes they were equals. He must resist this strong desire to please and to seek approval. It was inappropriate for a gentleman at his stage in life and of his standing.

Peter dressed hastily and, pausing in the hall to pluck the heavy iron key inscribed TRUSTEE OF LINCOLN'S INN FIELDS from its hook, slipped out of the house into the chill morning air.

The old watchman, on his way home after a long and uneventful night, touched his hat in deference to Peter and shuffled out of the square liked a tired nocturnal animal. Peter unlocked the iron gate that led to the private garden at the center of the square, the use of which was a privilege accorded to the already privileged residents of Lincoln's Inn Fields. The gate squeaked open and clanged shut, every noise vibrating and exaggerated in the dawn stillness. Peter made his way to the bench where he sat when he felt the need for reflection, his footsteps crunching over the gravel path.

If Peter had looked up, he would have seen Kate watching him from her attic room at the top of the house. It was in this room that she and Peter had made the blood pact never to return home without the other. It had been from this very window that the two twelve-year-olds had seen Tom betray Gideon to the Carrick Gang. That had been either a few weeks ago or nearly three decades—depending on your perspective. How much had changed since her last visit. Sir Richard Picard, then the owner of the house, who had done so much to help them, had passed away some years ago. Sidney Byng had inherited his uncle's London residence, though apparently he rarely stayed in it, preferring life in Derbyshire where his mother and most of his siblings still lived. Kate pictured Sir Richard's alert, fine-featured face and his gentlemanly stance, and it made her feel quite sick to think that he was now dead. And as for Sidney, who had been so taken with her on her first visit—much to Peter's disgust!—she wondered what kind of man *he* had grown into. Kate looked down at Joshua Seymour. He seemed lonely and rather sad. She wondered why.

Down below, Peter took out his pipe and a tobacco pouch and pressed down the pungent, golden flakes with his thumb, ready for his post-breakfast smoke. It suddenly occurred to him that he had better desist. Peter knew perfectly well that his contemporaries' assertion that tobacco had medicinal proper-ties was nonsense, but, as he enjoyed smoking a pipe, he had conveniently forgotten the truth of the matter. Besides, it had become a point of honor never to disseminate knowledge from the future. Although he did draw the line at drinking river water (he knew what had gone into it), eating anything with mold growing on it (despite accusations of being wasteful), and being served supper by servants with unwashed hands and black fingernails (he had shown great restraint over the years by *not* explaining the concept of *germs*). He emptied the tobacco back into the pouch. How his parents had detested the smell of smoke! And how appalled they would be if they saw the clouds of acrid tobacco fumes he was accustomed to sit in at the Chapter Coffeehouse! He had vague memories of seeing packets of cigarettes as a child with SMOKING KILLS! emblazoned on them—but this seemed so ludicrous to him now he wondered if he had merely imagined it.

Peter's thoughts turned once more to the broken antigravity machine. *What if,* he asked himself, *the Marquis de Montfaron could not mend it? What if no one could?* At that point he would have to admit who he was—but how would he explain his deception? He shook his head, as if trying to scatter the doubts that assailed him onto the dewy grass. It was too early to fear that the machine was irreparable. He would cross that bridge only *when* and *if* he had to. *In the meantime,* he told himself, *as soon as I reveal who I am to my father, he will discontinue his search. Of that I am certain. And if he finds the man, he loses the child. For the sake of everyone concerned I must now be strong. Too many lives will be damaged if I weaken. I shall help my father find my younger self. And if this Montfaron cannot repair the machine, we will search and search until we find someone who can. . . .*

Kate watched Joshua Seymour walk back purposefully, ignoring both the cat who wanted to brush past his legs and the coal man who, bent double with a large sack on his back, was struggling to lever up the heavy coal hole cover in front of the house. *There is something either strange or familiar about Joshua Seymour,* she thought. *I'm not sure which. . . .* Then she tried, for the third time that morning, to blur back to her own time. And for the third time she found that she could not. For a moment she thought she could sense luminous spirals reaching out toward her but then they vanished. *Perhaps,* she thought, *I'm trying too hard.* But she sensed that something had changed. Changed in her. It didn't feel quite like the last time. And she wondered if, or when, she would fast-forward again.

At breakfast the atmosphere was a little strained. Kate noticed that Joshua could scarcely take his eyes off Mr. Schock. He ate little and spoke even less. Hannah came in and out with fresh tea and butter and French rolls fetched fresh from the baker on High Holborn. Meeting Kate again after all this time had made Hannah emotional. She constantly dabbed her eyes and permitted herself to stroke Kate's hair.

"Such beautiful hair, Mistress Kate. To think so much has happened in my life, and time has stood still for you! Ah, would that I could be young again which I know I never can be."

"But time hasn't stood still for me, Hannah! It was a mistake! Someone must have tampered with the antigravity machine before we took it. We should have gone twenty-nine years further back in time—and if we had, then you'd still be young. . . ."

This made Hannah weep even more.

"I didn't mean that now you're old, Hannah. . . . Oh, dear . . ."

Kate did not know what to say as she watched the tears roll down Hannah's plump cheeks, so she gave her a hug instead. It had been a shock at first to see how she had aged, but unlike Queen Charlotte, she did at least instantly recognize her. After a while every other expression or gesture would put Kate so much in mind of the young Hannah that it was like seeing an older Hannah through the lens of a youthful one. She wondered if that was how her parents saw their friends—not just middle-aged folk with wrinkles and sagging cheeks, but faces that told a history, that had been kids and teenagers and young adults, too, and they could read all of that in their expressions because they had grown older together. . . .

It transpired that Hannah had left the service of the Byng household to marry and that she was now the mother of two grown-up sons, both of whom were tenant farmers in the Dales. Alas, she had been widowed some twelve years ago and had returned to work for Mrs. Byng at Baslow Hall. Gideon Seymour still managed the estate there. His employer could never speak highly enough of him and he was well-respected throughout the county. Indeed, Mrs. Byng lived in fear that one of the great Derbyshire estates would poach him. Hannah said that she had been reliably informed that Gideon had been made a most handsome offer, but he was too loyal to Mrs. Byng to accept. Although Gideon made regular visits to Lincoln's Inn Fields, he was currently trying to finish his book of memoirs and had, in consequence, rarely left Hawthorn Cottage these past few months.

"Oh, we must go up to Derbyshire and see Gideon!" cried Kate, bright-eyed at the thought of seeing her friend again and being able to ask him questions about Peter's life in a foreign century.

Peter gulped. He knew Gideon well enough to know that he would never be party to this deception, no matter how well-intentioned were his motives. If Kate saw Gideon he would have to reveal all—and yet he should have foreseen that Kate would want to meet with him.

"It is a long and arduous journey and the roads are dangerous," said Peter hastily.

"But, Joshua, I can't *not* see Gideon!"

"The journey there and back would take a week, probably more. Should not our main concern be the repair of the antigravity machine?"

"I have to agree with Joshua," said Mr. Schock. "The machine must come first and my leg is still recovering. I don't want to waste a week visiting an old friend just for the sake of it, Kate—not even Gideon. This isn't a holiday, after all."

"Besides," continued Peter, "Gideon's letters to me are full of accounts of murders and robberies. Derbyshire has become a dangerous county. . . ."

Hannah saw the look of disappointment on Kate's face and put her hand on hers. She gave Peter a withering look and sniffed. "Why, anyone would think that we did not *want* Kate to see Gideon. . . ."

Peter glared angrily at his housekeeper.

"But perhaps it is for the best," said Hannah quickly, meeting Peter's gaze over the top of Kate's bowed head, "that you remember Gideon the way he was, not 'old,' like me, but blond and heroic and not a single wrinkle on his brow! Do you remember how he taught that highwayman a lesson, Mistress Kate?"

"Ned Porter?"

"Yes. A handsome lad. 'Twas a pity the footpads shot him. . . . I still dream about that night. Of course, he was a bad man." Suddenly she laughed. "Do you remember scolding me for saying how I liked the looks of Lord Luxon? 'It doesn't matter what he looks like,' says you, 'he kidnapped Gideon!' I felt very ashamed, particularly when Gideon was nearly hanged on account of his false accusations. . . ."

"Ha!" commented Mr. Schock, a smile on his face. "So I am not the only one to be rapped over the knuckles by Miss Kate Dyer!"

Kate looked hurt, but Mr. Schock, unlike Peter, did not notice and carried on regardless.

"She has been reprimanding me for speaking out of turn at Kew. I only told Queen Charlotte that Kew Gardens would house the greatest collection of plants in the world. And that during World War II they drilled holes in all of the floors of the Pagoda so that scientists could drop their bombs down the shaft and study how they fell. I mean, where is the harm in that?"

Kate hesitated and then said softly: "Well, I don't think it was a good idea to tell her that historians believe King

George's madness was made worse by the medicine his doctors gave him. . . . What if Queen Charlotte does something about it and King George doesn't go mad again? . . . Who knows what effect that might have on history. . . ."

A flash of guilt streaked across Mr. Schock's face. Then he looked irritated.

"Naturally I stand corrected, Kate. We grown-ups need keeping in check."

Peter smiled to himself. His father never could not stand being in the wrong. And he was managing to rub Kate the wrong way just as Peter recalled he used to do to him. . . . *Poor Kate*, thought Peter. Saying sorry and backing down did not come easily to her traveling companion. It was wonderful, Peter realized, how, with the perspective of age, and the distance of years, and this mask of anonymity, he was able, for the very first time, to clearly *see* his father for the person he was. The stormy relationship they had when he was a child was no longer distorting his vision. And, in spite of any shortcomings his father might have—and he certainly wasn't alone in that—Peter found, to his delight, and a little to his surprise, much to *like* about his father. He admired his energy and his directness, he even appreciated his stubbornness. He actually *liked* his father. A glow of relief suffused him.

Kate, on the other hand, was still flushed with discomfort after Mr. Schock's tactless comments. Peter looked at her sympathetically as she stared fixedly through the tall windows at the goings-on in Lincoln's Inn Fields.

Peter pushed back his chair and stood up.

"I suggest we depart for Golden Square at eleven o'clock. Hannah, will you be so good as to help Miss Dyer to get ready? She may need to purchase some additional items."

He bowed to Kate and then turned to his father.

"My wardrobe is at your disposal, sir. It seems to me that we are of a similar height and build."

"Thank you, Joshua. I suspect the Marquise won't appreciate me turning up in these," replied his father. "May I call you Joshua?"

"By all means," said Peter.

"And you must call me Nick."

"If you wish it. Yes, thank you . . . Nick."

Peter left the room and closed the double doors behind him. He leaned against the wall for a moment, resting his back against the cool plaster. He closed his eyes and slowly let out his breath. *I cannot allow myself to be his son,* he thought, *but I can be his friend and I will treasure what little time we have together before we must say good-bye.* Then he ran up the curved staircase to his dressing room three steps at a time.

Hannah started to remove cups and saucers from the table, then called for John, the footman, to help her. Kate and Mr. Schock were left alone in the dining room and for a while there was an uncomfortable silence which was broken by Kate.

"Joshua has really taken to you, hasn't he? He's very . . . what's the word? Respectful."

"Well, why wouldn't he be?" joked Mr. Schock. "I'm a very nice fellow! But no, I think it must be because of Peter. They must have practically grown up together. Perhaps he can see a resemblance. In any case, I think we were lucky to bump into him as we did. Don't you like him?"

"I do. But there's something . . . oh, I can't put my finger on it. There's something . . . a bit *funny* about him."

"Not being blessed with feminine intuition, I don't know what you mean," said Mr. Schock sarcastically. "*I* like him."

Kate frowned. She wanted to say that it wasn't a question of not liking Joshua Seymour. It was more that she sensed he was hiding something. But she decided to hold her tongue.

"You have reached the voicemail of Dr. Anita Pirretti. Please leave a message after the tone and I will get back to you as soon as possible."

There was a long beeping sound.

"Anita, it's Andrew Dyer. For goodness' sake pick up if you're there! . . . Ed Jacob just called me from MIT to say that Russ Merrick's antigravity prototype has gone missing. You've taken it, haven't you? And I can guess what you're going to do with it. . . . Anita, I'm asking you, as a friend, please think of the consequences before you do anything drastic. . . ."

There was a click on the line. Dr. Pirretti put the receiver to her ear and looked out at her backyard. Golden bamboo rustled in the dry wind and strong Californian sunlight filtered through clumps of feathery grasses.

"I'm here," she said quietly.

"Anita!"

"Is there any news of Kate?"

"None."

"I'm so sorry, Andrew. . . . I've been lying low. NASA have been calling every five minutes to find out what's going on. Your Inspector Wheeler continues to wind everyone up at the office from the janitor upward. He's like one of those turtles that once it gets its jaws into you won't let go even when it's dead."

"Anita," interrupted Dr. Dyer. "I'm going to go after her. In the end Ed Jacob couldn't bring himself to destroy Russ's prototype. Did you?"

"No."

"Then why?"

Dr. Pirretti did not answer.

"You must know that Ed Jacobs isn't going to keep all this under wraps for much longer—NASA isn't just piling the pressure on you! And as for Tim Williamson, he is increasingly anxious to carve his name in the annals of great scientific discoveries. Of course they understand that we're playing with fire, but—"

"Playing with fire!" Dr. Pirretti exclaimed. "This is like letting a bonfire get out of control in your backyard and the whole world goes up in flames!"

"We all understand your point of view. We do. It's only natural to fear the unknown and I'm not saying that time travel might not have catastrophic consequences—but, you know, this is the third time that the machine has gone back in time and, well, we're all still here, aren't we? The universe hasn't collapsed. Napoleon hasn't won the Battle of Waterloo and America isn't suddenly a British colony again. . . . And sometimes good *does* come from taking risks! You've only got to think of radioactivity and heart transplants and gene therapy. . . . People used to think traveling at high speed in cars would bring on a heart attack. . . ."

"I'm on my own now in this, aren't I?" Dr. Pirretti shouted. "The bottom line, Andrew, is that you've changed your mind, you're retreating. Now you say, yes, keep it secret but don't destroy the machine. Soon it will be: Let's go public, this is too important to keep to ourselves. Somehow we'll find a way to contain it, to make it safe. . . . Well, my bottom line is that the past is sacrosanct. You keep your hands off history. If you could travel back in time and not change stuff, okay—but you can't!"

"And where do your high principles leave me and my family?" exclaimed Dr. Dyer. "I'm struggling here to do the right thing but my first duty is to them! All I want right now is to get my Kate back. Her mother is beyond comfort. I haven't seen her brothers and sisters smile or heard laughter in our house since she left. They've been through too much already. All our lives are in limbo. Are you going to let me have Russ Merrick's machine or do I have to go begging to Tim and ask him to help me build one from scratch?"

"The antigravity prototype is already packed up and ready to go. All I ask is that once you've brought Kate and Mr. Schock back, and hopefully Peter, too, you'll destroy the machine."

"Anita! You'd already made up your mind!"

"I'm not a monster, Andrew. I've seen you with Kate. I was hoping against hope that she would get back under her own steam. I'm not kidding myself—destroying the second machine won't stop the research but it *will* slow it down. It'll give me a window to build up an anti–time travel campaign. And trust me, there'll be more folk who agree with me than with the rest of you. I just hope that we can fine-tune the prototype to get you back to 1763. History is an awfully big place to get lost in."

That night Dr. Pirretti slept badly. She awoke a dozen times and each time, alone in the dark, she sensed the brooding, ominous finger of fate wagging at her to rouse herself before it was too late. At the crack of dawn she awoke again. She swung her legs around and sat perched on the edge of her bed, gripping her mattress. Her head was full of a jumble of transient sounds that mocked her and denied her any repose. She put her hands over her ears and shook her head from side to side, desperate for some respite. Suddenly she went rigid and her eyes opened wide with surprise and recognition. She stretched out her hand, switched on the bedside lamp and opened the drawer where she kept a pencil and notepad. She scribbled down a couple of sentences and lay back down again, puzzlement and relief flickering over her face. How can I know these things? And yet I do. . . .

The next morning she decided to follow in the tracks of the antigravity machine and booked herself on the next plane to Manchester.

TEN

THE SWING OF A CHANDELIER

*In which Kate takes a dislike to the Marquise de Montfaron
and the party makes the acquaintance of Louis-Philippe*

The Marquise de Montfaron had rented a narrow, Dutch-gabled house of red brick some six stories high, located at the better end of Golden Square. It was an attractive part of London, although not as fashionable as in former years, and while the square was far enough removed from the bustle of the main thoroughfares to be peaceful, it was not too quiet, either. Children played with hoops, small dogs scampered about, and a succession of carriages and sedan chairs picked up and dropped off the well-heeled residents and their visitors. The hackney coach moved away, having deposited the party in front of a highly varnished black front door which put Kate in mind of number ten, Downing Street. The door knocker was unusual for London houses: a lady's hand covered in rings emerging from a frilled cuff. Peter knocked smartly and they waited for an answer. Kate felt a sudden tug of anxiety at the thought of meeting a family of French aristocrats, particularly given what was happening on the other side of the English Channel. What should she say? "I'm terribly sorry to hear about the French Revolution but perhaps you could have been a little kinder to the peasants . . . ?"

The front door opened and a diminutive footman took the note which Peter had addressed to the Marquis de Montfaron. Soon he reappeared and admitted Kate, Peter, and his father into the hall.

"Pleez to enter," he said, and led them up a curved staircase to the first-floor morning room where large windows looked out over Golden Square. "Madame la Marquise will welcome you directly."

Unlike the simple furnishings of Lincoln's Inn Fields, the Montfaron residence was primped and preened and beautified in a most ornate manner. Although, curiously, Kate thought, the house did smell strongly of fish. She sat on a gold-framed armchair, upholstered in sumptuous silk the color of cherry blossom, feeling self-conscious and ill at ease. She sensed that the aristocratic residents would expect her to be on her best behavior which of course made her want to do the exact opposite. It seemed to Kate that Joshua felt as uncomfortable as she did. *He can't stop fidgeting!* she thought. It was true that Peter constantly crossed and uncrossed his legs and fiddled with the buttons of his waistcoat as if the presence of his father had made him forget all adult restraint. Mr. Schock, on the other hand, reclined on a chaise longue in front of the arched window looking every inch the gentleman, composed and elegant. His borrowed clothes fit him perfectly. In fact, as Joshua commented, anyone would have thought they had been made for him. Kate dearly wished she had taken Hannah up on her offer to walk down to the Strand to buy a silk shawl to smarten up her old-fashioned dress. She was now painfully aware that in this setting she must look seriously underdressed.

Everyone had time to make a detailed study of the morning room, since their hosts thought fit to keep them waiting a full three quarters of an hour. *This Marquis de Montfaron had better be worth it,* thought Kate. Despite Sir Joseph and Joshua's conviction that the machine could be mended, she wondered whether anyone from the eighteenth century was capable of repairing such a sophisticated device. On the other hand, she and Peter's dad, the two representatives of the twenty-first century, were no better. Kate sighed heavily and tapped her foot on the polished wood floor. She idly observed the massive ormolu mirror, which reflected blue sky and scudding white clouds, and some oil paintings of overdressed shepherdesses displayed in deep, carved frames. Kate could imagine the reaction of her sheep-farming neighbors in Derbyshire to such fanciful costumes. These pouting shepherdesses would be more at home floating across ballrooms than stomping through mucky fields. The room also housed several impressive pieces of Chinese furniture in red and black lacquer, the most impressive being a tall cupboard which Kate imagined was full of secret compartments. Every surface was decorated in shades of gold: pagodas and rocky landscapes and graceful trees weeping over streams.

Kate longed to pull open one of the many doors to see what was inside but did not dare.

Growing tired of looking at the comings and goings in Golden Square and at the fine examples of chinoiserie, Mr. Schock got up and paced around the room. He paused to stretch underneath a magnificent chandelier. It had six candle arms, all made of glass, and six spire arms, each pointing toward the ceiling like crystal stalagmites, while the whole was draped with cascades of pear-shaped drops of cut glass that sent rainbows skimming around the sunny room. As Mr. Schock's arms reached upward, his knuckles collided with the chandelier, which started to sway back and forth like an exquisite pendulum, and all the crystal drops started to tinkle like wind chimes.

Peter shot up to grab hold of it before the momentum pulled the fixture out of the ceiling, but Mr. Schock held up his hand to stop him. Instead, he moved his arm in time with the creaking chandelier as if he were conducting music. He laughed, as did Kate, and hummed a little tune in time to its swaying. Peter, however, did not find it funny. Having brought down a chandelier at Baslow Hall while still a teenager, the image of a livid Parson Ledbury, head ghost-white with plaster and wielding a stout stick, still haunted him. The Parson had pursued him through the orchard, intent on teaching him a lesson he would not forget. And, indeed, he had not forgotten it. Crystal chandeliers like these cost a king's ransom and Peter did not want to pick up the bill. He caught a glimpse of Kate giggling and her eyes sparkling with merriment, the value of this costly item the last thing on her mind. *I used not to give a fig for such matters,* he reflected. *Faith, I have become more sensible than my father!* And he looked at the chandelier beating out the passage of time but did not try to stop it.

"Have a care, gentlemen, that is one of a pair by William Parker. The other hangs in our château in Arras and I hope to reunite them one day."

It was a woman's voice, deep and resonant with only a slight French accent. Kate and Mr. Schock stopped laughing and looked—gawked was nearer the truth—at the woman who stood in the doorway. Viscountess Cremorne had not exaggerated. There are few true beauties in the world, but the Marquise de Montfaron was one of them: She was tall and blond with a graceful figure, dark blue-violet eyes, and a complexion that brought to mind ripe peaches. Her thick golden hair was artfully arranged to show off a swanlike neck to perfection.

She stood and smiled, in her lavender and ivory silk gown, perfectly conscious of the effect her appearance was having on the little group.

"And to whom do I have the honor of addressing myself?" She glanced down at the note which Peter had given to the footman. "Which of you gentlemen is Mr. Seymour?"

Peter stepped forward and bowed low.

"Madame la Marquise," he said, "thank you for agreeing to see us at such short notice. Permit me to present Mr. Nicholas Schock."

"How do you do?" said his father, holding out his hand to the Marquise.

Peter cleared his throat noisily to indicate that this simply was not done, but the Marquise, laughing at his forward behavior, took Mr. Schock's hand in her lace-gloved one and shook it.

"I do very well, Mr. Schock, despite the meanness of the accommodation which we are forced to endure since leaving France."

Mr. Schock glanced around him, incredulous.

"But your home is lovely. I've been admiring the view of Golden Square from your window."

Kate waited her turn to be introduced and looked expectantly at Joshua and Mr. Schock, but both of them seemed too overawed by the Marquise de Montfaron to pay any attention to her. The latter took in Mr. Schock's haircut and outfit appreciatively: cream worsted britches with black waistcoat and jacket over a snowy-white shirt and cravat.

"My dear sir, anyone who has witnessed the glory that was the Court of Versailles could not conceive of this," and here, with a graceful sweep of her arm, she indicated the morning room, or possibly Golden Square, or perhaps the whole of London, "as *lovely*. Whereas, if I close my eyes I can still fancy myself walking down the broad alleyways of Le Nôtre's gardens to the music of fountains. I can see Queen Marie Antoinette and her ladies-in-waiting gliding down the Hall of Mirrors, ostrich feathers swaying above their heads, a small army of courtiers bowing in their wake. Images such as these are lovely. To use the selfsame word to describe Golden Square would be to debase it. Why, if you can imagine such a thing, a coal merchant resides not twenty houses away from where we stand."

"You speak perfect English," said Mr. Schock, clearly bowled over by this beautiful woman who actually knew Marie Antoinette. Kate cleared her throat meaningfully but everyone ignored her.

"It is no hardship for me to speak English—my father insisted on an English governess when I was twelve years old. Miss Gunn's French was execrable and as a consequence my English became fluent. Her Latin was poor, too, and her knowledge of the classics little better, yet she taught me more about life than any other person had until then. My father would have been appalled, I am sure of it, if he had known the nature of some of our lessons. But we had a diverting time for a few years . . . and then I married."

The Marquise looked into Mr. Schock's eyes, eliciting precisely the response she had intended, and Mr. Schock felt weak at the knees. His grown-up son felt strangely annoyed. Kate began to feel impatient with her two companions and it was the Marquise herself who turned her attention to Kate. Her searching blue gaze hovered over her, scrutinizing her from top to toe, lingering on her hastily arranged hair, her none too clean fingernails, her lamentably provincial cotton dress, and the lack of stays. If Kate was being subjected to some kind of test, the Marquise de Montfaron had clearly given her bottom marks. She made no attempt to conceal her contempt. Kate was mortified. Rising from her curtsy she caught her heel on a small polished table. It toppled over and the porcelain bowl which had been displayed on it smashed into pieces.

"Oh, I am so sorry!"

Flustered and embarrassed, she got on her hands and knees and started to pick up the fragments. Without realizing it she had caught her finger on a splinter of porcelain and drops of blood plopped onto her skirt and, worse still, seeped into the cherry pink silk of her chair, which she grabbed in order to pull herself up from the floor.

"My footman will deal with it, Mademoiselle!" exclaimed the Marquise, far more horrified at Kate's lack of poise and her willingness to undertake manual labor than any minor damage to her property. "Émile!" she called through the open doorway.

Peter tried to catch Kate's eye to reassure her, but she was too upset to do anything other than look at the floor. He passed her a handkerchief which she took without comment and wound around her finger.

"May I have the honor of presenting Miss Kate Dyer, Madame," he said.

The Marquise inclined her head vaguely.

"*Enchantée*," she said, without actually deigning to look at Kate.

"Pleased to meet you," mumbled Kate.

The sight of the upturned table irritated the Marquise, but she evidently could countenance neither picking it up herself nor permitting her guests to do so. She stepped into the hall.

"Émile!" she called impatiently, but the footman seemed to have more important things to do. "This is not to be borne!" she exclaimed. "I have noticed that some of the best families in London have Chinese footmen—I think it is time that I hired one! Émile! . . . Louis-Philippe!"

Kate caught Mr. Schock and Peter exchanging glances, each of them raising the same eyebrow. The Marquise returned, a little sour-faced, into the morning room. Then the clatter of someone tripping on the wooden stairs announced the explosive arrival of an extraordinarily good-looking young man into the room. He was perhaps sixteen or seventeen, and his features so resembled those of the Marquise that there was no doubt in anyone's mind that this must be her son.

"May I present my son, Louis-Philippe de Montfaron," she said. But before the boy even had time to acknowledge the guests, his mother drew him to her and said in a low voice which everyone could hear: "If you must sleep in your clothes, at least have the goodness to change before appearing in company. And what, pray, is that foul stench?"

The young man bowed vaguely in everyone's direction. His colorful silk outfit was crumpled and none too clean and he wore a wet towel around his head. There were purple circles under his large blue eyes and he looked as if he would have benefited from the invention of aspirin.

"I wagered I could drink more glasses of wine than Lord Chesterfield's son could eat pickled herrings. He cheated, I am sure of it. . . ."

The Marquise did not look amused. "And how much did you lose?"

Louis-Philippe tapped the side of his nose. "Not a tenth as much, *chère Maman*," he whispered, "as I hear you lost last night. . . ."

Kate had to put her hand over her mouth to hide her amusement and Louis-Philippe flashed her a smile. The Marquise's eyes narrowed in annoyance. "Where is Émile?"

"I said he could read one of the books that Papa asked me to get for him."

"What possible interest could our footman have in your father's books? Tell him to come at once. . . ."

"Yes, Mother," replied her son unconcernedly. The turbaned Louis-Philippe left the room, bowing to the guests on his way out. The Marquise practically stamped her foot in irritation but soon recovered herself.

"Forgive me, as an émigrée in London, and without my husband to support me, my domestic arrangements are not all that I should desire. . . ."

"Émile! *Ma mère demande ta présence!*" they heard Louis-Philippe bellow from an upstairs window before closing it with a bang. He returned to the morning room, followed by two miniature lapdogs with silky black ears and large, shining eyes, that yapped excitedly at his heels. The Marquise shooed them away and Kate heard their tiny claws clicking on limestone as they scampered down the curved staircase. Louis-Philippe stood side by side with the Marquise and although mother and son radiated charm and allure, their audience suddenly had something else to preoccupy them. Kate, Peter, and Mr. Schock looked at each other in alarm.

"Madame, do I understand correctly that the Marquis de Montfaron did *not* accompany you to London?" asked Peter.

"Did you not know? Monsieur le Marquis remained in France—he will not abandon our estate. Although, sooner or later, I fear it will be taken from us anyway."

"And your husband has no plans to return to London?"

"My husband believes that the French people will see sense in the end and order will be restored. He is an optimist, *n'est-ce pas*, Louis-Philippe?"

"Papa is an optimist on principle and by nature."

"He is, in any case, perfectly content to be buried in the countryside—society bores him. It suits my husband to live like a hermit and conduct his experiments and correspond endlessly with every scientist and philosopher in Europe. Meanwhile we," and here the Marquise put her arm around her son's shoulder and tried to smile bravely, "must manage as best we can. . . ."

"I am sorry to hear of it, Madame," said Peter, "for to be separated from one's family is difficult at the best of times, but with the current situation in France . . ."

"Yes—it is a torment," said the Marquise.

Ha! She doesn't look exactly tormented to me, thought Kate, who, unsurprisingly, had taken against her.

"You have not told me, Mr. Seymour, why you requested an audience with my husband."

Peter took a deep breath and tried to formulate a suitable response.

"We are in possession of a mechanical device . . . er, the complex nature of which demands an understanding of the laws of natural science . . . and it is beyond our capacity to . . ."

"Our machine is broken," interrupted Kate. "We need your husband's help."

Peter raised an eyebrow and looked sideways at his young friend. He smiled at her—that was the Kate he remembered. The Marquise was on the point of replying when the errant footman reappeared and stood to attention at one side of the door. A pair of small, wire-framed spectacles were still perched on the end of his nose.

"Finally!" she hissed and pointed to the upturned table.

Unperturbed, the dapper footman who had opened the front door for them picked up the table and got onto his hands and knees to pick up the broken pieces of porcelain with white-gloved hands. Kate picked up a piece that he had missed and offered it to him, defiantly meeting the Marquise's stare and noticing the twinkle in Louis-Philippe's eye. *He seems fun*, she thought. *Unlike his mother.*

"I have no doubt," the Marquise continued, "that my husband would have been delighted to help you. But if you need his help you will have to find a path to him. I can assure you that he will not come to London."

"Did you say that your estate is in Arras, Madame?" asked Mr. Schock.

"Yes, a little to the north of the city. It is called the Château de l'Humiaire. Although, unless your errand is of the utmost urgency, I cannot recommend that you pay him a visit during these trying times. They call this the century of light but all I can see is *darkness*. . . ." Suddenly the Marquise's whole demeanor changed; she clenched her fists and the tendons in her neck stiffened. "You have heard, I am sure, what happened to the royal family in Paris last month? My cousin was there. He saw everything . . . what the mob did to the Swiss Guard. . . . They are animals! Animals! My husband still hopes that all will be well, but *that* is what he can expect—to be torn apart, without mercy, by the very people he has spent his life serving!"

Kate was taken aback by the icy hatred in the aristocrat's voice and the fear in her eyes, yet an instant later the Marquise had slipped on her habitual mask and had regained all the poise of the professional socialite.

"So, I regret to inform you, Mr. . . ."—the Marquise glanced at Peter's note—"Seymour, that you have had a wasted journey. . . ."

The meeting was over and Peter, Kate, and Mr. Schock found themselves once more on the front doorstep overlooking Golden Square.

"Now what?" asked Kate.

"Sir Joseph said that after Benjamin Franklin and Alessandro Volta, the Marquis de Montfaron would be his first choice," said Mr. Schock.

"Where can we find this Volta person?" asked Kate.

"Italy," said Peter.

"We can't possibly go to Italy—it would take weeks! . . . What about Benjamin Franklin?"

"He died two years ago."

"Ah."

"Arras is only about an hour's drive from Calais—if that," said Mr. Schock.

"Well, that's hardly the other side of the planet!" exclaimed Kate.

"France is at war with Prussia," said Peter. "The country is in the throes of a revolution!"

"And we'd need to cross the Channel," added Mr. Schock. "And ships don't have engines yet. They don't, do they?"

Peter shook his head.

"But if Sir Joseph says that Montfaron is our best bet, perhaps we should risk it," said Kate. "And anyway, the revolutionaries aren't *our* enemies. It's not as if we're French aristocrats!"

The two men looked doubtful.

"I'm just imagining what your parents would think of me taking you on a day trip to the French Revolution," said Mr. Schock.

"A day would not suffice," said Peter. "Even if the wind blows fair over the Channel it would take the best part of three days to travel from London to Arras."

"Unfortunately," said Mr. Schock, "the alternative could mean never getting home. . . ."

Peter suddenly turned away from his father, his attention

caught by some high-pitched cries of distress. He looked around and, unable to see their source, made his way toward the center of the square. Kate and Mr. Schock followed close on his heels. They instantly spotted a huddle of boys, perhaps thirteen or fourteen years old, who stood in a circle beneath a large plane tree looking down at something, shouting and gesticulating excitedly. It took Kate several moments to grasp what was going on. The youths had captured two small boys— street urchins by the look of the filthy rags they wore—and the poor wretches had been forced to lie on their backs, knees to their chests and feet together. On closer inspection, Kate realized that wooden broom handles had been forced behind the small boys' knees while cords attached their hands to the broom handle, locking them into this excruciating position. Each boy was being urged to kick out violently at the other's legs and each cried out pitifully with the pain of it.

Five big boys stooped over them, their fleshy hands resting on their thighs, and they were shouting and jeering at the little ones, egging them on to kick harder and taking bets as to which one would pass out first. One of them, with blond curls and a plump, angelic face, ground his pointed shoe into the ribs of the smaller boy, causing him to howl even louder.

"Lose me my shilling, you sniveling little rat, and I'll roll you into Brewer Street, and once the wagons have done their work I'll watch the crows pick off what's left of you. . . ."

The tormentor found himself hoisted into the air by the collar and then Peter Schock's boot propelled him at the other boys like a billiard ball, toppling two of them clean over.

"I never was partial to cockfighting, of the winged or of the two-legged variety," commented Peter. "And I am even less partial to bullies. Away with you before you feel my cane on your backside!"

When two other boys made as if to retaliate, Mr. Schock stepped forward and knocked their heads together, sending them sprawling over the cobblestones. The rest did not fancy their chances against these tall, well-made gentlemen and backed away, not without an oath or two, and sloped off toward Brewer Street with ugly expressions on their faces. Mr. Schock smiled at Peter and raised his hand into the air. Peter instinctively struck it in a perfect high five. Mr. Schock's smile transformed into a puzzled frown.

"Joshua, how did you . . . ?"

"Peter used to do it," said Peter swiftly.

"Don't worry, we'll soon get you free," said Kate as she crouched down next to the poor victims and started to untie their cords. Neither of them said a word but merely stared up at her, a mixture of gratitude and suspicion in their eyes. "Hateful pigs! How could they do such a thing?"

Peter and Mr. Schock knelt down to lend a hand and soon the boys were released from their shackles. They hobbled off without a backward glance.

Peter reached into his pocket and pulled out a couple of coins.

"Come back!" he called to the little boys. "I have something for you."

But neither of them stopped and, if anything, they speeded up.

"Poor wretches," said Peter. "Their legs are black and blue. . . ."

"Watch out!" screamed Kate all of a sudden. "He's got a stone!"

She pointed at the angelic-looking boy who now stood taking aim at them from the perimeter of the square. Peter and his father turned to follow her gaze and immediately ducked, only just in time, as a large cobblestone whistled past their ears and landed with a resounding thump somewhere behind them.

Kate was outraged. "He could have *killed* someone!" she exclaimed.

But the boy had already pulled up another loose cobblestone and was taking aim once more. He was starting his run-up, like a spin bowler in a cricket match, when a figure appeared from nowhere and threw himself at the boy in one long, magnificent dive, flooring him and pinning him to the ground.

"Good grief!" exclaimed Mr. Schock. "It's the Marquise's son!"

"It is!" beamed Kate. "It's Louis-Philippe!"

Louis-Philippe relieved the boy of his cobblestone, rolled him onto his belly and stood, one foot planted on the boy's shoulder blades, before looking over at them and smiling his charming smile.

"What should I do with him, do you suppose?" called Louis-Philippe. "Shall I feed him to our dogs?" He growled menacingly, revealing strong white teeth.

The party ran to help him, for the youth was struggling frantically to escape his captor and Louis-Philippe's body weight was not sufficient to keep him down for long. But before they reached him, and despite Louis-Philippe's best efforts, the bully had wriggled free and was now charging at top speed away from them. Louis-Philippe shouted something undecipherable after him and the boy reciprocated in kind.

"Thank you!" panted Kate.

"Yes, indeed, our grateful thanks, Monsieur," said Peter.

"It was nothing," Louis-Philippe replied smugly.

He gave a deep bow and the wet turban fell to the floor revealing a mass of golden hair. He winced and put his hand to his head as he stood up straight again.

"I should eat the herrings next time, if I were you," said Mr. Schock.

Louis-Philippe shook his head. "*Non, non,* I can assure you, sir, that the consequences on the stomach of an abundance of herrings are even worse than the consequences on the head of a surfeit of wine. You are all uninjured, I hope?"

"Yes, indeed," said Peter.

Kate noticed a small parcel lying on the ground nearby and pointed to it.

"Is that yours?" she asked.

"Yes, thank you," said Louis-Philippe, stooping to pick it up. "I would beg a favor, Mr. Seymour. In fact, two favors."

"By all means," replied Peter, his curiosity aroused.

"Do you intend seeking out my father?"

"Perhaps . . ."

"I think we may have no option," interrupted Mr. Schock.

"You would not regret it," said Louis-Philippe. "My father has prodigious talent in the sciences. If anyone could help you, it would be he."

"What are the favors you wish to ask of me?"

Louis-Philippe indicated his parcel.

"I have not received word from my father since the beginning of August, for the mail has been unreliable at best for many months. Will you give these books to him in person? He will be most gratified, I assure you."

"And the second favor?"

"Simply to beg my father to abandon our estate and join us in London. We fear greatly for his safety," said Louis-Philippe a little awkwardly. "He will not listen to me—perhaps he will take notice of a stranger. . . ."

"My dear sir," replied Peter, "I would, of course, be happy to oblige—*if* we decide to travel to France."

With his wide blue eyes and sparkling smile, Louis-Philippe de Montfaron was nothing if not persuasive. Before taking his leave of the party, he managed to get Peter to take the parcel of books with him. If they decided against traveling to Arras, he said, perhaps he would be good enough to have them delivered back to Golden Square and he would send them on to his father by the mail coach.

They walked past the rows of tall, red-brick houses toward

Brewer Street, where they were to hail a hackney coach back to Lincoln's Inn Fields. Mr. Schock idly examined the books. There were three of them: *The Rights of Man, Part I* and *The Rights of Man, Part II*, both by Thomas Paine and which Mr. Schock had heard of, and a book by Alessandro Volta himself, *Memorie sull Elettricita Animale*. Mr. Schock and Peter, neither of whom spoke Italian, were speculating as to the meaning of the title when they both noticed that Kate was not with them. On turning around they saw Kate standing in the gutter, a look of pure anguish on her face, flickering and fuzzy one moment, the next opaque. A beggar was jumping on the spot in horrified excitement a few yards away, pointing at her and screeching.

"Behold the ghost, the apparition! A spectre who dares walk in the light of day!"

Mr. Schock and Peter rushed toward Kate and stood around her protectively. Mr. Schock reached out his hand.

"Don't touch her!" Peter practically screamed at his father, remembering what happened when Kate had done something similar to him many years ago. "She is blurring—you could damage her! Yet something is not right. . . ."

Stomach lurching, Peter stared into Kate's face, trying to divine what was wrong. She was in agony, that much was plain. She was turning round and round as if caught in a glass cubicle, her hands pressing feverishly against its walls. He could neither hear her nor tell if she was aware of him, but she was shouting noiselessly and the words her lips formed were unmistakable: "Help me!"

It was over as suddenly as it had begun. Kate's form had returned to normal: opaque and solid. She slumped forward onto the cobblestones of the street, insensible and deathly pale. Mr. Schock looked on as Peter brushed the excitable beggar to one side and scooped up Kate in his arms. The bewildered Mr. Schock needed to jog to keep up with him.

"What ails the child?" asked a lady with two young children in tow. "May I be of assistance, Sir?"

"She has fainted, that is all," snapped Peter. "I must needs take her home."

A few minutes later, safely inside a hackney coach, both men had to struggle to control a sense of rising panic. They peered anxiously at Kate. Her closed eyelids fluttered and her limbs twitched. The skin on her face appeared waxy, almost bloodless, and her breathing was shallow and rapid. Peter held her hand. Very gradually, a little color returned to her cheeks and her breathing eased. Kate was beginning to stir but was still unconscious.

"Joshua, do you have any idea what is going on? Is this the 'blurring' phenomenon which Kate told me about? If it is, I hope she doesn't make a habit of it. . . ."

"When he was still a boy, I witnessed Peter blurring on more than one occasion," said Peter. "It is as if the body is connected in some fundamental way to its own time and tries to return to it. But it can only do so fleetingly and appears as a ghostly apparition. It is possible that only children are susceptible to the phenomenon for, although both Kate and Peter blurred, Dr. Dyer never did. Although, many years ago now, I recall we heard reports of a footman seeing the 'ghost' of the Tar Man. I wondered at the time if he had, indeed, reached the twenty-first century and had learned to blur. . . . I take it that you have experienced nothing?"

His father shook his head. "No, I'm relieved to say. It doesn't look much fun. . . ."

"I cannot be certain, but it seemed to me that Kate was trapped between this time and her own. . . . The process was not complete. I am fearful for her well-being. We should not delay—the antigravity machine must be repaired as quickly as possible. Kate needs to return to her own time. Of that I am certain."

"It sounds like a trip to France might be in order. . . ."

Peter nodded. "Alas, despite the Revolution, I think we have no option."

When Kate finally regained consciousness, as they approached Lincoln's Inn Fields, she opened her eyes to see Joshua and Mr. Schock bending over her. She burst into tears.

"What is happening to me?"

"It's all right," said Mr. Schock gently. "We're here, we're taking you back to Lincoln's Inn Fields. Don't be scared. . . ."

"But I am scared!" she sobbed. "I don't understand what's happening to me. . . . No one could help me where I went. I thought I was blurring back home but I couldn't get there. Something was stopping me. I thought I'd be stuck there forever. . . ."

ELEVEN

CUPID'S ARROW

*In which a chance encounter delights the Tar Man
and Anjali sees more than she bargained for*

Life cannot have been kind to him. He had an old face for
one so young, at least what you could see of it, for his features
were mostly hidden under the hood of a gray sweatshirt. The
boy was about fifteen years old, although he would have been
hard pressed to tell you his exact age. He was too thin for
someone with so much more growing to do and his pale skin
was stretched, taut and translucent, over his cheekbones. He
slipped through the exuberant weekend crowds of Covent
Garden alone and unnoticed, head down and hands thrust into
the pockets of his baggy jeans, but every so often he would
look up and scan the sea of faces that surged around him on
all sides. He had already walked up and down Drury Lane
three times and was becoming weary of searching. Now, like
thousands of other Londoners, he felt the pull of the bustling
Piazza and the market with its lively stalls, galleries of shops,
and tempting cafés.

As the boy made his way toward the market, he was surrounded by the incessant hum of a thousand conversations; he moved through shifting pockets of sound, each one gradually merging into the next. There were sudden waves of laughter and applause as a couple of street entertainers worked the large crowds, then he became aware of the electric chords of a blues guitarist which gradually transformed into a soprano's trilling notes, and presently her song too was drowned out by a hurdy-gurdy that invited customers to step onto an old-fashioned merry-go-round. The boy stopped in his tracks. He had never seen such an amazing contraption before and stood before it, captivated. He watched the troop of painted horses bobbing up and down as children beamed, holding on tight to the striped posts, flying around and around, a blur of red and gold. Yet it never occurred to him that he could have a ride himself. Such things were not for the likes of him. The boy soon turned away, for he was tired and hungry and, unlike the smiling faces that surrounded him, did not crave entertainment; he had a different motive for being here. So he continued on his way, walking relentlessly on as if it were the only thing he could do.

As he made his way forward, pushing against a crowd of people leaving the market, it struck him that everyone else appeared to belong in this world in a way that he felt he never had. In this century as much as in his own, his lot was to scrape the barrel of life's bounty, a scavenger roving around the edges of other people's good fortune. He mostly wished that his curiosity about the magic machine had not got the better of him and that he had never gone near the crypt at Tempest House on the day that Blueskin and

Gideon Seymour raced against each other. He remembered the shaft of light that had pierced the darkness as someone removed a couple of roof slates and dropped into the crypt next to him. The next thing he remembered was waking up, who knows how many hours later, with a poacher lying on top of him and three fine carp on his chest. The fish slime had ruined his footman's uniform and the fishy stink had lingered about him for days. But when he had thrown wide the crypt door, it had opened onto a new world . . . this one. For a long time afterward he kept expecting to wake up from his dream. But he never did. He lay low for several days and nights, observing this foreign place and trying to make some sense out of what he saw, creeping out after dark and darting back under cover as soon as anyone noticed him. In 1763 it was commonplace to be poor and hungry but in this unknown future, Tom knew himself to be part of that small ignored army that sleeps in shop doorways and on filthy mattresses in subways, whom people step over and pretend not to see. Tom felt so down and helpless, he thought he might even have been pleased to see the Carrick Gang—though not Joe Carrick. Not him. He had had enough beatings from Joe Carrick to last him a lifetime.

The smell of chargrilled steak made his grumbling stomach clench. He walked up to a waffle stall and pressed his nose against the glass display case. The sight of mountains of custard doughnuts and pastries and waffles dusted with vanilla sugar drove him half-wild. He reached into his pocket to pull out his white mouse and rested her for a second on the counter while he dug deep looking for coins.

"Get that vermin out of here, sonny," warned the stallholder, not unkindly, looking at the mouse's twitching whiskers and delicate pink ears. "You want to get me closed down?"

Tom grabbed his mouse protectively and backed silently away. A few seconds later and he had disappeared into the mass of people heading for Covent Garden's South Gallery. He needed to get some rhino. Five pounds would do. He made his way toward the big semicircle of folk who were watching a tightrope walker inch his way across a rope swung between two stone pillars of the portico of St. Paul's Church, arms outstretched and a cutlass clenched between his teeth. Tom hardly noticed him. He dreaded the act of stealing. He was not a natural cutpurse, for his movements were too jerky and he lacked confidence. His heart would thump and his hands would sweat as he stood behind his intended victim. Often he would lose courage and edge slowly away, not ready to risk all for an uncertain gain.

Tom was too short to see anything but a row of backs. Immediately in front of him was a couple in tight jeans, their arms entwined around each other. There was half an inch of wallet peeping out of the man's back pocket. Tom's best chance was to ease the wallet out while the audience was caught up in applauding a trick. He hovered uneasily, waiting for precisely the right moment. It should have been easy. He stretched out his trembling hand and, standing as close as he dared, touched the wallet with the tip of his fingers just as a cheer went up. But fear caused him to freeze, so he withdrew his hand, gritted his teeth, and waited for the next cheer. . . . After three attempts he sloped off, empty-handed and sick at himself, and sat down on the ground close to a pasta and pizza restaurant on the edge of the market. He rested his head on his knees and furtively pulled out the white mouse who was struggling to get out of his dark, cramped pocket full of crumbs. Tom placed her gently inside the hood of his sweatshirt. She immediately scurried around his neck and down his back, tickling him with her scratchy claws. The tiny creature seemed to vibrate against his skin. He laughed despite himself and sat up in order to extricate the animal. As he looked up his heart leaped—a family of four were walking away from their corner table leaving their generously-sized pizzas half-eaten. Tom flew up to snatch the remnants off their plates and ran outside. He crouched down against a wall and discreetly placed the mouse in his lap and offered her a morsel. The two of them sat and ate. Then the mouse washed her face with her paws and Tom wiped the tomato sauce from his lips with the back of his hand. The day had suddenly taken on a rosier hue.

Not for the first time, he fished out the carefully folded piece of newspaper from his back pocket and looked at the grainy photograph, trying to decide whether it was wishful thinking that the character on horseback charging down Oxford Street was indeed the Tar Man. The face was in darkness but the way the fellow held his neck, not to mention the display of horseman-ship, suggested that it was. . . . And if it *was* Blueskin, he would know just what to do. He wouldn't be scared of the twenty-first century. Lord Luxon aside, Blueskin was the cleverest man he'd ever come across, and he was bound to have a plan. Sooner or later he was certain to reappear in his old haunts. And when he did, Tom was going to be there, waiting for him.

Seated in a café on the lower level of Covent Garden market, the Tar Man watched the last of Anjali's shortlist of candidates leave and climb the stairs to the ground floor.

"Look how he struts, as if he expects the whole world to take note of him!" remarked the Tar Man with a sneer. "He has too high an opinion of himself to be eager to learn and is too conspicuous to be useful to me."

As the lad in the sharp suit reached the top of the stairs, he gave Anjali a wave and a cheeky smile.

"Ciao, Tony!" she called. Then, turning back to the Tar Man, she said: "He knows how to handle himself. And he's a good dancer. I like him. . . ."

"Then you are more of a fool than I give you credit for. Bless me if all of the rogues you have brought to me so far aren't like you—headstrong and cocksure with an aptitude for doing the opposite of what you are asked! Every last one of them would overreach himself and need pulling out of the hole he had dug for himself."

"You think I'm like that! I ain't given you no trouble! If you'd seen how I was with the teachers at school, you'd think I was an angel now. . . ."

"I believe you!" said the Tar Man. "I'll warrant you were whipped more days than you were not."

"Whipped! You think teachers are allowed to beat the kids up? There's laws, you know. Things have moved on since the bad old days."

The Tar Man snorted. "Then I pity the teachers. No doubt it is the teachers who get the beating. If they cannot demand obedience how can they teach the children to respect their betters? And the threat of a good whipping does much to focus the mind."

"That's rich coming from someone who breaks the law every day of his life! I can't see you respecting your 'betters' when you was a kid!" exclaimed Anjali.

People from adjacent tables looked over at them but soon turned away when the Tar Man stared back aggressively, challenging them to look in his direction again. Then he glared at Anjali.

"You would do well to control that tongue of yours, before you trip up over it," he snarled.

The Tar Man had realized by now that the girl would be impossible to tame. But she had proved useful, so he would tolerate her impudence—up to a point. Anjali knew she'd over-stepped the mark. *Me and my big mouth,* she thought.

"Anyway," she continued more sweetly, "I don't see why *I* can't be your apprentice. I've done all right, haven't I? I got you a passport and a bank account and your own place. *And* a smile good enough for Hollywood."

The Tar Man stared intently at Anjali in a long moment of dispassionate appraisal. Anjali stared back defiantly, but in reality wanted to hide from his searching gaze. It was a trick, she knew, but a good one. He made her feel as if he were stripping away all the little pretences with which she was in the habit of clothing herself. *I've got to go careful with this one,* she thought, *I can't second-guess him.* Finally he spoke.

"Spirit you have in plenty, Anjali, and intelligence, and you've proved your worth. But my apprentice must be my cat's paw when I need to hold back and I must never for one moment doubt that I can trust him, even though it means he must swear false in the highest court of the land. He would declare that a cow was a horse if I asked it of him. He should be dogged and tireless, and while he would nurse an ambition to follow in my footsteps, he would not expect too much too soon. Life will, you can be sure, have dealt him a few hard blows, for no one learns the self-mastery and persistence I would have him possess without a little suffering."

"So does that mean you *are* considering me?"

"So, in short, Anjali, be glad that I do not care to take you on as my apprentice. It means that life has let you get your own way more often than not, and no doubt will continue to do so."

Anjali looked away and sighed heavily. She knew he was right. She'd always been a rebel and she wasn't suddenly going to start liking taking orders. All the same she felt that she had been criticized in some subtle way and did not like it. She pouted slightly which brought an amused smile to the Tar Man's face. By way of diverting her from her sulk, he slid the car magazine they had purchased earlier across the table.

"Here," he said, "by all means choose whatever pleases you."

Anjali's expression brightened and she started to flick through the magazine, feigning boredom. She stopped at the luxury sports car section. It'd have to be red, she thought, or was black better? As she turned over the pages, she forgot to be indifferent.

"Wow!" she gasped. "Take a look at that! This has got to be the one! Me turning up at the club in this!"

The Tar Man glanced at a photograph of a sleek, silver car. "No man is a better judge of a horse, but I do not yet have an eye for cars. I am at pains to tell them apart."

"Trust me, this one's a thoroughbred. This one would have won the Derby. Three times."

"Very well, Anjali. Find me a merchant who will offer me a fair price and we will see."

"And we'll need a driver, of course. I bet Tony's good behind a wheel. . . ."

The Tar Man ordered himself another coffee, a beverage he had never been partial to in his own century. Whatever they did to it nowadays, it was good. Anjali had to remind the Tar Man that the girl was a "waitress," not a "wench"—which had not gone down at all well—and that you did not bellow out your order across the room. First you attracted the waitress's attention and then you waited for her to come to your table to serve you, at which point you politely gave her your order. And as for the coffee he was so fond of, he wasn't pronouncing it right. It was "cap-u-cheeen-o."

The Tar Man wore the patient expression he had learned to put on in response to Anjali's criticisms. He pretended to be happy to be corrected and she pretended that she did not enjoy catching his mistakes. Yet the Tar Man was satisfied with Anjali's twenty-first-century lessons. He had provoked fewer stupefied reactions in his dealings with people since taking her on. Little by little he was learning to blend in. As for Anjali, she still wondered why Vega Riaza, as he now insisted on calling himself, still persisted in pretending he came from 1763. She had been playing along for long enough now to half-believe it was true. But in her heart she knew that this couldn't be the case. Until she saw the evidence with her own eyes, how could she believe such a thing? She had satisfied herself, at least, that Vega Riaza wasn't mad, although *why* he should prolong this crazy game was beyond her. And he was more than generous—either that or he really didn't have a clue how much money was worth. But, whatever his game was, her little stash of savings was growing by the day . . . and what else was she going to do with herself? She went back to reading *What Car?* magazine while the Tar Man examined his gleaming white incisors appreciatively in the back of a coffee spoon.

Presently, and without turning to look at him, Anjali said to him, "There's a weedy, weaselly-looking kid, can't take his eyes off of you. Up there, next to the stairs, leaning over the railings."

When the Tar Man saw the stooped, young figure, his dark, anxious eyes staring out from under unkempt hair, he stood up, dropping the spoon on the floor and letting out an involuntary cry of surprise. He climbed the stairs three steps at a time and took hold of the boy's narrow shoulders. The Tar Man looked incredulously into his face.

"Do my eyes deceive me? Can this be Tom?"

The boy nodded vigorously, his body rigid, his eyes wide and dark. The Tar Man took hold of both his shoulders.

"Tom! How the devil did you end up here? I was told you had run away from the position I had secured for you at Tempest House! I thought you were once more in the pay of Joe Carrick."

"Not him! I did not run away—it was an accident. It was the magic machine that brought me here. . . ."

"You too!"

"I stole into the crypt at Tempest House to take a look at it . . . but I do not rightly know how I arrived here. . . ."

"Who's this?" panted Anjali, arriving at the top of the stairs.

"This, Anjali, is a fellow traveller from 1763, an acquaintance from the 'bad old days.'"

"Oh," said Anjali, trying to keep a straight face. "He just 'turned up,' did he?"

"As you can see. A more timely arrival I cannot imagine. He was due to become my apprentice. It is nothing short of a miracle."

"Wow. Very timely, as you say," said Anjali, wondering what on earth Vega was up to now. "It makes getting lost in the Sahara Desert and bumping into your next-door neighbor seem quite probable. . . ."

The Tar Man was too pleased to see Tom to chastize Anjali for her sarcasm and, in any case, he had not heard of the Sahara Desert. Exiles in a different century, he and Tom saw the world through the same lens and it would be a relief to have someone to share it with.

"So, aren't you going to introduce us?" asked Anjali.

"With the greatest of pleasure. This, Anjali, is Tom, and a more promising lad it would be difficult to find," said the Tar Man, interpreting correctly the expression on Anjali's face. "Despite appearances, you would do well to take a few leaves out of this lad's book. . . ."

"Hiya," said Anjali to Tom, plainly underwhelmed, and held out her hand.

Tom gazed at the most enticing creature he had ever beheld. When Anjali addressed him directly he blushed deeply, color flooding his pasty cheeks, and yet still he could not bring himself to tear his eyes away from her. Such spirit! Such beauty! And it was at that very moment, in the blink of an eye, that Cupid's arrow found its mark. Tom's faithful heart felt a pang of something that almost resembled pain. He took the girl's cool hand in his and bowed.

"I am your humble servant, Miss Anjali."

The three of them walked to the Tar Man's apartment on Floral Street in high spirits. The sadness and isolation which had so oppressed Tom vanished and in its place joy beat against his chest. How his life had changed in such a short space of time!

Not only did he have a powerful and fearsome protector, now his world had Anjali in it, shining bright as the sun.

They walked past a group of three mime artists at the edge of the Piazza, dressed all in gold, their skin painted gold also, pretending to be classical statues. One was a Grecian lady holding an urn, another a slave carrying a basket of bread, and the third a Roman soldier. They had developed the art of keeping perfectly still to such an astonishing degree that it was difficult to believe that they were flesh and blood. Anjali was entranced and wondered out loud what it would take to get them to break their poses. Tom, desperate to please, immediately gamboled about, leaping up high into the air and playing the fool in an effort to get a reaction. Finally, he put his face so close to the Roman soldier their noses touched. None of the living statues even blinked.

Anjali was impressed. "Awesome!" she pronounced, dropping a coin into each of the mime artists' collecting bowls.

The Tar Man, who had been watching Tom's antics from the sidewalk, moved forward and calmly picked up all three bowls and set off at a smart pace with them.

"Oi!" shouted the statue of a Roman soldier, brandishing his spear, "where d'you think you're going with that?"

The slave and the Grecian lady followed suit and all three golden statues set off in pursuit of the Tar Man. Anjali doubled up with laughter, as did half the street. Tom's face dropped. His master had stolen his thunder. The Tar Man soon stopped and stood facing the furious mime artists, holding out their bowls.

"Apologies, my lady and gentlemen, it was by way of a lesson for my young friend."

The statues looked daggers at the Tar Man, snatched back their bowls and returned grumpily to their pedestals. The Tar Man turned to Tom.

"Always strike where it hurts. Life rarely gives you a second chance."

They arrived in Floral Street and Anjali tactfully waited to make sure that her employer could manage to key in the security number to get into the building before taking her leave.

"I'll let you two catch up," she said. "I'll be back later."

Tom gazed after Anjali until she disappeared out of sight, unwilling to be removed from her presence so soon.

A hefty cash deposit and some fake references had secured the Tar Man a spacious penthouse apartment over a men's boutique. The building dated from his own day, but its innards had been ripped out and it had been converted into three urban lofts which incorporated every modern convenience. It amused him that the house where he used to keep a room in 1763 was but a few minutes' walk away, yet how the area had changed! Gone were the footpads who freely roamed the streets, gone were the assassins, gone were the anglers whom he'd seen plying their trade on this very street, hooking up wigs and great coats and valuables from the tops of carriages. Now the only robbers in Covent Garden were the landlords. When Anjali told him the monthly rent, he had laughed until tears ran down his cheeks.

It occurred to him that if such a vast sum could be charged for rent, he would be wise to add the acquisition of property to his growing list of ambitions.

The Tar Man took pleasure in showing off his new home to Tom. With Anjali he kept up his guard: She only ever saw that side of him which he permitted her to see. But the Tar Man knew Tom of old and trusted him. Despite his timidity, he thought, the boy had clung on to life by his fingertips. To have survived the Carrick Gang, he knew, was a feat in itself. Joe Carrick was a nasty piece of work even by his standards—vicious and unpredictable. And then, there was a truly dogged perseverance about Tom: It was a trait they both shared, and the Tar Man understood its value. When he had first scrutinized Tom's small face on the balcony in Covent Garden—at once earnest and edgy, sad and alone—he had been surprised to find that, for a fleeting moment, he was actually moved. And as he watched Tom now, the Tar Man realized that he reminded him of himself at the same tender age. Both of them, without the succor of friends or family, rejected by the world through no fault of their own, and strangers to the milk of human kindness.

And so the Tar Man and Tom flung themselves onto giant sofas in the cool, spacious living room, buried their faces in soft towels, warmed their hands under the hot tap in the kitchen sink, drank cold beer from a fridge the size of a wardrobe, and made the electric kettle boil five times in row, laughing heartily each time it switched itself off. And then, in awe of the miracle of modern plumbing, they turned on the power shower and flushed the toilet. The Tar Man gave Tom his mobile phone and sent him into the hall. When it rang, Tom pressed the button Blueskin had indicated and held it gingerly to his ear.

"Say something, you numbskull," bawled the Tar Man into his receiver inside. "It does not have teeth!"

"I have seen people with these in the street, Blueskin!" Tom whispered excitedly into the mobile. "The way they pressed them against their heads I thought it a cure for the earache. . . . It is wondrous indeed! Does everyone have such an object? Does Anjali?"

"Anjali! Ha! When is she *not* talking to some fellow on her mobile phone . . ."

There was a state-of-the-art television, too, but the Tar Man avoided using it. He had not touched it since Anjali told him that sounds and pictures traveled through invisible airwaves and were picked up by televisions and radios.

After a while the Tar Man and Tom grew tired of playing with these new toys and told each other of their adventures since arriving in the future. Tom could scarcely believe his change in fortune: Blueskin was treating him like an old friend! He would not, he was sure of it, have treated him in such a familiar way had they been back in their own time. So Tom was careful to show the utmost respect and not take anything for granted. *I am invited into the lion's den,* he thought. *Best to tread carefully and not speak out of turn . . .*

They drank more cold beer. Tom described how he had been sleeping by the river, under a railway bridge where the trains thundered overhead and rats scuttled about among the rubbish.

"So, tell me, young Tom, how do you find the future?"

"I like *this* future. I didn't care for it when I was on my own. . . ."

"I like it well," said the Tar Man. "This century is more bountiful by far than my own. Upon my word, Tom, this chance shall not come my way again and I shall not squander it! I should not return to 1763 now, not for a king's ransom. . . ."

The Tar Man described how he planned to make his mark in this new world. In time, just as Lord Luxon had done, he would court the great and the good, as well as the rogues and the scoundrels, and he would soon begin to cultivate a spreading network of men who would be only too pleased to do his bidding—or too scared not to.

"I shall become rich! Ay, and powerful, too, I do not doubt! For you see, Tom, I have a secret. . . ."

Tom listened, round-eyed, to the Tar Man and marveled at the scope of his ambition. But how would Blueskin scale such lofty heights? And what was his secret? He dared not press him. When the Tar Man asked if he would agree to be his apprentice in this new century, Tom did not hesitate. How could he survive here on his own? And how could he resist the strength of the Tar Man's purpose?

They drank some more beer and stood on the narrow balcony overlooking Floral Street, to get some air.

"London does not have the same odor," commented the Tar Man. "The air is foul. Which London stank worse—our London with its horses and putrid gutters or this one full of cars?"

Tom sniffed. "I smell nothing, Blueskin."

"Standing upwind of you, as I am, I say be glad you can smell nothing!"

The Tar Man slapped Tom roughly on the back. He was in excellent spirits and started to hum a tune under his breath, and Tom joined in, tapping his foot in time to the familiar rhythm. Soon they were both singing the words of an old highwayman's ballad with gusto while pedestrians on the pavement below craned their necks upward:

> *Our Hearts are at ease,*
> *We kiss who we please:*
> *On Death it's a folly to think;*
> *May he hang in a Noose,*
> *That this Health will refuse,*
> *Which I am now going to drink.*

When Anjali walked in and heard their none-too-melodious voices, she decided not to interrupt and went into the kitchen instead to make herself some toast. Before long the Tar Man heard her clattering about and, closely followed by Tom, came into the room. Anjali was going dancing later and had already changed into a satin skirt. She had just opened her mouth to say hello when the slices of toast popped up noisily out of the chrome toaster. Both the Tar Man and Tom jumped with the shock of it and looked wildly around the room for the cause of the alarming sound. Anjali realized that her new employer was brandishing a knife. It would have been funny except he looked ready to attack. It was an instant and genuine reaction. For the very first time Anjali contemplated the possibility that if these two people had never come across a toaster before, they might also have traveled here from a different century.

"Hiya," she said, trying to keep calm. "Anyone want some toast?"

The Tar Man shook his head, slowly put away his knife, and retreated from the kitchen. Anjali made no comment, as she now understood how much her employer loathed appearing foolish. She buttered her toast and took it into the living room where she turned on the television, flicking through the channels with the remote control. Tom stood watching her shyly from the doorway. He did not notice his white mouse peeping out from the cuff of his sweatshirt but Anjali did. She shrieked and pointed. The Tar Man came in from the balcony but was reluctant to pass between the remote control and the television for fear of what the invisible waves might do to him.

"I am sorry, Miss Anjali, I did not mean to frighten you," said Tom timidly.

"You didn't," she said, waving her hand at him as if to shoo him away. "I'm a bit jumpy today. You didn't think I was scared

of a mouse, did you? Just keep it away from me is all, I don't
like 'em. . . ."

Tom put his mouse back into his pocket. The Tar Man
beckoned for Tom to join him again on the balcony, which he
did, although he was wary of the television, and the hairs on the
back of his neck stood up as he imagined the room full of those
magical airwaves Blueskin had told him about. . . . The Tar
Man waited for Tom to come through and pointedly closed the
French doors behind them.

"I must ask you something," said the Tar Man quietly. "Can
you *fade*?"

"I do not understand. . . ."

"Have you returned to our own time, even if only for a few
moments, as if in a dream?"

"No."

"You remember how Master Schock and Mistress Dyer
escaped from us in the rainstorm?"

"*You* can do that!" exclaimed Tom.

"Ay, and more. It is not for the fainthearted and I have made
mistakes—but I am resolved to master it. Already I have a
secret skill which would make me the envy of every thief in
Christendom. . . ."

"Where do you go when you fade?"

"Ha! A good question, indeed! I fade back to our own time.
It is not in my power to stay overlong, for invisible forces will
always pull me back. But while I am there I can see and hear
and speak and *move*. Indeed, although things do not feel the

same when I am in that precarious state, I have even learned to *transport* whatever I can hold in my hands from one century to another. And if I stay five minutes in the past, five minutes have elapsed when I return. If I take a dozen paces, I reappear in that selfsame spot. Truly it is miraculous! And this has not happened to you?"

"Never, Blueskin."

"Why should that be so? Perhaps some have a propensity for it and some do not. . . . But, no matter, you shall see it with your own eyes. Watch, and be amazed!"

The Tar Man stood tall and closed his eyes. His brows furrowed in deep concentration. Nothing happened. The Tar Man opened his eyes, paced up and down for a moment, and tried again. Tom stood awkwardly in the corner of the balcony, waiting for something to happen. Nothing did.

"God's teeth! Why can I not do it?" growled the Tar Man. Then, turning to Tom, he barked: "Leave me!"

Tom scurried back into the sitting room and cowered behind the curtains. Anjali observed him silently as she crunched through a crust of toast.

The Tar Man rested his hands on the cold balcony rail and breathed in deeply, closing his eyes and trying to reach that state of calmness which seemed to aid the process. He pressed the palms of his hands hard against his eyeballs. It was a trick he had recently discovered. It made him see luminous shapes floating through infinite blackness, which mimicked what he saw as he faded. He focused his energies once more but was soon shaking his head again in frustration. He could not do it.

Let my brains be knocked out if I let one mishap stop me! It did not kill me! The Tar Man knew very well the cause of his difficulty. The previous night, in Southwark, he had faded in the grounds of the cathedral. When he materialized, he found that his right side was trapped inside the trunk of a plane tree. Instantly, a process started whereby the atoms of his body in his altered state repelled the object in which it found itself, causing the Tar Man to slide slowly from the tree like molasses dropping from a spoon. The intense pain had taken his breath away and he all but lost consciousness. A terrified cat, back arched and electric green eyes flashing, stood hissing at him throughout. Exhausted and in shock, the Tar Man had made no effort to resist the forces that always pulled him back but just stood, limply, awaiting the inevitable. Like falling off a horse, however, the Tar Man knew that he must immediately fade again lest his courage fail him the next time. He had given himself ten minutes to recover, made sure that he was well out of the way of the tree and faded back once more to pay a visit to 1763 and the petrified church cat. This time, things went without a hitch.

Now, standing on the drafty balcony in the twenty-first century, the Tar Man stood tall and centered himself. *I shall fade,* he told himself, *it is the key to all that I desire!*

Tom continued to peep at his master through a gap in the curtains. He stood motionless, head bowed and shoulders a little stooped, in a posture of intense concentration. After what seemed a long time, Tom's patience was rewarded. He watched, dumbfounded, as Blueskin gradually became transparent and finally vanished. Tom rushed out onto the tiny balcony and paced up and down, scratching his head, his heart thumping in his chest with the shock of it. Anjali, too, now positioned herself behind the curtains to steal a look outside, curious about what was going on. Unprepared, for she had heard nothing, she suddenly felt a hand squeeze her shoulder. She let out a piercing scream. Tom flew in from the balcony and stared in disbelief at his smiling master.

"Calm yourself, Anjali; you have no cause to creep about like a spy. I have no secrets from you. . . ."

Anjali stood, wide-eyed and rigid, as the Tar Man offered a pewter tankard half-full of ale to Tom.

"Drink," he ordered.

Dumbfounded, Tom drank. He grimaced, and swallowed, and then his face slowly lit up. "It's warm!" he said. "And it's from our time!"

"Who *are* you two?" Anjali cried. "Are you dead? Are you ghosts?"

TWELVE

GHOST FROM THE FUTURE

*In which the Tar Man confides in Tom,
discovers the joys of haunting, and clears
up an unresolved matter with Lord Luxon*

After instructing the hairdresser to cut Tom's hair short and spiky, Anjali had taken him shopping. There was something about shops, especially clothes shops, that made Tom want to bolt like a wild horse. He had refused to try anything on, even for Anjali, and she had struggled to get him to stand still long enough for her to hold up items of clothing against him. Tom was so unused to looking at himself in a mirror that seeing his startled reflection return his gaze made him start with fright. But finally the torture was over, and they returned to the flat with armfuls of shopping bags. Anjali pushed him into his room, pulled out an outfit for him to try on and closed the door behind him.

"I'd rather tread on broken glass than go through that again," said Anjali to the Tar Man, sinking into a sofa and pulling off her shoes.

The Tar Man laughed. He laughed even louder when Tom

appeared with his new haircut, dressed in tight black jeans and black-and-pink-striped T-shirt that displayed his midriff. Tears of mirth came to his eyes.

"If this is your century's version of the gentleman of fashion, then I am obliged to tell you, Anjali, that mine has produced better dressed lapdogs!"

Anjali left for the evening, apparently in a huff, after the Tar Man's remark but not before she had retorted:

"Well, at least even our century's dogs smell better than your century's humans!"

In truth, much as the two exiles from 1763 were amazed by the power shower in their ultramodern bathroom, their relationship to it took the form of a sincere appreciation rather than an intention to use it. In any case, the Tar Man mistrusted the concept of daily bathing and found the idea that he should aim to have no odor quite ludicrous. It was not the first time that his twenty-first-century adviser had commented on his attitude to personal hygiene, but he was not unduly perplexed.

"I am a man!" he had replied. "Would you have me smell as a flower?"

Anjali slammed the door behind her for effect, but she had a smile on her face. She was getting good at judging how far she could go with Vega Riaza or, as Tom called him, Blueskin, on account of his dark stubble, as well as, for reasons she had yet to discover, the Tar Man. If his attitude to names was anything to go by, she thought, here was a character who did not like to be pinned down. She knew that her cheekiness appealed to his sense of humor, which was just as well, for the Tar Man was definitely someone you wanted on your side. . . . When they'd gone over to Bethnal Green at lunchtime, to meet with a sleazy-looking bloke in a long leather coat, she had observed the Tar Man display his darker side. It was this aspect of his character which Anjali herself had witnessed in the underground station and which Tom had often hinted at, and which, no doubt, was the reason the boy took such pains never to overstep the mark. The meeting had been arranged because the Tar Man wanted to talk about the disposal of some goods that had been acquired in a manner which demanded more than a little discretion. The fence, unfortunately for him, displayed the merest suggestion of discourtesy to the Tar Man, whom he was meeting for the first time. Then he outlined the deal he was proposing, the substance of which impressed the Tar Man even less than his manners. Without saying a word, the Tar Man had stood up, levered the man up by his elbow, which he held in a pincerlike grip, digging his thumb into the nerve, and marched him out of the restaurant. Tom and Anjali had watched through the plate glass window as the Tar Man spoke quietly into the fence's ear. When they returned to the table, the fence's complexion was the color of mushroom soup and he could scarcely hold his fork for trembling. Anjali had noticed that Tom had looked away and put his hand in his pocket in search of his precious mouse. But she also noted, with some satisfaction after her lecture on discretion in an age of mobile phones and security cameras, that the Tar Man had at least gone *outside* before pointing out the error of his ways to the unfortunate fence. Life looking after this pair was certainly not boring.

The Tar Man had gone for a late-night stroll by the Thames. Tom had accompanied him but was dragging behind, lost in his own thoughts. The Tar Man breathed in the cold river air. Gone were the boatmen and the sailing ships and gone was the stench, too. They walked across Waterloo Bridge and stopped at its center. An illuminated barge sailed under the bridge below them, breaking up stripes of neon pink and turquoise that shone onto the shimmering surface of the water from the South Bank. People were dancing and drinking on deck, and music drifted up and reached him for a moment before dissolving into the breeze and the noise of traffic. The Tar Man never tired of seeing this London at night. Night meant something different in his time. With it came the enveloping darkness under whose shroud he had plied his trade and had done whatever needed to be done. Gone now the velvet blackness and the silence. In its place, permanent light and the drone of a city that does not sleep. The Millennium Wheel and the Houses of Parliament rose up to the west, St. Paul's and the Gherkin to the east. All these buildings were flooded with impossibly powerful lights. He did not comprehend this cityscape, formed, it seemed to him, from a million twinkling lights, yet he felt an almost parental pride in seeing what London had become. Reflected in the swirling river, he admired the architecture of a city whose foundations rested on centuries of the wealth and power that the Tar

Man so badly craved. The cold wind blew at his face and his vivid white scar tingled. He felt at the center of the world. He soaked up the ripples of energy that came from his city. Here, anything was possible.

As they descended the staircase that leads to the South Bank, their footsteps disturbed a homeless youth who stirred beneath filthy blankets, and, in a reflex action, his hand shot out for money. His voice was slurred.

"Spare some change for a cup o' tea?"

The Tar Man stopped and looked coldly down at him and kicked at a can of beer that peeped out from under the blankets. The youth's head slowly emerged, suddenly uneasy at the attention. He was fourteen at most. All at once the Tar Man reached down and picked him up, blankets and all, and carried him, seemingly without effort, the few steps up to the bridge. For an instant, Tom thought he was going to throw him into the river, and the youth was too shocked and disorientated even to struggle. Instead, the Tar Man lifted him up high above his shoulders and rotated him three hundred and sixty degrees, showing him the panoramic view.

"Are you then blind?" he cried. "Is there anywhere on earth more ripe with possibilities than this city? Open your eyes and see! You are in a prison of your own making!"

And he dropped the malodorous bundle onto the freezing concrete.

Tom looked back at the startled young vagrant and watched him picking himself up from the floor. He scurried back into the stairwell like a rat into a gutter. The Tar Man walked on and did not look back.

As they were passing the Globe Theatre the Tar Man paused and, pointing toward the City on the opposite bank, said: "I have a fancy to live at the top of one of those buildings that touch the sky. What say you, Tom? We could acquire a monstrous flying bird and our feet need never feel the earth beneath them. . . ."

Tom did not reply, for his attention was taken by a girl with silky, short black hair in a satin skirt who had just walked past him.

"Anjali!" he called.

The girl turned around. It was not Anjali. A look of intense disappointment suffused Tom's face, and with a tinge of annoyance, the girl went on her way. The Tar Man observed his apprentice.

"I had a prancer once," he said to Tom. "Black as the night. Curb her even a little and she'd kick up and threaten to throw me in the ditch. But she was the fastest horse I ever had, so I tolerated her temper. Now I warn you, Tom, for I have eyes in my head, don't entertain fanciful thoughts about Anjali. She has her uses and it amuses me to keep her on a long rein, but with you, Tom, I have a notion she'd do worse than throw you into a ditch. . . . You are but a boy. Do not let Anjali distract you from finding a foothold in this new world."

Tom bowed his head and did not reply.

They continued walking and after a while Tom asked: "Was that the black horse you rode the day Lord Luxon had you race against Gideon Seymour?"

"No, lad! Can you not tell a stallion from a mare? Lord Luxon, damn his eyes, chose the finest horses in five counties for that race. Two stallions of Arab blood. 'Tis a talent to spot evenly matched mounts and I cannot deny that my erstwhile employer has an eye for horseflesh. . . ."

"That day," said Tom, "was my first day as footman to Lord Luxon and my last day in our time. We left ahead of you to be at Tempest House for the finish, but I dearly wish I could have watched you and Mr. Seymour race one against the other for you were as evenly—" Tom suddenly stopped, realizing what he was about to say might give offence.

"Finish your sentence, lad! For we were as evenly matched as the horses? Doubtless it was precisely that idea which was in Lord Luxon's mind also. But if Gideon is the more elegant rider, I am the stronger."

"To be sure," said Tom quickly.

The Tar Man nodded. "And had that pernicious Parson not poisoned my horse I should have proved it, though, upon my word, all that matters little now. . . . But I do have a mind to tell you something that will astonish you, young Tom."

Tom looked at him, all attention. An unfathomable expression had appeared on Blueskin's face. He stared vacantly at the river flowing past until suddenly he spoke.

"It is on account of Gideon Seymour that I broke with my employer on the day I journeyed to the future."

"You broke with Lord Luxon!"

"Yes, at least my actions on that day make it doubtful that

Lord Luxon would desire my return to his employ. I was lately informed, by someone I have no reason to mistrust, that Mr. Seymour is . . ." The Tar Man was all at once unnerved by the reality conferred to the notion by expressing it in words. He finished off the sentence quickly. "It is possible that Gideon Seymour is my brother. Not only that, but, I am reliably informed, it was my relationship to Gideon that was the principal reason Lord Luxon took me on as his henchman."

"Gideon Seymour is your brother! And Lord Luxon knew! But 'twas Lord Luxon that sent him to the gallows!"

Tom sank down onto a bench overlooking a replica of the *Golden Hind* and he looked so slack-jawed with shock, the Tar Man almost laughed. But, instead, he found himself sitting next to his apprentice and talking about a matter which, like an itch he could not scratch, had been bothering him a sight more than he was prepared to admit.

The Tar Man related how, on the eve of Gideon Seymour's execution, and in a fever of apprehension about what Lord Luxon would do to him, the new gamekeeper let slip that he and the condemned felon were, in fact, brothers. The gamekeeper's father, a resident of the village of Abinger in Surrey, used to know a fellow named Seymour who married a widow from Somerset. She had left the county to start a new life with her children after her eldest son, still a teenager, was hanged as a thief. There was an unconfirmed rumor at the time that the boy was cut down too soon, had escaped, and had been spurned by everyone that knew him when he had burst into the village hall during a dance. Other people reckoned that it was his ghost that had appeared pleading for assistance, while in fact his body had been snatched and sold to a surgeon for dissection. In any case, the widow herself always refused even to acknowledge that she was mother to the boy.

The Tar Man paused to gather his thoughts and Tom sneaked a look at his master's face. His expression betrayed no bitterness and his tone of voice was matter-of-fact. Tom wondered which was worse: never to have known your mother or father, as was the case for him and most of the children he was brought up with, or to have been disowned by your own family like Blueskin. Probably the latter, he decided, and, for an instant, although he could not have articulated his feelings, he perceived the sheer strength of will and self-belief required to propel Blueskin out of the deep, dark hole that his early life had dug for him. Presently the Tar Man continued with his tale. Several years after the widow's arrival in Abinger, an epidemic of scarlet fever devastated the village. The Seymour family was all but wiped out. There had been several children; the game-keeper did not rightly know just how many, but only one boy from the widow's first marriage and one boy from the second survived. The eldest boy was called Gideon. . . .

The Tar Man told Tom that when he had confronted Lord Luxon at Tyburn, he had refused either to confirm or deny any knowledge of the matter.

"That my Lord Luxon hoards secrets like other men hoard gold is something I have long known," said the Tar Man. "It pleases him to pull a man's strings, and his satisfaction is all the sweeter if the object of his attention believes he is moving of his own accord."

"In your heart, do you believe Gideon to be your brother?"

"It is possible. I had a young brother named Gideon and I have him to thank for this scar when he was too young to realize what he had done. However, our family name is not the same and I am loathe to put all my trust in one man's word. Perhaps my mother did remarry. . . . But many is the time I have been wrong-footed by rumor and hearsay. Now that fate has sent me to the future, I may never learn the truth. In any case, what use have I for a brother? Yet I swear to you, were I to discover that Gideon Seymour shares my blood and that Lord Luxon has deceived me, then, one way or another, I shall extract payment from him. I'll be no man's puppet. . . ."

"Perhaps Gideon knew."

"Ha! Not him! If Gideon had that knowledge you can be sure he would have endeavored to turn me from my wicked ways. . . ." The Tar Man laughed. "Or more likely put as many miles as he could between himself and the black-hearted villain he knows me to be! I should be the last man on earth he would choose for a brother and it is a sentiment that I reciprocate. . . ."

"And yet I saw him steal back the diamond necklace from the Carrick Gang in front of their very noses," said Tom. "A more skillful bit of thievery I never saw in my life."

"Ay, confound him, were it not for his prickly conscience, I could have put him to good use."

"When you fade back to our time, do you not have the power of speech? Could you not ask Lord Luxon face-to-face if you have a brother?"

The Tar Man regarded the boy in utter astonishment.

"Tom, lad! Was I not right to choose you as my apprentice! Suddenly I have a strong desire to go a-calling to Bird Cage Walk. . . ."

The Tar Man smiled so broadly at Tom that the lad was emboldened to say what was on his mind.

"I am not so surprised as you might suppose, that you and Master Gideon might be brothers. Though your faces are as different as day and night, you're both as strong and agile as may be and . . . there is an air about you both that . . . commands men's attention. You might almost say, begging your pardon, that you and Gideon Seymour are like two sides of the same coin."

The Tar Man sat in an armchair by an open casement window in Lord Luxon's bedchamber. It was the dead of night and Bird Cage Walk was silent apart from the eerie hooting of an owl that echoed over St. James's Park. The moon was waning, and what moonlight trickled into the room did little to dispel the inky darkness. By now the Tar Man's eyes had adjusted to the lack of light and he could just make out the bulky shape which was, in fact, the sleeping form of Lord Luxon. He listened to his steady breathing.

"Lord Luxon," he whispered.

Lord Luxon moaned in his sleep and threw the linen sheets off him. He wore a white nightgown and lay in a high, four-poster bed which Louis XIV had reputedly once slept in. It was draped with heavy, ornate cloth and had clumps of dusty ostrich feathers sprouting out of each of the top four corners.

"Lord Luxon!"

Suddenly the recumbent figure sat bolt upright, his long blond hair loose around his shoulders. Lord Luxon froze, holding his breath and straining to hear. He was not alone. Then, with a start, he saw, or imagined that he saw, a shadowy figure sitting in the chair next to the window. He reached his hand under his pillow and drew something out.

"Good evening, my Lord. Or perhaps I should say good morning."

"Who is there?"

The Tar Man heard his involuntary gasp and the fear in his voice. Lord Luxon slipped out of bed and stood up, peering blindly into the darkness.

"Who dares come into my chamber?"

But the Tar Man did not have the opportunity to reply, for the figure in white came at him, one arm raised high. The Tar Man felt a long, cold blade pierce his heart. He clutched at his chest and let out a long, agonized scream.

"Aaaaargh!"

The Tar Man staggered toward the bed and collapsed onto the mattress headfirst, causing the dagger to sink further into his chest.

Lord Luxon ran to the door, struggling in his panic to find the key in its lock and to turn the brass doorknob that was always apt to stick. Finally he flung open the door and fled into the corridor. A night light still burned on a small console table beneath an oil painting of his mother as a young girl. He lurched toward it and clung on to both sides of the table like a shipwrecked sailor to flotsam, breathing as heavily as if he had been running at full pelt. Presently, rising up through the turmoil of confused thoughts that beset his mind, the idea came repeatedly to him that the owner of that chilling voice was known to him. Suddenly it struck him who it was.

"Blueskin! By all the gods, I have killed Blueskin!"

He lit a candle from the night light and returned, swaying, to the scene of the crime, steeling himself to look at the bloody corpse of his henchman. He hesitated at the doorway and held on to the wooden frame. He re-entered his chamber and locked the door behind him. Then he forced himself to walk across the room. With a trembling hand he held the candle up high. The flame guttered a little in the sweet air that entered the stuffy room from the park. As he reached down to pull the body over so that he could look on Blueskin's face, the corpse stirred. Then the Tar Man rolled over onto his back. Lord Luxon's jaw dropped open in shock. The Tar Man groaned and his face contorted in pain. His arms twitched limply at his sides and he shook his head this way and that against the blue counterpane embroidered with flowers. Did his eyes deceive him? Was Blueskin more than a little transparent? Then he noticed that there was no blood. Not a single drop. His hench-man had no blood in his veins! Was he raving? Was this a waking dream? Or did he behold a ghost? A movement on the Tar Man's chest caught his eye. He stood up again and moved his candle closer so that he could see. Little by little the blade of his dagger was, unaided by any human hand, pushing itself up, emerging, unstained, from the Tar Man's diaphanous flesh. Lord Luxon stepped backward, away from the dreadful appa-rition. He felt nauseous. The veins in his temples throbbed and although molten wax dripped onto his wrist he was oblivious to the pain.

"What nightmare is this?" he cried.

Abruptly someone turned the door handle and, finding it locked, rapped sharply on the door instead. Lord Luxon was in such a heightened state of alarm he all but screamed at the interruption.

"May I be of assistance, my Lord? I heard a cry," his servant called.

"No, no. . . . All is well. A bad dream, that is all. . . . I bid you good night."

"Very well. Good night, my Lord."

The dagger fell onto the wooden floor with a clatter and Lord Luxon watched, unable to move, as the Tar Man heaved him-self up and sat on the edge of the bed. There was a small, frayed slit in his shirt over his heart and he clutched at his stomach and prodded his face and his arms and his legs as if to reassure himself that they were still there.

"Do I yet live? I feel I have been turned outside in and pummeled in a butter churn for good measure," groaned the Tar Man. "By heaven, I feel sick to my stomach."

He let his head drop forward between his knees and his back started to heave as if he were about to vomit. After a moment, though, he revived a little and sat up. The Tar Man looked directly into Lord Luxon's eyes, and when he read the horror-struck expression on his old master's face, a wafer-thin smile flickered over his lips. Then the Tar Man chose to vanish into thin air, but very slowly, like condensed breath evaporating from a cold mirror. He kept eye contact to the end. Lord Luxon staggered backward and fell into the armchair, where he contemplated the full horror and mystery of what he had seen until dawn's watery light announced the break of day.

Once he had recovered from the physical shock of experiencing his blurring body repulse an object from a different time, the Tar Man rejoiced in the possibilities which this encounter suggested to him. Just as materializing in a tree had caused him no lasting hurt, he had been stabbed in the heart and yet had suffered no injury. Was he, the Tar Man wondered, to all extents and purposes, invincible when he faded back to his own time? Not, he thought, that he was in any hurry to repeat such a nauseating experience. However, what gave the Tar Man most satisfaction was that Lord Luxon had plainly taken him for a ghost. Which, in a way, he was. A ghost from the future. And it seemed to him that even the duplicitous Lord Luxon might think twice before concealing the truth from a visitor from the spirit world. . . .

Had he been able to compare notes with the young Kate Dyer, the Tar Man would have discovered that soon after his first experience of fading on the Golden Gallery of St. Paul's, by dint of practice and perseverance he was able to blur for substantial periods of time, longer by far than Kate had been able to, before feeling the inevitable and irresistible force that hurled him back to the twenty-first century. In the same way that pearl divers gradually build up the length of time they can spend underwater, on his trips back to 1763 the Tar Man always resisted, with gritted teeth, the pull of the future for as long as he possibly could before the luminous spirals covered his vision like a migraine. Soon he could manage a full half an hour with little discomfort—three times the length of time, at least, that Kate had ever been able to manage. But, unlike Kate, the Tar Man was planning a whole career around his ability to blur at will.

He blurred back to Bird Cage Walk three times over the following few days, reasoning that the more fear he could instill into Lord Luxon's heart, the more likely it would be that he could tease the truth out of him. In general, the Tar Man hurt people to get what he wanted from them and, unlike Joe Carrick, did not take any particular pleasure in seeing them suffer. However, the prospect of watching Lord Luxon squirm was not without its attractions. The Tar Man therefore appeared fleetingly at the end of his bed on the following night, and the next evening stepped out suddenly in front of Lord Luxon as he walked out of his front door. The day after that he materialized at supper-time while Lord Luxon was sipping some chicken soup alone in his parlor. When Lord Luxon saw the ghostly apparition yet again in as many days, with his nerves already torn to shreds, he dropped his silver spoon, staining his silk waistcoat and the spot-less linen tablecloth. The Tar Man was just about to sit down next to him and engage him in conversation when footsteps in the corridor announced the imminent arrival of a servant. The Tar Man walked to the window and concealed himself behind the long, red velvet drapes. Lord Luxon continued to look in horror at the curtain while his footman took away his half-empty soup dish and replaced it with a platter of grilled Dover sole. Noticing the look of anguish on his master's face, the footman asked if he could be of any assistance.

"I fear not," replied Lord Luxon, who had convinced himself that, like Macbeth and the ghost of Banquo, he alone could see the vengeful spirit of his old henchman. The Tar Man came so close to laughter he had to return immediately to the future for fear of ruining the effect of his haunting and decided to wait for a couple of days before attempting to extract the truth from Lord Luxon.

Exciting new challenges were presenting themselves in the twenty-first century and the Tar Man's preoccupation with his relationship to Gideon Seymour diminished. Instead, forg-ing relationships with a handful of key figures in London's underworld became his priority. Back in the eighteenth century, however, Lord Luxon, for his part, could think of nothing but the next ghostly visitation. Any unexpected movement in his peripheral vision was apt to make him jump out of his skin. Not only that, his sleep was shattered, he had lost his appetite, and his consumption of wine, already high, increased further. Habitually fastidious with regard to his dress, the aristocrat was seen to arrive at his club, White's on St. James's, looking somewhat disheveled. This provoked much comment among his gambling cronies, and when one of them suggested that the black circles under his eyes were a result of his guilty past catching up with him, he had to be restrained from challenging the impudent fellow to a duel.

But, at last, the Tar Man took it into his head to revisit his old master in Bird Cage Walk. Certainly one reason was to clear up, once and for all, the troublesome matter of his relationship to Gideon Seymour, but now he had another reason. He had it on Anjali's good authority that the paintings and engravings of certain eighteenth-century artists would, as she put it, "fetch a packet" in London's great auction houses. Anjali had done her homework and had given him three names to remember: Thomas Gainsborough, Joshua Reynolds, and George Stubbs. The Tar Man had not heard of any of these gentlemen, but he was actually acquainted with another artist she mentioned, William Hogarth. They both frequented the same chop house in Covent Garden, and Lord Luxon, he knew for a fact, had purchased several of his engravings to grace the hall at Bird Cage Walk.

And so it was that Lord Luxon arrived back from White's Club one evening to find Blueskin draped over his Italian marble staircase with a small pile of Hogarth engravings neatly stacked next to him. Gray with fright and unable to bear this haunting any longer, the aristocrat sank to his knees in despair.

"How much longer must I endure this, O Spirit?" he cried.

It was then that the Tar Man chose to pose the question he had delayed putting to Lord Luxon for so long.

"Was it well done, my Lord, to bring two brothers together only to deceive them as to their true identity and then condemn one of them to death?"

Lord Luxon covered his face with his hands. When he removed them, his cheeks glistened.

"It was wrong of me, Blueskin, and I do most sincerely repent my actions. I assure you that I had intended to tell you . . . at an apposite moment."

"Before or after Gideon Seymour was hanged!" exploded the Tar Man. "So it *is* true then."

Lord Luxon was all confusion.

"You did not know? The dead are then as ignorant as the living?"

"I am not dead, you fool! I am transported to the future by the magic machine. I am able to return to my own time only in this altered form. Ha! You have used me ill, my Lord! I deserved better!"

"The machine transported you to the future!"

"Ay, my Lord. Hundreds of years into the future. I have seen things the like of which would make your hair stand on end. . . . And already I am rich!"

Lord Luxon remained speechless and stared at him in astonishment. Had the Tar Man not been so angry, he might have noticed the sparks of desire and cunning that suddenly blazed on Lord Luxon's features before he smothered them, as fast as they had appeared.

"I must inform you at once, Blueskin, that I cannot swear that you and Gideon are brothers. It was based on mere conjecture, that is all."

The Tar Man stood up and said angrily: "Is Gideon my brother or is he not?"

"Without further investigation, I can neither confirm nor deny it. And, alas, your informant, the gamekeeper, is dead."

"Dead!"

"An accident. An encounter with a poacher, I believe."

"Do not play with me, my Lord!"

"Upon my word, why should I play with you?"

"And yet you knew there was a possibility that Gideon Seymour and I were brothers the day you hired me!"

Lord Luxon did not reply.

"Do not deny it!"

"Ah, how the past does ever hold us in its thrall," replied Lord Luxon. "Even if you and Gideon *were* brothers—would it change your life one whit?"

"But why did you not tell me of the possibility, damn your eyes!" hissed the Tar Man. "The truth, my Lord!"

Lord Luxon opened his mouth and closed it again. His mouth twitched.

"Because it amused me."

The Tar Man gave a hollow laugh. "I believe you! The day of the race, how you must have relished your secret . . . to pit brother against brother . . . I could have *killed* him!"

"I told you! It is a possibility, that is all!" Then Lord Luxon added petulantly: "But what a pleasure it would have been to see the look on Gideon's self-righteous face on being told that *your* black blood runs in his own veins."

The Tar Man leaped up, beside himself. "Blood is blood, my Lord Luxon, and we'll soon see the color of yours!"

The Tar Man took a furious swipe at Lord Luxon but his former master did not end up in a huddled heap on the stairs as he had intended. Instead, the Tar Man found that his fist sank into his victim's chin as if it were jelly. He pulled it out straightaway with considerable repugnance. Lord Luxon, meanwhile, retched uncontrollably. His henchman had touched the roots of his teeth, grated his bones with his nails; for an instant their flesh had mingled. His pale complexion grew even paler and he repeatedly stroked his chin to reassure himself that all was well. The Tar Man was cradling his fist in his other hand but refused to admit to any discomfort or surprise. *So,* he thought, *I might be invincible when I fade, but neither can I do more damage than make a man heave.* . . . He sat down again, a little breathless, on one of the marble steps and gazed down at Lord Luxon in distaste.

"I've often heard say that Gideon Seymour is your conscience. 'Tis no wonder, then, that you wanted to kill him."

Continuing to rub his chin, Lord Luxon considered his reply. The two men eyed each other.

"Come, Blueskin, let us not quarrel. It is true that Gideon had a rare talent as a cutpurse. But his conversion to a righteous existence was ill timed. . . . I lost a tidy sum—and more than I could afford—when he refused to ply his trade. But, all's well that ends well, and with your arrival my troubles were over. Your reputation is well deserved. I have been unable, in truth, to conduct my affairs properly in your absence. . . ."

The Tar Man did not care to acknowledge the compliment, mistrusting, as he did, his old master's motives. *What is he about, now?* he wondered. *My Lord is as slippery as ever. . . .*

"I have not had news of Gideon since his rescue from Tyburn," Lord Luxon continued. "Did the magic machine also transport him through time?"

"No. He remained here with Master Peter Schock. I journeyed to the future with Miss Dyer and her father."

"So the boy is still *here*! How really very intriguing! . . . Then is the machine in your possession?"

"No."

"Then how . . . ?"

"I am able to fade back here, but for a short time only, before I must return to the future."

"In the same manner in which you told me Mistress Dyer and Master Schock faded! But the machine allows you to travel from one century to another as you will?"

257

"Ay, that would seem to be the case. . . ."

"Then you would do well to track down this ingenious device!"

"I know nothing of that," said the Tar Man, irritated that something so obvious had not occurred to him before. He was beginning to feel strained. Invisible forces were clutching at him. "And now, my Lord, I must bid you adieu. I trust you will not begrudge me these worthless engravings by way of recompense. . . . It was wrong of you to withhold this secret from me. . . ."

Lord Luxon laughed. "What, do you mean to tell me that Mr. Hogarth's pictures have a value in the future? Take them with my blessing, Blueskin! For I shall do my utmost to make amends for the wrong I have done you. I have always admired you and thought you deserved better. . . ."

In some pain, the Tar Man grimaced and clutched the engravings to him. He managed to whisper: "I could buy Tempest House twice over with the proceeds from these."

He half closed his eyes and luminous spirals began to cloud his vision. He was beginning to fade. Lord Luxon rushed toward his increasingly transparent henchman, his hands outstretched. The Tar Man heard him calling after him as if from a great distance. . . .

"Promise me that you will come again, Blueskin! I, too, desire to see the future! If you agree to help me, I shall give commissions to every last painter in London! And I shall leave no stone unturned until I discover the true nature of your relationship with Gideon Seymour. Just say the word and it shall be done!"

THIRTEEN

THE SIX CONSPIRATORS

*In which the six conspirators make plans
in the Derbyshire farmhouse and
Dr. Pirretti makes a confession*

Dr. Dyer kept the promise he had made to Mr. Schock in Middle Harpenden. He immediately contacted Mrs. Schock to explain that both her husband and his daughter were currently in the mid-eighteenth century attempting to track down Peter. Unsurprisingly, Mrs. Schock was outraged that Dr. Dyer would taunt her in this ludicrous manner and questioned whether the balance of his mind had been disturbed by the stress both families had been under. She had slammed the receiver down and burst into tears. But when her husband still had not contacted her after twelve hours, Mrs. Schock had telephoned the Dyers. Kate's mother had confirmed the story and also arranged for Mrs. Schock to speak with Dr. Pirretti in the States. There had been a short delay while Dr. Pirretti located a secure landline, for she was concerned that her telephone might have been bugged.

Now Peter's mother stood at her sitting-room window, gripping the receiver and staring out at a sunny Richmond Green, as Dr. Pirretti repeated the same story. Mrs. Schock doubted neither her sincerity nor the feelings of sympathy and professional regret which she expressed. And even under such devastating circumstances, she warmed to the Californian scientist.

Dr. Pirretti was honest enough to admit that she had been against revealing the truth to her. She also spoke of her dismay at the unexpected side effect of their antigravity experiment and her determination, one way or another, to kick over all traces of the existence of a machine capable of time travel.

"I'm so sorry that you've been burdened with this knowledge when you've already got so much to deal with, but please," urged Dr. Pirretti, "I'm begging you to be discreet. It will be a catastrophe for the world if this gets out."

When Mrs. Schock put the receiver down she felt curiously detached from the world. Her gaze followed the progress of a group of children and their small dog along the diagonal path that crosses Richmond Green until they reached the red postbox on the opposite side. She had never felt more alone.

Megan had promised Kate to keep an eye on Sam. She was visiting him the following day after school when, unannounced, Mrs. Schock arrived at the farm. She had driven up to Derbyshire to speak with Dr. and Mrs. Dyer in person. Megan and Sam were sitting around the kitchen table munching on peanut butter biscuits when Kate's mum brought in a pretty woman with dark, bobbed hair to say hello.

"This is Peter's mother," she said.

The grown-ups shut themselves up in the dining room where they talked for three hours without a break. Megan gingerly opened the dining-room door to say good-bye when it was time for her to go home. Mrs. Schock immediately got up and asked Megan if she would be coming again soon because she wanted to hear all about Kate and what, if anything, she had told her about the time she spent with Peter in the eighteenth century. Megan took to Mrs. Schock. She looked sad—which was hardly surprising—but she was smart and quick to smile.

"Kate takes after her dad," Megan told her. "They're both incredibly determined."

"And stubborn!" said Mrs. Dyer.

"Thanks!" said her husband.

"I know Kate and Peter's dad will find him—you'll see. . . ." said Megan.

Mrs. Schock gave her a grateful smile and put an arm around her shoulders.

"So you think there's hope yet?"

"Definitely!"

Mrs. Schock had booked herself into a nearby hotel but was persuaded to stay on at the farm. She never left. It was so much easier to be with people who knew exactly what she was going through, and it was good not to be forever watching her words. Megan came most days to spend some time with Sam and, in an unspoken pact of secrecy and support, the five of them—two children and three adults—in their own very different ways, shored up the collective morale against those negative thoughts that inevitably assailed them all.

When Dr. Pirretti let the Dyers know that she would be traveling to Manchester along with Russ Merrick's antigravity prototype, Kate's dad offered to pick her up from the airport. He was on the point of leaving, and eating a quick snack, when something caught his eye in the Sunday paper.

"Just take a look at this!" he cried out from the dining room, sloshing coffee into his saucer in his excitement.

He walked into the kitchen holding open the flapping newspaper for everyone to see. "This, if I am not very much mistaken, is our fugitive from the eighteenth century!"

"Let me have a look," said Sam, ducking under Dr. Dyer's sweater-clad arms and popping his head between his dad and the newspaper.

"Oooh! Is that the Tar Man? Mum, look! He's blurring!"

Mrs. Dyer looked over her husband's shoulder. "How do you know it's the Tar Man? He's got his back to us."

"I'd recognize that crooked neck anywhere."

"What on earth is he doing with a painting of a horse?"

"Not any painting of a horse—it's by George Stubbs. The National Gallery paid a lot of money to keep that picture in the country. . . ."

"Has the Tar Man stolen it?" asked Mrs. Schock.

"Strangely, no. . . ."

"What's he doing, then?"

"From what they can tell, all he's done is stuck a red dot on the bottom right-hand corner of the painting!"

"What, like it's been sold, you mean?" asked his wife.

"Exactly!"

Mrs. Schock laughed. "What do the police think he was up to?"

"They're treating it as a stunt—they can't figure out how or why he did it but, as nothing has been stolen, I doubt they'll be spending much of the taxpayers' money pursuing the matter. . . ."

"Once a thief, always a thief. . . . Do you think we should contact the police?" asked Mrs. Dyer.

"You can't, Mum!" said Sam. "Not without telling them about time travel."

"If he starts murdering people, rather than sticking red dots on equestrian paintings," said Dr. Dyer, "then we'll have to think again. But right now we've got other priorities. . . ."

The arrival of Dr. Pirretti, and with her Russ Merrick's antigravity machine, brought renewed optimism to the farm. Dr. Dyer had the machine transported from Manchester Airport to Derbyshire disguised as a fridge-freezer. The machine was not complete, and working from Tim Williamson's notes which Dr. Dyer had smuggled out of the NCRDM laboratory along with a large suitcase of equipment, the two scientists toiled, almost without a break, in the old dairy until they were satisfied with their modifications. By the time they had finished, the only difference, to the best of their knowledge, between Tim's original machine and this copy was the addition of a security device. The latter had been Dr. Dyer's idea and it demanded the input of a code before it could be switched on.

"What happens if you forget the code?" Sam asked the day the work was completed.

"I won't!" said Dr. Dyer.

"I'd write it on my wrist!" said Sam. "And how are you going to get back to the right time?"

"That's at least the third time you've asked me the same question, Sam! We're going to set the power to an identical level as before—six point seven seven megawatts, as it happens. The antigravity machine *should*, in theory, travel back the same distance in time. So, hopefully, I *should* arrive in the summer of 1763."

"What happens if you miss?"

"Then I'll just have to come right back again, won't I?"

Dr. Dyer was in favor of telling their colleagues in the antigravity project what they were attempting to do, but Dr. Pirretti refused.

"As far as they are concerned I've already destroyed the machine along with all the documentation. And that's how I'd like it to stay, for now, anyway. If we fail . . . perhaps I'll have to think again."

Dr. Dyer knew from bitter experience how long it took to travel even a few miles in 1763. He wanted to get as close to Peter and Gideon as possible and so made the decision to transport the machine to Hawthorn Cottage, for he suspected that Gideon would take Peter back to Derbyshire rather than risk staying in London. The only problem was that they did not know the location of Hawthorn Cottage, or, indeed, if it still existed. Mrs. Dyer and Mrs. Schock, helped by Megan and Sam, visited the local records office and combed through old manuscripts and maps. By the end of the second afternoon they had found a legal document dating from the early 1800s which clearly indicated a certain Hawthorn Cottage which was situated around a mile away from Kate's school.

"It has to be it!" Megan cried when she spotted it. Mrs. Dyer and Mrs. Schock agreed, and they all dived into the Land Rover, intent on taking a look at it before it got too dark. Mrs. Dyer found that she already knew the cottage, with its pretty garden, whose gray stone walls had been more carefully preserved than its original name. She had often passed it although she was not acquainted with its owners. It brought a lump to her throat to associate it with Gideon Seymour, who now seemed so real a person to her.

It was the eve of Dr. Dyer's departure. Dr. Pirretti and Dr. Dyer had taken a turn around the farmyard. Before they entered the farmhouse, for they did not want to cause any upset on this of all nights, the scientists agreed between themselves that Dr. Pirretti should stay behind. If Kate's father failed to return, Dr. Pirretti would have to decide whether—or not—to build another machine.

When they entered the red and cream dining room, they found

that they were the last to sit down around the long table. The little ones had been in their beds long ago and the six conspirators, as Megan had dubbed them, had helped prepare what, to his wife's annoyance, Dr. Dyer kept referring to as his last meal. Every time he had done so, Mrs. Dyer had flicked him hard with a tea towel.

Everyone had been as upbeat and cheerful as they knew how. Mrs. Dyer had laid the best check tablecloth and lit the room with candles, Sam had lent his dad his lucky stone, a fragment of Blue John from the underground caverns in Castleton, and Dr. Pirretti had brought along two bottles of rosé champagne—one to toast Dr. Dyer on the eve of the rescue attempt and the other, she explained, to toast him on his return. Mrs. Schock asked Dr. Dyer if he could take a small photograph to give to Peter. It had been taken by his granddad a couple of years ago at the seaside in Devon. Peter was lying on a Hawaiian towel on the sand between his mother and father. All three of them were fast asleep and Peter had one arm under his mother's neck and one under his father's.

"Tell him I want it back," she said. "It's one of my favorite pictures. . . ."

Dr. Dyer looked down and nodded. His wife squeezed his hand under the table.

They were all biting into the rich chocolate truffles which were Megan's contribution to the supper when Dr. Pirretti spoke.

"I have a confession to make," she said abruptly.

Everyone looked at her expectantly.

"I've been talking to myself."

There was general laughter around the table.

"Never mind, Anita," said Dr. Dyer. "It comes to us all. . . ."

"What I mean to say is that I've been talking to myself in what I believe to be a parallel world."

An awkward silence descended on the low-ceilinged dining room. A burning log fell onto the grate and Mrs. Dyer put it back on the fire with a pair of tongs.

"I don't understand, Anita," said Mrs. Schock.

"Neither do I. I sure wish I did. But, at the risk of appearing ridiculous in your eyes forever, there is something I feel compelled to tell you. . . ."

Dr. Pirretti now had everyone's undivided attention.

"You see, I get the distinct impression that the voice I have been hearing is extremely concerned about something. . . ."

"The voice? What are you talking about, Anita?" asked Dr. Dyer in alarm.

"I think you know that I've been suffering from headaches and tinnitus since I first came to Derbyshire. I happened to be in St. Paul's Cathedral a while back. In the Whispering Gallery. There were all these echoey, distorted voices. It's merely an intriguing side effect of the architecture—the sound waves bounce off the walls in such a way that someone whispering on one side of the dome can be perfectly audible on the other. Anyway, after a while it struck me that there was something about them that reminded me of the noises I'd been hearing in my head for some time."

"You mean that you are hearing voices?" asked Mrs. Dyer.

"Not exactly. If this doesn't sound too crazy, I am *seeing* voices. Actually, I now realize, *a* voice. It just seems like I'm hearing noises until I . . . tune in . . . and then it's more like seeing but there is an element of hearing, too. . . . I'm sorry but it's difficult to explain. You'd have to experience it yourself. And accompanying it there is always an intense sensation of recognition, of having lived through it before, of knowing what is going to happen next. . . ."

"So, er, who do you think is talking to you?" asked Dr. Dyer apprehensively. The memory of Dr. Pirretti talking to him in her sleep when she was in hospital suddenly came back to him. Could his respected colleague be losing her grip?

"It might be easier if I start with *what* I think she is saying to me. . . ."

"She? All right. Start there. What is *she* saying?"

"She says the same thing over and over until I get it. You must understand that it's a little like listening to a radio where there is practically no reception. It's confusing, and an excruciatingly slow process . . . and there's a danger that I've misheard or am misinterpreting what she is saying. . . . Oh, Lord, this sounds such a crackpot thing now that I'm saying it out loud. . . ."

"Anita! Get on with it for goodness' sake!" said Dr. Dyer. "If we think you're mad we'll chuck you in the duck pond after coffee. . . ."

"Okay, okay." Dr. Pirretti took a deep breath. "My overwhelming fear when we discovered time travel was that the one thing we thought we could be one hundred percent sure about—the past—could, in fact, be rewritten. The voice seems to be telling me that this is not the *only* problem. Going backward and forward in time has created multiple parallel worlds. I think she's saying that one of the fundamental laws of nature is that you can't destroy what has already happened. . . . So you get two worlds: one where things *are* altered; one where things stay the same. If she's right I guess there must be a parallel world where Peter and Kate never went to 1763 in the first place but came back to the farmhouse for the lunch. . . ."

"Which also implies," said Dr. Dyer, "if she—you—are right, that there could be an infinite number of parallel worlds. . . ."

"And that *we* are responsible for the creation of them," said Dr. Pirretti.

"Are you seriously suggesting," asked Mrs. Schock "that there could be many worlds in which there are duplicate Derbyshires and Richmond Greens and Atlantic Oceans . . . and Sams and Megans?"

Dr. Pirretti nodded. "It's impossible to imagine, isn't it? And so, to answer your original question, Andrew, the person I believe is speaking to me is *myself* in a parallel world."

Dr. Dyer slowly let out his breath in a long, low whistle.

"Anita, this is, I'm sure you will understand, a little difficult to take onboard all at once. . . ."

"I know. But I couldn't keep it to myself any longer. My anxiety that she—I—could be right finally overcame my professional embarrassment. I freely admit that the situation is ludicrous. It's like playing 'I spy' in the dark."

"It sounds more like 'Simon says' to me," said Dr. Dyer. "Only the identity, location, and reliability of Simon are all extremely questionable. . . . I mean, is this some kind of advanced telepathy or what?" asked Dr. Dyer.

Suddenly he felt very tired and found himself becoming intensely irritated with his colleague. Voices! Duplicate worlds! "Anita—is this a long and convoluted way of telling me I shouldn't go tomorrow? Because I *am* going back in time to find Kate and Peter and his dad and I *am* going to bring them back whether your voice says so or not. Is that what you're trying to tell me—that it's not a good idea?"

"I don't know! If it is true, how am I expected to know the effect of creating multiple worlds on the universe?"

"Well, I wish my duplicate self in a parallel universe would try and communicate with me, too, and then perhaps I could help out . . . ," said Dr. Dyer archly.

"Apparently he's been trying," Dr. Pirretti replied. "He's been doing the equivalent of bawling in your ear, but you won't listen."

FOURTEEN

PETER'S NOSE

In which Mr. Schock gets a close shave, the party
encounters a traffic jam, and Kate becomes suspicious

The morning of September 11, 1792, found Peter Schock in an
agitated frame of mind. He was beginning to take delight in getting to know his father on equal terms; he even dared hope that
they could become friends for the short time they would have
together. So while he desired to put off the day of his father's
departure as long as possible, what he had witnessed happening
to Kate in Golden Square had created in him a renewed sense
of urgency to repair the antigravity machine. Like a strong light
whose afterimage stubbornly refuses to fade and glows, in lurid
shades, at the back of the eye, the sight of Kate, terrified and
alone, battling with forces beyond her control, was imprinted on
his mind. He had felt something which he could confide neither to Kate nor his father. Something long dormant had stirred
within him and he sensed, rather than saw, the fluorescent spirals which he so vividly associated with blurring. Yet something
had gone wrong: Rather than moving between two different
centuries, Kate appeared to be trapped between them. Could the

hooks that bound her to her own time have become damaged in some way? The look of abject terror in her eyes haunted him. He wanted to protect his childhood friend who had traveled willingly back in time to rescue him, and it made him sad that his extra years were not enough in themselves to find a solution to her predicament. As a child he had taken it for granted that the grown-ups would always know what to do. Now he understood the reality of it: Despite appearances they often feel as unequal to the task as the children, but with no one else to turn to they must do the best they can. And then, what Augusta, the Reverend Austen's daughter, had said about Kate flitting about like a bat came back to him. What could it mean? *We must depart for France this very day,* he thought. *Let us hope that this Marquis de Montfaron is as resourceful as Sir Joseph believes him to be.*

There was a soft knock at the door.

"Come in, John!"

The footman carried a large jug over to the washstand and, two fresh linen towels draped over his arm, poured steaming hot water into a basin decorated with birds and flowers. He stifled a yawn, having been up in the middle of the night to open the back gate for the night-soil men. They had come to empty the stinking cesspit by moonlight, as was their custom, so as not to offend the nostrils of the sleeping gentlefolk. John had already been up two hours, during which time he had cleaned and polished the entire household's shoes and boots in a basement room set apart for the purpose. Then, using the force pump, he had pumped up enough water to fill the cistern at the top of the house, from whence, via a simple system of lead pipes, water was available on every floor of the house. Now, after brushing and laying out Peter's clothes in the adjoining dressing room, it was time to help his master prepare himself for the day.

Dour-faced John, who had been poached from Lord Chesterfield's household by Sir Richard Picard more than thirty years ago, had always been a favorite. He affected a world-weary air which belied a wry sense of humor and a fondness for practical jokes which he would never admit to. Hannah now refused to walk up the stairs in front of him after an incident with a feather and a large house spider. For all his gentlemanly appearance now, John still thought of Mr. Peter Schock as the clumsy, fidgety youth who had broken more crockery in his first few visits to Lincoln's Inn Fields than the entire Picard family had in a century. John had grown used to his master's eccentric ways. For instance, he had a mania for cleaning his teeth, which he did after *every* meal, such was his fear of dental surgeons and what he called their barbaric ways. This fear had always seemed absurd to John. After all, if you did not like surgeon dentists no one would force you to consult with one (what was wrong with some strong twine and a swiftly shut door?). Yet Master Peter frequented them at least twice a year for what he termed "checkups," and the dentist was more than happy to take his gold. And then there was the annual birthday request to the cook to fry little beef patties which he would eat between chunks of bread with a slice of melting cheese, golden-fried onions, and fried potatoes cut into long sticks. Cook always tried to tempt him with delicacies such as raw oysters or calf's head pie or tripe in vinegar but, incomprehensibly, he always refused. John liked Peter Schock. He was a good employer—which many weren't—and he had even paid for a doctor to tend him when he contracted bronchitis the previous January.

Master and servant conversed little but fell into the comfortable routine of a thousand mornings. Peter pulled off his nightcap, loosened his voluminous nightshirt, and sat on the mahogany chair in front of the washstand where John laid out the toiletries and shaving equipment. When still new to the century Peter had found his relationships with the household staff problematic. Being waited on made him uneasy and he would try to help. His well-meaning attitude more often than not backfired, for it embarrassed the servants, drawing attention to their inferior status and ignoring any satisfaction which they might have felt in a job well done. After a few years, however, Peter had grown so used to his social situation he rarely questioned it and, if the truth were told, would now find life difficult without the constant support and companionship of Hannah and John. The footman took the attar of rose shaving cake and mixed it into a sweet-smelling lather which he applied liberally to Peter's face with a soft badger-hair brush. His master always closed his eyes to avoid getting soap in them and it was not unusual for him to drift off to sleep again. It amused John to pull faces at Peter at this stage in the proceedings—touching his tongue to the tip of his nose and blowing out his cheeks as far as they would go, ever ready to snap back to a more appropriate expression should his master's eyelids flicker—but he had never yet been caught out.

Next John took his strop, a long leather strap, which he used to sharpen the already lethal blade of his cutthroat razor. Then, yellowing teeth biting his lower lip in concentration, John attacked his master's stubble, scraping away at the bristles with expert, rasping strokes until Peter's face was as smooth and pink as was to be expected of a well-groomed English gentleman. John handed Peter a towel, for he knew he preferred to dry his face himself.

"Will you be requiring me to accompany you to France, sir?"

"No, John," said Peter, rising from the chair and returning the towel to his servant. "I do not intend to be away upward of four or five nights, and I should prefer you to attend on Miss Dyer in my absence."

"Very good, sir, I shall pack your trunk directly."

There was a second knock on Peter's door. John stepped forward to open it and they saw Mr. Schock standing in his night-shirt holding a handkerchief spotted with blood to his chin.

"I'd like to take you up on your offer, John. I've tried but I just can't manage it. I'd grow a beard but I haven't seen a single man who isn't clean-shaven since I arrived here. It doesn't help that one look at these cutthroat razors and I conjure up pictures of a fountain of blood spurting from my throat. . . ."

Master and servant exchanged glances but remained straight-faced.

"I have been shaving the men of the household for nigh on

three decades and most of them have lived to tell the tale, have they not, sir?"

"Indeed, John. In fact I cannot recall the last time we saw a *fountain* of blood, nor even a stream. A trickle perhaps . . ."

"Yes, yes, yes. Have your little joke," Mr. Schock retorted. "But without a bit of help, either I shall be scarred for life or I shall bring shame to the image of the English gentleman abroad. . . ."

"Quite, sir," said John, guiding Mr. Schock to the chair and lathering his face, "and that would never do."

Peter watched as the footman took out his strop again and gleefully sharpened the glinting blade with great vigor only an inch or two from Mr. Schock's face. The latter's gaze followed the rapid movements of the cutthroat razor with dismay and he craned his neck backward as far as it would go. The footman plucked a coarse gray hair from underneath his powdered wig and let it fall over the cutting edge. Peter's father gulped as he saw that the single strand of hair had been bisected. The next instant the razor was at his throat and John paused momentarily, adjusting with a flourish the angle at which he held the blade.

"I am pleased to see your hand does not tremble as much as it has of late," commented Peter.

John held out the cutthroat razor at arm's length and they all observed the visible tremor.

"Yes, my affliction is much improved, sir."

The hapless victim gripped the arm of the chair throughout

the operation, scarcely daring to breathe as the footman scratched away at him, lopping down the forest of bristles with precise, authoritative strokes. Beads of perspiration appeared on Mr. Schock's forehead. But presently, to his vast relief, he felt the cool touch of linen against his skin and John was holding up an ebony looking glass for him to admire his handiwork.

"Have I shaved you close enough, sir?"

"Yes, thank you, John, quite close enough!"

Only then did Peter allow himself to burst out laughing and John, holding out his hand which was as steady as a rock, assured Mr. Schock that he had never been in any danger.

John left to help Hannah with the breakfast and Mr. Schock stood up and thumped Peter good-naturedly on the back.

"Far be it from me to resent anyone having some fun at my expense but, be warned, I might have to get my own back one of these days. Just because we twenty-first-century-ites can't mend an antigravity machine doesn't mean to say that we're totally clueless. . . ."

"When we are in France, I shall teach you how to shave with a cutthroat razor. It is easier than you might think."

"I shall have to show Peter what his old dad has learned to do in the eighteenth century, although he's unlikely to be impressed. I don't often come up to scratch as far as my son is concerned. Not that I blame him. . . ."

Peter was surprised and sad to hear his father voicing concern about how his son perceived him but said nothing. Mr. Schock hesitated for an instant, wondering if he could confide in Joshua, and then, deciding that he could, continued: "Do you know the last thing he said to me?"

Peter shook his head but of course he could remember. Their argument in the kitchen of the house on Richmond Green, the argument which had started off this whole calamitous train of events, and which Peter had relived a thousand times over three decades, came flooding back. He could even hear the metallic clang of the pedal bin as his father shoveled overcooked eggs into it, berating him for being a spoiled brat. Then he could remember charging upstairs, so angry with his father because he had gone back on his promise of a birthday treat for the third time that he thought he would explode with the injustice of it. He had turned around at the top of the stairs and shouted at his father loud enough to hurt his throat. And those terrible words which had sprung to his lips had been etched onto his mind as if by acid. . . .

"'I hate you!'" said Mr. Schock. "That was what he shouted down at me before slamming his bedroom door. 'I hate you!' I can hear him still . . . and I can see the expression on his face."

"He cannot have meant it. . . . It was certainly said in the heat of the moment."

"Peter was angry but I have no doubt that he meant it. I put my work before my son once too often. I should have paid him more attention. . . ."

"No, no, I . . . In truth . . . You see, Peter confided in me. He was so very young at the time. You must believe me, Nick, for years your son bitterly regretted what he said and I know he wished with all his heart that he could have turned back the clock and swept those words away."

"No, Joshua. Thank you for trying to make me feel better about it. But I know my own son."

Peter looked away. He did not want his father to know who he was and yet his success in concealing his true identity was almost too much bear. He wanted to peel away the years and shout at his father, "Surely you must know who I am?" But he could hardly blame his father for his own deception.

"Joshua?"

"Yes, Nick?"

Mr. Schock put his hand on Peter's arm.

"You must have been very close to my son. Please, could you tell me about him? What kind of man he was . . . What he achieved . . . If he was happy?"

Peter controlled his emotions with difficulty and with clenched jaw stopped himself suggesting the question which his father might ask of him: Would I have been proud of my son? He paused for so long before replying that his father began to look uneasy.

"Was I wrong to ask, Joshua?"

"Upon my word, no. . . . I shall tell you all about your son and his life in a foreign century, Nick. I'll tell you everything I know about him. But not now. Let us talk on our way to France. We must set out on our journey and we must make haste if we are to reach Dover by nightfall. . . . And perhaps . . . perhaps you could tell me about his mother. Peter talked about her so often. . . . I should like to learn more of her."

Kate pushed away her plate of bread and butter and stood up in the sunny morning room, her freckled face creased in consternation.

"Please don't leave me behind! I *want* to go."

"It could be dangerous, Kate—there's a revolution happening and, believe me, it's a bloody one. Not to mention that France is at war with Prussia . . . !"

"Would *you* like to be left behind? Besides, I'll be useful, I've started to learn French. . . ."

"I lived there for a year," countered Mr. Schock. "I'm fluent."

"But I can blur!"

"Precisely! And look what happened to you yesterday. You're not well—it would be much better if you stayed safely behind in London."

"I'm not *ill*! Something weird happened to me, but I'm not ill! Do you really think it'd be better for me to be stuck here on my own, worrying about whether you'd made it or not? Peter and Gideon kept going off without me, too. I hated it. Is it because I'm a girl?"

Mr. Schock threw up his arms in exasperation.

"I'm only trying to do the right thing! I'm trying to think what your parents would want me to do. . . ."

"I believe we should listen to Kate," said Peter quietly. "I can understand her fear of being left alone hundreds of years away from anyone she knows. . . ."

"Why thank you, Joshua!" said Kate.

Mr. Schock looked at her intently and then sighed. "All right. It's against my better judgment, but if that's what you want . . . Just don't go getting yourself into trouble, okay?"

"If Mistress Kate is going to France," exclaimed Hannah, "then it's only right and proper that I go too, despite the Revolution and the rich sauces. You gentlemen would defend her to the death, I am sure, but Mistress Kate seems pale and out of sorts and you might not notice if she was tired or needed nourishment or a cheerful song."

"You misjudge the male sex, my dear Hannah!" Peter protested. "Are we so insensitive to the needs of our companions?"

Neither Kate nor Hannah would deny it and Peter looked offended.

"Trust me, Joshua," said Mr. Schock, "things don't get any easier for us menfolk in the twenty-first century—a lot worse, if anything. At least you don't feel obliged to cultivate your feminine side and then get derided for not being manly enough. . . ."

"For goodness' sake!" cried Kate in frustration and Peter laughed at his father's ability to wind Kate up. He was unaware, Peter realized, quite what a talent he had for it.

"Let them believe in their superiority, Joshua," continued Mr. Schock. "Everyone needs encouragement."

Kate threw a pellet of bread at him and Mr. Schock ducked, winking at Peter.

"Only kidding, Kate! You're a clever girl but you'll have to learn how to take a joke."

Kate stamped her foot with impotent rage. *I can understand why Peter got so fed up with his dad,* she thought.

"Well, that's decided then," said Peter quickly, smiling at everyone in an effort to smooth the waters. "We shall be a party of four. Two persons of the fairer sex and two of the . . ."

". . . unfairer," prompted Kate.

They would set sail from Dover to Calais on the first available ship. If they caught the early stagecoach which left from the George Inn in Southwark, they should reach the seaport by the evening. They were already running late because Hannah needed to pack a trunk for Kate and herself and needed reminding that they were going away for a few days only, not a few months. Peter, who had promised the driver of the hackney coach an extra shilling if he got them there in good time, was forever looking at his pocket watch. Alas, their journey across the Thames proved to be neither as straightforward nor as swift as he had hoped.

As they left Lincoln's Inn Fields, they were enveloped in a mushrooming cloud of dust as the small army of workmen demolishing the innards of number twelve succeeded in knocking a wall down. The driver and John (who was to accompany them as far as the coaching inn to help with the luggage) were sitting on top and had violent coughing fits and were half blinded for a time by the acrid dust in their eyes. The passengers passed up handkerchiefs and a flask of water and then had to wait while the driver was recovered enough to continue.

Hannah tutted. "It was a perfectly nice house to begin with," she said. "I do not understand why the gentleman must pull it down only to rebuild it again. His cook told me that her employer has a mania for collecting statues and relics and whatnot from his trips abroad and that it takes an eternity to do the dusting."

"As John Soane is commissioned to build the Bank of England, Hannah, I think we must at least allow him to redesign his house," said Peter. "He was kind enough to show me his collection not so long ago—statues from Greece and Rome and all manner of fascinating ancient artifacts. However, the next time I see him I shall warn him to think twice before adding to his collection on account of the grave danger of its attracting dust. . . ."

Hannah sniffed haughtily, which made Kate giggle, and Peter glimpsed for the first time since the Golden Square incident a hint of the spirited girl he knew. Hannah was right: Kate did seem pale and out of sorts. Suddenly he shivered, although he was not in the least bit cold, as he was gripped by a strong sense of foreboding.

They set to talking about the Marquis de Montfaron, whom Sir Joseph had assured them was as close to a genius as any man he had met.

"How ludicrous it seems that someone from the *eighteenth*

century, for goodness' sake, knows more about electricity than me!" commented Mr. Schock.

"We aren't so ignorant in this century, Mr. Schock, if you pardon me for saying so," said Hannah, affronted by his implication. "Why, I had an aunt who was treated with electricity at the Middlesex Hospital after she was laid low by an apoplexy. And that was twenty years ago at least!"

Peter laughed out loud. His father really did have a knack for rubbing people the wrong way without meaning to—he wondered why he could never see that it was unintentional as a child.

"I am certain that Mr. Schock did not mean to imply that people in this century are in any way inferior, Hannah."

"No, I certainly did not, Hannah. I meant no offence. . . ."

"Then none taken, Mr. Schock."

Peter's head disappeared out of the window. When it reappeared he said: "This journey is taking an eternity. I cannot understand it."

They were indeed making slow progress. The traffic was heavy and the coach crawled toward Fleet Street past Temple Bar. Kate stared out of the window and lost herself for a while in the sights of the city. The lively London crowd streamed by on both sides of the carriage, rich and poor, fat and thin, young and old: an ever-moving stage on which an infinite number of stories were constantly being played out. She watched a boisterous bunch of young bucks tossing one of their party into a horse trough, though he did not seem to mind too much, and when he stood up, knee-deep in water and long hair dripping in a curtain over his face, he even made an elegant little bow for the benefit of the rowdy onlookers. And then, where Shoe Lane meets Fleet Street, they had to stop to let a wide load through, and Kate spotted a forlorn young woman in a silk dress the color of autumn leaves. She stood still as a statue on the street corner, clutching her fan, her large, dark eyes full of sadness. A second later they moved off again and the beautiful lady was lost to sight.

The street vendors were out in force that morning. "Who will buy my sweet oranges?" called a pretty orange-seller to her through the window. The muffin man rang his bell at them and the pie man leaned through the window with a steaming steak and oyster pie. Hannah pushed him away good-humoredly, but the smell of rich gravy that lingered in the carriage afterward made everyone's mouths water. Halfway up Fleet Street, Kate was convinced she recognized the chop house where she and Peter had dined with Parson Ledbury in 1763 and she wondered what had happened to her friend all those years ago. Was he lost or was he dead? And if he was dead, how did he meet his end? She could not bear to think about that and looked fixedly at her lap until the lump had gone from her throat.

Presently the coach stopped moving altogether and the driver called out to a chair-man going in the opposite direction and asked him if he knew what the problem was. Peter got out of the carriage the better to hear the answer. Hannah nudged Kate and pointed to the occupant of the sedan chair as it drew to a halt next to them. One arm and the head of a purple-nosed old gentleman were lolling out of the window, wig askew, and he was snoring noisily, oblivious to everything. When the rear chair-man saw Hannah and Kate laughing, he called out to them, sweat pouring down his face, but refusing to lay his heavy burden down even for a moment.

"Would you ladies have the kindness to push 'im back in for me? He is a sea captain. The old fellow has had one sup o' rum too many after seeing the pirates that sunk his ship hang at Execution Dock. I fear 'is 'ead will get tangled in a wagon wheel and then we'll never get our fare and we've carried 'im all the way from Wappin'."

Hannah, who was nearest, obliged and, leaning out of the window, gave the man's head a hearty shove which failed to wake him up. The chair-man called out his thanks and a moment later the chair-men were off, careering at breathtaking speed down Fleet Street and shouting "By your leave!" at the crowds who fell this way and that out of their way.

It transpired that a heavy wagon carrying barrels of ale had collided with the landau of the Swedish ambassador on London Bridge. Both vehicles had overturned, the barrels causing several more incidents including a concussed donkey. The ensuing chaos meant that traffic bound for the other side of the river was at a standstill and would likely as not remain so for some time to come.

"Driver!" called Peter. "Do you know a route to get us to the watermen? I fear crossing by boat is now our only option."

The driver maneuvered the hackney coach out of the traffic jam and by dint of some backtracking and taking some short cuts down alleys barely wide enough for the Hackney coach, they arrived at the slimy green banks of the Thames where they were greeted by its distinctive odor.

"Yuk!" said Kate, holding her nose. "I don't want to sail in a rowing boat on that filthy water. What happens if you fall in?"

They watched a dead cat float past by way of an answer. Peter told them that mostly all you had to do was to stand on the bank and shout "Oars!" and you would immediately be overwhelmed by offers to take you to your destination by dozens of watermen in their distinctive red jackets. Today, though, as Hannah commented, there wasn't a wherry to be found for love nor money. All of them were already hired, and the stretch of the river close to London Bridge was covered with a flotilla of wooden boats while the watermen rowed furiously, making the most of this unexpected windfall.

Peter was beginning to despair of getting the party to the George Inn on time. The driver, however, suggested that if they proceeded up Thames Street, past Billingsgate and the Tower of London, they would be sure to find a wherry there. No one could bear the idea of returning back to Lincoln's Inn Fields and being forced to wait another twenty-four hours and so they took the driver's advice. Soon they reached Billingsgate but there were still no boats to be had. There had been a fish market here for centuries and the very ground seemed to be permeated with the stink of fish.

"It's actually making my eyes water!" exclaimed Mr. Schock. "How can *fish* make your eyes water?"

They drove past two fishwives having a violent argument, and Hannah clapped her hands over Kate's ears.

"I have never understood," she complained, "what it is about selling fish that causes these women to have such foul tongues in their heads."

Before long Kate found herself looking up at the White Tower, which seemed the same as she remembered from visiting the Tower of London on a family trip to see the Crown Jewels—although she couldn't remember the moat being filled with water. At first she thought she was imagining the sound of big cats roaring and monkeys screeching, but Hannah informed her that there was a menagerie inside which members of the public were allowed to visit for a small fee. She also told her, which, as Mr. Schock said, was definitely one piece of information too many, that she had visited the zoo with an aunt and uncle who had donated a sick, old dog to the lions in lieu of an entrance fee, a practice which was not uncommon.

But at last, on the other side of the Tower of London, just beyond Traitors' Gate, they caught sight of two red-jacketed wherrymen taking their ease and smoking clay pipes in a long, narrow boat which bobbed up and down on the green-brown water. Peter shouted over to them and the watermen jumped to and rowed toward them.

John helped them with the luggage and stood by as everyone clambered with difficulty into the boat. In fact it was fortunate that he did, for the vessel listed this way and that, and Hannah, who was endeavoring to keep her balance while she clasped a bag with one hand and clutched the generous flounces of her skirts with the other, wobbled violently and would have fallen in had John not come to the rescue. Kate fared better because she lifted her long skirts right up above her knees and draped them over one arm while she took hold of John's proffered hand. Hannah was scandalized at the sight of her charge showing her legs to all and sundry and pursed her lips. However, a smile soon came to her face as she saw John imitating the ladies and pretending to lose his balance before leaping out onto the slimy shore. The wherry was twenty feet long, and by the time four passengers, several items of luggage, and two watermen were installed, it lay very low in the water. The Thames was turbulent on this stretch of the river and waves lapped against the wooden sides of the boat, and there was a satisfying *thwack* as the front of the wherry rose up and then slapped the surface of the water as it fell back again. They became accustomed to the stench surprisingly quickly and the fresh breeze which ruffled Kate's hair put her in mind of the sea journey that was soon to come.

John took his leave of them, as there was not enough room in the boat to take him too, and he wished everyone a safe journey. He bade Hannah be strong in the face of all the rich food she would shortly be obliged to eat and prayed that she would not return home all French-ified and triple their butter bill. . . .

The watermen were attuned to the river's ways. Not for an instant did they lose their balance as they moved about the boat, and when they started to row it was in perfect unison, with powerful, athletic strokes. The boat cut through the choppy water and soon John was left behind, waving from the bank. John's cry was carried away in the breeze, only just audible, and neither Hannah nor Mr. Schock heard him. But Kate did. And so did Peter.

"Good luck, Master Peter!" he cried to his master.

Kate turned around as sharply as if she had been slapped in the face and stared questioningly at the man whose identity was suddenly in doubt. Could she have misheard? Peter smiled innocently, pretending not to have noticed John's slip of the tongue, and then turned to look fixedly at the opposite bank and their destination. His father was facing the same way. Kate caught sight of both of them in profile. Joshua and Mr. Schock had similar builds, she thought, but very different coloring and features. Mr. Schock's chin was bigger and his ears were smaller than Joshua's. But their noses . . . Kate gave a sudden gasp. They had the same nose! *Could* this man—easily as old as her father—really be Peter? She felt a little giddy as the possibility sank in and her heart started to beat wildly. As for Peter, he could feel Kate's eyes burning into him, but he did not once return her gaze.

Halfway across the Thames they had to stop on account of a small ship, with billowing, dun-colored sails, which had emptied its cargo of mackerel at Billingsgate and was now returning to the coast. Hannah grabbed hold of Kate's arm.

"Look, Mistress Kate! Did you ever see a better view of the city?"

Kate nodded distractedly. She had other things on her mind than the panorama of domes and towers, bridges and steeples that rose up to the west of them. She had to decide what to do. By the time they had reached the opposite shore, Kate had come to a decision. She would confront Joshua and ask him to his face who he really was, but she would wait until they were alone. . . . In the meantime she looked first at one nose and then at the other to compare the two. A sliver of a doubt set in. Was there *really* a family likeness between these two noses? She turned her head to and fro so many times she could have been watching a tennis match. Hannah observed Kate's behavior anxiously—not only did she look pale and tired but now she had developed a nervous tic. And they hadn't even reached the stagecoach yet, let alone France. . . .

Kate now stared quite blatantly at Joshua, not caring if she was being rude. She studied this eighteenth-century gentleman in his fine clothes, observed his quick, dark eyes that took in everything, looked at his feet which could not keep still when the rest of him could, and, finally, recognized something familiar about the cast of his mouth, the way that he held it, like the young Peter Schock was apt to do, in a crooked half-smile when he was self-conscious or embarrassed. He *was* Peter! He *was*! All at once she was certain of it. How could she have missed something so obvious? But what possible reason could Peter have for concealing his true identity so cruelly?

FIFTEEN

THE DOVER PACKET

*In which a supporter of the revolution flees
the country and receives a hero's welcome,
Kate confronts Peter, and the party arrives on French shores*

At nightfall a fresh northeasterly wind blew up, which boded well for the passage of the Dover packet across the English Channel. It sent ribbons of clouds scudding across the luminous sky while high above the cliffs, Dover Castle, bathed in moonlight, looked out over a silvery sea. Below, facing the harbor where giant, rusting chains draped themselves over stone quaysides and masts creaked and waves lapped against the prows of sailing ships, stood a whitewashed inn.

Inside the low-ceilinged dining room, Hannah, Kate, Peter, and Mr. Schock were looking forward to their beds. A roaring fire, a bellyful of pigeon pie, and the tang of sea air after a long journey would make anyone sleepy, yet the fatigue that could be discerned in Kate's face was more than that. Her skin was waxy pale and her eyes hollow. To Hannah's disappointment Kate had pecked at her food even though she had said she was hungry. But now, warm and satisfied, everyone drooped over the table, snug inside a large inglenook, and only Hannah was alert enough to be interested in what was going on around them.

The bustling dining room was full to bursting, and it was difficult to make oneself heard above the good-humored din. One group, however, sat silent and subdued at a corner table. There was a boy, a little older than Kate, who stared blankly in front of him with large, dark eyes that spoke of fathomless despair. Hannah nudged Kate's arm.

"They are come from France. Look at that poor child; why, he should be abed, just as you should, Miss Kate."

Kate was sure that it was more than lack of sleep that was wrong with him. He wore a shirt with long, flowing sleeves and an embroidered silk waistcoat of the highest quality, but it was grimy and finely spattered with mud or perhaps red wine.

The landlord, a broad-shouldered man with ruddy cheeks, was trying to squeeze between their table and the neighboring one in order to attend to the fire. He carried a bundle of wood and was panting with the effort of holding it up. Neither Kate nor Hannah had noticed him.

"By your leave, my ladies," he said.

"Oh, I'm sorry," said Kate, as she and Hannah drew in their chairs. The landlord dropped the logs onto the fire, causing a shower of glittering sparks. As he made his way back, he noticed the pile of books intended for the Marquis de Montfaron, which Peter had placed in front of him and was intending to dip into before he retired for the night.

The landlord nodded at a volume of Thomas Paine's *The Rights of Man*, which was on the top of the pile.

"I am proud to have the author of that book sleeping under my roof tonight. Are you bound for Calais, sir?"

"Yes, we sail with the tide in the morning."

"In which case, you and Mr. Thomas Paine will be fellow passengers," said the landlord before disappearing into the kitchens. "He'll have a warmer welcome in France than he's been used to of late, and that's for sure!"

"Upon my word," said Peter, "we shall be traveling in distinguished company!"

"Who *is* Thomas Paine?" asked Kate.

"Mr. Paine is an Englishman and a thinker of some repute—at least, according to some. . . . He played no small part in encouraging the American colonists to break away from British rule—"

"Oh!" said Kate. "Isn't America a British colony anymore!"

"Did you not know, Mistress Kate?" said Hannah. "It must be nigh on ten years since the war ended."

"I bet Parson Ledbury didn't take the news too well!"

"Not to mention King George," said Peter. "And now Mr. Paine turns his attention to the French Revolution—which he defends in no uncertain terms in his renowned book. It has won him friends and enemies in equal measure. . . ."

"'Renowned' isn't a word I'd care to use about that book, sir, if you'll pardon me for saying so," said Hannah. "I've heard John and his cronies talk about it. . . ."

"John has read it!" said Peter in surprise.

"Well, no, but Mr. Soanes' footman has. . . . He and John were sitting around our kitchen table half the morning last week, while his master was away and John was busy polishing the shoes. And Mr. Paine's book had set him off on talking about the rights and freedoms of the common man and I know not what. . . . Though they were very happy for a common woman to wait on them. . . . And then the butcher's lad came in to deliver a ham, and lingered awhile to listen to the conversation, and *he* said that in his opinion it was a fine thing that the French people had thrown off the shackles which had so long oppressed them! And he's barely fifteen, if you please! So I asked him," continued Hannah, "if he thought that we should do likewise and rise up against our masters. To which he replied that if he could stop being a butcher's boy, and have a share in some of what he sees his betters enjoying, he'd be all for it!"

Hannah looked so outraged it made Kate laugh.

"You'd better watch yourself, Joshua!" said Mr. Schock. "It sounds like there's rumblings below stairs. . . ."

For the first time in many years, Peter saw himself through twenty-first-century eyes—a gentleman of means who was used to having servants at his beck and call. Suddenly he felt very uncomfortable.

"I know I'm not an educated woman," continued Hannah, "but I say that coffee house philosophizing is all very well, but whoever has an ounce of common sense would not wish what is happening in France to happen here! Faith, we've already had one revolution and where did that get us?"

"Actually, Hannah's got a point," said Mr. Schock, "after all, in a very few years the French will . . ."

Kate stared meaningfully at Mr. Schock and stroked a finger across her lips as if to zip them up. He smiled and stopped mid-sentence. *She's learning to handle my father better than I ever could,* thought Peter.

The fire suddenly blazed as the new logs caught fire and great orange flames flew up the chimney.

"Why does our host not baste us with a little goose fat and have done with it, for his guests are already slowly roasting," said Hannah.

Kate laughed and fanned poor Hannah's scarlet cheeks with her napkin. "You know," said Kate, "you can get a really good breeze around your legs if you just lift your skirts up and down. Look, like this."

Kate hoisted her skirts above her knees and let them drop. Hannah put on a severe expression and slapped her hand on Kate's skirts, but then smiled.

"Are you trying to teach your grandmother to suck eggs, Miss Kate? There's all sorts of things you can do with a long skirt, but there's a time and a place for everything."

On their way to their rooms they passed an alcove just big enough for one table. Someone, a youngish man from what Kate could tell, was slumped forward, his fingers still wrapped around a tankard of ale. He was facing away from them, sound asleep. His golden hair glowed in the soft candlelight. Two serving wenches stood over him, craning their necks to look at his face.

"Have you ever seen a more handsome lad in your whole life?" Kate heard one say to the other.

"Never," said the other, gently trying to extricate his fingers from the handle.

"And such happy manners . . ."

"When he started to sing, and asked me to join him in a verse, and he put an arm around my shoulders, oh, I fair near swooned!"

Kate looked back at him as she climbed the stairs, idly hoping that the sleeping youth would turn over so she could see his face, but he merely snored contentedly and did not stir.

As soon as they retired to bed, Kate fell instantly into a deep sleep, from which she did not stir until Hannah awoke her in the middle of a dream in which the persons of Joshua and young Peter and Mr. Schock had all become confused. When she tried to make sense of it, the shreds of the dream dissolved into the day like ice into water.

The rest of the party had spent a tolerably comfortable night at the inn but were eager to continue with their journey and had little appetite for breakfast. Before they set off, however, they witnessed a distressing incident. The innkeeper and his son were setting up half a side of beef on a spit in front of the fire in the dining room. As the men returned to the kitchen, carrying long butchering knives, they passed in front of the table occupied by the party recently arrived from France. The boy was staring vacantly into space, showing no interest in his plate of bread and butter, but when his attention was unexpectedly caught by the bloodstained blades, he started to scream hysterically and to fight with an unseen foe. It was several minutes before he would allow himself to be calmed and even then he sat, shaking and mute, his body safe and sound in the confines of the inn, his mind elsewhere, still trapped in some dark and terrifying place. The distraught innkeeper hurriedly sent his son back to the kitchen with the knives and went to offer his assistance to the young demoiselle who was trying to comfort the boy. They exchanged a few words in broken English and Kate saw the bighearted innkeeper pass a hand over his face. She had the impression he was close to tears. Then he pressed some gold into the young woman's hand which she would not accept, but he insisted, closing her fingers around the cold coins.

Before they left, Hannah asked the innkeeper what ailed the boy.

"Freedom comes at a price, madam. The poor lad was caught up in events in Paris and has seen things the like of which no child should see. I will say no more with ladies and children present, particularly those who are bound for France. But I do say, have a care, for these are dangerous times. I do not know your politics but you would be well advised to wear a tricolor cockade to show your allegiance to the Revolution. After last week's turmoil in Paris, the whole country is as jumpy as a March hare."

At eight o'clock they were on the quayside, and Hannah and Kate warmed themselves in the morning sunshine while white-shirted sailors stowed cargo on the Dover packet. They were a little late after the incident at the inn, but it was of no consequence, for the captain was still awaiting the mail coach, without which he could not leave. There were few passengers on the outward journey, but the captain said that with the recent news of events in Paris, he would be surprised if he did not have a full ship on his return home.

The tall sailing ship creaked and groaned as she rose and fell with the waves, for the sea was choppy, even in the shelter of the harbor. Kate looked up at the mast and the young sailor climbing along the rigging like a monkey, and she longed to be away. Hannah had kept a chunk of bread from breakfast, and she and Kate amused themselves by throwing crumbs high into the air for the sharp-beaked seagulls who swooped and dived to take them with unerring accuracy and breathtaking acrobatics.

Kate watched Peter and Mr. Schock bend over today's copy of *The Times*. The pages flapped about in the energetic breeze. Every so often Mr. Schock would recognize a name and he would read it aloud: "Danton!" he would exclaim. "Robespierre!" "Marat!" These people meant nothing to Kate, but she supposed they must be famous if even Mr. Schock had heard of them. He seemed at once dismayed and excited by it all, while the only thing of immediate interest in 1792 for Kate was finding her friend. Unless, of course, she had, in point of fact, *already* found him. She adjusted her position until she could observe both men's noses in profile. *As soon as I can get Joshua by himself,* she thought, *I am going to ask him. And if it is Peter, I'm going to tell the liar exactly what I think of him!*

Mr. Schock folded up the newspaper. "It's hard even reading about this carnage," he commented. "Joshua, my friend, we haven't chosen an exactly brilliant moment for our little French holiday."

"Arras isn't Paris," said Peter. "As long as we are discreet, and do nothing to draw attention to ourselves, I'll warrant that we encounter few obstacles."

The yellow stagecoach, with its cargo of mail destined for France, arrived on the quayside with a thunderous clatter of hooves on cobblestones. A handful of sailors immediately jumped to and started transferring the mail boxes to the ship. Meanwhile, amidst some commotion, the final passenger arrived. He was an intense, dark-haired man, dressed in sober clothes, crumpled from traveling. He had a portly companion who wore a red, white, and blue rosette on the side of his large black hat. They heard the captain order a couple of sailors to escort Mr. Thomas Paine and his companion on board.

"So that's him!" said Mr. Schock.

Some of Mr. Paine's supporters followed on behind. They were being jostled and threatened by a rowdy group of locals who shouted insults and made as if to snatch the man's luggage. However, once the sailors had got Mr. Paine on board, the troublemakers soon dispersed. One of his trunks, however, ended up in the water and it bobbed up and down next to the gangplank until one of the sailors fished it out with a grappling hook. As the creaking vessel left the shelter of Dover harbor, Mr. Paine's supporters sent him off with a rousing alternative version to the national anthem,

"God Save Great Thomas Paine." They heard the captain offer the use of his cabin to Mr. Paine and watched the two men disappear down below. Neither reappeared until the Dover packet was entering Calais.

The party, on the other hand, chose to remain on deck. The wind was fair for France and the giant sails billowed noisily above them. The sun shone on the soaring, white cliffs, the English Channel sparkled, and the good sea air somehow filled everyone's hearts with hope. They spotted a large shoal of mackerel, clearly illuminated by the rays of the sun just beneath the surface of the water, and, barely visible on the horizon, they saw what the captain of the ship assured them was a whale.

By noon they were growing tired and cold and spent more time sitting on the little wooden benches provided for passengers and less time looking at the sea. Kate took a surreptitious photograph, with Megan's mobile, of Joshua cutting a fine nautical figure, shading his eyes and looking out toward France. He was nicely framed against a background of sea and ship's sails. Then she snuggled up next to Hannah to keep warm and pulled her paisley shawl tight around her. She had been working herself up to confront Joshua for some time and was rehearsing her words. The more she thought about how he had deceived them, the angrier—and the more puzzled—she became. Why had he done it? Didn't he *want* to go home? But just as she had mustered up enough courage to stand up, she saw Mr. Schock approach Joshua where he stood on the bow, looking toward France. He tapped him on the shoulder and soon they were deep in conversation, and judging from the intense expressions on both their faces, she thought it best not to interrupt them.

"It would be comforting to know a little more about my son's life in this century," said Mr. Schock. "If you are willing . . ."

Mr. Schock looked intently into Peter's face. Peter was taken by surprise and, for a few moments, was tongue-tied. Mr. Schock waited patiently while he marshaled his thoughts. Where to begin? Oh, this was hard, Peter thought. Too hard.

But he took a deep breath and plunged in. He began to tell his father something of his early life with Gideon at Hawthorn Cottage. Those early, mostly happy years seemed so long ago that, as he spoke, he half convinced himself that he was talking about someone else. He tried to paint the best picture that he could of his teenage years in Derbyshire, of riding and hunting and of being tutored with Sidney at Baslow Hall, of the kindness of Mrs. Byng and his fondness for Parson Ledbury, of the excitement of weeks spent in London in the company of Sir Richard Picard, of learning how to dance with the Byng girls and how to behave in high society. But his memories of the long summer days spent exploring the craggy hills and dales of the county with Gideon Seymour were the brightest. He described how Gideon had taught him how to skin rabbits, track deer, and defend himself against a footpad in a dark alley, as well as counseling him on love and honor and keeping faith with himself. Peter did not talk of the hard times, when he had cried into the night because he could scarcely recall what his mother and father looked like and because he felt like an exile in a foreign century. Nor did he mention how Gideon had proved his friendship to him over and over again during those times and had remained steadfast and true even when Peter had screamed at him to go away because it was his father that he wanted and not him. But it was precisely because Gideon's own life had not been easy, and he had himself faced grief and regret and despair, that he was able to help. Gideon would always be patient with him and would wait until his young friend came to himself again. But how could Peter tell his own father the truth of how it had been? What good would it do? So, instead, Peter spoke from Joshua's point of view of other, lighter, things, of harvest balls and Parson Ledbury's gambling and how, on warm nights, they would build a fire under the oak tree at Hawthorn Cottage, and Gideon would tell him stories far into the night.

Peter keenly observed his father as, hanging on his every word, Mr. Schock tried to imagine how his son had lived his life with neither mother nor father and how he must have had to learn so many things as well as unlearn much that his own technological age had taught him. Peter read in his father's face the pain and the fleeting pleasure which his words provoked. He suddenly felt exhausted with the effort of it and stopped. Mr. Schock gripped his hand.

"How can I ever begin to thank you, Joshua? And how much I find I owe to Gideon. I hope I might meet him one day. If we are lucky enough to find a way back to my son and I can return home with him, I swear I'll spend time with him just as your brother did. Childhood is short and that time can never be recaptured. I wouldn't make the same mistake again."

Mr. Schock walked away and stood alone gazing at the swell of the sea. But no sooner had he gone than Hannah joined Peter, leaving the frustrated Kate on her own on the bench.

"Forgive me, sir," she whispered, "but I have rarely seen two gentleman warm to each other's company so well as you and Mr. Schock. It is breaking my heart that you do not tell him that you are his son. Please, sir, I beg you to reconsider."

All emotional energy spent, Peter was caught off balance by Hannah's request and he turned furiously on her.

"I will thank you to remember your place, Hannah!" he hissed. "You gave me your word to help me in this and I shall expect you to stick to it."

"Yes, sir," she said simply, "if that is your wish." And she walked sadly away.

Seeing Joshua alone again, Kate made her move. *Now or never,* she said to herself.

He was looking toward the cliffs of the Côte d'Opale, which were looming ever larger on the horizon. He did not notice her at first. She tapped him on the shoulder and he turned round with a start. Kate took a deep breath and spoke.

"Joshua, I think you have lied to us. I think you are really Peter Schock."

Peter's heart missed a beat and his gaze slid anxiously over toward his father, hoping that he was out of earshot. What was he going to reply? He needed a moment to reflect.

"Kate! I was deep in thought, you shocked me. Forgive me, what did you say?"

Kate repeated her question but she did not manage to say it with such conviction this time. Peter forced himself to laugh, which he did most convincingly.

"I know that Peter and I resembled each other, for Gideon oft remarked on it, but to accuse me of lying to you about my identity! What should cause me to do such a thing? You are not serious?"

Kate stared back at him. She had been so sure that he was just going to admit it. . . . Could she really be wrong about this? Were the shape of his nose and her instinct not sufficient evidence?

"Upon my word, Kate, you *are* serious. . . . I assure you that you are wholly mistaken in this. Do you not think my own father would have recognized me, even after such a passage of time?"

Peter saw doubt flickering across Kate's features and quickly pressed home his advantage.

"I do hope you will not refer to the matter again—it would be deeply distressing for Mr. Schock to hear of such a suggestion. And, as I am sure you must be aware, your accusation is deeply insulting to my person."

One look at Kate's distraught gray eyes, peering up at him from her pale, freckled face, and he knew. He had won this round. She had believed him. Kate gulped and mumbled her apologies and went back to the bench. Her cheeks burned with the embarrassment of it. She wanted to run away and hide. What a fool she was! Why had she let her imagination run away with her like that? And it suddenly occurred to her that if Joshua *were* Peter, it would mean that Hannah and Queen Charlotte herself would have had to have been involved in the deception—and how could that possibly be true? She picked up *The Times* and buried her head in its pages.

What a skilled liar I am, thought Peter, not without a twinge of guilt. He looked over at his father, who had regret and sadness written on his face. *How strongly he desires to prove the father he could be to his son—I must not doubt that what I do is for the best.*

Clouds had been gathering as the afternoon progressed and the sea and sky had gradually taken on a gray and dismal hue. The ship was now hugging the coastline of northern France and they had just passed Wissant and Cap Gris Nez. All being well they would reach Calais in half an hour. The motion of the waves proved to have a soporific effect on Hannah, who had been drifting in and out of sleep for some time, while poor Mr. Schock, who had felt increasingly sick, now hung over the side of the ship, back heaving. Kate, meanwhile, had recovered herself and had come to a decision. She must try and make amends with Joshua. If she didn't, she reasoned, it might make the journey awkward. And he had been so very generous to them. . . . So she carefully eased Hannah's dozing head from her shoulder and walked over to Peter.

"Will you shake hands with me, Joshua?" she asked, holding hers out toward him. "I am really sorry for upsetting you. . . ."

But Peter did not reply. In fact he did not move. His face was frozen in a smile. Kate looked at him expectantly for a moment and then her blood ran cold. She whipped her head around but she had already guessed what scene would confront her. She was fast-forwarding. The ship was littered with statues. Hannah slept, her head tipped backward and mouth half-open. Mr. Schock stood with a handkerchief to his mouth, his windswept hair rigid as cardboard. The ship's cook was throwing a bucket of scraps on to waves sculpted as if out of ice and a gull dived toward them, wings folded backward in a *V*, curved yellow beak open in what would have been a raucous cry. Kate put her hands over her ears, for the roar of the wind and the waves had slowed down into an unbearable and deafening growl. She looked slowly around at her frozen, lonely world. How long would she have to endure it this time? Peter still smiled warmly at her, his hand outstretched. She tried to smile back bravely at him.

"You don't think I'm going to be stuck here forever, do you, Joshua? . . . I only wanted to say that I was sorry but it looks like it's going to have to wait. I *am* sorry, though. . . ."

Something made her want to reach over to take his hand, perhaps for comfort, but no sooner had she touched it than her stomach lurched, and like the explosive vertical descent of a roller coaster, she re-entered the torrent of normal time. The roar of the waves deafened her and the sea breeze hit her like a violent slap in the face.

"Is anything wrong, Kate?" asked Peter.

He hadn't noticed a thing! It must have all happened in the blink of an eye! What had brought her back so quickly? Was it Joshua's touch?

"No, no, I'm fine . . . I just . . . I just wanted to say that I was sorry."

Kate, Hannah, Peter, and his father were the first to disembark at Calais. The party now stood on the quayside in front of the Dover packet, surrounded by their luggage and ignored by everyone. But they all detected a palpable feeling of excitement and anticipation in the air. Groups of official-looking gentlemen stood in huddles, deep in conversation. There were soldiers, too, milling about near their ship or standing at their ease, laughing and joking among themselves. Kate wondered what was going on. If this was supposed to be the French Revolution, she thought, it felt more like a holiday. . . . It was beginning to drizzle, and although they had expected to find a carriage without difficulty, they could find none free to take them. Peter announced that he would go into the town in search of one and Mr. Schock, because he spoke French well, insisted on accompanying him.

"All this fuss couldn't be on account of Thomas Paine, could it?" asked Kate.

"Surely not! He's only a writer," said Hannah.

As Kate watched Mr. Schock and Joshua walk away, side by side, she could not help noticing that their backs were of a similar width and that they both had square shoulders and swung their arms in the same way. *Stop it!* she told herself. *You're becoming obsessed. . . .*

"How are you, Mistress Kate?" asked Hannah kindly. "Are you very tired?"

"No, I'm fine, thank you. . . . How are you doing?"

"Me, Miss Kate? Oh, there's never anything the matter with me, thank you for asking. I have the constitution of an ox, always have had."

Hannah had an instinct for diagnosis. She had always known when Master Peter was going to be ill before he did, and she was certain that all was not well with Kate. It was her pallor that bothered Hannah and it reminded her of something. It was, she thought, a little like what happened to fabric or wallpaper that is exposed to sunshine. Over time, imperceptibly at first, the colors become less vivid, the pattern less clean and defined. She scolded herself for being so fanciful. But then she scrutinized Kate's face again and thought, no, she was not mistaken. If she didn't know better she would have said that Miss Kate was fading.

"Why are you staring at me like that, Hannah?"

"Forgive me, Miss Kate, I didn't mean to . . . but if I was, I wasn't the only one. Look."

Kate followed Hannah's gaze and looked around her at the bustling harbor. Soldiers, in their blue and white uniforms trimmed in red, balanced the ends of their muskets on the quayside; fishermen mended their nets; old women, dressed in black, sat in doorways, making lace or spinning; a young lad, stick-thin, swept the cobbles in front of them. But every last one of the good citizens of Calais, as far as Kate could tell, was wearing a revolutionary cockade. And Hannah was right, they *were* beginning to attract people's attention. If Kate returned their gaze they quickly looked away, but as soon as she turned back again she could feel their stares burning into her. The hairs rose on the back of her neck.

"Why are they looking at us like that?" whispered Kate to Hannah.

"No doubt they take us for spies or aristocrats. Unless I grew an extra head while I was asleep!"

"I don't like it . . . ," started Kate, but then gasped in fright as someone took hold of her arm.

"Does Calais not please you, mademoiselle?"

Kate wheeled around, half expecting to be arrested on the spot.

"How did *you* get here?" she exclaimed in surprise.

"Are you acquainted with this young gentleman, Mistress Kate?" asked Hannah, taking in the stranger's glossy hair and firm jaw, his aquiline nose and limpid blue-violet eyes.

"Yes, I am! This is . . ."—Kate dropped her voice to a barely audible whisper—"This is Louis-Philippe de Montfaron, son of the Marquis de Montfaron."

Hannah tried hard not to gawk at the striking young man. Unfortunately her eyes kept sliding back despite her best efforts. Handsome was too poor an epithet. But Louis-Philippe was plainly so accustomed to provoking this kind of reaction, that he took no notice whatsoever. Kate introduced Hannah in her turn. Louis-Philippe inclined his head.

"Welcome to France, madame!"

"Were you on the Dover packet?" asked Kate. "I didn't see you."

"Had I known you were on board, I should have come up on deck—even though the sight of so much water makes me melancholy. I played cards instead, down below, with the ship's cook and a Dutch farmer who shared his bottle of Madeira wine. The journey passed most agreeably."

"Was that you I saw last night at the inn?" asked Kate. "Asleep on the table?" She tried not to smirk.

"It might have been—traveling is very tiring."

"But why are you here?" asked Kate.

"It occurred to me—after you left Golden Square—that despite my mother's fears, I should not be sending messages to my father. I should go in person and persuade him to leave our estate. And, as you did not return the books, I hoped that I might encounter you en route. Now *you* shall have a guide to direct you to the Château de l'Humiaire and *I* shall have companions for my journey. Naturally Maman will be *enraged* when she finds that I am gone, but, if all goes well, we should soon all be back in London. . . ."

"Your mother doesn't know where you are!"

Louis-Philippe shrugged his shoulders. "She would only have refused me permission. . . ."

"I'm not surprised! You're an . . ."—Kate whispered the last word—"aristocrat."

"Am I?" said Louis-Philippe, taking off his hat with a flourish and indicating the tricolor cockade. "And how, pray, would anyone guess such a thing?"

Kate and Hannah exchanged glances.

Louis-Philippe was in the middle of explaining how the Swedish ambassador's son had purloined his father's carriage to take him to Dover, when a large, mud-spattered coach pulled by four scraggy horses appeared. Peter and Mr. Schock were inside.

"The Swedish ambassador's son!" said Kate quickly, as the men clambered out. "You weren't by any chance involved in an accident with a wagon and a donkey on London Bridge?"

"How could you possibly know that?" asked Louis-Philippe. "But it is true that I was forced to catch a mail coach instead. . . ."

When Peter and his father saw who had turned up so unexpectedly, and they heard the reason for Louis-Philippe being there, they both shook his hand warmly and offered to take him with them to an inn.

"I am vastly pleased to renew our acquaintance," said Peter. "And I hope that we may be of some service to you, for in these dangerous times it is imprudent to travel alone."

"I assure you, sir, that I feel no anxiety on that account," said Louis-Philippe, patting his jacket and opening it just wide enough for Kate to spot a pistol tucked into the pocket of his waistcoat. "I have come well prepared."

Kate and Hannah wasted no time clambering into the stuffy coach which, to Kate's delight, was lined with sheepskins. She took a corner seat and brushed her face against the soft white fleeces and watched the driver making light work of their heavy luggage. He sported an impressive mustache and long jackboots in black leather. Louis-Philippe squeezed in between Hannah and Kate. Kate wondered how old he was. Sixteen? Seventeen at most, she thought. And, much as the grown-ups, even Mr. Schock—at least most of the time—were nice, it was going to be great to have someone young to talk to.

"So much for not drawing attention to ourselves," whispered Mr. Schock to Peter. "Have you noticed how people stare at him?"

But even Louis-Philippe was only of minor interest to the crowds on that day. The coach had barely set off when a huge cheer went up. The driver pulled on the reins and his passengers craned their heads out of the window to look. The cheer was, indeed, on account of Mr. Thomas Paine. As his feet touched French soil, an officer embraced him and presented him with a tricolor cockade. Then the artillery, who were now assembled in a neat line, fired a salute above the crowd's heads.

"By heaven," said Hannah, "the innkeeper was right—that man finds more favor here than in his own country!"

The coach set off again, through gathering crowds. Peter watched Kate looking up at Louis-Philippe, bright-eyed and a little flushed, as he made her giggle with his imitation of the ship's cook. Peter felt a twinge of an emotion he did not like to put a name to. When he was a boy, had Kate ever looked at him with that expression in her eyes?

The driver recommended an inn which was barely five minutes' ride from the harbor. The rooms were clean and comfortable and Kate was helping Hannah unpack their night things when they heard a sharp knock on the door. Kate answered it and found Louis-Philippe standing in the corridor.

"Have you seen the crowds? We must find out what is going on! Will you join me? It will be more diverting than sitting in our rooms."

He held out his hand, and when Kate took it, he pulled her out of the doorway toward the window, which overlooked the street. It was true, hundreds of people were lining the streets.

"What do you say?"

"I'd like to . . . but I should check that it's all right with Hannah or Joshua first. . . ."

Louis-Philippe put his head on one side and smiled his irresistible smile.

"Do you really need to ask permission to go outside? We won't be long. . . ."

SIXTEEN

THE SCENT OF BLOOD

*In which Kate and Louis-Philippe
meet a fugitive from Paris
and Peter loses his temper*

Holding her hand tightly so that they did not become separated, Louis-Philippe pulled Kate through the drenched crowds in the direction of the town square. It was raining heavily, and Kate was only wearing her dress, the hem of which became quickly soiled with mud.

"Please slow down!" she panted, but soon Louis-Philippe came to a halt in any case, for a wave of cheers had erupted from the crush of people that lined the street as the carriage carrying Thomas Paine drove past.

"What is everyone shouting?" cried Kate.

"'Long live Thomas Paine! Long live the French nation!'" Louis-Philippe shouted back.

The crowd pushed forward and they were swept along behind the carriage as it bumped and vibrated over the potholes toward the town hall. Kate was by now soaked to the skin and could see nothing but a sea of heads as they hurried blindly on. Presently the carriage came to a halt and a hush fell on the crowd. She could hear raindrops pattering onto the roof of the carriage.

Kate could see little, even on tiptoes, but she heard a strong and resounding voice echo around the square, although she did not understand a word.

"It's the mayor of Calais," said Louis-Philippe helpfully. "He's making a welcoming speech. . . ."

He looked back up at the mayor, but Kate tapped him on the arm. "I think I should go now—Hannah will be wondering where I am. . . ."

Suddenly the crowd roared and drowned out Kate's words. People next to them were clapping enthusiastically and there were more cries of "*Vive* Thomas Paine!"

"He's been elected to represent Calais at the National Convention!" said Louis-Philippe. "An Englishman! And the fellow can't even speak French!"

The rain trickled down Kate's neck and the thought kept coming to her that she was standing next to an aristocrat in a crowd of people who supported the revolution—even if he was wearing a tricolor cockade in his hat. She felt increasingly uneasy. Did Louis-Philippe enjoy taking risks?

"I'd *really* like to go now, please," she said.

Although Louis-Philippe appeared to be interested in what was going on, Kate was relieved that he only delayed for a few moments before shepherding her out of the crowd. They started to head back toward the inn and had soon left the square behind.

"What if someone had recognized you?" asked Kate.

"But I'm in disguise!" he answered, indicating his outfit. "Who would recognize me in clothes such as these? Besides, I don't know anyone in Calais."

"Weren't you *scared* in the middle of that crowd?" asked Kate.

"I am Louis-Philippe de Montfaron. I refuse to fear them. If I fear them they have already won!"

Kate looked up at Louis-Philippe and she suddenly sensed that, underneath his bravado, scared was precisely what he was. Had he stood in the middle of the crowd just to show that he *could*? She did not mind admitting how frightened she had been, but then, Kate did not belong to a noble family on the verge of losing everything, and she, unlike Louis-Philippe, did not have anything to prove.

They walked on. They had just turned a corner when, without warning, Louis-Philippe ducked behind Kate, then dived into a doorway and crouched down as low as he could.

"Hide me!" he said in an urgent whisper.

Kate stood in front of the doorway and pretended to have something in her eye while she scanned her surroundings to see what—or who—had so alarmed her companion. They found themselves in a narrow, cobbled street, rather run-down and lined with tall terraced houses. It was deserted apart from a mangy cat drinking from a puddle and an old woman sitting on her doorstep, a shawl pulled over her head against the rain. The gutters stank. Coming toward them, she saw a man

317

approaching at a fast pace. There was something aggressive in his demeanor. He was searching for someone. His sandy-colored mustache was even bushier than their coach driver's had been, and he wore long, red-and-white-striped trousers that came down to his ankles. A cockade was pinned to the soft red cap which covered his hair, and he wore a sleeveless jacket. It was like a uniform, Kate thought, although she was certain he wasn't a soldier. As the man grew nearer she saw him peer down every alley and into every doorway. Kate felt Louis-Philippe pulling out the hem of her dress to conceal himself better. When the man reached Kate, she stood her ground and refused to budge and stubbornly rubbed her eye. She was so frightened she forgot to breathe. He paused for a brief moment and scowled at her. For a moment she feared he was going to push her out of the way but then he moved on, staring at her as he did so with piercing, pale eyes, as if committing her appearance to memory.

"He's gone," she said, when he had finally disappeared from view.

"A thousand thanks!" said Louis-Philippe, standing up and stretching out his cramped legs. "I know that foul fellow, and more to the point, *he* knows *me*. He's called Sorel. He married a woman who works on our estate. When the troubles started he joined the *sans-culottes*—the revolutionaries—in Paris. They pulled down the old prison, the Bastille, stone by stone, and I remember he brought back a piece of it to break up and sell as souvenirs."

Louis-Philippe stood immobile, and Kate couldn't tell what he was thinking.

"Come on," she said, taking his arm. "It's not safe here—let's get back to the inn."

They had barely set off when a door creaked opened ahead of them and a woman peeped timidly out into the street. She spotted them immediately and darted back inside like a creature into its burrow. Presently one eye reappeared and a fragile, dark-haired figure stepped out uncertainly into the street.

"De Montfaron?" Kate heard her say. When Louis-Philippe nodded, she broke down in tears of relief, and spoke rapidly, without pausing for breath, making great, sweeping gestures with her expressive hands.

"What is she saying?" asked Kate after a while.

"That she was a personal maid in the royal household. That she had often seen my mother at the Court of Versailles before the revolution and that she recognizes me, too. She says that no one who had ever seen the Marquise de Montfaron could ever doubt that I am her son. . . ."

"And why is she so upset?"

The woman's large, dark eyes flitted between the two of them while Louis-Philippe translated.

"She went into hiding after the King and Queen surrendered to the Assembly in August. She is intent on fleeing to England but was denounced as an anti-revolutionary by a woman who traveled in the same coach. That man—Sorel—has been trailing her since Béthune. Will you help me get her to the

Dover packet? I fear she is a little hysterical. If we go now, the crowd will be busy listening to the mayor."

A part of Kate wanted to say that they should return to the inn to tell the others what they planned to do. But how could she? They might miss their opportunity to get the poor woman to the ship. All the same, Hannah would be so worried. . . . Suddenly Louis-Philippe turned to her.

"You are not like other girls. All the young ladies of my acquaintance would already have scampered back to the inn, weeping about the mud on their skirts."

Kate could certainly not ask to go back now, so she replied: "I'm glad you think I've got bottom!" and blushed when she realized what she had said.

They frog-marched the woman between them as fast as they could through the streets of Calais toward the harbor. The woman talked ceaselessly, and in great bursts, of what she had witnessed, as if, like lancing an abscess, she needed to find a way of getting rid of the poison that had been building up inside her. At first Louis-Philippe tried to translate for Kate, but after a while he slowed down and finally stopped. Kate was glad of it, for the images the woman conjured up were the stuff of nightmares and gripped their imaginations so tightly that the damp, gray streets of Calais began to seem unreal.

By the time they reached the harbor, Kate understood that the woman had been in the Tuileries Palace on that fateful day in August when the royal family had decided they had no option but to surrender themselves to the Revolutionary government. Fearing to go with them, the terrified maid had hid in the palace, wedging herself on top of a tall wardrobe in one of the children's bedrooms. From this elevated position she had a view, through a gap in the shutters, of the Swiss Guard defending the palace. She saw hundreds of the rampaging mob mown down by the artillery. Their broken, bloodied bodies littered the courtyard in front of the palace. But worse was to come. Gradually, she heard fewer and fewer shots as the artillery's ammunition became depleted, and then she heard them barricade themselves inside the palace. It was useless. Soon the rabble broke through, and the soldiers were overwhelmed by waves of men who, having trodden over the corpses of their friends, now waged a frenzied attack on their killers. The maid had clamped her hands to her ears but was unable to blot out the agonized screams as the Swiss Guards below were ripped apart with as little mercy as they had shown in their turn. Afterward, for what seemed like an eternity, she had been forced to listen to the mob search the palace, room by room, looking for new victims. Her heart beat so fast she thought her chest would explode. She started at every creak, at every footstep. When she heard the bedroom doorknob turn and the hinges whine open, her terror was so great she passed out. And when her eyes opened again, the first thing she saw, through the gap in the blinds, was the severed head and entrails of a man alive and whole but an hour before, now paraded about on a pike in the courtyard to the rousing cheers of those who fought for the rights and freedoms of man.

What she remembered most, she said, was the scent of blood. The smell permeated her clothes, her skin, her hair—and no matter how much she washed, the smell would not leave her. . . . She sniffed her hand and then proffered it for Kate to smell.

"She wants to know if you can smell blood," said Louis-Philippe.

Kate looked sadly at the woman and shook her head.

"Please don't translate anymore," said Kate. "I don't think I can take it."

Soon, the Dover packet was in sight. Compared to how it had been when they had disembarked, Calais harbor was almost deserted. It was windy outside the protection of the town, and in her wet clothes, Kate was chilled to the bone. Still the woman talked, her words tumbling out in a constant stream. Louis-Philippe came to an abrupt halt.

"La Princesse de Lamballe!" he exclaimed. He put his hands to his mouth and stood, swaying slightly, on the edge of the quayside. Kate thought he was going to be sick.

"Sssh!" Kate said to the woman and put her finger to her lips. "*S'il vous plaît*! Stop now! No more! . . . Are you okay, Louis-Philippe?"

Kate pulled him back from the edge and he turned to look at her.

"She was our friend. . . . Was it her fault she was born into that elevated rank?"

"What happened to her?"

"She was dragged through the streets and . . ." Louis-

Philippe shook his head vigorously and refused to complete his sentence.

"Once, when I was small, she held me under a fountain at Versailles to cool me down. It was like a thousand rainbows. . . ."

The sound of galloping horses of which Kate had been vaguely conscious suddenly grew loud enough to cause her to turn around. They all saw a coach hurtling toward them. The woman let out a bloodcurdling scream as it drew to a halt and a tall man, wearing a furious expression and a tricolor cockade on his hat, jumped out next to them. At the same moment that Kate cried "Joshua!" the woman, crazed with fear, and willing to do anything to avoid capture, ran to the quayside and leaped into the choppy water below.

For a split second, Kate, Peter, and Louis-Philippe all looked at each other, and then, without a word, Peter started to tear at the buttons of his jacket, kicked off his shoes and jumped in after her.

"I can't swim!" cried Louis-Philippe.

"Never mind that," said Kate. "Tell her to stop struggling! She's drowning Joshua!"

Louis-Philippe did as he was asked, but if the woman heard him, it did no good. She thrashed about in the waves, her skirts billowing in the water like a giant jellyfish. She kept pushing Peter's head below water, though whether this was from panic or fear of his intentions, it was difficult to say. Kate ran, screaming and pointing, over to the Dover packet and alerted a sailor to what was happening. He rushed over with a grappling hook, and with everyone's help they managed to heave the sodden pair onto dry land once more. Kate held the woman's hand as the sailor carried her, now limp as a rag doll, onto the Dover packet. Then Kate sprinted back to see how Joshua was faring.

He lay on the cobblestones, spewing up seawater and trying to get his breath back. After he had recovered a little, his eyes met those of Louis-Philippe. Peter pushed himself up on his elbows. Even a dip in the freezing waters of the Channel had not cooled Peter's anger.

"If you choose to put your own life at risk, sir, that is your affair, but do not drag an innocent young girl along with you on your reckless adventures! You are irresponsible and rash, and I *forbid* you to see Mistress Kate again!"

"Joshua!" said Kate, aghast, not knowing what else to say. She glanced over at Louis-Philippe, whose expression displayed, in rapid succession, surprise, distress, a sense of injustice, and finally anger.

"You are not my father, sir! Nor, indeed, Mistress Kate's!" And with that, Louis-Philippe turned on his heels and walked smartly away from them toward the town.

"Louis-Philippe!" cried Kate. "Come back! It's dangerous!"

"Do not be anxious on his account," said Peter, shivering uncontrollably as the strong wind bit into him. "The young gentleman can clearly look after himself—if not those in his care. And I am disappointed that *you*, Mistress Kate, could be so thoughtless as to accompany Louis-Philippe without leaving word where you had gone. We were all beginning to fear the worst. . . ."

SEVENTEEN

THE QUEEN'S BALCONY

*In which the Tar Man displays his talents
and Inspector Wheeler becomes obsessed
with a new master criminal*

A fine drizzle fell silently onto London's Pall Mall. Scene of
innumerable royal processions, the broad, tree-lined avenue,
with its flagstaffs and its pinkish tarmac, resembled a vast red
carpet leading to the gates of Buckingham Palace. Pall Mall
culminates in a roundabout at the center of which is set, rather
incongruously, the large and imposing Victoria Monument.
Black cabs and diplomats' cars constantly whizz around it, and
it has long been a popular vantage point at times of national
celebration, when people clamber over it and hang off the
statuary. Today, however, was an ordinary working day in mid-
winter. Victory, represented by a golden angel at the top of the
monument, pointed, as usual, toward the heavens, her magnificent wings dazzling against the leaden sky. Halfway down the
monument, carved out of white marble and with the royal orb
and scepter on her lap, Queen Victoria surveyed the damp tourists arriving to see the sights. Looking up at her from the steps

below stood a burly man. His cashmere coat was sprinkled with droplets of moisture like morning turf with dew.

"Grumpy-looking old trout, wasn't she?" he said.

He was speaking to a gangly youth who was failing to keep the rain off him with an umbrella too small for the purpose. The big man trained his binoculars on the curiously blank facade of Buckingham Palace and then zoomed in on a scarlet-jacketed guard standing to attention in front of a sentry box.

"There's discipline for you. I saw one of them guards keel over once. Fainted clean away on account of the heat."

His binoculars swept across a straggly line of tourists and hovered over the only three people who were not peering at Buckingham Palace through the tall black and gold railings.

"And there's our man if I'm not mistaken. . . ."

He observed the athletic figure of the Tar Man, known to him as a certain Mr. Vega Riaza. Although the man wore a woollen hat and scarf which covered everything but his eyes and nose, he recognized him on account of the way he held his neck. The Tar Man had impressed him—a rare occurrence, for he found the majority of the human race to be a disappointment. He could not understand where Vega Riaza had suddenly sprung from. He had put feelers out without any success. No one, it seemed, could provide any information on him. Either that or they weren't talking, for the big man knew, having climbed a harsh route to the top of the criminal profession himself, that only experience can teach you the kind of self-possession which this mystery man had in plenty. Vega Riaza already had an interesting history—of that he was certain.

The Tar Man was again accompanied by the pretty girl who dressed, he reflected, in clothes designed to look as if they'd come from a charity shop. That stunted youth was with him, too. He was the runt of the litter and no mistake. There was something about his face that reminded him of sepia photographs of starving East End kids before World War II.

"What a shower! If he's wasting my time, I'll pull his arms off for him. I've got better things to do than hobnob with Queen Victoria in the rain. We shan't be amused, shall we, Ma'am?"

Tom and Anjali both carried large umbrellas. Suddenly, in a movement that reminded the big man of assistants helping a magician do his trick, they drew the umbrellas together so that the Tar Man was hidden from view.

"What's 'appening, boss?" asked the gangly sidekick. "I can't see nothing."

Tom and Anjali separated again. The Tar Man had disappeared.

"How did he do that!"

Anjali turned to face the Victoria Monument and took out her mobile phone. A second later the big man answered her call.

"Keep your binoculars trained on the balcony," she instructed. "Whatever happens—and I mean *whatever happens*—if you're still interested, meet us as planned in Mayfair. Think of it as a free trial. If you don't want to go ahead, no problem—we're not short of interested parties. . . ."

Anjali did not wait for a reply but hailed a black cab, and she and Tom, staring straight ahead, drove down Pall Mall toward Horse Guards Parade.

The big man frowned as he watched them sail past. He had the uncomfortable sensation that he was being led like a bull with a ring through its nose. It didn't do to have small fry like these give him the runaround. He had his reputation to consider. His sidekick accidentally poked him in the face with the umbrella. The big man swore at him and shoved it angrily away, but the youth was not listening. Instead he was pointing, slack-jawed, at the palace.

Like butter melting, a grin slowly spread over the big man's face. The last time he had seen anyone on that balcony it had been members of the Royal House of Windsor, waving at the cheering multitudes while RAF jets roared over Pall Mall leaving patriotic vapor trails in red, white, and blue. But now it was Mr. Vega Riaza who stood calmly in the center of the balcony and he was waving at the Victoria Monument.

"That," he said, "I *wasn't* expecting. . . ."

Soon people were pointing and cameras were flashing and a couple of guards ran out into the forecourt of the palace to see what the fuss was about. The big man became anxious despite himself and shouted pointlessly up at the tiny figure.

"Get out of there, you idiot!"

He snatched up his binoculars and zoomed in on the Tar Man who simply stood there, quietly observing the frenetic activity which his presence had initiated. The big man was puzzled.

"What's his game?"

Moments later there was a flurry of activity, and a huddle of uniformed soldiers and security guards appeared on the balcony. They forced the Tar Man to the ground at gunpoint although he put up no visible resistance. Soon the sound of multiple police sirens echoed all over Pall Mall.

"Bang goes tea and cakes in Mayfair," said the gangly youth. "Shame. I was feeling a bit peckish."

"Use your head," said the big man. "He let them take him. Our Mr. Riaza is a risk-taker. Let's go and see what his messenger has got to say for herself. . . ."

When they arrived at Brown's Hotel a quarter of an hour later, smoothing down their hair and giving their shoes a quick polish on the back of their trousers, a uniformed valet showed them the way to an elegant private room, bedecked with flowers, where Anjali and Tom were already waiting for them. The big man gave a guarded nod to Anjali, and he sank down into one of the sumptuous upholstered sofas. His sidekick dithered, unsure whether he was supposed to sit down or not.

"Why don't you take the weight off your feet," said Anjali, patting the seat of her sofa. "I've already ordered. Tea should be here in a minute."

Almost immediately the door opened and a waiter came in carrying a large tray of tea, cucumber sandwiches—crusts cut off—and petits fours. He bent over and placed it carefully on the low mahogany table and started to pour tea from a silver teapot into china cups. Interestingly, the waiter then proceeded to sit down next to Anjali and help himself to a pink, iced cake which he popped into his mouth and dispatched in one bite.

There was total silence as the assembled company watched the Tar Man take a sip of his tea. The big man started to clap, slow at first and then louder. And then he began to laugh. Soon the room was resounding to applause and raucous laughter. Anjali was doubled up and clung on to Tom trying to catch her breath. Tom felt the warmth of her hands through his shirt and wished that the moment could have lasted forever.

"A clever trick, Mr. Riaza," said the big man and then, suddenly serious, "How did you *do* it? And, more to the point, how the heck did you get away?"

"It is more than a clever trick, my friend. It is a priceless one—and, believe me, I am aware of its worth. I have a skill which is unique in all the world. I have the power to go wherever I please—be it a lady's bedchamber or the Bank of England—and no man can stop me. Capture me and I will slip through your fingers like water through a sieve. Can you begin to comprehend the possibilites? From your expression I see that you can. . . ."

"What do you want, Mr. Riaza? Are you offering me something or asking me for something?"

The Tar Man smiled, showing all his newly whitened teeth. He liked a fellow who came to the point.

"Both."

"You don't think you're becoming a bit . . . fixated with this Houdini character, do you, sir? You can't pin *every* unsolved crime on him. There's no proof that it's the same person." Sergeant Chadwick put on a concerned but respectful expression.

"Don't try to be tactful, Sergeant. 'Obsessed' is the word you're looking for, and I've already been called that once today. And if I'm becoming obsessed, it's for good reason!"

Inspector Wheeler's voice was getting louder. Sergeant Chadwick closed the office door.

"We're only dealing with hints and rumors so far. No one's talking—and that's worrying in itself. I cannot understand why I am the only one who thinks that this constant trickle of disparate information points to the same man. But I'll tell you one thing for nothing—if I'm right, I've never seen anyone move in on so many different territories so quickly. Either this is one very scary guy or he's got something that people want. . . ."

"Or both," suggested Sergeant Chadwick.

"Obviously. You see, we're not just talking about the East End, this guy has already gone south of the river, he's into the warehouse district around Heathrow, he's infiltrated the City. It's as if he's spinning a spider's web across London. . . ."

"Do you still think there's a link between this Houdini and the Schock/Dyer case?"

"Of course there is!" snapped Inspector Wheeler. "The scientists are lying through their teeth, but they are plainly not criminals. I am sure the key to this has some connection with the antigravity experiment. And as for the latest nonsense from the Dyer family! Holiday indeed! Kate Dyer has gone into hiding. But from whom? And now Mr.

Schock has decided to go incommunicado. . . ."

"His wife says he's gone off to be by himself—which seems a bit tough on her."

"Aye, well, I'm taking *that* explanation with a large pinch of salt."

Sergeant Chadwick sucked in his cheeks and frowned. "You know, the thing that baffles me most is their clothes. Why was Kate Dyer wearing the long green dress in Bakewell? And then she *and* the Schock boy were in fancy dress in the supermarket car park and Covent Garden. And the horseman on Oxford Street was wearing a three-cornered hat. You don't think it could be some weird secret society on a fantasy trip, do you?"

The Inspector raised his eyebrows. "I don't think a case has ever got to me like this one. It's driving me nuts. I can't sleep. There's a missing piece to this puzzle that must be as plain as the nose on my face—but I'll be blowed if I can see it. . . ."

"Do you want a cup of tea, sir?"

"Aye, I do. Thank you, Sergeant."

Sergeant Chadwick picked up Inspector Wheeler's mug and opened the door but stopped halfway when the telephone rang. He picked it up and after a brief conversation replaced the receiver.

"Here's something that might interest you. . . . The guy doing surveillance on Dr. Dyer has just phoned in to say that he's at Manchester airport picking up a large piece of equipment and that Dr. Pirretti was on board the same flight."

EIGHTEEN

HELICOPTER!

In which the Tar Man sends his calling card,
Detective Inspector Wheeler finally learns the truth,
and the Tar Man tries out his new toy

"It's a wonder he agreed to treat you after what you did to him the first time," said Anjali, after showing the chiropractor out. "His eye's still swollen."

The Tar Man wiped down his neck and shoulders with a thick white towel. The three of them stood in the vast sitting room of the new apartment with its panoramic view of London now bathed in evening sunlight. Below, the river reflected mirrored skyscrapers and the giant cranes that seemed to stalk this part of the city like dinosaurs. Tom held out a fresh shirt for him while trying to avoid making any kind of eye contact with Anjali. The Tar Man had already noted that his apprentice did not seem quite himself today.

"'Tis a wonder he has survived in his profession for so long!" said the Tar Man. "Pinning me down with a knee in my back! When he pulled back my shoulders, the crack was as loud as pistol fire. I thought he had broken my neck, confound him!"

"But that's how they make you better—they manipulate you . . . Anyway, is your neck loosening up yet?"

"Ay, it is. I am obliged to you, Anjali. I had thought the pain in it would end only with the grave. . . . See how I can turn it and hold it straight. I'll warrant that popinjay of a doctor will have me cured before the month is out. My head will swivel like a barn owl's. I never thought to see the day."

Anjali was pleased to be thanked so graciously.

"You won't be so easy to spot now, neither. I reckon you could have your trademark scar sorted 'n' all. . . ."

The Tar Man looked shocked but interested at the same time.

"I could find out. If you liked."

"Who would I be without this scar?"

"Well . . . It's up to you."

"I could scarce stop myself from laughing," said Tom, "when the doctor made so bold with his remark. . . ."

"What remark?" asked Anjali.

"Why, imagine if you can," said the Tar Man, "that the gentleman had the impertinence to suggest that the nature of my injury was such that if he had not known better, he would have guessed I had been hanged!"

The Tar Man laughed heartily and so did Tom. Anjali didn't get the joke.

"So?" she asked, but they were laughing too much to answer.

"Right, then, I'd better be off." Anjali dropped two slim booklets on the low glass table in front of the leather sofa.

"Homework," she said. "Practice makes perfect 'n' all that. Oh, I nearly forgot. You were in the paper. . . ."

Anjali fished about for the newspaper behind the sofa, opened it up, and jabbed at the rustling pages with a finger.

"See. Quite the celebrity . . . First Buckingham Palace and now this."

The Tar Man grabbed hold of it and peered at the grainy image of himself blurring in front of Stubbs' glorious oil painting of a chestnut horse at the National Gallery.

"Upon my word they did not hurry themselves to report my daring exploit!"

"They're dismissing you as a publicity stunt—what with the red dot and you all fuzzy. Some high-tech trick or something! Like it was all done with mirrors!" Anjali laughed. "I could make a bundle if I went to the papers with what I knew. All these priceless items going walkies from galleries and bank vaults and nobody none the wiser. Not to mention a never-ending supply of eighteenth-century antiques . . ."

"Ay, you could," said the Tar Man, "but you wouldn't live to see the next day dawn."

"I was only joking!" Anjali protested, suddenly uncomfortable.

"As was I, Anjali, as was I. We had a particular punishment for snitches, eh, Tom? If we were feeling merciful . . ."

"What?" asked Anjali.

The Tar Man stuck out his tongue and mimed snipping it off.

"Charming!" said Anjali, and glanced at Tom for moral

support. Tom, however, knowing that the Tar Man, in this, at least, was not joking, stroked his mouse and would not look up.

The Tar Man smiled a knowing smile and gave the newspaper back to Anjali. Then he walked over to a black-lacquered sideboard and slid open a drawer. He returned with a small embossed card in his hand.

"I want you to have the newspaper delivered to this gentleman."

Anjali glanced at it. "You're moving in high-class circles all of a sudden. Is this Mr. Red Dot?"

The Tar Man nodded. "Put it in a box. Let it be tied with silk ribbon. . . ."

"Gift wrap it, you mean? Like for a present?"

"Yes. And deliver it with all haste."

"Right now? But I was about to—"

"*Now*, Anjali."

She sighed, disgruntled. "Do you want me to say who it's from?"

"He'll know."

"Am I allowed to know what this is about, Vega?"

"I have it in mind to join a particular gentlemen's club in Mayfair."

"Gentlemen's club!"

"As I say. Money I can acquire. I am short of a more valuable currency—influence. For a while in this century I shall need to be a cuckoo in the nest of the great and the good. . . . This gentleman is chairman of the membership committee. I put it to him that I had a strong desire to join his club. Then I asked him if there was anything in the world that might persuade him to push me to the top of his list. A list, they say, that is so long that most of the applicants die waiting."

"And what did he say?"

"The gentleman is a lover of art. He said that he had a weakness for a certain oil painting of a horse. By a Mr. George Stubbs."

Anjali left to deliver the newspaper to the Tar Man's powerful new acquaintance. Her high-heeled boots clicked as she walked across the pale ceramic tiles. Tom closed his eyes, straining to catch her scent as she passed him. Then he felt something soft tickling his ear. At first he thought it was his mouse, but it was Anjali.

"Don't let him open and close the balcony windows too much, like he's been doing," she whispered. Tom could feel her breath. "The electrician said he's nearly burned the circuits out. . . . And . . . no hard feelings about last night, eh?"

The Tar Man watched his apprentice's cheeks flush scarlet as Anjali vanished into the hall. Tom listened to the lift doors clanging shut, followed by the whirring of machinery as the lift carried its precious cargo down the vertiginous shaft. Tom gave an involuntary shiver as if he were suddenly cold.

"By heaven, you'll have to overcome your fear of lifts, Tom, else never go out—and then what use will you be?"

"I cannot help myself, Blueskin. . . ." Tom's voice was still breaking and it dipped from high to low and back again in the space of a few words. "I have tried, I swear it. No sooner have I stepped inside than an awful dread comes over me. The walls close in and I fear I shall be dashed into a thousand pieces when the contraption plummets to the ground. . . . I can run down as fast as may be!"

The Tar Man laughed. "Where is your bottom, Tom? Faith, you've lived cheek by jowl with the Carrick Gang for two years and put up with Joe's murderous threats from dawn to dusk— and yet, you are defeated by a lift! Stop your bleating, else I shall be forced to find a new apprentice!"

Tom looked at the ground. He hoped Blueskin did not mean what he said but did not dare look into his face in case he did. He liked it here. He felt safe with the Tar Man—at least most of the time.

The Tar Man picked up one of the slim books which Anjali had left for them and threw it to Tom. He picked up the other one himself, and master and apprentice sat on the leather sofa side by side and read together as they did most afternoons. Sometimes they practiced texting each other on their mobile phones, but today Anjali wanted them to focus on their reading. The Tar Man complied, for he realized that being illiterate in the twenty-first century was not an option. They took it in turns to read a line, the Tar Man needing to follow the words with his finger. Tom was already a much better reader than the Tar Man, but as he knew this annoyed his master, he tried to disguise it by speaking slowly.

"Mum was c-r-oss and D-ad was cr-oss but B-illy did not c-are," read the Tar Man.

338

Then it was Tom's go: "'You must not pull your sister's hair. It is not kind,' said Dad."

"You h-ave made her c-ry, B-illy. . . . What are you go-ing to say to her?"

"Sorry, Mum. Sorry, Dad," read Tom. "I will say to Amy that I will—"

"Drop her from the roof and that will cure her of her whining," quipped the Tar Man. "Confound this nursery fare. Where is the intrigue? Where is the wit? Where are the fulsome wenches?"

The Tar Man grabbed the remote control and the balcony window started to glide open. As soon as the opening was wide enough he flung the reading primer high up into the air with all his force. It spiraled up toward the dark blue heavens and then it started its descent. Tom dashed out into the freezing air and his delighted gaze followed the arc the book made as it dropped twenty-one floors toward the river. Red sunlight illuminated his face, and his green eyes, fringed with thick lashes, sparkled. He was already less painfully thin than he had been and it suited him. The Tar Man joined him on the spacious balcony and together they watched the tiny speck of white as it landed on the gray river below and floated away.

"Who hit you last night?" asked the Tar Man suddenly.

Tom's cheeks colored. "No one!"

"Was it Anjali?"

Tom would not answer and cringed in discomfort.

"Don't lie to me, lad! You still bear the mark. Someone

slapped you—and hard. Only a girl would do such a thing."

"No! You are mistaken."

The Tar Man grabbed hold of Tom's ear and twisted it until he cried out.

"Tell me! I need to know that I can trust her!"

"It was nothing, Blueskin. I swear to you. . . ."

The Tar Man released his ear a fraction.

"I followed her to the dancing club she goes to. There are some evil-looking fellows and the streets are dark. She wanted Tony to dance with her, but he was with another girl. Anjali was crying and I pulled her away, but she didn't want to come."

"So she slapped you. . . ."

"Yes. Only a little."

The Tar Man let go of his ear. "Then you should have slapped her back."

The memory of the night before came flooding back. Tom stuck his nails into the palms of his hands. It had been so dark in the club, and so very hot. The dance floor was a snake's nest of bodies writhing to the music that pounded in his ears and in his chest. Powerful lights flicked on and off, generating intermittent blue-white snapshots of gyrating figures. He felt giddy, disorientated. This barrage on his senses was too much for him and he longed to escape into the cold and the quiet of the night. He saw Anjali at the other side of the steamy room. He could not hear a word, yet it was clear that she was making a fool of herself. He had to stop her. The shifting throng of dancers obscured his view, and as he beat a path through the crowd, he caught fleeting glimpses of Anjali shouting and crying, her long, metallic earrings reflecting the pulsing lights like miniature beacons. Her hands were clenched into tight fists and she was shaking her head. Observing her dispassionately were Tony and his new girlfriend and a gaggle of his mates, all of whom had stopped dancing to stare at Anjali's performance.

As he drew close he heard Tony shout out: "What do I care if Vega Riaza can walk through walls? So can a bulldozer." He saw Tony's mates double up with laughter. "You think you're so cool, Anjali. Take it from me. You're not."

Tom darted in front of Tony and his new girlfriend and grabbed hold of Anjali's hot hand.

"Come, Miss Anjali. Best come with me."

Anjali looked down at him, incandescent with rage. She tried to pull away her hand, but he would not let go. Tom heard the howls of derisive laughter. He read contempt and loathing and humiliation in her eyes.

"Get away from me, you little creep!" she screamed.

"Please, Miss Anjali! These are not your friends. . . ."

Anjali wrenched away her hand and slapped him so hard he staggered backward a step. Slowly he raised his head and met her gaze.

"Will you come now?" he asked.

She took a step toward him and delivered another stinging slap to the other cheek.

There were guffaws of laughter. All he knew was that he had to save her from this. He held out his hand toward her. She knocked it to one side and struck him again. *Slap!* Tom's jaw was knocked first to one side and then the other. *Slap! Slap! Slap!*

"You're mental, you are," commented Tony. He turned his back on Anjali and moved away with his entourage.

Finally Anjali stopped, ashamed and defeated.

"Get out!" she shouted at Tom. "Why didn't you fight back? What's *wrong* with you?"

Tom fled into the cooling rain and ran through the dark streets without stopping. Then he slumped down onto the pavement under the orange glow of a street lamp, his heart as bruised and numb as his poor face, and he let his mouse crawl up his sleeve and through his tousled hair and slide down the sheet of tears that covered his cheeks.

"Does she have a loose tongue when she talks with her friends?" asked the Tar Man.

"No! Anjali knows how to hold her tongue. You need have no fear on that account!"

The Tar Man scrutinized Tom's face.

"You think I am wrong to doubt her. She is no squeaker, of that I am certain, yet no more is she as careful as she needs to be, and perchance one day she'll find that out to her cost—or ours—and that makes me uneasy. But I do not deny that she is a good guide. I have been pleased with her efforts."

The Tar Man paced up and down the balcony. A blackheaded gull landed on the handrail and immediately took off again when it realized it had company. It flew, squawking, toward the sun. Master and apprentice watched the bird's strong wings beating a course downriver. The *whup-whup-whup* of a helicopter made them look overhead. It was a police helicopter. The Tar Man recollected his dramatic entry into the future and smiled a broad smile of satisfaction. "I hope you have the bottom to attend me when I take delivery of the flying machine."

Tom gulped. "Will we fly in it?"

"Why else would I buy one, numbskull! We will see the world as a bird sees it! What say you we follow the course of the Thames to the sea?"

"Yes, Blueskin," Tom said doubtfully. "I think I should like to see the oceans. . . ."

Suddenly the Tar Man laughed and thumped Tom on the back.

"See how far we have come so soon! The view from this place is very pleasing to me. . . . Life is sweet in the future, eh, Tom?"

"Yes, Blueskin, it is very good."

"And as for our friend Anjali, stick hard by her for a while. Keep her out of harm's way. The lovesick make mistakes—and I do not wish to have the trouble of being obliged to find another guide."

"You're a good dog," said Sergeant Chadwick. Molly had sat at his feet all this time without even a whimper. He leaned down and patted her golden head and she looked up at him with her dark, soulful eyes, pleased to have some attention. Sergeant

Chadwick wriggled his toes. They were fast becoming numb. He stamped his feet on the frozen lawn and rubbed his hands together. He could see his breath. If he had known he was going to be standing guard over an oversized fridge, he would have brought some gloves and a hat, not to mention a flask of sweet tea. It had been nearly an hour since they had apprehended Kate Dyer's father and Dr. Pirretti. They had been unloading equipment from a Land Rover into the garden of this chocolate box cottage on the outskirts of Bakewell for a reason which had yet to be ascertained.

When questioned, the scientists had not been exactly forthcoming. However, when Detective Inspector Wheeler had threatened to arrest them for obstructing the police in their inquiries, Dr. Dyer had turned to his American colleague and said: "Anita, if it's a choice between telling him or not going after the children, I vote we tell him. . . ."

Dr. Pirretti had argued vigorously with her colleague while the bemused Inspector Wheeler, barely able to get a word in edgewise, tried to remind them that they were, in point of fact, trespassing on this resident's property. He also pointed out that, after being copied in on some of the curt missives from NASA concerning her recent conduct, he doubted that she possessed the requisite authorization to be carting NASA-funded equipment all over Derbyshire.

There had then been a long silence during which Sergeant Chadwick had tried to interpret a series of meaningful glances between the scientists. Eventually it was Dr. Pirretti who spoke.

"Against my better judgment, Inspector, we're going to let you in on a little secret that will blow all of your theories about the missing children straight out of the sky." Then she had glared at Sergeant Chadwick. "This information is for your ears only, Inspector, and is given strictly on the condition that, under formal questioning, should it arise, we will always deny all knowledge. . . ."

Sergeant Chadwick had been unceremoniously relegated to guard duty. Sergeant Chadwick's gaze strayed repeatedly over to the steamed-up windows of the Land Rover. The Inspector sat in the driver's seat, twisting his neck around awkwardly to look at Dr. Dyer and Dr. Pirretti. Mostly the Inspector listened, bushy eyebrows raised in amazement, staring at them incredulously. At one point he just sat there with an astonished grin on his face. Whatever they were telling him, it was certainly compelling stuff. What *was* all this about? Molly yawned noisily.

"I know just how you feel."

Suddenly Detective Inspector Wheeler was out of the car and was buttoning up his heavy Harris tweed coat. He bounded over to Sergeant Chadwick. "Right, Sergeant, I need you to come with me."

The Inspector's Scottish accent always seemed to intensify when he was excited.

"You're looking cheerful, Inspector."

"Aye, Sergeant, I am. I am indeed."

They opened the cottage's wrought iron gate and walked up the front path. When they could no longer be seen from the road, Detective Inspector Wheeler gave a little leap and punched the air triumphantly.

"I knew there had to be a missing piece to this puzzle! But never, never in a million years did I think it was going to be this!"

For a moment Sergeant Chadwick thought he was going to hug him.

"But I take it that you're not allowed to tell me. . . ."

The Inspector tapped the side of his nose. "Don't fret, Sergeant, I'll put you out of your misery later. . . ."

It took a while for the bleary-eyed occupants of the cottage to come to the door, and they were none too pleased to be informed that their home was needed for urgent police business for a couple of hours and that Sergeant Chadwick would assist them in vacating the property without delay. As soon as the Sergeant had driven off with his unhappy passengers, Inspector Wheeler helped Dr. Dyer and Dr. Pirretti carry the antigravity machine into the three-hundred-year-old cottage that in former centuries used to be known as Hawthorn Cottage. Moving the machine indoors had, in fact, been Inspector Wheeler's idea. Since, from past experience, it could be assumed that Dr. Dyer would be in an unconscious state for some time once he had, with any luck, arrived in 1763, it made sense for him to recover indoors rather than lying in the garden for any ne'er-do-well to see.

Dr. Dyer requested that his two assistants leave the cottage before he attempted to start up the antigravity machine. So Dr.

Pirretti and Inspector Wheeler stood outside the sitting-room window at what Dr. Dyer suggested would be a safe distance while he keyed in the security code and checked the settings for the twentieth time. Dr. Dyer had said his good-byes to the children the previous night and told them to be good and that he would see them again very soon, but, as he waved to his wife who stood at the kitchen door refusing to cry, he saw Sam, Issy and Alice, Sean, and even little Milly peeping out from behind the curtains. *Why,* he thought, *did this have to happen to us?*

His finger hovered over the button and he spoke a silent prayer. Molly lay at his feet and Dr. Dyer stroked her soft ears. "Good dog," he said. "You found her the last time; let's see if you can do it again."

In a state of high excitement the Inspector peered through the window at the antigravity machine, incongruous against the cottage's bare-brick walls and slate inglenook. Dr. Dyer smiled at Dr. Pirretti. She smiled back at him and gave him the thumbs-up sign. Then he pressed the button. For several seconds Inspector Wheeler was aware of something happening to the surface of the machine—it seemed to be dissolving, liquefying, transforming. . . . The hairs rose on the back of Inspector Wheeler's neck. Then Dr. Dyer, too, appeared to lose some of his opaqueness, and an instant later no trace remained of either man, machine, or Golden Labrador. Dr. Pirretti let her face drop forward against the pane of glass in relief.

"Thank God," she said.

Detective Inspector Wheeler was trembling. Dr. Pirretti turned her head a fraction to look at him.

"So now you know," she said.

Tucked away in a quiet corner of a country pub that evening, Inspector Wheeler drank bitter lemon and gave Sergeant Chadwick a blow-by-blow account of the incredible story that Dr. Pirretti and Dr. Dyer had told him and what he had seen happen to the antigravity machine.

"Are you sure you should be telling me this, sir?"

"I'm not telling you anything, Sergeant. You are like the three brass monkeys: blind, deaf, and dumb. I happen to be talking to myself. You happen to be sitting next to me."

Inspector Wheeler's relief was palpable. During his talk with Dr. Dyer and Dr. Pirretti, all the missing pieces of the case which had tortured him for so long appeared in their entirety, as if summoned by magic, slipping into place and revealing the complete, astounding, picture. His narrative was punctuated with exclamations from Sergeant Chadwick: "You've got to be pulling my leg!" and "Time travel!" and "I don't believe I'm hearing this. . . ."

When the Inspector finally ran out of steam, they sat in silence for a while, sipping their drinks and aware for the first time of the clinking of glasses and the hiss of the wood fire and hum of conversation. The cozy scene inside the pub somehow increased the sense of unreality they were both feeling. After a while Sergeant

Chadwick started to chuckle quietly and commented: "The fancy dress thing had really been getting to me. . . . Who'd have thought the explanation was so much more logical than all the incredible theories we'd been coming up with."

"*You* had been coming with!"

"And the Dyer girl appearing between the goalposts at the school . . . And the photocopying room incident at Lincoln's Inn Fields . . ."

"And how they vanished from the laboratory without trace and with no witnesses," said Inspector Wheeler. "Not to mention Kate Dyer's convenient loss of memory and Mr. Schock's so-called 'holiday.' Do you remember how we struggled to come up with a reason for them scraping off the graffiti at the Dyer girl's school, Sergeant? Turns out she'd left a message—'Kate Dyer wants to come home—July 1763.' It was the first evidence they had found that the children had gone back in time."

"No wonder the NASA scientists wanted to keep a lid on it. They'll never manage it, though. Not something like this. If *they* managed to invent it, someone else will work out how to do it eventually. And I don't rate Dr. Dyer's chances of find-ing the kids and Mr. Schock, either. Talk about a needle in a haystack. . . ."

"No. Indeed."

"It's a brave thing that he's doing but then, when it's your own kid I guess you'd do anything. . . ."

Inspector Wheeler suddenly sat upright and gripped Sergeant Chadwick's arm.

"But I was forgetting—there's something else I haven't told you! When Peter Schock got left behind in 1763, his place was taken by a certain eighteenth-century criminal called the Tar Man. A pretty scary guy by all accounts who—"

Sergeant Chadwick's face lit up.

"Who doesn't by any possible chance have a crooked neck and a scar down one cheek and was last seen riding a horse down Oxford Street?"

"The very same."

Sergeant Chadwick thumped the table and whooped. Inspector Wheeler put a crumpled five-pound note on the table.

"And if you get me another drink, Sergeant, I might be persuaded to tell you how he got that crooked neck of his. . . ."

Inspector Wheeler was listening to a comedian on the radio as he headed for home. The eleven o'clock news bulletin came on, and he was not in the mood to hear it. It occurred to him that it would make a pleasant change to go back to the eighteenth century and escape mass communication and with it the daily diet of war and political maneuvering and gloomy economic, not to mention gloomy weather, forecasts. Actually, he did not *want* to know that a thick bank of cloud was moving over the British Isles and that it would be several days before the sun was able to break through. *Ignorance,* he thought, *is becoming an increasingly rare and desirable commodity.*

Driving back through the deserted country roads after such a memorable and exciting day, Inspector Wheeler wanted to listen to some music. Something haunting and beautiful to soothe him and stop his agitated brain thinking any more about time travel and blurring and the Tar Man. He slowed down to a crawl and ferreted about in the glove compartment, chucking CDs and empty cases behind him onto the backseat to sort out later. Even as he threw them over his shoulder, he already knew that he would not find the time to finish the job. His car was, like his life, strewn with the detritus of good intentions. He could do with an antigravity machine, he reflected. It would be good to think you could have another bite at the cherry. . . .

He put in the classical CD he had found and turned up the volume until the strains of Debussy's *The Cathedral under the Sea* transported him to an altogether lovelier and more mysterious place than the scruffy interior of his car. But he soon became dimly conscious of a noise, a rhythmic engine noise above the loud music, although he had not seen any other vehicles on the road for miles. He drove on, the hawthorn hedgerows flashing past him, their bare, thorny branches illuminated for an instant before disappearing into the engulfing darkness. It had been drizzling for a while, but now a real deluge was beginning. Fat raindrops rolled across the windscreen. The wipers scraped the glass out of time with the music and the headlights lit up sparkling ropes of rain. Inspector Wheeler leaned forward and peered out at the pitch-black countryside. Suddenly a light bounced off the rearview mirror, strong enough to dazzle him momentarily. He checked the road behind, but there was nothing there. It happened again. Then he realized that the noise of which he had been intermittently aware was becoming louder—or nearer. The uneasy feeling which he had been experiencing immediately intensified. He turned off the music and jammed his fingers on all four switches at once to open the electric windows and listen to what was going on. He heard his tires splattering over the wet tarmac, the grating of the rubber wipers on the windscreen, and then the *whup-whup-whup* of a helicopter. He thrust his head out of the window and looked up. A helicopter was mirroring the course of his car perhaps one hundred feet above him. A small warning light blinked on its tail. Inspector Wheeler looked away just in time—the road had swerved to the left and now he was driving on the wrong side of the road and was about to topple into a ditch. The tires squealed as he corrected his position.

Suddenly the car was caught in a perfect circle of dazzling light and a voice boomed out above him. It was a man's voice, with an American accent.

"Sir, you've driven into a military exercise, please pull over."

Inspector Wheeler was so astonished he carried on driving. The helicopter flew lower.

"Sir, for your own safety, please cooperate and stop your car."

Inspector Wheeler put his foot on the brake and drew slowly to a halt. This was absurd! How could the military take over a country road like this? There hadn't been any signs. . . . Surely he would have been informed!

The helicopter ascended vertically into the air, circled for a moment overhead and then landed twenty yards in front of him, its propellers rotating deafeningly over the open road. Finding himself once more in darkness, Inspector Wheeler stepped out of the car into the rainy night and was buffeted by the blast of wind that nearly knocked him off his feet. He was furious. And he was going to demand to speak to the pilot's senior officer. The Inspector had taken only a few steps when the blinding beam of light was again directed straight at him. He covered his eyes and squinted through the gaps in his fingers.

"What on earth do you think you're playing at?" he shouted.

The glass door of the helicopter slid open. He was expecting to see a figure in military uniform emerge. Instead, a slim, athletic man in jeans and a black leather jacket dropped lightly to the ground. His dark hair was scraped back in a ponytail, and when he stepped into the light, Inspector Wheeler saw something which made his blood run cold: The man sported an impressive scar on one cheek, a lurid white slash of a scar which started above one eyebrow and curved down to below his jaw.

The Tar Man! Inspector Wheeler did not hesitate. He turned on his heels and ran toward his car. The Tar Man immediately launched into a sprint, accelerating effortlessly so that by the time the policeman was at the car door he was upon him. Inspector Wheeler threw himself into the driver's seat and slammed the door shut. The Tar Man grabbed hold of the handle and pulled it open again. With both hands the policeman tugged at the door with every last ounce of his strength, and for a moment, the door remained half-open with neither of the two men gaining the advantage. Then the Tar Man lost his grip on the wet chrome and in that instant the policeman was able to pull the door shut and lock it. The Tar Man immediately started aiming high kicks at the driver's window with his powerful legs but was taken aback when it would not break. Inspector Wheeler switched on the ignition and put the car into reverse. As the car careered backward, the Tar Man dived onto the hood. The Inspector steered sharply to one side, but the Tar Man grabbed hold of the wipers to avoid slipping off and pulled himself up again toward the glass, leering at him through the windscreen. Inspector Wheeler prepared to reverse diagonally across the road, but as he looked up their eyes met. In that split second, as the Tar Man's eyes bore into him, the policeman sensed the chill of fear rise up in him and, to his shame, knew he had been unable to conceal it.

Suddenly, agile as an acrobat, the Tar Man jumped up and balanced on the center of the hood, hands on hips, and looked down at Inspector Wheeler.

"I would talk with you, policeman," he shouted through the window. "Must I persuade you or will you accept my invitation?"

Inspector Wheeler jammed his foot on the accelerator pedal. The Tar Man leaped nimbly to the ground before he was thrown off and bounded back toward the helicopter. Inspector Wheeler turned the car in a full circle, came out of reverse gear, and drove off into the darkness at top speed. He needed to find cover as soon as possible, somewhere where a helicopter could not get at him. There was a small wood, not much more than a thicket, perhaps a mile or two away. Inspector Wheeler drove like he had never driven before. The countryside flew by and the needle of his speedometer soon flickered over maximum. Yet moments later he could sense the shuddering vibration of the helicopter behind him—and it was getting closer.

The machine hovered overhead like a hawk, still and deadly, waiting for the right moment to strike. Inspector Wheeler was in a cold sweat. How much longer before he reached the cover of trees? Then, to his horror, he saw the helicopter descending in front of him, blocking his path. Instinctively he braked hard to avoid crashing into it but instantly realized his mistake. He should have kept on going, for the pilot would assuredly have got out of the way in time. But it was too late now. A burned, acrid smell laced the air, the car went into a slow skid and finally came to a halt, sideways on, only feet away from the helicopter. Inspector Wheeler was thrown forward over the steering wheel and when he looked up he could discern the Tar Man and the ex-marine who flew the machine looking down at him, smiles of satisfaction on their faces. Anger began to win out over fear and Inspector Wheeler growled with rage. The Tar Man leaned over toward the microphone.

"Have you had enough sport, Inspector Wheeler, or shall we continue awhile? For my part, rarely have I been more diverted, yet I can see that you are no longer in the bloom of youth. . . ."

Thin-lipped, Inspector Wheeler revved up the engine and pulled violently on the steering wheel, turning his car around in one smooth maneuver. He raced down the road the way that he had come, plunging ever deeper into the black country-side. The helicopter immediately took off and hovered only a few feet above the roof of the car. Trying to shake it off, the Inspector performed an emergency stop, immediately followed by a three-point turn, and set off again in the direction of the wood. He could see nothing but the rain teeming down like shining needles in front of his headlights. All at once the helicopter found him again, and, to his joy, as the beam of light was directed on him once more, he was able to distinguish, ghostly pale, the bare skeletons of winter trees a short distance away. If he had been riding a horse instead of driving a car he would have dug in his spurs and cracked his whip. Anything to get into the safety of the wood. As it was, he pushed down the accelerator pedal with all his might, uselessly, as his foot could not go any farther.

Moments later Inspector Wheeler penetrated the wood while, frustrated, the helicopter pilot was forced to make a rapid ascent. The Inspector released his foot from the accelerator and the car glided through the trees. His mobile phone, he realized, was in the pocket of his tweed coat in the trunk. He debated with himself whether or not he wanted to risk getting out of the car and calling for reinforcements. . . . In the heat of the moment it seemed like a good idea to turn his headlights off to make tracking him more difficult.

BAM!

Something came crashing out of the darkness at him, and the car rocked violently forward and backward, throwing the

Inspector, who was not wearing a safety belt, against the steering wheel. Pain stabbed at his forehead and garish colors clouded his vision, and in those few seconds before he lost consciousness he berated himself for his stupidity. . . .

When he started to come round, a few minutes later, he pushed himself up and sat upright, dazed and nauseous. His rib cage ached where it had slammed into the steering wheel, and he felt a sharp pain in his neck. It was still night, but it was no longer pitch black, for the first thing he saw, in his rearview mirror, was light streaming into the wood from the helicopter. Walking away from the car into the light, and sharply silhouetted against it, was the figure of a tall, powerfully built man. The body of a young deer was draped around his shoulders. Its head flopped up and down with each stride. Dazed, the Inspector leaned back and rested his head on the neck rest. He rubbed his forehead, palmed his sore eyes, and groaned.

"I am fond of roast venison," said a voice quietly from the back of the car.

Inspector Wheeler cried out and his whole body jolted with the awful shock of it. The Tar Man was behind him! He fumbled to reach the door handle, but the Tar Man had a cord around his neck before he could get a grip. He clutched at the Tar Man's arms, trying to pull him off. He gasped for breath and kicked out futilely, feeling the cord burning into his skin and pressing against his windpipe.

"Keep still and I shall be gentle with you. Do you understand?"

Inspector Wheeler made a nodding movement with his head. The Tar Man relaxed his grip a little.

"What do you want?" asked the Inspector in a strangulated whisper.

"I have need of some intelligence. I seek an antigravity machine. . . . I believe you know of what I speak."

Inspector Wheeler's mind raced. The Tar Man wanted to get his hands on the antigravity machine! He was wreaking enough havoc in the twenty-first century with his ability to blur. He did not like to think what he could do with a time machine. . . . Initially he had been shocked when Dr. Pirretti said she intended destroying all evidence of their discovery of time travel. In that moment he totally understood her reasoning.

"Why are you asking me? If you want to know about an experimental machine you should be asking NASA. . . ."

The cord tightened a notch.

"Inspector Wheeler, I would not for the world detain you any longer than need be, but please be assured that I shall squeeze the last breath out of your body if you do not tell me what I need to know. I shall, in any case, find it out one way or another. It is remarkable what means spies have at their disposal in your century. . . ."

"In *my* century?" said Inspector Wheeler.

"Pray don't try to hoodwink me, Inspector. You know precisely who I am and where I come from. And I have had you followed. Snippets of a conversation overheard not an hour since have already been conveyed to me. What I want to know is this: I am now of the opinion that there are two antigravity machines. Where are they?"

The cord tightened again. Inspector Wheeler remained still and silent.

"'Tis a pity that you display so little common sense and that I must resort to violence," remarked the Tar Man. "But I am a man of my word."

He pulled steadily on the cord until the policeman started to choke. He was not even aware of his arms and legs thudding against the window and the steering column, and soon he barely had the strength to struggle. His eyes were open, and as the functioning of his brain slowed down, it seemed to him that the roof of the car was a gray sea and that he was drowning in it. . . .

"All right . . . !" he gasped.

The Tar Man loosened the cord at once and gave him a few seconds to recover.

"You and your kind would gladly wipe me from the face of the earth, would you not, Inspector Wheeler? That much hasn't changed. But I shall show you more mercy than ever was shown to me. I give you a final chance."

The Inspector spoke with difficulty and in a rasping voice. "I'll tell you where they are, but it won't do you any good. You can't get at them. . . . Kate Dyer and Peter Schock's father stole the first machine shortly after your arrival here. They went back to 1763 to find the boy. They haven't been seen or heard of since. Dr. Pirretti brought a second version over from the States last week."

"The States?"

"America. I witnessed Dr. Dyer return to the past only this morning. He means to rescue all three of them. But I don't rate his chances."

"Are there any other machines?"

"No."

"And . . . what is the name of the handsome woman who was with you in the car this morning? This is not the first time our paths have crossed."

Inspector Wheeler hesitated but realized that the information could be readily obtained—and his windpipe had taken enough punishment. . . .

"Dr. Anita Pirretti of NASA."

"Pirretti," said the Tar Man, rolling his r's. "Thank you, Inspector."

The Tar Man withdrew his hands and slipped the cord from around the Inspector's neck and got out of the car. Inspector Wheeler, trembling with shock and holding on to his throat with both hands, observed his nemesis depart in the rearview mirror and did not dare move until he saw him disappear into the helicopter which, seconds later, took off and was speeding over the desolate countryside back toward London.

Inspector Wheeler staggered to the back of his car and felt for his mobile phone deep in the pocket of his great tweed coat. "Nobody," he croaked, "does that to Dan Wheeler and gets away with it. . . ."

NINETEEN

THE LIGHTNING CONDUCTOR

*In which the town of Arras suffers a violent thunderstorm
and the party reaches its destination*

Louis-Philippe did not appear at supper and the innkeeper told
them that he had asked for something to be sent up to his room.
Peter knocked at his door before retiring for the night, but there
was no reply. Immediately on rising, at daybreak, Peter knocked
at Louis-Philippe's door again, only to find that he had already
left, having hired a fast horse procured for him by the innkeeper.
The atmosphere at breakfast was, in consequence, tense.

"If anything happens to him," said Kate, looking around her
to make sure she would not be overheard, "it will be our fault!
He's an aristocrat in the middle of the French Revolution!"

"It is a day's ride to Arras and he is familiar with the route,"
returned Peter. "I scarcely think he needs our protection. . . .
And if he does, he should not have acted so irresponsibly."

Mr. Schock and Hannah held their peace, even though both
had been badly frightened and had spent half of the previous
evening coping with wet clothes and arranging a passage for the

Frenchwoman on the Dover packet. Kate could tell at a glance that Joshua was still as furious with her as she was with him. Before they left, the innkeeper's wife remembered to tell them that the handsome young gentleman had asked her to pass on his compliments to them and, as he would be traveling on alone, to wish them a pleasant journey.

"That was kind of him to wish us a pleasant journey," said Hannah.

"*Yes*, it certainly *was*," said Kate pointedly.

The open carriage they had been obliged to hire was not comfortable. They felt every stone they rode over, although the quality of the gravel road impressed the English visitors; it was broad and paved in the middle and did not have the same number of bone-shaking potholes that they were accustomed to in England. At first they passed through a series of verdant valleys, but soon the countryside started to look parched and less fertile; they saw herds of swine grazing on the low hills and, occasionally, fields of thin cows. The laborers who worked the land appeared malnourished and worn down by their toil.

It was early evening before they caught their first sight of Arras. When the town and its cathedral came into view in the far distance, a spontaneous cheer erupted from the coach, causing flocks of tiny birds to rise up from the scrubby undergrowth and the skittish mare to come to a halt. Everyone was exhausted from being jolted and shaken around the entire day and—despite the handkerchiefs which Hannah had tied around them—Peter's hands were bleeding from pulling on the ropes that harnessed the horses to the dilapidated coach.

The sun was now hidden behind thick clouds, and the air was heavy and humid. Swallows swooped low in search of midges, and as the hours and miles passed by, the landscape took on an ominously dark cast. Billowing, purple clouds edged with yellow raced across the sky and a great, gusting wind blew up from the west. Soon they saw a flicker of lightning on the horizon and then, several seconds later, the first rumbles of thunder reached them. They saw gray curtains of rain appear which were headed in their direction. Forked lightning was now striking the countryside repeatedly, and thunder rolled across the landscape, so loud that Kate clapped her hands over her ears. Peter and Mr. Schock exchanged glances. This was a bad storm. Abruptly the wind dropped and the air felt curiously warm. Kate realized that the birds had stopped singing. All around them the countryside was enveloped in threatening stillness.

"We're in the eye of the storm!" she murmured.

The horses stopped of their own volition and stood, ears pricked back, waiting. . . . Peter dropped the reins and for a moment no one spoke, looking around them, hardly daring to breathe. A second later several jagged flashes of electric blue streaked simultaneously across the heavens. It was instantly followed by an explosive crack of thunder. Kate jumped with the violence of it. Then the rain hit. It came at them in horizontal, icy sheets and lashed at them mercilessly. It set off the horses and before Peter could catch hold of the reins again, they were galloping, out of control, headed for some tall trees.

"Let's get under cover!" shouted Mr. Schock.

"No!" screamed Kate. "Isn't that the last thing you should do in a thunderstorm?"

But her cries were drowned in the wind and the rain and the thunder and the clatter of hooves and the groaning of the old coach. Little by little, Peter managed to get the horses under control and they ground to a halt at the entrance to a long avenue of chestnut trees, easily a hundred years old. They scrambled out of the carriage.

"Further in Master Pe— Mr. Joshua!" said Hannah. "Look, the ground is scarcely wet beneath the trees. Mistress Kate is soaked as it is—I don't want her to catch a chill on top of everything else. . . ."

"You were going to say Peter!" cried Kate in astonishment. "Weren't you!"

Peter glared at Hannah as she stared back at Kate, round-eyed, and began to mouth a reply. But before she could utter a word, there was a deafening explosion, not fifty yards from them, as lightning struck one of the chestnut trees. The ground shuddered beneath their feet and hundreds of terrified birds flew up into the teeming rain, squawking and cawing. For a moment the party clung on to each other and a bitter smell of scorched bark met their nostrils. They had to raise their hands protectively over their heads as they were pelted by a shower of twigs and leaves falling down from the sky. Then, in quick succession, they heard a terrible creaking and saw the crown of the tree slide sickeningly sideways.

"Oh no!" cried Kate.

The rest of the party looked where Kate was pointing: A man and a woman, dwarfed by the giant tree, were darting out from under its broad boughs toward them. There had been people sheltering under that very tree! There was nothing they could do to help them. Kate watched, aghast, as the ancient horse chestnut started to fall. The two small figures ran the race of their lives.

"Faster! Faster!" shouted Kate, quite beside herself.

Steam was now rising from the boiling sap and a plume of dirty white smoke rose into the air. They could discern a few bright orange flames where the lightning had struck the trunk, but these were rapidly being extinguished. There were small hissing sounds as raindrops instantly evaporated in the intense heat. The woman slowed down momentarily in order to look behind her, but when she saw the towering structure about to crush her she froze like a rabbit in front of headlights.

"Don't stop!" cried Kate and then, "Joshua! No!"

With a burst of adrenalin Peter had sprinted forward toward the woman. He reached out for her nearest hand and pulled with all his might but almost immediately lost his grip on account of the rain. They both rolled over and over, and as half the tree hit the ground with a shuddering crash, the two of them were covered with a tangle of foliage and gnarled branches the size of a small ship. All around them hand-shaped leaves were fluttering down and there was the soft pitter-pattering of prickly, semiripe chestnuts landing on the gravel avenue. The man had managed to reach safety and now stood, along with Kate, Hannah, and Mr. Schock, in front of the settling debris. In that fraction of a second, Kate felt a flash of recognition; she had seen the man somewhere before. . . . Immediately everyone sprang into action and dived into the foliage, shouting and pulling frantically at branches where they had last seen Joshua and the woman.

"Marie!"

"Joshua! Make a sound if you can hear us!"

The rescuers were making so much noise themselves they were drowning out any potential replies. Mr. Schock suddenly stood up and put a finger to his lips.

"Sssh! I heard something."

Everyone followed suit and stood up, ears straining to focus in on anything that could indicate movement. There was a faint rustling sound and a tanned, work-worn hand emerged from the canopy of leaves.

"*Au secours*!" came a faint, high-pitched voice, pleading for help.

"Marie!" shouted her companion in response.

He dived in and reappeared with the woman, supporting her under her shoulders. The woman's hair and dress were strewn with leaves and small twigs and her face was scratched and smeared with mud. She also had a black eye. Clutching on to the man's arm, the woman staggered out of the foliage. Kate saw her feel around her neck for a silver crucifix which she held for a moment in her hand, then she sank to her knees in thanks, making the sign of the cross as she did so.

"Joshua!" called Mr. Schock. "Can you hear me?"

There was no reply.

Kate dropped to the floor and started to crawl under the branches, constantly hindered by her skirts that snagged and tore as she pushed her way through to where she had seen him vanish.

"He's here!" she called. "Help me!"

Mr. Schock dived in behind Kate and pulled away armfuls of foliage until Peter was partly visible. He was pinned down by a branch the width of a man's arm which straddled his waist. Had he been a hand's breath further to his left he would have been crushed by the main trunk. As it was, he did not appear to be moving. He was lying on his stomach, spread-eagled on the ground as if he had been hit with a gigantic flyswatter.

"Joshua!" cried Kate. Oh, he mustn't be dead! He had still been angry with her! What if he were Peter?

So slow as to be almost imperceptible, Peter raised his head. His eyes met Kate's.

"Ouch!" he said with a flicker of a smile, and let his head sink back to the floor.

"Can you move your legs?" cried Mr. Schock.

"I do not know. . . . Yes."

"And your arms?"

They could see both his hands forming into a fist.

"I am winded, that is all, as far as I can tell. . . ."

"Thank the Lord for that!" exclaimed Mr. Schock.

"But something is stabbing into me. . . ."

Another deafening thunderclap boomed overhead as Mr. Schock struggled, vainly, to break off the branch that covered Peter. He suddenly found himself being pulled away by the Frenchman, who pushed in front of him brandishing a wood axe that glinted in the greenish gloom. He chopped away at the branch, pulling it upward as he did so in order to cause Peter the least amount of pain. He had soon cut it through. Mr. Schock tugged at the severed branch and then, with the Frenchman's help, slid it off Peter, pulling it out from under other branches. They needed to walk backward for several yards before the tip of the branch was clear of him. Peter struggled to his feet unaided, his face contorted in pain. Kate immediately saw the problem and rushed forward to help him. He had landed on a cluster of chestnuts in their prickly green cases and they had pierced through his cotton shirt and were sticking into the flesh of his waist like so many baby hedgehogs.

"Argh!" He winced as Kate plucked them off one by one.

"You seem to be making a habit of saving damsels in distress!" Mr. Schock said to Joshua as he brushed leaves off the back of his jacket. "That's two in as many days!"

"You showed great courage, sir," said Hannah. "Mr. Gideon would have been proud."

Kate nodded in agreement and smiled broadly at him, hoping that he would understand that she wanted to put yesterday behind her.

While Hannah examined Peter and the woman, as best she

could, and pronounced them both to have got away with nothing worse than cuts and bruises, Kate observed the two strangers. It was then that Kate realized where she had seen the man before. It was on account of him that Louis-Philippe had hidden in the doorway! She remembered his name, too: Sorel. Hannah heard Kate's sharp intake of breath and glanced up at her. Kate shook her head discreetly as if to say "not now."

Sorel's wife had kind eyes and a somewhat fearful, doelike demeanor. She was still young but, like everyone they had met in the countryside that day, painfully thin and hollow-cheeked. It transpired that her black eye was not, in fact, a result of her encounter with the chestnut tree, though she would not say how the injury came about. Despite the fact that the storm was still raging and that his wife was visibly shaken, the man was anxious to set off again. He took his leave of them in a halfhearted, unfriendly manner, but judging from the suspicious sideways glance he gave her, Kate was convinced that he recognized her from the previous day. Sorel stood looking into the distance, his chin jutting in the air, while Marie thanked the English ladies and gentlemen. When she made a curtsy of sorts, the gesture appeared to provoke his disapproval. Husband and wife marched swiftly away through the torrential rain, the husband walking three yards in front of his wife. The damp and disheveled party watched them from under the cover of the trees on the assumption that lightning doesn't strike twice in the same place. The storm was beginning to abate, but it was far from over.

"Mr. Schock, sir, might it be an idea to ask for directions?" suggested Hannah.

"It's a good job someone's got their wits about them! Thank you, Hannah!"

Mr. Schock hurried after the couple. *"Monsieur! Madame! S'il vous plaît! Nous cherchons le Château de l'Humiaire!"*

The pair turned around, raindrops streaming down their faces, and Marie looked puzzled for a moment, then gave a short reply and pointed at something through a gap in the trees.

"She says we're already there!" said Mr. Schock, and they all rushed forward to see what she was pointing at.

It became clear that the avenue of chestnut trees was nothing other than the château's long and sweeping front drive.

"Oh, it's beautiful!" Kate exclaimed.

The Château de l'Humiaire resembled a compact medieval castle, built of a mellow-colored stone, complete with two circular towers with pointed roofs and a moat. Formal gardens radiated out from it and a flock of sheep grazed on the lawns. The château had a benign and welcoming air, even in this weather.

"'Tis no wonder the Marquis is reluctant to leave," commented Peter. "Rarely have I seen a happier prospect than this view of his property."

As the group stood admiring the château, a fiery spear of forked lightning burst through the dark, dense clouds and struck the roof of the nearest tower like a guided missile. It was accompanied by a curious electric sound, somewhere between

370

a prolonged hiss and a crackle. The crack of thunder which it engendered resounded, like a detonation, for miles around. Kate gasped and waited for flames to appear or for the roof of the tower to cave in—but nothing happened. By some miracle the château appeared to have sustained no damage whatsoever. Suddenly Marie started to laugh delightedly. Kate looked at Marie's face, all aglow. She gabbled something to Mr. Schock, but in the middle of a sentence Sorel interrupted her and pulled her away. With a curt good-bye they set off again.

"What *is* his problem?" asked Kate as the couple strode away. "I'd better tell you that Louis-Philippe knows that man. I saw him yesterday. He's a Revolutionary."

"Him and millions of others!" exclaimed Mr. Schock. "We are in the middle of the French Revolution! And, speaking personally, I'd be hard pressed to say whether I was for or against it."

"And he did try and help me . . . ," said Peter.

"But it was him who was following the maid!" said Kate. "Oh . . . Never mind—but I don't trust him."

"What did his wife say?" asked Hannah.

"She said that the Marquis has been out in every storm for the last three years, waiting to test out his lightning conductor, and now he has the proof that it works! Her husband warned us that the Marquis is stark, staring mad. And if you look over there, you'll see the alleged lunatic himself, or, as Sorel referred to him, Citizen Montfaron, formerly le Marquis de Montfaron. Can you see? There, on the front lawn."

Mr. Schock pointed. There, in the distance, only just visible and surrounded by sheep, a tall, thin man in a white shirt appeared to be dancing a jig in front of the château in the pouring rain.

"The time has come, my friends," said Peter, "for us to introduce ourselves to the man we hope will find a solution to all our problems."

TWENTY

LE MARQUIS DE MONTFARON

In which the party finds itself on the receiving end
of the Marquis de Montfaron's hospitality, Kate's grip
on time is diminished, and Mr. Schock predicts the future

The storm departed as quickly as it had arrived. The wind dropped and the heavy rain became a fine drizzle. Tiny cracks of blue appeared in the sky and the birds started to sing again. Then a chink of sunshine appeared just long enough for a rainbow to form over the Château de l'Humiaire.

"Bless me, there's a good omen and no mistake," said Hannah, whose sodden clothes, heavy with water, were, like everyone else's, beginning to steam gently.

The party left the horses to graze beneath the dripping trees and they walked down the gravel road that curved around in a graceful sweep. Soon the avenue broadened out into a forecourt which was scattered with lead sculptures of wood nymphs and satyrs set onto square limestone plinths. They walked slowly for Peter's sake, as he had not yet recovered from his encounter with the tree. As they approached the gardens, which had appeared so pristine from afar, they began to notice signs of neglect.

"I doubt that Mrs. Montfaron would be too impressed if she could see this," said Mr. Schock.

"I wonder if Louis-Philippe has arrived yet," said Kate.

While the sheep kept down the grass on the vast lawns, weeds were growing up through the gravel paths and the forecourt was peppered with ruts and deep, muddy puddles. Many of the statues were frost-damaged, and ferns grew out of cracks in the masonry. Specimens of box, which once upon a time had been meticulously pruned into pyramids and spheres and positioned to highlight the geometrical design of the gardens, were now growing out of control. Bright new foliage escaped, chaotically, from the form that had imprisoned it. Ornamental fruit trees lined the paths, and many crab apple, plum, and pear trees had shed their harvests on the ground. As a consequence there were circles of rotting fruit everywhere they trod. Mr. Schock stepped on a moldy, liquefying pear and skidded onto the grass where he landed in a pile of sheep droppings.

"Don't say a word," he said when he saw Kate's face. He wiped himself down. "What wouldn't I give for a nice, hot shower. . . ."

The idea of a hot shower puzzled Hannah, who found it difficult to imagine such a thing, but she thought it best not to comment as Mr. Schock was apt to be a little abrupt.

They stopped of one accord when they arrived at the draw-bridge, uneasy about crossing it. It spanned a small moat, bright emerald in color on account of all the algae. Small white ducks swam in it, tracing black patterns through the solid surface.

Everyone's instincts told them to beware breaching the château's defence without prior permission from its owner.

Kate looked up and saw a mass of rampant ivy. It scrambled up the walls and penetrated the interior of the château through broken windows.

"It's like the castle in *Sleeping Beauty*," said Kate in a whisper.

It was then that she heard it.

"Oh, listen!" she cried. "Come on!"

Kate led the way over the slimy ancient planks of the drawbridge into an inner quadrangle. A bedraggled peacock strutted around, and half a dozen speckled hens, alarmed by the strangers' appearance, darted about *po-o-o-ck-pock-pock-pock*ing indignantly. In front of them, heavy carved doors were thrown wide open, and exquisite music drifted out into the quadrangle.

They stole up to the threshold and peeped in. Kate looked around her in wonder. She saw a great galleried hall with a flagstone floor. Light streamed in through windows high above them. The room was so large it appeared misty as the eye traveled to its furthest edges. A mountain of furniture, silver and porcelain, partially covered in dust sheets, dominated the hall. All the furniture and valuables in the château had obviously been stacked up, here in this one place, guarded by the lone figure who sat at a harpsichord in the center of the room, his back arched over the instrument, his hands moving with precision over the black and white keys.

A modest wood fire smoked in the center of the giant hearth, and in front of it Kate saw a table and chair, both piled high with books and papers. Dirty plates and goblets and jugs were balanced precariously on heaps of letters tied with ribbon. Above the Marquis de Montfaron's head hung a beautiful crystal chandelier which was, without any doubt, the twin of the one the party had seen in Golden Square.

Streams of tinkling notes cascaded from the Marquis de Montfaron's nimble fingers. The music sent shivers down Kate's spine and put tears in Hannah's eyes. It was sad and uplifting at the same time.

"It's beautiful!" said Kate.

But the sound of her voice broke the spell and the elegant figure at the harpsichord wheeled around, white shirt glowing in the gloom. His startled dark eyes beheld an uninvited audience. Before the party could understand what was happening, his arm shot up and he tugged at a cord dangling from the ceiling.

All at once, their vision was filled with yellow. A soft, buttercup yellow. Floating down on top of their heads came yards and yards of silk. It enveloped them. It was as if a tent had collapsed on them, and they all thrashed around, flaying their arms about in an effort to get to the edge of the material.

"Heaven preserve us!" shouted Hannah.

"Run! It's a trap!" cried Peter, but the end of the word was transformed into a cry as what felt like red-hot wires landed on their heads and shoulders. Everyone shook violently and fell to the ground. . . .

Kate was walking through an alien landscape. Past, present, and future were one. She must always have been here. Walking, walking. The only human soul left alive. Not a blade of grass. The carcasses of trees reached up their bony arms to a desolate sky. The stench of corpses. Great muddy pits gashed into once-fertile earth. She could scarcely breathe; the acrid air burned her throat. She was searching for something or someone but she could no longer remember what or who. . . .

"Kate, oh, Kate! Come back!"

Suddenly she was aware of the warmth of a human hand, and as she found herself gripping it, the hellish landscape slowly faded away. In its place rose up the flickering flames of a wood fire and Peter's anxious face staring at her. She gasped with relief and recognition.

"Peter!"

Peter's heart skipped a beat. How happy it made him feel to be called by his own name. Despite the passage of time and his denial, she knew. Whatever it was that made him uniquely Peter Schock was still recognizable.

"No! No, it is I, Joshua," he said. "We feared we had lost you!"

"That's twice you've rescued me—you must be my guardian angel."

"The second? How so?"

"On the ship. I fast-forwarded. . . ."

"Fast-forwarded?"

"Oh . . . I . . . Sometimes I move faster through time than everyone else—but when I touched your hand it stopped."

"On the ship? I was not even aware of it. . . . The girl at the vicarage told me that you were flitting around like a bat in the garden. I think you terrified the poor creature."

"I terrified myself! When it's happening it doesn't feel like I'm going fast. It just seems that everyone else is going very, very slowly. I hate it."

Hannah arrived. "The Lord be praised!" she exclaimed.

"What happened?" asked Kate. "How long have I been like this?"

"An hour or more," replied Peter.

Kate pushed herself up on her elbows and looked around her. She found that she was lying on cushions in front of the fire in the great hall of the Château de l'Humiaire. It was dark. The light of the fire cast giant shadows behind them, and the mountain of furniture next to her seemed so high as to be about to topple down on her. A gleaming silver soup spoon suddenly came at her out of the dark.

"Have a little broth, Mistress Kate. It will give you strength."

Kate sipped a little of the steaming liquid. It was good. She finished it and Hannah gave her some more.

"The broth was prepared by Marie," said Peter. "The Marquis told us that she has been secretly preparing food for him ever since the last of his servants left, six months ago. . . ."

"And unless I'm no judge of character, her husband gave her a black eye for her trouble," said Hannah.

Soon Kate had finished a whole bowl. Hannah refilled it. Peter and Hannah did not take their eyes off her. Kate saw the relief in their faces but also their continued concern.

"Thank you, Hannah. . . . I feel much better. Where is Mr. Schock?"

"He is gone with the Marquis of Montfaron to fetch the wagon and our trunks. In all the excitement we had forgotten the horses. Not that he has anything to feed the poor beasts other than rotten fruit."

Suddenly Kate remembered the yellow silk and the searing pain. She sat bolt upright.

"What did he do to us?"

"The Marquis of Montfaron electrified us!" said Hannah. "He took us for thieves or Revolutionaries come to imprison him. He told us that his late friend, Mr. Benjamin Franklin, used to kill turkeys using the same method with which he was pleased to welcome us into his house! The Marquis realized his mistake as soon as Mr. Joshua gave him Sir Joseph's letter of introduction, and he has scarcely stopped apologizing since. . . . What a terrible thing is electricity! I never felt such pain in my whole life even though it lasted but a second. . . ."

Peter pointed toward the doors that opened out onto the quadrangle.

"Do you see all those great glass jars? They are filled with water, and by some means which is beyond my understanding, they store an electrical current which was transmitted through copper wire threaded through the silk carapace which fell upon us."

"And after the Marquis pulled the silk off," said Hannah, "the rest of us were able to get to our feet, shaken though we were, but not you, Mistress Kate. I do not know the words to describe what happened to you. . . ."

Kate looked from Peter to Hannah and back again in alarm. "What did happen to me? I don't understand. . . ."

"You blurred, Kate," said Peter gently. "Only intermittently. It was as if you were in between states: sometimes solid, sometimes transparent. I know not where you journeyed, but sometimes you put your hands over your ears and your whole body shook as if caught in the blast of some explosion. You wandered into the yard and were looking around you, sometimes frightened and sometimes so sad. . . . Wherever you were, it was a nightmarish place. Once you stooped down as if to pick a flower. And sometimes it seemed as if you were moving far quicker than you normally would and sometimes far slower. . . ."

Kate listened mournfully.

"I saw long trenches cut into the ground. I was in a deserted battlefield. There wasn't a sign of life, not even any birdsong. . . . I picked up someone's broken spectacles. I saw a rifle, half-buried in the mud. I think a lot of people had died there. I could smell it. . . . I've only ever blurred to my own time before. I don't know whether it was past or future! What's happening to me? Every time it happens, I wonder if I'll go back to normal."

Hannah sat down next to her and pulled her close.

"Hannah tried to get you to lie down," said Peter, "but every time she tried to touch you, it was as if she was pushed backward. . . ."

"Maybe the next time I might . . ." Kate's face crumpled. "I might just drift away—and never come back. . . ."

Hannah stroked Kate's hair and wiped away the single tear that rolled down her cheek.

"Don't be anxious, Mistress Kate. Now we've found the Marquis de Montfaron, he'll mend the machine and we'll soon get you home and all will be well."

"The Marquis saw everything," said Peter. "There was nothing we could do to hide it from him. He is convinced that it is an unusual side effect of the electrical shock which you received!"

The fire spluttered as the heavy doors creaked open and a gust of wind seemed to blow the Marquis de Montfaron and Mr. Schock into the galleried hall. A smell of damp night air and horses came with them. All solicitude, the Marquis de Montfaron approached Kate's impromptu bed.

"How fares your mistress?" he asked Hannah. His English was, as Sir Joseph had told them to expect, impeccable, although he spoke with the accent of the South, rolling his r's at the tip of his tongue and pronouncing every syllable with equal and lilting stress.

"She has drunk two bowls of broth, sir; I fancy she is on the mend at last."

"Yes, I'm feeling much better now, thank you," said Kate.

"Mademoiselle," he said, bowing low to Kate, "there are not words enough to express my sorrow for the injury I have inflicted upon you. You travel from England, you brave a terrible storm, you bring me books and news of my family—and how do I respond? I electrocute you like one of Mr. Franklin's turkeys! Although, I admit, never have I witnessed a more dramatic reaction to electricity. It was remarkable, I assure you!"

Kate took a liking to Montfaron the moment his large eyes, the color of ripe chestnuts, smiled at her. He was half a head taller than Mr. Schock, stunningly tall for a man born in his century, but neither stooped nor scrawny. His nose was prominent and aquiline, and he had a strong, angular jaw. Although Kate had spotted no less than three wigs on stands perched on the mountain of furniture, Montfaron wore his own springy hair scraped back in a ponytail. It was black but with streaks of white spreading out from his temples. Now in his middle years, Kate guessed that in his youth his looks must have been striking. She noticed a dimple in his chin. Now his tanned, wrinkled face announced a man who was prone both to laughter and frowning in concentration and who was predisposed to take delight in the world.

"We did not mean to sneak up on you, sir, although it might have seemed that way."

"No, I was at fault. I was too hasty and I hope you will accept my humble apologies."

"Of course, sir. Thank you," said Kate. *He's much nicer than his wife!* she thought.

"Mr. Schock tells me you met my son in Calais and that he is on his way to persuade me to decamp to London."

"Oh dear," said Kate in alarm. "Has Louis-Philippe not arrived yet? Should we go and look for him?"

"No doubt Louis-Philippe has found something to divert him en route. I am afraid I shall have to disappoint him, however. I have no intention of leaving. I have a profound belief in the common sense of the French people. The situation *will* improve sooner or later."

"Have you been able to keep up with the news, sir, despite living in a state of siege?" asked Peter.

"Thanks to Marie, a little. She was in the middle of telling me about the latest atrocities in Paris when her strutting cockerel of a husband arrived and dragged her away. . . ."

"I fancy he'll make her pay for her trouble, sir," said Hannah.

Montfaron sighed and nodded. "I shall do what I can for the poor girl. Her family has worked in this house for generations. . . . Arras is presently overrun with excitable young men with something to prove, and Marie's husband is one of them. An ex-priest, a man by the name of Lebon, is in the ascendant and the young bloods are vying with each other to impress him. . . . And, of course, our Monsieur Robespierre's spectacular success in Paris is boosting morale in the camps. . . ."

"Robespierre!" muttered Mr. Schock under his breath to Kate. "You must have heard of him! He was a key figure in the Revolution—he started off with high ideals but in the end sent thousands and thousands to the guillotine. They called him 'The Incorruptible.'"

"You must have been living in fear for your life, sir," said Peter. "Were you not tempted to join your family in London?"

"And have all our lands and possessions confiscated? No!

While hope remains, so shall I. Besides, I am making progress with my research into the nature and storage of electrical current. I cannot leave my experiments now!"

Peter and his father exchanged anxious glances.

"I am not without friends here," continued Montfaron, "and it may surprise you that I even have some sympathy with the goals of the Revolution. However, I agree that the current madness in Paris makes my situation precarious. Of course, I shall defend myself if I must—it is for that reason that I have been experimenting with my electrical equipment whose efficacy you have unfortunately proved. . . ."

"Yes!" said Mr. Schock, with feeling. "I doubt I shall ever again be able to bear that particular shade of yellow. . . ."

Montfaron laughed. "Ha! I was fortunate to obtain that silk when such quantities of material are so difficult to come by. . . . I scavenged it from a hot-air balloon. It came down in the village pond. The peasants who found it thought that the moon had fallen to earth! And what, I ask you, did they do? Did they examine it or call for a man of science to inspect their marvelous discovery? No! They tried to *kill* it with pitchforks! But I am a poor host. Food is in short supply, alas, but I can at least offer you wine while you explain the meaning of Sir Joseph's message and describe to me the mysterious machine of which you spoke."

Montfaron soon returned from his cellar. "From my cousin in Bordeaux: a Saint Émilion, bottled in 1783. An excellent year."

Mr. Schock gulped. "Oh my . . ."

Peter smiled as he watched his father hold up his glass in front of a candle flame, the better to appreciate its color, and savor every last drop with a look close to ecstasy on his face. Deprived of civilized company for too long, Montfaron was delighted to be entertaining a guest who appreciated his cellar. He slapped Mr. Schock enthusiastically on the back.

"I am happy that my wine gives you pleasure!"

"I have some chocolate," said Kate. "Has anyone seen my backpack?"

Peter passed her the canvas backpack. She untied the cord and rooted about at the bottom of the bag. Unable to find what she was looking for, she pulled out the contents one by one and placed them on the floor: a flashlight, her Swiss Army knife, Megan's mobile, the small brown bottle containing penicillin, and, finally, the bar of chocolate. Montfaron eyed them curiously. She tore open the wrapper, broke the bar into pieces, and passed it around.

"Chocolate, you clever girl!" said Mr. Schock. "And you've managed to resist eating it until now! I *am* impressed."

Peter took a piece; it had been twenty-nine years since he last tasted Cadbury's chocolate. He placed it reverently onto his tongue and let it melt slowly. His eyelids closed and he sighed.

Montfaron, in his turn, offered everyone a clove of raw garlic, whose medicinal properties, he said, were too little appreciated. Hannah looked so scandalized that Peter felt he should answer for her. "I think garlic and chocolate are flavors which do not marry well. Perhaps on another occasion . . ."

"As you wish," said Montfaron.

The Marquis popped some garlic into his mouth and went to fetch a couple more logs for the fire. No sooner was he out of earshot than Peter said to the others: "We shall have to tell him the truth. Else we will be hard pressed to persuade him to return with us."

"I think you're right," said Kate.

Mr. Schock nodded. "Agreed."

Montfaron returned and threw the logs onto the glowing embers; yellow flames licked around them. Kate was glad, for the château was cold.

"So," said Montfaron. "Who will tell me about this curious device?"

It was Peter who began. He decided to speak plainly.

"Kate and Mr. Schock have traveled from hundreds of years in the future to our time by means of a machine which, although it was not designed to do so, has the capacity to transport people across the centuries."

Kate studied Montfaron's expression. Other than a slight twitch in one eyebrow, his face remained impassive.

"It appears that one of the side effects of time travel is a tendency for the subject to return for short periods to their own time—although they are never wholly successful in this attempt. Miss Dyer, in particular, is prone to episodes of 'blurring,' and you have yourself witnessed one of these, which was brought on, or so it seems, by the electric shock."

Peter paused in case Montfaron wished to say something but he merely nodded as if to say, "Continue."

"Our reason for seeking you out is this: The machine was damaged when it landed on uneven ground and is currently stored in secret at Kew Palace in the hope that we can find someone who can attempt to mend it. The President of the Royal Society himself, Sir Joseph Banks, has examined its workings and is of the opinion that you are one of the very few men in Europe to whom he would dare entrust its possible repair. If it cannot be repaired, Miss Dyer and Mr. Schock will be stranded forever in a time which is not their own."

Montfaron stared at Peter and then busied himself poking the fire until he could contain himself no longer and exploded into laughter. He could not stop; tears started to flow down his cheeks and he dropped the poker. His laughter was infectious, and soon Kate and Hannah started to snicker. Peter resisted for longer but when he saw Montfaron leaning against the mantelpiece, his whole body vibrating with merriment, alternately holding his stomach and wiping his eyes with his sleeve, it set him off too.

"It's not funny! It's true!" said Mr. Schock, which made everyone laugh even more.

"I have always admired," panted Montfaron, "the Englishman's sense of the absurd. . . ."

"But I *am* from the future!" spluttered Kate. "You see this? It's a flashlight powered by a battery. It produces a beam of light you can direct anywhere."

She pointed the flashlight at the ceiling and switched it on. Nothing happened.

"Oh dear . . ." Kate started giggling again. "I've got some spare batteries somewhere."

Montfaron wiped his eyes and blew his nose. "Upon my word, I have not been so diverted in months. How I have missed good company. But I must tell you straightaway that even if your machine existed, I could not possibly abandon all of this. . . ." Montfaron made a sweeping gesture with his arm and the general hilarity immediately evaporated. Montfaron, however, still seemed highly amused. "Describe to me how you travel backward in time. Do you witness events unfolding backward? Do you see old men growing younger until they are newborn babes?"

"No," said Kate. "You are flung into a long, dark tunnel and are surrounded by spirals of light. You lose consciousness and then, when you wake up, you find you are in a different time."

Montfaron scrutinized Kate's face. Her sincerity was plain. The smile faded from his face.

"So your tunnel is a kind of corridor which leads to many rooms. . . . You are not obliged to pass through each room in sequence to reach your destination, for the corridor gives you access to the room of your choice . . . which implies that individuals can exist in different times simultaneously . . . which, in turn, implies that all times could be seen as unfolding in an eternal now. . . . How fascinating!"

"Have you heard of the guillotine?" asked Mr. Schock abruptly.

Montfaron looked puzzled. "Yes. There is one in Paris; it was used for the first time in the spring, I believe. Dr. Guillotin invented it as a humane way of dispatching criminals. He is to be applauded. Death is instantaneous—better that than to be burned or hanged or broken over the wheel. . . . Why do you ask, Mr. Schock?"

"As a student I took classes in French history. Most of it went in one ear and out of the other, but some of it stuck, despite my best efforts," said Mr. Schock. "If I scour my memory for a few pertinent historical facts, I think they'll add up to a pretty accurate prediction of your future."

"You have my ear, my dear sir. . . ."

"Over the next few months the Revolution enters a new period: the Terror. And the guillotine becomes its symbol. Even the King himself is not spared. . . ."

Montfaron gasped. "*Non!*"

"Robespierre is the guiding force. Anyone suspected of anti-Revolutionary tendencies is killed. There is a bloodbath: Tens of thousands are slaughtered all over France. As for the ex-priest, Lebon, I remember him, too. He became known as the Butcher of Arras. The town square will soon be stained with the blood of all the citizens he sends to the guillotine. . . ."

"This is not so diverting," said Montfaron and started to pace around the room in the darkness.

There was silence and everyone looked at each other uneasily.

"Was all that true?" whispered Kate in Mr. Schock's ear.

"You think I'd make something like that up?"

Kate shrugged and searched in her bag for spare batteries. After a while Montfaron broke his silence.

"Robespierre was born and brought up but a few miles from here. It was on account of him that I grew interested in lightning conductors. A fellow in St. Omer erected one which his neighbors feared would *cause* fires rather than *prevent* them. . . . He was ordered to take it down, but the stubborn fellow resisted. A certain lawyer named Robespierre defended his right, very eloquently, I might add, to keep it. True eloquence, as they say, consists of saying all that needs to be said and nothing more—he possessed that very rare gift. That case made his name. I recall that we were both guests at a supper given by the mayor before the Revolution."

"You met him, then?" asked Mr. Schock.

"I did. He was articulate and dressed with great care. I recall that we both enjoyed the cherry tart, but he would not permit himself a second helping. I should never have taken him for a mass murderer. . . . How can you expect me to believe such terrible things?"

"But even if you don't believe me," said Mr. Schock, "don't the wishes of your wife and son mean anything to you?"

Montfaron glared at him. "You have already made it perfectly clear that you would have me return with you to London, sir. I believe I have already given you my answer."

Peter put his hand on his father's arm. "It would be best to say no more," he whispered.

"Let there be light!" said Kate suddenly.

She switched on the flashlight and directed it at the galleried landing above. Montfaron's eyes widened. Ropes of cobwebs were illuminated and giant shadows appeared. Motes of dust could be seen dancing in the beam of light. Montfaron walked over to Kate and held out his hand.

"Will you permit me?"

Kate handed it to him and he swept the narrow beam across the room, illuminating objects in the near, middle, and far distance. Kate took it back briefly and unscrewed the bottom, revealing the batteries.

"See these? Electricity is stored in there, I think. . . . They're called batteries. Of course it's only a cheap flashlight—you can get much better ones."

"If only I could show this to Volta!" cried Montfaron.

Kate smiled. She was glad her little stash of twenty-first-century artifacts was coming in useful. . . . "And this is a mobile phone. You can use it to talk to people at the other side of the world if you want to. . . . Not that you can use it here, of course. But I can set it to play some music."

Kate took back the flashlight and gave him the mobile. Strains of Megan's favorite song echoed around the château. The Marquis was speechless. He examined the two miraculous objects and took hold of Kate's backpack, zipping and unzipping a compartment.

"You have given me much to think about," said Montfaron finally. "I suggest that we continue our discussion in the morning. My answer, however, will remain the same. I cannot abandon the

Château de l'Humiaire. I should like nothing more than to study your device, but, you know, the greatest skill is that of understanding the true cost of things. In this case the cost is too high."

Kate, Peter, and his father looked at each other in despair. They had come all this way only to have to return to London and be back at square one. Mr. Schock opened his mouth to argue, but Peter put his hand on his shoulder again and shook his head. His father sighed noisily.

They slept as they could, uncomfortably for the most part, using dust sheets to keep warm. Kate heard the Marquis toss and turn, doubtless trying to make some sense of what he had heard and seen that evening. Two or three times she saw the glow of flashlight under Montfaron's sheets—he had taken it to bed with him! Kate smiled to herself. She wished she could give him one as a present.

Nor could Kate find any repose. It suddenly came back to her how Hannah had addressed Joshua as Master Peter earlier that afternoon. She said it a moment before lightning struck the tree, and so much had happened since then, it had slipped her mind. She could not very well accuse Joshua a second time in so many days, but she could try to get the truth out of Hannah.

Kate slept fitfully for a while and dreamed that she was back home. She could see the farmhouse in Derbyshire on a misty, late winter afternoon. The last of the sunshine slanted onto the glistening slate roof and onto bare-branched trees. A robin's sweet melody rose up from the hedgerow, and she could hear the trickling of the little stream. There was another sound: the crunching of tires on the dirt drive, and then she saw her dad and Peter in a large white police van. Inspector Wheeler stepped out, followed by that sergeant who was always with him. . . . Then Molly pushed in front of Peter, barking joyfully, and bounded toward the house. Now Peter got out and stood for a moment on the drive, dazed and unsure what to do. There was a dark-haired woman standing at the front door whom she did not recognize. When the woman saw Peter, she let out a little cry and started to run toward him, arms outstretched. "Mum!" he cried. And they clung on to each other, sobbing and smiling and exclaiming, beside themselves with joy. But then she saw her own mother, rooted to the spot, watching the reunion. Her dad was walking toward her. "Kate?" her mother mouthed. Her dad shook his head slowly. Her mum put her hand over her mouth and her eyes filled with tears. Molly was running from one person to another barking excitedly. . . .

Kate awoke with a start. "Don't cry, Mum," she found herself saying. "I'm okay. Please don't give up hope. We'll find a way to get back home!"

Never had she had a dream like it. It seemed more real than real life. . . . The images were vivid and crystal clear, the colors rich and intense. And unlike other dreams, which leave traces so fragile that the merest breath of conscious thought wafts them away, the memory of this dream stayed with her, solid and unchanging. She lay there listening to her companions' rhythmic breathing. The fire was almost out. A few embers glowed red in the grate. But moonlight poured in through the high windows above, painting the top of the furniture mountain a silvery blue. . . . All at once Kate knew, with the same certainty she felt when solving a puzzle, or putting a name to a face, or matching a memory to a certain taste, she knew with every atom of her being. She had not dreamed it. Kate suddenly started to tremble and could not stop. Now she could see the future!

TWENTY-ONE

DUST AND ASHES

*In which Tom shows his mettle, Anjali
has cause to regret her actions, and Lord Luxon
plants an idea in the Tar Man's mind*

Tom was alone in the apartment that night. He was lying in one corner of the capacious sofa watching television, knees up, white mouse scampering up and down his trouser legs. Every so often Tom would help himself to a handful of honey-roasted cashews, a recent discovery. He offered one to the mouse who immediately began to gnaw her way through it, rotating it in her delicate paws. He did not understand why people minded so much about his mouse. Anjali complained that she smelled. He picked her up by the tail and sniffed her soft belly—*he* couldn't smell anything. Worse, she had got into trouble with Blueskin. He kept bundles of twenty-pound notes in a cardboard box in the sideboard, and when he was delving into it in order to pay the ex-marine who was to pilot the helicopter, he found that the notes were covered with mouse droppings and were nibbled around the edges. Not that Blueskin cared much for currency that could fly away in a gust of wind or that you could *burn*.

Gold, which you could bite to test its purity and whose weight you could feel in the palm of your hand and which grew warm in your pocket, was better. And how was the mouse to know that she was nibbling her way through a small fortune?

Tom had eventually lost his fear of the remote control and he flicked through the TV channels, holding it well away from him, mesmerized by the moving images but too unused to interpreting this medium to properly appreciate and enjoy what he saw—although the magic box did stop him from feeling lonely. When a character on the television pointed at someone off the screen, Tom found it hard not to look around to see who it was. If Anjali saw him she would crack up laughing. She was fond of what she called "sitcoms." Sometimes Tom would stand in the doorway watching Anjali watching television. It still struck him as odd to see her sitting by herself and laughing out loud at the flat glass screen. Even more curious was the laughter apparently coming from audiences inside the television set. Tom correctly took this as a signal that he, too, should find whatever was happening on the screen very funny. But more often than not he did not understand the joke. He wondered if he ever would.

It was true that Tom found a number of things in the twenty-first century confusing and worrying and would go to great lengths to avoid them—public transport, for instance, and supermarkets, and the sort of coffee shop where people invariably jumped the queue in front of him while he gawked at the number of ways he could order his coffee. On the other hand, never in his wildest dreams did Tom imagine he would experience this level of comfort. Anjali, who currently had a room in her granddad's maisonette that overlooked a railway junction, said that this was luxury. Tom should see where they lived—not that she would ever let him, he thought, for Anjali was proud. Blueskin was becoming so wealthy, he thought, from the sale of the pictures procured for him by Lord Luxon, perhaps he might dare suggest that he buy Anjali an apartment too. Like this one. She would like that. Perhaps one in this very building. . . .

From time to time Tom would awake convinced that he still lived in the filthy wreck of a house, if you could dignify it with such a name, that he shared with the Carrick Gang on Drury Lane. At night only a little straw came between him and the cold, damp floor, where lice, fleas, and hunger were his constant companions. Apart from those rare occasions when the Carrick brothers would tolerate his presence in the Black Lion Tavern, he was cold from October to April. But here all was comfort and warmth and cleanliness and light. He sniffed his sleeve: He smelled of soap! He pinched his waist. There was flesh and not just skin between his fingertips! Who would have thought it? He blessed the day that he had found Blueskin. Tom laughed out loud. But immediately an awful thought made his stomach clench. How long could he stay here? And would he have to go back to his old life one day?

It was usually Anjali and occasionally Blueskin who answered the telephone, so when it rang Tom shot up from the sofa but then stood uneasily next to it, his hand hovering over the receiver, unable to bring himself to actually pick it up. It rang four, five, six times, and then stopped. Tom breathed a sigh of relief, but then the answerphone kicked in and he heard the reassuring sound of Anjali's prerecorded voice inviting the caller to leave a message after the beep.

BE-E-EP!

"Tom! Tom! . . . Pick up. Please!"

The voice sounded scared and out of breath. Tom snatched up the receiver.

"Anjali!" he said.

"You gotta help me, Tom! There's someone after me. . . ."

She was running as she spoke and her breath came out in big bursts.

"Where are you?" cried Tom in alarm. "I shall come to you at once."

"Sssshh! Don't say nothing for a sec. . . ."

For some moments Tom could only hear indistinct sounds— distant traffic, a door slamming perhaps, footsteps echoing in an empty street—but he could not be sure what he was listening to. Keeping the receiver glued to his ear, he ran over to fetch his sneakers, knocking the handset off the table in his panic. He pushed his feet into his shoes and stood awkwardly, every muscle tense, straining to hear anything. Finally he heard Anjali's voice once more. She sounded relieved.

"It's okay. False alarm—he's gone. I lost him."

"Who?"

"That lowlife who attacked me in the underground. You

remember I told you how Vega Riaza dislocated one of his gang's shoulders?"

"Yes, I remember."

"It was him. Must have followed me."

"Tell me where you are!" Tom realized he was shouting. "If he hurt you, I'll—"

"Keep your hair on! I told you, I lost him. I'm a couple of minutes down the road. If you put the kettle on, I'll be with you by the time it boils."

"No! Let me come for you," he started to say, but Anjali had already switched off her phone.

Tom walked to the sink like an automaton and put water in the kettle. Then he paced frantically about the kitchen for a couple of minutes. He got out her mug and put a tea bag in it. The minutes seemed to drag into hours. How did she *know* she'd lost him? What if he was waiting in some dark alley for Anjali to make the first move and show herself? That is what the Carrick Gang would have done. . . . He could no longer stand the torture of waiting. He dashed toward the stairwell but skidded to a halt outside the lift. If Anjali *was* in trouble, he did not have time to run down twenty-one floors. The down arrow was illuminated, the lift was already there. All he had to do was press the button for the doors to open. He had seen Blueskin and Anjali do it enough times. . . . Sweat pricked at him. Suddenly he started to run down the first flight of stairs, for he could not muster up the courage to incarcerate himself in that terrible metal box. But then, from far below, echoing up the emergency stairs, noises of a scuffle reached him. He stopped in his tracks and listened with all his might. . . . Nothing. Had he imagined it? Adrenalin pumped around his body. He no longer had any choice. He turned on his heels and bounded back up the stairs and jammed his finger on the lift button. The doors swooshed open and he stepped inside.

When the doors closed and sealed him in, his heart leaped into his mouth. He was trapped and alone. He took a deep breath and waited. Nothing happened! What did he have to do? Panic set in. Then he saw the long row of illuminated buttons, and he realized he was going to have to press one of them. Kettles, telephones, TVs, power showers—everything had a button to make it work in the future. . . . But which one should he press? And what would happen if he pressed the wrong one? He ran his fingers through his hair, beside himself with anxiety, imagining all the while that Anjali was in mortal danger. Then he saw the numbers next to them and it occurred to him that they might refer to the floor. One? Surely that must be it. Could "one" stand for the first floor? But then what did the "G" stand for below it? And the "B" below that? Should he get out of the lift and run down? But how, at this point, did he get out? Tom hit the button with the number one next to it and stepped back, eyes closed, fists clenched at his sides. He heard the terrifying sounds of machinery engaging and then the floor of the lift lurched. . . . The descent! It was beginning! Tom's stomach felt that it had been left behind on the twenty-first floor. He stared wildly about him and put the flat of his hands on the walls, bracing himself for the impact when it hit the ground. . . . But after a few seconds he could no longer detect any motion. Cautiously he unpeeled his hands from the walls and watched as, ever so slowly, the doors slid open. He shot out of the lift backward before they closed again and found himself in a narrow corridor with stairs at one end.

Tom ran downstairs three steps at a time before he heard muffled sounds coming from above. He zipped around and started climbing upward instead. He turned the corner to go up the next flight of stairs just in time to see a tall, blond youth throw himself at Anjali's legs and bring her down so that she lay sprawled out over the hard steps. For a second everything seemed to slow down: Anjali was screaming and holding on to the back of her head and the youth was pulling her up by her hair. Now he was pinning her against the wall, his left forearm pressing against her collarbone. Blood dripped from her nose. The youth drew back his right arm. Bracing herself for the inevitable blow, Anjali strained to turn her face to the wall as far as it would go. She could smell his breath.

"I told you I was gonna teach you a lesson. . . ."

Tom flew up the half-dozen steps and sprang onto the blond youth's back, grabbing hold of his right wrist before it smacked into Anjali's face. For an instant Tom looked into Anjali's eyes and they were dark pools of terror. Tom's weight pulled the youth off balance and he was forced to take a step backward, allowing Anjali to slip out and escape up the stairs. She turned around at the top and watched, too shaken to help him, as the youth, a good foot taller than Tom and at least twice his weight, set about shaking him off. Tom clung on tightly like a monkey and put both hands over his opponent's eyes so that he could not see. The youth reached up and grabbed hold of Tom's wrists. Tom was no match for him. The youth levered open his arms, heaved him off his back and pushed him violently away. Tom fell backward, rolling over and over, his thin body juddering over every step, until his head cracked against the corner of the wall adjacent to the lift shaft. The sickening sound reverberated around the stairwell. For an instant Anjali and the blond-haired youth struck strange poses on the stairs, like statues, staring, with unblinking eyes, at Tom's motionless body. Then Anjali hurtled down the stairs and knelt down next to him. She laid her cheek on his chest and listened, staining his sweatshirt with her blood; she felt for a pulse on his wrist and on his neck; she took his limp hand in hers and squeezed it. Finally she looked back at the youth in wild-eyed despair.

"You've killed him!" she shrieked.

The youth started to come slowly down the stairs, his eyes fixed on Tom's white face. "It wasn't my fault! I didn't mean to do it!"

Anjali leaped up and pounded his chest with her fists.

"Murderer!!"

He shoved her roughly away.

"First time I saw you I knew you was trouble. You're a jinx, you are. . . ."

The youth disappeared down the stairs to the ground floor.

Anjali dropped heavily to the floor and sat on her heels, looking down at Tom, holding his hands in hers. Blood and tears
trickled down her white face and her lips trembled. She sat
in the silence for she did not how long, her mind numb with
shock. She gave a start as cables clanked and machinery suddenly whirred into action next to her. Someone had called the
lift and would soon be on their way down. Anjali panicked. It
was her fault, in the end, that she was kneeling next to Tom's
lifeless body, wasn't it? She looked at her blood on his clothes.
She couldn't risk being discovered here and there was nothing
more she could do for him. Anjali stood up, but as she did a
small movement caught her eye. Tom's white mouse appeared
at the neckline of his sweatshirt, whiskers twitching. Anjali
hesitated for an instant, bent over, and grabbed hold of the
tiny creature. Then, very gently, she kissed Tom's cool forehead.

"I'm sorry, Tom. . . . I'm sorry for everything. . . ."

Anjali fled from the building, unseen, and blinded by her
own tears.

It was a Sunday, and most Londoners slept on under a thick
blanket of slate-gray clouds that, as forecast, would not shift.
Hyde Park was deserted apart from the odd jogger. The Tar
Man strode around the Serpentine. His face was drawn, his lips
pressed together; there was a bitter expression on his face. On
the other side of the lake a lone swimmer dived into the freezing water with a splash. A moorhen squawked, its cry echoing

around the quiet park as its oversize, webbed green feet scurried across the surface of the water.

The Tar Man had been invited to dine in Mayfair the previous evening with the entrepreneur who had expressed an interest in the oil paintings of George Stubbs. He had anticipated that he would walk away from the evening with a commission for a major art theft and an invitation to become a member of the most exclusive club in London. Instead, the hypocritical, puffed-up socialite had looked down his superior nose and had harangued him until the Tar Man's self-restraint broke. At least he had managed to hurt him before he found himself escorted off the club premises by four liveried thugs and kicked, literally, out onto the pavement. When he had tried to hail a cab, a nod from the doorman, who clearly put a lot of work the cabbies' way, meant that none of the taxis would stop for him, and he was forced to walk down the street knowing that all eyes were upon him and with the barrage of abuse still ringing in his ears.

"You're scum," the entrepreneur had said. There was something about his face that reminded the Tar Man of an emaciated eagle. Grandeur, cruelty, Olympian disdain. Like Lord Luxon, he was old money. How the Tar Man resented all those centuries of unearned privilege, looking down his hawk-like nose at him.

"You're the scum of the earth and always will be. How could you *possibly* think I was serious? All the cash and the Rolex watches, all the fancy apartments and designer labels, all the trappings of what you think is success don't fool anyone. Do you really think we would tolerate your kind in this club? Do you really imagine that you could threaten me with your sordid little blackmail threats? Half of the greatest political minds, scientists, lawyers have passed through our doors at one time or another, with the finest pedigrees. . . . But who are you? *What* are you? I'll tell you what you are: You are a gnat, a nothing, a deluded grotesque, and we would not have you taint the air that we breathe. . . ."

The Tar Man's headbutt had split open the skin of his noble forehead, though his blood was not blue but red like anyone else's. . . .

The Tar Man walked on around the Serpentine. After this little incident he had visited Lord Luxon and, making light of it, told him what had occurred. He noted that Lord Luxon did not attempt to refute the insults but merely suggested that he try another club. He had gone on to say that although gaining power and influence was important, his priority should remain the acquisition of the antigravity machine. After all, with such a device, would it not be possible to change the course of history? The words had resonated in his mind, but it was only now that the idea grew, like yeast, as the Tar Man reflected on who he was and what he had become.

The entrepreneur's words had stung so much, he thought, because they were not so far from the truth. All the money in the world would not change who he was: a thief, a talented villain, a manipulator of men, a black-hearted rogue, a murderer. Other men might command respect, admiration, love—what did he inspire? Fear? Horror? Hatred? And why should he care if he *did*? What would he have become if he had been meek and respectable and weak-willed like the rest of humanity? Ground down with daily toil until his body gave out? Starving in a flea-pit? Dead in a ditch? And if he *had* done bad things, the world had done worse to him. All the same, he pondered when it had all started to go wrong. Was it the day he had been imprisoned for a crime he did not commit? Or was it earlier? The first time he had stolen a loaf of bread, shortly after his father had died? Suddenly he saw the face of Gideon Seymour, with his direct blue eyes and his priggish view of the world. The mere thought of Gideon being his brother brought with it a powerful spurt of anger in his chest which he could not explain. Yet the thought still tugged at him. Why had his brother chosen one path while he . . . He refused to continue with the thought but the thought continued despite him. What if, he reasoned, the antigravity machine could change the course of history, change the course of *his* history. . . . If he could press a button and change that pivotal moment in his life, would he press it?

Dring-dring . . . Dring-dring . . . Dring-dring . . . With a start the Tar Man realized that his mobile phone was ringing. It would be Anjali. It was only ever Anjali. But what was she doing calling him at this time in the morning? He idly wondered if she could still contact him if he had faded back to 1763.

"Vega?"

"Faith, Anjali, who else would it be?"

"You gotta stay away from the apartment for a while. There's police cars and ambulances crawling all over the place. . . . There's been an accident. . . ."

"Your voice is shaking."

The Tar Man listened in silence to what Anjali had to say, looking all the while at the water and the trees and the clouds reflected in it.

"Vega? Are you still there?"

The Tar Man stood motionless, holding the mobile phone to his ear.

"Vega?"

"I do not wish to see your face again, Anjali."

There was a long silence, then Anjali said: "I . . . I have Tom's mouse. Do you want me to—"

"His *mouse*!" shouted the Tar Man. "Should his mouse be some kind of consolation?"

The Tar Man flung the mobile phone into the center of the Serpentine and started to run. He ran halfway around the lake, over a small bridge and along Rotten Row, the dirt bridle path where, even now, Londoners exercise their horses. A girl trotted past him on a glossy black mare. All at once the Tar Man was sick of the future. He wanted to return to his own century. He wanted to feel horseflesh between his knees and the wind in his face. He grabbed hold of the reins and pulled the girl off the saddle so that she fell backward onto the soft ground. She lay, helpless, in the dirt as he mounted her horse. He shrugged off the gold Cartier watch from his wrist and threw it at her. It landed on her belly. She picked it up and looked from the watch to the Tar Man and back again.

"For your horse," he said and galloped out of the park into Knightsbridge.

The Tar Man rode without thinking for many miles through the quiet streets of Belgravia, Chelsea, and Westminster. He galloped on and on, but no matter how fast he rode, the once heady scent of the twenty-first century had lost its appeal, contaminated with a whiff of the despair that had dogged him all his life and had turned him into what he was. The Tar Man allowed the steaming mare to come to a halt at the north side of Westminster Bridge. London had not changed, but all he could taste was dust and ashes.

TWENTY-TWO

THE CHALK MINES OF ARRAS

In which the party finds itself in
a difficult situation

In the still of the night Kate did not at first realize that she was fast-forwarding. She had been unable to sleep since her startling vision of young Peter arriving back safe and sound with her father at the farm. Nor could she get her mother's distraught face out of her head. Alone, in the dark, she felt that she was clinging to a reality which was constantly shifting: What would happen to her next? What *could* happen next? First blurring, then fast-forwarding and now this . . . She did not *want* to see the future. While it was a relief to know that Peter was back in the twenty-first century, what if she started to see her own future? What if she saw terrible things, wars and natural disasters that she could do nothing about but live in dread of them happening? Nor did she want to know how her own life was going to pan out: what she would do for a living, if she would marry, the children and grandchildren she might have . . . how her parents would die, how *she* would die. Kate suddenly grew angry at what a truly dreadful thing the scientists had unleashed. Peter had once told her that fish must always swim forward through water else they drown. Surely it was the same for humans moving through time? Humans can't fly, they can't breathe in water, their lives can only unfold through time in one direction. *We're not* meant *to know how it will all end,* she thought, *and once we've moved on there's no going back. At least, that's what it should be like. . . .*

Kate felt drained, utterly wrung out. How she wished she could feel her mother's arms around her right now. How she wished she could share her problems with Megan. Instead, she was falling further and further away from the life that she knew and loved. Worse, she was transforming into this strange, frightening creature who was blown about space and time like a leaf in an autumn gale.

All of it would be easier to bear, Kate thought, if she had some control over these unpredictable episodes. She had almost given up trying to blur back to her own time since leaving Middle Harpenden. What talent she had for it seemed to have been left behind in 1763 with Peter. Kate idly wondered if she could *make* herself fast-forward. She tried to imagine becoming detached from the broad reaches of time that carried everything along with it like a great river; she pictured stepping out of it and plunging into a faster-flowing current. But this did not work and nothing happened, or at least, so she thought.

Hannah was snoring and Mr. Schock kept mumbling half-finished sentences. Once he called out for Peter. She was too alert now to get back to sleep and in the end decided to get up and explore. It was only after she had crept up the stairs and roamed up and down the moonlit corridors and poked her head through slits in the deep stone wall to look at the stars that she realized that her attempt to deliberately fast-forward had, at some point, been successful. Kate happened to find herself in yet another high-ceilinged room that smelled of damp and dust. A harvest moon, large and yellow, hung in the clear sky and by its light, in a corner of the window, she saw a fat spider sitting at the center of its web. As she gazed up at the spider, waiting for it to move, the quadrangle below entered her angle of vision. It was at that moment she realized she was fast-forwarding. She could have been looking at a photograph. A man in striped trousers and a soft cap was entering the yard. He held a pistol in one hand and a flaming torch in the other. Captured in that instant of time, the blue and yellow flames looked like billowing silk. . . . It was Sorel! She was sure of it. Behind him trotted two horses pulling a large wagon, and following the wagon were four more men. All were frozen in mid-step. She could not see the other four as clearly since they were half in shadow, but all were burly, powerfully built men. Kate could easily guess the purpose of this visit: the capture of four English spies caught plotting together with an aristocrat. That would boost Sorel's reputation with his Revolutionary friends. . . .

Kate pelted out of the room, along the corridor and down the stairs three steps at a time. She tried to wake Mr. Schock, but it was like trying to shake a tree trunk. Could she *stop* fast-forwarding at will too? Poor Hannah did not respond either.

Kate ran around the room, peering through the window, examining Montfaron's electric booby trap with all its jars full of water and wires leading from them, and wished she knew how to set it up again. Then she considered going outside and disarming Sorel and his gang, but the heavy door was locked and she could not find the key anywhere. Finally she gave up. Her father's voice came to her. Use your head, Kate. No good ever came from panicking. *All right,* she thought, *I can't disarm them, and I can't warn anyone but at least we can be prepared. . . .*

By the time Kate fell backward on Peter while trying to pull out an ormolu table from the furniture mountain, the doors were barricaded against all comers. Tables, chairs, chests, piles of books, a statue of Venus, a globe . . . Peter cried out more in surprise than in pain. Kate sighed with relief. She was back.

"That's the third time, Joshua!" she said. "You *are* my guardian angel!"

Then she hurried from one person to another, shaking them.

"You've got to wake up! Sorel has come for us with some men and they're armed!"

"Is this your work, Kate?" cried Mr. Schock incredulously, indicating the barricade and struggling to disentangle himself from a dust sheet.

Kate nodded.

"Why on earth didn't you wake us up so we could all help?"

Suddenly there was a gigantic crashing and splintering of glass and timber as a casement window at the far end of the room imploded under the impact of axes. Getting in through the window had clearly been an easier option than breaking down the door. Kate berated herself: "Stupid, stupid, stupid . . ." Montfaron ran to the mantelpiece and plucked two swords that were hung on the wall above it. He tossed one to Peter, who caught it by the hilt and raised it above his head with both arms in readiness. A second later they saw five men jump through the window carrying flaming torches and pistols. Flickering flames exaggerating the shadows on their faces, Sorel's men immediately trained their pistols on the five of them.

The heavy wagon wheels rolled over the pitted road under the stars. Sorel drove, two men walked ahead with flaming torches, and two went behind to guard the prisoners. Everyone winced with every jolt, for with their hands tied together they could not brace themselves against knocks. The air was chill, and a ghostly mist rose up from the land after all the heavy rain of the previous day. They heard frogs croaking in the silence of the night, and as they approached Arras, a nightingale sang its heart out in a walled garden filled with apple trees.

At first the party had been in genuine fear of their lives, but Montfaron's unfailing courtesy and quiet acceptance of events had, at least for now, defused a dangerous situation. Peter did his best to hold Kate's hands in his and gave her reassuring smiles every time their eyes met. Peter was impressed with Montfaron. He had nerve and good instinct and he clearly had the measure of Sorel. After Montfaron had failed to convince him that the motive behind his English guests' visit was not espionage but science, he applauded him for his good citizenship and agreed that the party would accompany him on condition that their case be formally submitted to the proper authorities first thing in the morning.

Sorel's brooding temperament, however, put the party on their guard. He reminded Kate a little of Joe, the leader of the Carrick Gang, in that he put everyone on edge, even the men he had brought with him. While being careful to address them as "Citizen," the men mostly treated their prisoners with respect. The Marquis de Montfaron had, after all, been an important figure in their community, and the memory of how things had been could not be sponged away so quickly. Sorel, however, was provocative and unpleasant. He had spat on the floor, clearly aiming for Montfaron's shoes, and would not allow anyone to take anything with them other than the clothes they stood up in, although, in the darkness, Kate had managed to secrete several items from her backpack in the lining of her dress.

Montfaron insisted that as Sorel was acting purely on his own initiative and had not brought with him a formal warrant for their arrest, the authorities would be obliged to release them in the morning. "Sorel does this for personal glory," he whispered. "Do not fear, all will turn out well, you will see. . . ."

Kate kept opening her mouth to tell Mr. Schock about her vision of the future, but it was not an appropriate moment to announce to Mr. Schock that she believed Peter would manage to get home—even if they might not. Meanwhile Montfaron hummed a tune and tapped his feet.

"I am pleased that you are able to keep so cheerful, Sir!" said Mr. Schock.

"A man's happiness or unhappiness depends as much on his temperament as on his good fortune. . . ."

By now they had entered Arras itself, and Montfaron pointed out a small sapling surrounded by protective iron railings.

"Behold," he said. "The Tree of Liberty. I saw it was planted amidst great celebrations in the spring. It was the last time I dared come openly into the town. I pity the person who has the responsibility of keeping that young tree alive. . . ."

Soon afterward they came to a halt in a great square surrounded on all sides by houses built in the Flemish style. The storm had swept the heavens clean and above them the velvet sky was studded with stars. The moonlight was strong enough for Kate to see ornate, curved gables and, below, covered arcades which would protect pedestrians from the elements. Sorel climbed down from the wagon and disappeared down a narrow passageway, leaving the four men to guard them. His footsteps echoed into the night. After what Mr. Schock had said, Kate wondered how long it would be until the shadow of the guillotine fell over this beautiful square.

"I fear he plans to hold us in the subterranean tunnels," whispered Montfaron. "Pray do not be alarmed when they take us underground. There have been chalk mines here for many centuries and there are miles of tunnels underneath the town. People store cheese here, and wine, as well as, it seems, those suspected of being against the Revolution."

"Are we to be thrown into a dungeon, Mistress Kate?" asked Hannah.

"If we are, I'm sure the Marquis will soon get us out."

Peter looked at his father and Montfaron. "We are three against four," he whispered. "Should we not attempt to escape now, before it is too late?"

Five against four! thought Kate but restrained herself from correcting him out loud in the circumstances.

Mr. Schock lifted up his tied wrists and shook his head. "We're unarmed. . . . We wouldn't stand a chance."

"Sorel would be happy to have an excuse to shoot us," said Montfaron. "And, in any case, such an action would be an admission of guilt. Do not fear, the people of Arras have common sense and good hearts. When we are brought before the authorities we shall be accorded our rights."

Suddenly Kate turned to Mr. Schock. "I must ask you something while I can. Does Peter's mum have short, dark hair with a fringe that flicks up like this?"

Kate indicated the shape with her hand.

"Well, yes," said Mr. Schock, puzzled.

"I thought so. . . . I think I'd better tell you something in case I don't get another chance. I saw the future tonight. And you're just going to have to believe me because I know that it's true. I

416

saw it as clearly as if I were there myself. My dad has brought Peter home. I saw them arrive at the farm and I saw him running into his mum's arms."

Peter's stomach lurched and Hannah stared meaningfully at him.

"The Lord be praised," she said.

Mr. Schock was not sure how to react. "I'm sorry, Kate, but how can you possibly know that?"

"You'll just have to take my word for it. I've never been surer of anything in my life: Peter is safe."

Mr. Schock scrutinized Kate's face and could not doubt her sincerity. "In which case the sooner we get out of this little mess and go home to see if you're right, the better for all concerned."

Peter slowly drew in his breath. After everything else that had happened to Kate, why should she not be able to see the future, too? Soon they were all bundled out of the wagon, but for Peter all thought of immediate danger was banished as a picture of his twelve-year-old self running into his mother's arms burned itself onto his mind. How many lives could one person lead? How was it possible to make any sense out of the mystery of time and existence?

When Peter opened his eyes again, he was surprised to see Sorel reappear with a woman. It was Marie. He held her firmly by the elbow with one hand while in the other he held a sheet of paper. He marched his wife right up to the Marquis and wafted the document in his face. Marie could not bear to look

417

at Montfaron and she turned her bruised and swollen face as far to one side as she could, biting her lip. Sorel said something to Montfaron and then pushed his wife roughly away. Peter watched the Marquis pale visibly. He did not need his father to translate what Sorel had said. Marie was going to testify against them. She had declared them to be spies and enemies of the Revolution.

They were made to descend a steep stone staircase. Kate peered down into the gaping darkness and her heart sank. Les Boves, the ancient chalk mines of Arras, were eerily beautiful. At first there were stone columns and vaulted ceilings, but as they progressed deeper into the subterranean tunnels they walked on dirt paths which were treacherously slippery while the walls were of roughly hewn stone. Twice the Marquis de Montfaron cracked his head on the ceiling. These mines were not constructed to accommodate men of his height, and he had to walk with a stoop. They could scarcely see where they trod, for the stinking tallow candles that guttered in alcoves above them cast too weak a light. Cool, damp air rose up from the depths as if from a crypt. It was a maze: Kate doubted that she could find her way back up to the surface unaided. They walked past a shrine of sorts and Kate noticed fossils embedded in the tunnel walls. Eventually they arrived at a man-made cave, dug out of the limestone. There were some oak wine barrels in one corner and metal bars enclosed it. One of the men opened up the creaking door with a large, rusting key and indicated that Hannah and

Kate should enter. Peter watched in horror as the door was locked and he saw Hannah and Kate cling to each other. There was only just enough room for the two of them. Water trickled down the walls.

"This is intolerable!" Peter shouted suddenly. "Kate and Hannah must not be held in such conditions!"

The men did not understand what he said, but their response was to push him forward down the passage. He lost his footing and fell heavily, owing to his hands being tied, and he hurt his elbow and shoulder. Sorel kicked out at him. Mr. Schock and Montfaron protested and struggled against their captors in order to help Peter up but he slipped and grazed his temple against the limestone. Kate watched in despair as her three companions were manhandled down the tunnel. Before they disappeared out of sight, Peter managed to turn around. Their eyes met.

"Peter!" she found herself crying, but he had disappeared.

Soon Kate could not even hear their steps. She and Hannah were left alone in the semi-darkness. Hannah started to cough and the sound of it seemed to echo forever in the interminable, cool tunnels.

"It is Peter, isn't it?"

"How could you say such a thing, Mistress Kate?"

Kate held her peace and her eyes gradually became accustomed to the semidarkness. She took out the items she had secreted in her skirts.

"Here," she said, passing Hannah some chocolate. "Perhaps this will make us feel better."

Kate tested the flashlight. It still worked, although she knew she must save the batteries. She had also brought her Swiss Army knife, Megan's mobile, and one of the watches. Now that things could not get much worse Kate felt strangely calm. Slowly it dawned on her that there was only one person who stood a chance of getting them all out of here. And a plan started to form in her mind. Even if she failed, it was worth the attempt . . . but it all depended on her ability to fast-forward at will. She flipped open the pen knife and started to saw through Hannah's bonds as best she could with her bound hands.

Kate had been calling at the top of her voice for some time before one of Sorel's cronies eventually responded. She pointed at Hannah, who was slumped against one of the barrels. Hannah started to cough violently.

"Very sick," Kate said slowly and loudly. "*Malade. Très malade.*"

The man nodded and shrugged his shoulders. Kate mimed picking up a cup and drinking from it, while trying not to let her loosened bonds fall off. When the man did not rush off enthusiastically to fetch them refreshments, Kate held up the wristwatch, mimed drinking from a cup, then pointed first at the watch, then at the man. He looked more interested and put his hands through the bars to reach for the watch. Kate stepped backward and the man grinned. He nodded and disappeared.

"Just don't say anything for a bit, Hannah, I've got to concentrate. . . . And, Hannah?"

"Yes, Mistress Kate?"

"Good luck. . . ."

Hannah sat on the cold, hard floor with her hands on her lap and watched Kate as she stood, eyes closed in concentration, her forehead resting against the iron bars. Minutes passed. The guard did not reappear and Kate remained stubbornly solid. Any hope that the plan might actually work began to evaporate. But then Hannah heard footfall echoing in the distance and she looked toward the dark tunnel.

"He's coming back, Mistress Kate!"

When Hannah turned to the spot where Kate had been, there was nothing but empty space. Hannah shivered. *'Tis no wonder Kate is looking so pale,* she said to herself. *All this is enough to make your blood freeze.* Then, as planned, she lay out on the floor and allowed her mouth to flop open. When the guard arrived, and saw that one of his prisoners had gone and that the other was lying unconscious, he set down the jug of water he was carrying and took out a bunch of keys. He hesitated for a moment, wondering if this was a trap, but then opened the door anyway. He did not feel someone brush past him. Nor did he notice the bunch of keys vanish into thin air. . . .

Speed and time being relative, once Kate was fast-forwarding, it seemed that she had to wait for an eternity while the man unlocked the door. His movements appeared so slow to her as to be barely perceptible. She could not bear to watch his progress because it made her feel so impatient. She had to make up ways to occupy the time, like trying to remember every girl's name in her class and then how many people she knew in the entire world. All the while she paced up and down the tiny cell in order that she might appear invisible to the man.

At last Kate was able to squeeze through the gap in the door and then, with difficulty, for nothing felt quite the same when she was fast-forwarding, she grabbed the flashlight and her knife, pulled the rusting set of keys out of the lock, and ran into the dark tunnel. She switched on the flashlight and hoped that the batteries would last longer when she was fast-forwarding. Soon there was a fork in the tunnel and she chose to go right. Immediately afterward there was another fork and she was about to turn left when she realized that she was bound to get lost. So Kate retraced her steps and, using the corkscrew attachment of her Swiss Army knife, scraped a continuous fine line on the wall. She walked on and on. Where had they put the others? A panicky feeling started to rise up inside her. The tunnel forked yet again and there were some rough steps leading to a higher level. She could not decide which direction to take, and for the first time since their arrest, Kate's courage failed her. She crouched down, resting her chin on her knees and clutching her ankles. She shivered in the cold and immense silence and felt oppressed by the unimaginably colossal weight of the rock above her. She wondered if she would ever see the light of day again.

It was some time before she felt able to continue. She walked across the entrance to one tunnel, about to go down another, when something stopped her in her tracks. Garlic! She could smell garlic! It had to be the Marquis de Montfaron! Kate ran helter-skelter down the tunnel and soon came across a series of caves used for storage. She walked past mountains of cheeses and dozens of barrels of beer and then she saw them. She trained the flashlight on two frozen figures.

"There you are!" she cried.

The men were in the middle of an animated conversation. Montfaron had his mouth open in a small *O* shape, and Peter was gesticulating with his hands. But there was no sign of Mr. Schock. Kate took the set of keys and tried one after another until she found the right one.

"I can't stop, I've got to find Mr. Schock!" she shouted as she pulled wide the door and continued down the tunnel, training her light on the floor to avoid tripping up. But there was no sign of him, and no more storage caves, so she decided to return the way she had come. By the time she passed Montfaron and Peter again, they were both looking and pointing at the open door.

"Yes!" she exclaimed. "Get a move on! You're free! I could do with a bit of help!"

She ran up the rough stairs she had passed earlier and now charged down that tunnel. At least she no longer felt cold. There, to her great relief, a short way down the tunnel, she discovered Mr. Schock seated on a small barrel and surrounded by giant cheeses—and he was not alone. Kate gasped and put her nose through the bars to confirm her first impression. Mr. Schock was in the process of wrapping his pale blue jacket around someone's shoulders.

"Louis-Philippe!" she cried.

Kate peered at him. He looked terrible. There were beads of sweat on his forehead, he was hollowed-eyed and his face had lost all its color.

"Poor Louis-Philippe!" she said.

She fumbled with the keys, becoming increasingly impatient. "Done it!" she said finally.

Kate gently stroked Louis-Philippe's hair. She spoke, even though she knew that they could not hear her, or that she would sound like a buzzing insect. "I hope you're strong enough to walk. . . . Try to get upstairs, if you can. I daren't leave Hannah alone with that man any longer."

Kate ran so fast she got the stitch and had to slow down, stumbling along the uneven, treacherous paths, following the marks she had left on the walls, holding her skirts and the keys in one hand and the flashlight in the other. Finally, she reached her destination and skidded to a halt.

The scene which confronted her was surreal, and one which, in other circumstances, would have made her laugh out loud. The man was cowering, holding his arms protectively over his head. Smashed pieces of a crockery water jug lay on the floor, while Hannah stood half in, half out of the doorway, holding the jug handle in her hand. She looked as fierce as a hissing cat.

Kate stood for a moment and scratched her head, looking rather like a moving man weighing up how he was going to get a large piece of furniture up the stairs. Then she grabbed Hannah round the waist and pulled with all her might to get her out of the cell. Her flesh felt hard, like wood. Kate was getting nowhere pulling so she decided to push instead. She crawled in front of Hannah and, using the weight of the man as leverage, shoved with head, shoulders, and the flat of her hands until her face grew red and her breath came out in short grunts. All at once Kate felt something give. She wriggled out to admire her handiwork. Hannah was falling backward, but very, very slowly. While Kate waited, she sorted out the correct key and put it into the lock. Then she pulled off the man's jacket, folded it into two and placed it where she estimated Hannah's head would hit the ground. Kate could not help laughing as Hannah's body seemed to float in midair before coming to rest, featherlike on the ground. Like thunder after lightning, the crashing sound came several seconds later. "Ouch," said Kate sympathetically.

Kate closed the door, locked it, and tossed the keys out of reach. She felt rather pleased with herself. Hannah's expression slowly turned from one of surprise to pain. "Sorry, Hannah!"

Kate stood and willed herself to stop fast-forwarding. She tried to banish the thought that perhaps this time she would *never* return to normal which meant, of course, that she thought of nothing else. Kate started to panic and decided to distract herself by going to see how the others were getting on, particularly Louis-Philippe, who had looked so ill. At the back of her mind, too, she wondered if her lighthearted comment about Joshua saving her had any truth to it. And it *had* happened three times. . . . Could it be possible that, like a lightning conductor grounds the electricity in a storm, Joshua was able to ground *her*?

By the time Kate reached Peter and the Marquis de Montfaron, they were beginning to run toward her, up the tunnel. In the weak light cast by a guttering tallow candle, the men looked like two magnificent sculptures, punching the air with their fists and kicking back their heels. She walked all around them as if she were in a gallery. Was Joshua her guardian angel? She noticed the tiny dark hairs on his fingers. Kate reached out her hand slowly toward his. His warmth seemed to flow into her even before she touched him, and as she gripped his hand, Kate exploded back into the normal flow of time. The noise of the men's pounding feet, their panting, and their exclamations of surprise all but deafened her. *It has to be Peter!* she thought. *It has to be! There must be some link between us!*

"It *was* you that opened the door!" said Peter. "I was certain it was! You are an extraordinary girl, Kate! I always knew it!"

She stared back at him with glittering eyes. "There's no time to lose," she cried. "I've let everyone out and I've locked the guard in the cell where they put me and Hannah. Let's get out while we can!"

They followed her up the tunnels and after a few moments they heard the sound of more footsteps behind them.

"That will be Mr. Schock and the other prisoner," said Kate.

"The *other* prisoner?" asked Montfaron.

"Yes," said Kate, deciding to let him discover for himself who it was once they were safely out of the chalk mines. "Follow us!" Kate shouted behind her.

Soon they reached Hannah and the angry guard.

"Oh, thank the Lord!" she said. "He's been throwing himself at the bars like a caged bear! I fear he might break through if he carries on much longer."

The guard glowered furiously at them through the bars. Kate was now so out of breath that she did not answer but merely grabbed hold of Hannah by the elbow and pulled her along with them. Mr. Schock and Louis-Philippe were still trailing behind. The desperate group ran onward and upward until they reached the final set of stairs. Peter went on ahead to the entrance to see if all was clear, and when he saw that it was, he motioned silently for everyone to follow him.

Kate and Hannah stole out into the cold night air, walking on tiptoes, their hearts pitter-pattering as their eyes darted anxiously around them. The covered arcades were dark and the many pillars obstructed their view of the square. Suddenly, behind them, a shot rang out, echoing down into the tunnels, and there was a cry. A man's cry. Peter tore back as did Kate and Hannah. A powerful smell of gunpowder met their nostrils and then, at the bottom of the first set of stairs, they saw Sorel with a smoking pistol in his hand. Across his feet lay a motionless figure in a pale blue jacket.

"Dad!" screamed Peter and hurtled down the stairs blind to everything, pushing both Montfaron and his father out of the way. He hurled himself at Sorel like a madman, knocked the pistol out of his hand, sending it skidding across the floor, and punched him repeatedly until he collapsed, insensible, and slumped against the wall of the tunnel. When Peter turned around, breathless and wild-eyed, the figure in the blue jacket was pushing himself up off the floor, bruised by his fall but otherwise uninjured. Peter stared at him in confusion. And then Montfaron hurried down the stairs.

"Louis-Philippe?" they both exclaimed at the same time.

Nobody moved.

Kate gasped. "It *is* true, then!"

Mr. Schock slowly descended the staircase, his eyes wide in disbelief.

"Peter?" he said incredulously. "Can it really be you?"

TWENTY-THREE

A BARGAIN, A GIFT, AND A REQUEST

*In which the Marquis de Montfaron strikes a
bargain with the party, Peter sends a gift to the future,
and the Tar Man requests Lord Luxon's help*

The party commandeered Sorel's wagon without scruple and made their way out of Arras through a maze of quiet back streets, wrapping sacks over their heads and shoulders in the guise of peasant farmers. Peter drove, which gave him an excuse to keep his eye on the road rather than face his companions. Louis-Philippe, so feverish as to scarcely understand what was happening to him, dozed fitfully on his father's shoulder. A deep, hacking cough frequently disturbed him, but he would soon drift back into sleep. Soon they had left Arras behind. They traveled without speaking through the quiet of the night, listening to the croaking of toads and to the hooting of owls. No one liked to break the silence. Kate sat smoldering behind Peter, her gaze boring into the small of his back as she tallied up the sum total of his deception. It was Montfaron who spoke first.

"What it is to be a father, *n'est-ce pas*, Mr. Schock? Our offspring never fail to surprise us."

Mr. Schock had been staring at the palms of his hands, deep in thought.

"I don't understand! *Why* couldn't you tell me, Peter? Now I know the truth, I'm happy but sad at the same time. Don't you *want* to come home? When I first saw you in Kew Gardens . . . there was something about you—I couldn't put my finger on it. But when you said that you were Joshua, I never dreamed . . . I just don't know what to say."

Kate could contain herself no longer. "Well, I know what to say," she cried. "How *could* you lie to us like that! After everything we've done to find you! And you must have persuaded Hannah and Queen Charlotte to lie for you too. . . ."

"I didn't *want* to do it, Mistress Kate," said Hannah. "But, in fairness to Mr. Joshua, I mean Master Peter, he did it with the best of intentions. . . ."

"What? It's okay to imply to your best friend and your father that you're dead? Peter should be ashamed!"

"Kate . . . ," said Mr. Schock weakly. "No doubt Peter had his reasons. . . ."

Peter pulled on the reins, bringing the wagon to a halt in the middle of fields bathed in moonlight. He twisted round to face Kate and his father.

"I wish with all my heart that I could have kept my secret to the end. I regret the distress that I have caused you—above all since the motive behind my deception was to *spare* you pain."

"What are you talking about?" cried Kate.

"I have waited to be rescued my entire life. And I have lived a good life, with good people. Although, sometimes, preoccupied by the possibility of my rescue, I have forgotten to appreciate what I had. A lesson I learned, long ago, is that timing is all. Through no fault of your own, you arrived too late. For you did not come back for *me*, the man you see before you. Rather, you came back for a Peter aged twelve years old with his whole life in front of him. I can assure you that the memory of these precious days which I have been allowed to spend with you will stay with me forever. But your search is not yet over; you have not found that boy. I wanted to spare you the pain of knowing that you were forced to leave me behind."

Peter took up the reins and clicked his tongue; the horses strained against the heavy load and soon the wagon was juddering along, once more, down the dark and lonely road.

Dawn was breaking, gray and cold, by the time the Château de l'Humiaire came into view. At first they mistook the wisps of smoke for cloud, but when they smelled fire, the Marquis de Montfaron immediately jumped off the wagon and ran on ahead. Soon they caught up and found him staring, stony-faced, at a smoldering bonfire in the quadrangle. The heavy doors into the château gaped open like a wound. The hall was empty, gutted. Anything the looters had not wanted was already ashes.

"Oh, sir," gasped Hannah, when she recognized the charred remains of decades of correspondence. "It is too cruel."

Mr. Schock picked off a blackened book from the top of the bonfire. It was Volta's book on electricity which they had brought from Golden Square. The Marquis de Montfaron turned on his heels and walked away without saying a word.

"I suspect," said Mr. Schock, "that the Marquis will be returning with us to London."

Kate ran into the hall to see if her backpack had been taken. It was nowhere to be seen, but she still found what she was looking for, tossed to one side and lying in a dusty corner behind the door: the bottle of penicillin for Louis-Philippe.

When they inspected the ravaged hall, they made one consoling discovery. The looters had either forgotten or missed the valuable chandelier. Standing on a horse's back while the rest of the party held the animal still, Peter managed to cut the exquisite object down, and afterward Hannah packed it up with scraps of an old curtain.

Presently they heard the Marquis de Montfaron calling to them from the other side of the drawbridge. He refused to set foot back in his home. He had, he said, too many good memories of the Château de l'Humiaire to wish to contaminate them with bad ones. If ever there could be a signal to him that it was time to cut his ties with the past, it was this. Kate, Peter, and Mr. Schock walked over to the drawbridge to hear him better.

"After what I have witnessed these last few hours," he shouted over to them, "I am persuaded that you have told me the truth. I therefore have a proposal to put to you. I will accompany my son and yourselves back to London, and I shall attempt to repair your machine on this condition: that, were I to be successful, you will allow me to travel to the future with you. What say you?"

Kate and Mr. Schock exchanged glances. "I reckon it'd be better to arrive home with an eighteenth-century aristocrat than not to arrive at all," said Kate.

Mr. Schock nodded his head. "Agreed," he said.

"Agreed," said Kate.

So it was that Kate and Hannah, two fathers, and two sons, set off on the arduous journey back to London. To Montfaron's surprise, Louis-Philippe showed a remarkable improvement after only two doses of Kate's penicillin, although his twenty-first-century companions were at a loss to explain what it was or how it worked. Even so, they decided to stay overnight at a comfortable inn in the village of Inxent in the Course Valley so that he could recuperate a little before the sea journey. After supper, while the sun set over the lush valley, the party left Louis-Philippe to rest and walked by the trout stream. Hannah and Kate soon returned to the inn so that father and son could talk alone. There, until well after dark, they talked and reminisced and, sometimes, argued by the gently babbling water. Mr. Schock talked about Peter's mother, and Peter, in his turn, told his father the story of his life. There were tears and there was laughter and there were heavy silences.

Meanwhile Kate sat for a while with Louis-Philippe while he sipped beef broth in bed. It had been prepared for him by the innkeeper's wife, who was so taken by the handsome invalid that she could not do enough for him.

"It must be great to be so good-looking," Kate said to

Louis-Philippe. "But doesn't it get on your nerves? Getting so much attention, I mean?"

"You flatter me!" he replied. "You would call me plain if you saw my cousins."

Kate laughed. *What a family!* she thought.

"Have you forgiven Peter yet? I saw him sneak in to speak to you before supper. . . ."

"Forgiven him! That pompous, sanctimonious fellow . . ."

Kate's face dropped. "Oh, don't say that!"

Louis-Philippe laughed out loud. "I was teasing. Of course I have forgiven him. He feared for your safety. I understand that. I *might* have been at fault . . . a little. Though I paid for it by not changing out of my damp clothes! Had Sorel not captured me in Montreuil, I should still be lying in a ditch too weak to move! In truth, he probably saved my life!"

"Peter is all right, you know. . . ."

Louis-Philippe laughed again and nearly said something, but stopped himself.

"What?" asked Kate. "Go on. . . ."

"I took Peter, at least at first, for a sensible, quiet fellow, but now I see a more passionate vein. There is something in his manner. . . . He is very . . . protective, I think. As a boy, he must have been fond of you."

Everyone could see that Mr. Schock was torn. He was at once desperate to persuade Peter to come back with them and, at the same time, aware that if Kate's prediction was correct, his young son might already be there waiting for them in the twenty-first century. It was a conundrum no one could solve. Peter, in any case, refused to be persuaded. His father had come back in search of a twelve-year-old boy, not a man who had already reached middle age.

"You might be worrying over nothing, Mr. Schock," commented Hannah none too tactfully, at breakfast. "For all his learning, the antigravity machine might flummox even the Marquis de Montfaron—begging your pardon, sir."

Now that his secret was out and her anger had cooled, Kate felt curiously shy with Peter. She kept stealing glances at him and tried to see the boy within the man and the man within the boy, fascinated and moved by the transformations effected by time. Kate wished that her young friend could see the man that he would become; she thought that he would be pleased.

She contrived to sit next to Peter on their way to Calais to catch the Dover packet.

"If we *do* manage to mend the antigravity machine," she said to him, "and the twelve-year-old you *has* managed to get back home, what should I say to him about you? And is there anything *you* would like to say to *him*?"

Peter burst out laughing. "Upon my word, Kate, your questions are challenging! Where do I begin . . . ?"

"Take your time," she said. "It's ages till we get to Calais."

After another mile or two, Peter turned to Kate and said: "I cannot tell you how you should describe me—that is your affair. But I have three pieces of advice for myself at twelve years old.

The first is this: no life is perfect, but he is luckier than he can possibly imagine with the one that he has. For years, I went to sleep picturing every detail of the life that I had lost. It makes me sad to realize that it was only when I no longer possessed it that I understood how lucky I had been. The second is this: that his father truly loves him and he must never doubt it. And as he grows up, he will see the truth of this more and more."

"And the third?"

"That he should never let go of you."

"That's a strange thing to say!"

"Yes, I suppose it is—yet it is how the words formed in my head."

Despite a rough crossing and heavy rain all the way between Dover and Shooters Hill, two days later the party arrived in Lincoln's Inn Fields. John pronounced them all to look thinner and paler and more fatigued than when they left. When Hannah was once more restored to her favorite chair in the kitchen, her face was wreathed in smiles and she took hold of Kate's hand and squeezed it.

"Perhaps it is wrong of me to wish it," she said, "but I hope that the Marquis de Montfaron does not find a way to repair the machine too quickly. . . ."

The Marquis did not delay, to his wife's disappointment and Kate and Mr. Schock's relief, traveling to Kew Palace to meet with Sir Joseph. He examined the machine and declared it to be a mystery to him. He did not dare dismantle it for fear of being unable to put it back together. His strategy, he declared, would be to draw it.

"*Draw it!*" exclaimed Mr. Schock as he read Montfaron's note, brought to Lincoln's Inn Fields by the Queen's messenger. "What good will that do?"

"Perhaps it's his way of paying attention to detail," suggested Kate. "Like dissecting frogs in biology lessons and then drawing what you see. It helps you . . . get it."

Mr. Schock did not seem convinced and his mood grew gloomy and pessimistic. Kate, too, wondered if her prediction was correct. Perhaps they would never get home.

The following day they had an unexpected visit. The Honorable Mrs. Byng's youngest daughter, Lizzie, had come down to London from Baslow Hall with her husband, who had business to attend to in the city. She had been charged by Gideon Seymour with delivering a precious present for Peter. Gideon had ordered a copy to be made of his book, which finally, after all these years, he had completed to his satisfaction: *The Life and Times of Gideon Seymour, Cutpurse and Gentleman*. Gideon had also sent a message. It had been too long since he had seen Peter; he urged him to come home to Hawthorn Cottage as soon as he was able. They would go trout fishing at Ashford-on-the-Water and persuade Parson Ledbury to come too.

"Dear Gideon," said Kate to Peter after Lizzie had left. "I do understand why you wanted to keep all this from him. All the same, I should have liked to have seen him again."

⊷⊨◉○◉⊨⊶

Ten days later, at breakfast time, another messenger arrived from Kew Palace. The Marquis de Montfaron summoned the party to come as quickly as they were able. He would await them in the Red House.

By three in the afternoon quite a crowd had gathered on the top floor of Kew Palace, where the antigravity machine had been secreted. Queen Charlotte was present, as was Sir Joseph Banks, the Marquis de Montfaron, of course, and Kate, Peter, Hannah, and Mr. Schock. The anticipation was unbearable. Kate was feeling pessimistic and tearful. How could anyone from the eighteenth century even begin to understand the workings of a NASA antigravity machine? Was this to be good news or bad? She steeled herself; perhaps she had better get used to the idea that she would never see her family again.

The Marquis turned to the expectant group. He held up a pile of papers covered with intricate and beautifully executed drawings of the antigravity machine.

"I have examined this miraculous device to the best of my ability and must admit defeat: Its workings are clearly so advanced in comparison to anything our century has produced that I find myself as helpless as a young child told to mend a pocket watch."

Kate's heart dropped. *I knew it*, she thought. *We're stranded.* She looked out of the window at the view of the Thames and the fields beyond and tried to hold back the tears. She felt Hannah take hold of her hand and squeeze it. But then she looked over at Mr. Schock and Peter, and they did not look the least bit downcast. Montfaron was smiling at them; his eyes were twinkling.

"However," he said. Never had Kate been happier to hear a "however." "Yesterday evening I noticed a small panel at the back of the device which I had neglected to investigate, so concerned was I with the inner workings of the machine. I unscrewed it with a fruit knife and found what appeared to be a narrow glass tube filled with mercury. A wire was attached to one side of the tube and I could see plainly that a wire *should* have been attached to the other side—but it had become detached and hung loosely next to it. This gave me reason to think that were the tube of mercury level, and were both wires attached as intended, an electrical current would flow through it. I consulted with Sir Joseph and he concurred. I reattached the wire and . . . perhaps a demonstration is in order. Sir Joseph, will you help me tilt the machine so that it is level?"

"With pleasure, sir."

"Miss Dyer, Mr. Schock," said Montfaron, "is it true that the antigravity machine will only function if it is level?"

"Yes!" they both cried at once.

"It has a fail-safe device built into it," said Kate. "It won't even start unless it's on the level."

"As I thought," Montfaron smiled.

The two gentlemen scientists manhandled the machine until it was perfectly level.

Suddenly there was a humming noise like a fridge being switched on.

"Oh, my goodness!" gasped Kate. "I don't believe it! You've done it! You've actually done it!"

"Bravo, Montfaron! Bravo!" cried Peter.

Mr. Schock slapped his hand to his forehead. "All that for a loose wire!"

It was decided that they would leave the following day, at dawn. Montfaron returned briefly to Golden Square. When his wife heard of his plans to abandon her again to go on a expedition of great scientific interest, the details of which he was unable to disclose, she was too angry even to say good-bye. He shouted— through the locked door of her boudoir—that he was a man of science and this was an opportunity which would never arise again. The Marquise declared that she would have preferred to have had a husband who took any number of lovers rather than one who worshipped at the altar of knowledge—for she would never be able to tempt him away from *that* rival's compelling attractions. Louis-Philippe, who was by now fully recovered, tried to understand his father's need to constantly push at the boundaries of human knowledge. Nevertheless he was hurt that his father would leave his family again so soon to go on a journey from which he might never return. He kissed his father good-bye but the pain in his expression was not lost on the Marquis de Montfaron.

Footmen carried the antigravity machine downstairs and laid it carefully in a part of the grounds which, as a frequent visitor to the gardens in the twenty-first century, Mr. Schock knew to be relatively quiet.

Kate, Hannah, and the Marquis de Montfaron held back and watched father and son from afar in what they knew would be their final conversation. In the distance, walking across the emerald turf toward the pagoda, Queen Charlotte took Sir Joseph's arm and would not, as she had promised, look back after saying farewell.

"My dear Mr. Schock," she had said, "I can only imagine how full your heart must be on this difficult day, and yet, as a parent I tell you this: You have the unique good fortune of knowing that your son will become a man you can be proud of. And I hope that it is of some consolation to you that Peter has found happiness with his adopted family. I have kept a weather eye on your son since his arrival in our century, and I promise you that I will continue to do so. God bless you and your family, Mr. Schock. May you be soon reunited with your young son and may you cherish him as he deserves to be cherished."

Kate and Hannah had said their good-byes too, and now stood, arms about each other's waists, watching the two men walking away quietly together. It was almost too much to bear, and both fought a losing battle to hold back their tears. Kate had lain awake thinking of a good-bye speech to say to Peter, but in the end all she had been able to do was run up to him and hug him.

Peter had kissed the top of her head. "You are an extraordinary person. I thought so as a boy and I know it now."

"You thought so then!"

"I did. When I was left stranded here, I often cried myself to sleep because I wished you were still here with me." Then he reached into his pocket and drew out a slim parcel. "This is Gideon's diary. I want you to give it to the young Peter. He can read of the life that he might have had. . . ."

"And if we don't find him?"

"In which case, I hope *you* will find something of interest in it. . . . I used to love Gideon's stories. He would sit me under the oak tree at Hawthorn Cottage and transport me to places I would never see, nor would I want to. And, as time went on, as you will see, I became a part of those stories."

Kate took the precious parcel and held it in her hand.

"You asked me if there was any advice that I could give to him. I have written it down in a letter which he will find within the pages of the book. God bless you, Kate. I wish you every happiness that life can afford."

Kate's throat felt too constricted for her to say even another word. She nodded vigorously. Kate watched him walk away, but suddenly he turned round again.

"I'm still the same, you know—on the inside. But you'll find out. Perhaps, in another life, I might have found out with you."

In her hand, along with the book, Kate clutched the miniature frame which displayed a silhouette, black on white, of Peter's profile, cut by Queen Charlotte herself. It would be a permanent reminder of Peter's nose and the proof of his ancestry.

Meanwhile the Marquis de Montfaron stood silent and

respectful, close by, his arms behind his back, surveying the pale sky streaked with pink. Inwardly he was ablaze with excitement at what he knew would be the most important journey of his life.

Peter and his father now stood looking at the antigravity machine, an incongruous object in this beautiful garden. "And you're not afraid of what will happen to you if we find your younger self?" asked Mr. Schock.

"A little. I asked Montfaron for his opinion, now that his fate is tied up with mine. He believes that nothing in the universe is ever lost. A life lived, surely cannot be *un*lived. He said that he does not profess to understand how Nature will contrive to accommodate the consequences of time travel, but contrive it she will. . . ."

"I hope he's right. . . ."

"When the powers of the intellect prove insufficient, blind faith is, I believe, our only alternative. If I cease to exist, at least I shall not be aware of it!"

Peter laughed. His father did not. He put an arm around his father's shoulder. "Much good has come out of our brief time together, has it not? I shall grieve, but I shall also rejoice. It is strange that by traveling into the past, you have seen a vision of the future. You came in search of the child and found the man he may become."

"Look at me," said Mr. Schock, wiping his eyes, "a pathetic, quivering wreck. While my own son stands next to me, a rock, with more strength and self-restraint and wisdom than I suspect I shall ever have. I shall tell your mother how proud she would be of you. How I wish that—"

"It was not to be, Father," interrupted Peter. "I knew from the start that it was not to be . . . and yet, I feel blessed, for you have shown in your actions that you are proud of who I have become, and in that knowledge I feel at peace. Child of the future, I now accept with all my heart that it is *this* century which has made me and that I shall never leave it. No longer will I forever be looking over my shoulder to see if my history has caught up with me."

The two men, one blond, one dark, stood in silence together, close and distant at the same time and more aware of the hand of fate than they ever had been before in their lives.

"I am so thankful," said Mr. Schock finally, "that 'I hate you' will no longer be the last thing which my son said to me. Those three words have eaten into me like acid for so long. . . ."

"I think it must surely be clear to you that your son loves you and always did," said Peter.

There was nothing left to say.

With no witnesses other than the blackbirds and thrushes and chaffinches that chirruped and twittered in the branches, the antigravity machine liquefied in the bright morning light and vanished into another century. Peter and Hannah joined Sir Joseph and Queen Charlotte at her cottage, and they stood watching the kangaroos hopping between the trees, and the Queen talked about the carpet of bluebells which in the future, she now knew, would be visited each year by crowds of Londoners, grateful to be welcoming in the spring.

"My Lord!" called the Tar Man in the darkness. "I have come to request your help."

Lord Luxon groaned and heaved himself up onto his elbows to peer at his ex-henchman at the bottom of his bed. He blinked and tried to focus on his insubstantial form.

"Blueskin?"

"You told me that if I were to find the machine, I could change history. Of late your words have given me much cause for thought and I have come to a decision. Fate has not been kind to me in my life. I have a mind to go back in time to tip the scales in my favor. I want to start my life afresh."

"Blueskin! You intrigue me! Indeed, you astonish me! Has life in the twenty-first century lost its flavor? Do you already tire of wealth and luxury?"

The Tar Man shook his head.

"To speak plainly, Lord Luxon, time is of the essence and this is not the moment for idle conversation. I have hired spies to keep watch on the policeman and the scientists. They have ingenious devices. I can hear their conversations as if I myself were in the room! I have this very hour learned of the location of the machine. It is in a valley in Derbyshire. But I have also learned that the scientists fear the consequences of time travel and plan to destroy the machine as soon as they are able."

"Destroy it!" exclaimed Lord Luxon. "Are they mad?"

"As you say. I plan to bring it back to 1763 where they cannot touch it. But I also know that the journey will render me as helpless as a newborn babe. It will be some hours before I am myself again. I need an accomplice whom I can trust. I would ask of you, my Lord, that you meet me at an agreed place to stand guard over my person and the machine. . . . I shall, of course, make it worth your while. I may even take you to visit the future which so holds you in its thrall. . . ."

Lord Luxon's eyes shone. "Blueskin, to be able to go some way to make amends for my disservice to you in the past will be payment enough. Where should I meet you?"

The Tar Man threw down a map onto the bed. "You will need to set off directly and travel through the night, for there is no time to lose. I have marked the precise spot. Wait for me there, by the stream, under cover of the trees."

TWENTY-FOUR

THE HARVEST BALL

*In which Peter attempts eighteenth-century dancing and
Gideon finds that someone has been sleeping in his bed*

Twelve-year-old Peter Schock awoke with a start when one of the carriage wheels dropped abruptly into a deep rut. He was propped up between Gideon Seymour and Parson Ledbury, and found that he was slumped, cheek creased, and dribbling ever so slightly, against the Parson's solid shoulder. As they bumped over the rough track that led to Hawthorn Cottage, Peter's nose rubbed up and down the Parson's sleeve. It smelled of port and snuff and hair powder. Peter blinked until the world came back into focus and breathed in the pure, cool air. He was content for a while to watch Bess, the Parson's bay mare, trot calmly along, pulling the chaise through the fragrant night. The fiddler's tune continued to play in his head and lines of girls still formed and re-formed, swirling in front of his eyes in their skirts of billowing pastel silks. Peter had barely been able to follow, let alone imitate, the intricacy of the steps which seemed second nature to the rest of the room. A small shoal of Byng girls had continually swum around him at the Harvest Ball, alternately demonstrating the dance steps and collapsing on each other's shoulders in fits of giggles at his ineptitude. Their elder brother, the Honorable Sidney Byng, who had been surprisingly kind to Peter since Kate's departure, was forever shooing the "gels" away and had made it clear to Peter that if he did not care to dance, he should not feel obliged to do so.

The small glass of punch pressed on him by the Parson, whose special recipe it was, had immediately caused his head to spin, and Peter had retreated to a corner of the ballroom at Baslow Hall where he had stood, swaying in time to the music, a vacant smile flickering over his face. After a while, a tinge of the sadness and loneliness—which this evening's festivities had eased for the first time in a month—returned. He had hoped to have been rescued by now and the uncertainty of his situation was hard to bear. If Kate had been there with him, this would have been such a different evening. He would not even have minded if she had laughed at him—which doubtless, knowing Kate, she would have done. Not, he suspected, that *she* would have fared any better.

From the dance floor, Gideon had flashed him an encouraging smile and had signaled for Peter to come and join the throng. But Peter had shaken his head. With a slight shrug of his shoulders Gideon had continued to swing his partner energetically around in time to the music which soon swept the pair back up the room. His current partner was Hannah, whose sparkling eyes and pink cheeks were the picture of gaiety, for she loved nothing better than dancing and she had found a partner whose steps were as light as her own. As the Honorable Mrs. Byng's new estate manager, Gideon had been in great demand at the ball, and he had barely sat out a dance during the entire evening. He had been the object of much curiosity, as newcomers to that part of Derbyshire were few and far between, but Gideon had swiftly secured a favorable verdict and he was pronounced to be both handsome and personable by one and all.

Mesmerized by the interweaving rows of dancers, Peter had started when Mrs. Byng spoke into his ear.

"I am pleased that Mr. Seymour finally persuaded you to come, Master Schock. It is a merry occasion, is it not? And, see, I am wearing the necklace which family tradition dictates I wear to the Harvest Ball and which you and Mr. Seymour did so much to protect from thieving hands."

"Yes, thank you for inviting me, Mrs. Byng, I'm . . . er . . . having a great time. . . ."

Mrs. Byng permitted herself to put an arm around his shoulder.

"I want you to know, Peter, that you will always receive a warm welcome at Baslow Hall, and I hope that until your—predicament—is resolved, you will undertake to visit us very often. We have all grown most attached to you."

The warmth in Mrs. Byng's voice, the Parson's punch, and the unbearably sweet strains of a violin all conspired to break Peter's resolve never to cry about his situation. He stared fixedly at the precious necklace which adorned Mrs. Byng's neck while he struggled to rein in his emotions, but the glittering diamonds grew misty and began to sparkle in all colors of the rainbow. Peter turned his face as far away from Mrs. Byng as he could.

"Peter," she said. "There is no shame in grieving for what has befallen you—and you are among friends. Come, the hour is late and you are grown pale with fatigue—I shall ask my cousin to take you to your bed."

Several of the ladies had looked more than a little disappointed as Gideon escorted Peter out of the ballroom alongside a perspiring Parson Ledbury, who dabbed at his brow and bid his farewells in a booming voice over the clamor of the crowd.

Now Gideon, Parson Ledbury, and Peter rode under the infinite dome of the night sky toward Hawthorn Cottage, which would be, for who knew how long, Peter's home. Peter sat up and stretched.

"Ah-ha! The young master awakes!" said Gideon. "I feared I would have to carry you to your bed. I am glad of it, for my feet are sore with so much dancing."

"You dance well, Gideon, but as for you, young Master Schock, I think it fair to say that you are the worst dancer I ever clapped eyes on! Indeed, I'll warrant folk would pay to see your attempts, for you would be certain to put smiles on their faces."

"Do not heed the good Parson," laughed Gideon. "If the

tables were turned, Parson Ledbury's mastery of twenty-first-century dancing might also be the cause for merriment. What say you, Peter?"

A grin appeared on Peter's face as he pictured Parson Ledbury gyrating in a disco. "You have no idea!" he said.

As they turned a bend in the dirt track, they saw moonlight reflected on the slates of Hawthorn Cottage above the trees. "Whoa!" called Parson Ledbury, pulling sharply on the reins.

The chaise rolled to a slow halt in front of the gate and Gideon prepared to jump down. "My thanks to you, Parson. You have saved us a long walk home."

"I am happy to oblige—"

Gideon interrupted him.

"But see! There is a light within!"

He slid down from the chaise, quietly opened the gate, and hurried up the path. Peter and Parson Ledbury looked at each other in consternation and followed him. The door was slightly ajar and Gideon pushed it with his finger, causing it to creak open, and then stepped inside the dark hall. Peter and the Parson tiptoed behind him. There was no one to be seen, but a candle burned brightly on the table, illuminating the journal which Gideon had been writing before they set off for the ball. In front of the fireplace, however, stood a large metal object, the same height as Gideon, and cuboid in shape.

"Oh!" whispered Peter in amazement. "It looks like an anti-gravity machine! They've come back!"

Gideon ran into the kitchen but when he found no one there

he sprinted upstairs, three steps at a time. Peter hurried after him and pushed him to one side in order to see what he was staring at. The Parson peeped over Gideon's shoulder. No one spoke. The sound of slow, rhythmic snoring came from Gideon's bedchamber. Peter laughed out loud. There lay Dr. Dyer, flat on his back and mouth open, and beside him was Molly, one paw over her nose.

Gideon cleared his throat noisily and the unconscious figure stirred.

"Greetings, Dr. Dyer," said Gideon. "What an unexpected pleasure it is to see you!"

"Yes, indeed, welcome back, sir!" said the Parson.

Kate's father sat up with a start and clasped his hand to his head as if he were in pain. Then Molly shot up and started to growl until, a moment later, she caught Peter's scent and then Gideon's and the Parson's, and she started to jump up at them excitedly and lick their faces.

"Molly! Down, girl!" chuckled Peter, wiping his wet cheek on his sleeve.

"Where am I?" Dr. Dyer cried. "Gideon? Is that you? And Parson Ledbury?"

"Hello!" said Peter.

"And *Peter*! Oh, thank the Lord! Is Kate here?"

"No," said Peter doubtfully. "Did you expect her to be?"

Dr. Dyer's face fell. "I was rather hoping that she might. . . ."

"Oh," Peter replied. "Did you get separated? And why have you come with a new machine?"

"We had to build a replica. Kate and your father, shall we say, ran off with the other one. . . ."

"What!" exclaimed Peter. "Kate *and* my dad! Dad's here?"

His heart leaped. His own dad had come to rescue him!

"Yes. They returned to 1763 only a couple of days after Kate arrived back home. Unfortunately, their antigravity machine will have materialized in Middle Harpenden, a small village in Hertfordshire."

"Why on earth did they choose to go there?" asked Peter.

Dr. Dyer rubbed his eyes. "That's a long story. . . . But I was convinced that they would have made their way here by now. I'm guessing that Kate and your dad will have reasoned, like I did, that Gideon would head for Derbyshire, and if they found Gideon, they'd find you. . . ."

"Your reasoning is correct," said the Parson, "although, mercifully, our friends are no longer fugitives. No sooner had the beneficiary of the news fled for his life along with Peter than—with impeccable timing—the confounded messenger arrived with the King's pardon! Sir Richard and I raced up to Derbyshire to bring the good tidings, but this pair dawdled all the way home and we beat them to Baslow Hall by three days!"

"But where are they?" Peter asked anxiously. "Even in the eighteenth century it doesn't take *that* long to get up to Derbyshire!"

"I would guess that there are but two possibilities," said the Parson. "Either they never arrived in Middle Harpenden or something has befallen them on their way to Derbyshire—as we know to our cost, these are dangerous times."

The Parson was right, Peter thought, though he wished he had not put it quite so bluntly. Images of Ned Porter, the highwayman, and the gang of footpads flashed through his mind. How on earth would his dad cope with eighteenth-century villains, not to mention less perilous inconveniences such as weevils and the lack of flushing toilets? And his dad hadn't even been a boy scout—he was hopeless at anything practical. Peter looked downcast. "We've *got* to look for them!" he said.

"I'm afraid I think we must," said Dr. Dyer. "Even though, now that I've found you, Peter, I wonder if I didn't ought to take you back to your mother straightaway."

"No!" said Peter. "We can't go back without them! I know what it feels like to be stranded!"

It was a full week before Peter, Dr. Dyer, and Gideon returned from Hertfordshire. As harvesting was finished, Mrs. Byng had spared Gideon from his duties, and Parson Ledbury had lent them his coach and four. It took them three days to find Middle Harpenden, relying on a poor map and even poorer directions from innkeepers on their way. Finally, Dr. Dyer recognized the village green and the pond, although the pond was smaller and there were fewer trees. The cottage, which in the twenty-first century would become a post office, had recently been built. Behind it, on the exact spot where the garage would stand and the antigravity machine must have materialized, there were several rows of cabbages. They spoke to a certain Reverend Austen, a shy young man, who was the new vicar of the parish. He offered them tea and seed cake in the vicarage and was very kind to Molly; he could not, however, recall anything of note happening in the village recently—other than the doctor's wife giving birth to triplets and a curious, warm wind that brought with it clouds of fine sand although they were a hundred miles from the sea. Certainly he would have remembered if any of his parishioners had come across a strange girl with red hair and a forty-year-old man, both dressed in unusual attire. . . .

They doggedly inquired at every inn they passed between St. Albans and Bakewell before they finally admitted defeat. Both Peter and Dr. Dyer nursed a forlorn hope that when they returned to Hawthorn Cottage, Kate and Mr. Schock would be waiting for them. But when Gideon pushed open the front door to find an empty house, everyone knew in their hearts that only one course of action was left open to them. Peter looked sadly over at Gideon—he was not only going to have to prepare himself for another difficult parting, but a difficult homecoming, too.

TWENTY-FIVE

DINNER OF THE CENTURIES

In which the party has much cause to celebrate,
Dr. Pirretti makes an impression, and
Sergeant Chadwick takes Molly for a walk

When Kate's mother asked her to fetch some extra desserts for the little ones, she was glad of a brief respite from the celebrations. As she searched at the back of the freezer for more chocolate chip ice cream, she took a moment to pinch herself. Had she ever felt happier in her whole life? Gone was the anxiety that had been weighing her down ever since she had first woken up to find herself in a field full of thistles in 1763. She was home! Peter was home! Everyone was home! She felt as light as air, as if she had been given a temporary reprieve from the laws of gravity!

It was late morning on a Saturday when Kate, Mr. Schock, and the Marquis de Montfaron arrived at the farm. Kate had persuaded the others to leave the van they had rented in the lane so that she could go on ahead. She had run, as softly as she could, to the front door and then had paused, almost reluctant to knock, as she savored the intense glow of anticipation. How she had hoped for it to be her mother who answered! Then she had rapped smartly on the familiar cracked red paint, and had heard footsteps in the hall, and the loose floorboard that creaked. Slowly, or perhaps it had just seemed slowly, the door had glided open. And there, in front of her, blinking in the sunshine, was her mother.

Mrs. Dyer had stepped backward and put both hands to her mouth, quite unable to move or speak.

"Mum! It's me!"

Her mother had let out a little scream and had drawn Kate to her and held her so tightly she could scarcely breathe. Suddenly Kate had disentangled herself and had looked up.

"What is it?" cried Mrs. Dyer in alarm, seeing Kate's distraught face.

"We didn't find Peter. . . . I didn't check the settings—it was my fault. . . ."

But her mother had merely broken into a huge smile and had turned to shout down the hall: "Peter! Everyone! Come and see who's here!"

Hearing his name, Peter had popped his head out of the kitchen and walked up the dark hall toward the dazzling daylight. Suddenly there was someone running at him at full pelt, red hair flying, and Kate had collided with him with such force that they had both ended up on the floor.

"You're back!" she had shouted. "And you're short again!"

"What!" Peter had exclaimed.

"Never mind," Kate had said, laughing. "I'll explain later. And look—your dad's here, too!"

❖═◉○◉═❖

There were scenes of jubilation that day which no one present could ever forget. As Kate and Mr. Schock and the bemused Marquis de Montfaron entered the crowded farmhouse kitchen, there were gasps and shouts and cheers; people embraced and clung to each other, talked without stopping, shouted questions, lifted each other into the air, danced and cried and laughed.

A trestle table from the dairy had been butted up to the long kitchen table in order to accommodate everyone. Now both were groaning with food and packed around with folk who elbowed each other cheerfully as they laid out plates and cutlery. Almost everyone helped prepare the impromptu lunch. Milly was too young, of course, while the Marquis de Montfaron and Inspector Wheeler—who, along with Sergeant Chadwick, had accompanied the antigravity machine and its passengers from Hawthorn Cottage—proved to be abject failures in the kitchen. Instead, the policeman and the eighteenth-century aristocrat perched on the staircase, quite oblivious of being in the way, and took great delight in probing another enquiring mind from a different time. Sam clung to Kate while Megan, who had rushed over as soon as she received the call, now stood next to her friend holding her precious mobile phone once more.

"You know," shouted Dr. Dyer above the hubbub into his Kate's ear, "if happiness could be measured like temperature with a thermometer, the reading in this room would go clean off the scale."

Sixteen people plus one golden Labrador gathered around

the kitchen table for the celebratory lunch: the Dyers, the Schocks, Dr. Pirretti, Megan, an eighteenth-century French aristocrat, and the two English policemen. Everyone was pink with the heat and the excitement and the champagne. It was, Sam commented, the most amazing celebration ever. It was the dinner of the century! To which his big sister had replied that, given the Marquis de Montfaron's presence and where they'd come from, it was the dinner of the centur*ies*. Numerous toasts were made. Peter raised his glass to Gideon Seymour, who had been so good to him during his stay in 1763, and Kate raised her glass to the Marquis de Montfaron, who had mended the antigravity machine. When Mr. Schock stood up, the whole table emulated him and rose to their feet.

"To Gideon Seymour! To the Marquis de Montfaron!"

Montfaron bowed his head in acknowledgement. He sat at the head of the table, flanked by Dr. Pirretti on one side and Inspector Wheeler on the other. He still wore eighteenth-century costume and his dress, like his height, attracted much attention. Halfway through the meal little Milly was to be found under the table examining the buckles on his elegant, heeled shoes. She soon contrived to find a way onto his lap from which vantage point she could stroke the gold brocade on his cuffs and trace, with her plump little finger, the roses embroidered onto his waistcoat. He ate little, and while too polite to rise from the table and pick things up, his wide eyes surveyed the modest farmhouse kitchen, observing, analyzing, noting. . . . He allowed himself just one question. When Mrs. Dyer switched the light on, he looked up at her and asked: "Electricity?" She nodded and the biggest smile lit up his face. It was Montfaron who suggested the last toast: "To progress," he said.

Peter sat between his parents. His mother rested her head on his and his father stretched out his arm around both of them. The overwhelming sense of loss Mr. Schock had felt only a few hours before had been replaced by joy at the prospect of a second chance, of proving to his son the father that he could be. His heart was full; he was still close to tears. When his father looked into his twelve-year-old face, Peter wondered which face he was seeing. He had already told Peter how proud he was of the man that he became (or might become?). And while really pleased and desperate to find out more about this mysterious older self, nonetheless uncomfortable questions—about his identity and how his father could have left him behind in 1792, no matter *how* old he was—were already beginning to surface in Peter's mind. But it was not appropriate to voice them in the middle of a celebration.

"Who knows what life has mapped out for you," said Mr. Schock suddenly to his son, "but of one thing I'm certain: You've got it in you to be a better man than I. There's so much to say and so much to tell you. . . . But there'll be time enough for that when we've all calmed down and made some sense out of all of this. Now we've got all the time in the world together. . . ."

Peter looked at his father, in no doubt, for once, about his father's feelings for him. Kate, too, was squeezed between her parents. She caught Peter's eye and fanned herself with a paper napkin. He panted like a dog with his tongue hanging out. They both laughed. It was so good to see each other again. But was it his imagination, Peter asked himself, or did Kate look a bit strange? Like his favorite T-shirt when it had been put through the wash too many times. . . .

Megan was looking at the photograph which Kate had taken on the Dover packet with her mobile phone. She reached over Mrs. Dyer to touch Kate's arm and get her attention.

"Are you telling me you only took *one* picture, Kate! *One*!"

"I was too busy to take pictures!"

"And all you can see on this one is great white sails and sea!"

"No," said Kate. "If you look carefully, you'll see a man in eighteenth-century costume too."

"*I* can't see anyone. . . ."

"You must be blind," said Kate. "Give it here—let me show you."

Kate peered at the tiny picture. The grown-up Peter Schock had been in the picture too, staring out to sea—she was *sure* of it. She looked closer and tipped the mobile at a slight angle. Yes, he was there! Just a trace of him, but he was there. . . . But then Kate looked again—and she couldn't make him out. What on earth was going on? Suddenly she doubted her own judgment. She no longer knew what she could see. . . . An unwelcome sinking feeling prompted her to pass the mobile phone quickly back to her friend. "My mistake," she said.

Megan looked back at her, unable to read her expression.

⊷⊶○⊷⊶

"Is anything wrong, Inspector?" asked Mrs. Dyer.

The policeman was leaning back in his chair and looking out of the kitchen door into the yard. He got up and looked at the sky. "I keep thinking I can hear a helicopter," he said.

"There's nothing unusual in that," said Mrs. Dyer. "We often get them flying over the valley."

Inspector Wheeler rubbed his bruised neck.

"I'll go and have a look around," offered Sergeant Chadwick. "I could do with a quick breath of air after that wonderful dinner." He smiled at Mrs. Dyer.

"You're very welcome, Sergeant."

"Why don't I take the dog for a walk while I'm at it. Do you want to keep me company, Molly?" he asked.

Molly's golden ears pricked up. She had been lying in front of the Aga and now sat up expectantly.

"Is that okay, Kate?"

"Molly never says no to a walk!"

Dr. Pirretti sat smiling in Peter's direction, delighted to see that, contrary to all expectations, everything had turned out well in the end.

"My mind is reeling," she said. "How can we be living in a universe where Peter reached adulthood, lived, and, presumably, died in the eighteenth century, and yet here Peter is today, sitting in our midst, a child once more! The more I try to figure it out the more my brain hurts. . . ."

"My dear lady," said Montfaron in his lilting accent, "whatever is the truth, is the truth, and our inability to comprehend it alters nothing."

"I feel I owe it to you to tell you," said Dr. Pirretti, "that my instinct is that we should attempt to return you and the Tar Man to your own times as soon as possible."

"Alas, I agree with you, dear lady, but not just yet. I hope that I might be allowed to stay awhile. . . ."

Montfaron put his head on one side and smiled so winningly at Dr. Pirretti, his clear brown eyes twinkling, that the entire table started to laugh. His charms were difficult to resist.

Kate's attention was caught by Dr. Pirretti, and she kicked Peter's legs under the table and nodded in her direction. She was passing her hand over her forehead and frowning a little as if she was trying to focus on something in the middle distance. She opened and closed her mouth as if she were about to say something but kept deciding against it. Others saw Peter and Kate looking at her, and soon the entire table grew quiet and turned to her expectantly.

"Is anything the matter, Anita?" asked Mrs. Schock, solicitously.

Dr. Pirretti's gaze swept around the table, and when her eyes met those of Dr. Dyer she said: "I'm sorry, Andrew. . . . On such a lovely occasion as this . . . I am aware of your doubts. . . . It's just that I am experiencing a quite overwhelming feeling that I've passed this way before."

The silence around the table deepened. Montfaron blinked

at her like an owl and the Inspector cleared his throat.

Finally Dr. Dyer said: "Could you tell us what's on your mind, Anita?"

But to everyone's astonishment Dr. Pirretti mouthed his exact words at the very instant he uttered them. Shivers went up and down Kate's spine and she exchanged glances with Peter.

"What's going on?" asked Dr. Dyer and Dr. Pirretti in unison.

Now everyone looked alarmed. Dr. Pirretti did not seem herself. It was as though she were speaking through a wall to people that she could not see.

Dr. Pirretti continued: "And then you say . . ."

She paused, as if waiting for a prompt.

"Why are you doing this?" they both said together.

"Because," said Dr. Pirretti, "I need to prove to you that I have already lived through this moment. You are witnessing the splintering of time."

"The splintering of time?"

"Yes. You cannot destroy something which has already existed. If you travel to a different time, you *can* alter the course of events—but, as a consequence, the universe will make a copy of itself rather than allow *what has already happened* to be wiped away. We now live in a universe where worlds and times overlap, duplicate themselves. . . ."

"I don't understand what you're saying!" said Inspector Wheeler. "Are you seriously suggesting there are duplicate worlds out there?"

"I mean that there is now a parallel world where Peter and Kate found Molly in the antigravity lab and all returned safely home to the farmhouse for lunch—but there is also *this* world, in which Peter and Kate were catapulted back in time and in which many other things have now occurred as a consequence."

"But . . . how could that continue? There could be an infinite number of worlds, of duplicates. . . . "

"Precisely—as long as people continue to travel through time . . . and not just in *your* world."

Mrs. Dyer clutched her husband's hand.

"This isn't the Anita I know," she whispered.

Peter saw the expression of horror on Kate's face and felt it too. It wasn't over, was it? His friend looked desperate.

"Why do you say *your* world, not *our* world?" asked the Inspector.

"Surely that is clear?" said Dr. Pirretti. "I mean what I say."

No one spoke. Everyone stared at Dr. Pirretti. She had seemed calm but was now beginning to look strained. She started to speak again, but this time her words came out in short bursts, as if she were out of breath.

"So, if you believe the evidence of your own ears . . . I am proof that parallel worlds do exist. . . . Haven't you ever said: It's like someone just walked over my grave; or, I *knew* what he was going to say before he even opened his mouth; or, it's fate, it was *meant* to happen. . . ."

"Déjà vu," Mrs. Schock whispered to her husband. He nodded.

"It's as if, for a few moments, you coincide with an alternative existence and you make a fleeting connection. . . . This past I share with you, though we do not share the same future. . . ."

"And what prompted you to try so hard to contact us?" asked Dr. Dyer.

"To warn you," she said. "*You* can change time. *I can't* . . ."

These last words came out as a gasp. And all at once everyone could see by the expression on Dr. Pirretti's face that it was over. She slumped forward for a moment and, like coming out of a trance, when she pushed herself up she was herself again.

"Oh my," she said, taking the glass of wine which Montfaron was offering her and taking a sip. "I'm sorry. My first public performance. Not good timing . . ."

"On the contrary, Madame, your timing was impeccable," he said. "I suspect we were all called on to be witnesses."

"Anita," said Mrs. Dyer. "Are you all right?"

Dr. Pirretti nodded. "I felt such a strong sense of *urgency*. I sense that she fears that something awful is about to happen. If only I could understand *what* she wants me to do."

"Is it possible that you have it in your power to do something which she cannot?" asked Montfaron.

"But if she wants me to do something, *why* can't she do it herself in her world? She certainly seems to know more than I do. . . ." Dr. Pirretti sighed, but all at once her face lit up. "Unless she's in a duplicate world and we are in—for want a better word—the master, and it's possible to alter history in our world but not in hers. . . . Does that make sense? Could that be what she meant?"

Kate gasped. "Can't you all see? It's obvious! She wants us to put things right. She wants us to go back in time to the beginning of the Christmas holidays and stop Peter and I going back to 1763 and everything that happened as a result! She wants us to prevent the first time event!"

Everyone looked at one another.

"I can understand Kate's reasoning," said Montfaron. "You do not fell a great tree by snipping off its leaves one by one. You take an axe to its trunk."

"And what do you think might happen if we don't?" asked Peter.

"I don't think *I* want to find out," said Kate.

Exhausted and overwrought, Dr. Pirretti excused herself and escaped upstairs to her room for a while. The celebratory dinner was over.

"So much for our plans to destroy the machines," said Dr. Dyer.

"I'm not letting Kate go back in time again!" exclaimed his wife.

"Nor Peter!" said Mr. Schock.

Dr. Dyer leaned over the table and put his head in his hands. "I have to admit that I remain highly skeptical about Anita's 'funny turns.' Convincing as she was, I don't want to base vital decisions on what could be the ravings of someone who's been under too much pressure for too long. . . ."

"If you will permit me to say so," commented Montfaron, "he who lives without madness is not as wise as he thinks. . . ."

"If only none of this had ever happened," exclaimed Dr. Dyer angrily. "If only we could turn the clock back!"

"*Exactement*, my dear sir," said Montfaron. "It appears that you can. . . ."

Mrs. Schock turned to her husband and spoke quietly, too unsure of her ground to want to address the whole company. "When I'm working on a script, I keep a master version and then, every time I make an important change—kill somebody off or create a new character—I make a backup. Like a snapshot in time of the story immediately before the point at which the change occurs."

Mr. Schock looked puzzled. "What's that got to do with anything?"

"Well, isn't it like the world Anita was talking about, potentially our world, in which everything is up for grabs and open to alteration? While she was speaking, I just kept relating it to my master script. In the master script the story keeps changing and evolving and you just keep adjusting stuff so that there are no loose ends. . . . Do you see? Whereas the backups are snapshots of the story at a certain point, frozen in time so to speak, though all of them could potentially carry on as a separate story—like parallel worlds. . . ."

Mr. Schock shook his head like a wet dog. "Well, if there's any grain of truth in that analogy, I sure would hate to be the universe's script editor."

The sound of distressed barking reached them from the yard.

"Something's up with Molly," said Kate, and squeezed past the line of chairs to the back door. It was several minutes before she reappeared in the doorway, very out of breath and holding Molly by the collar. There was blood smeared on her golden fur although there was no visible wound. Molly was trembling and when she staggered forward a few steps it was clear that one of her hind legs was hurt. She sat down heavily on the quarry tiles next to the Wellington boots.

Kate, too, was trembling. She did not want her young brothers and sisters to hear what she had to say, so she motioned to her parents to come closer and then whispered into Inspector Wheeler's ear: "I found Sergeant Chadwick. He was tied up to a gatepost by the stream, one field up from the farm. His head was drooping forward and . . . blood was dripping from his nose. . . . I don't think he could hear me. . . ."

TWENTY-SIX

TIMEQUAKE

*In which Kate and Peter renew an old acquaintance
and this story comes to an end*

Inspector Wheeler threw down his napkin, shot up from the table, and ran out of the kitchen door. Mrs. Dyer immediately gathered up the little ones and, in a very calm voice, asked Megan and Sam to sort out a cartoon for them to watch in the sitting room. As Megan disappeared, she flashed a questioning look at Kate. But Kate was too disturbed to notice her friend and followed the Marquis de Montfaron and Mr. and Mrs. Schock out into the yard.

"Not you, Kate!" cried Mrs. Dyer. "I have no idea what's going on, but you've been through enough. I want you to stay here."

"But, Mum!"

"Peter," said Mrs. Dyer. "Will you stay with Kate?"

"I will if you want me to."

"Yes. Please. I'd be very grateful. I'll be back in a minute. . . ."

And Mrs. Dyer disappeared outside too.

Peter and Kate found themselves alone in the kitchen

together. Kate sat next to Molly at the foot of the long table, its red-and-white-checked cloth strewn with the wreckage of the celebratory lunch. Kate wiped away the blood from Molly's golden fur with a dishcloth. All the color had drained from her cheeks.

"Are you okay?" asked Peter.

"It's not Molly's blood," she said. "It must be Sergeant Chadwick's. She must have been trying to protect him."

Molly moaned and rested her head on her front paws.

"My poor Molly. I'm going to tuck you in with your blanket. Come on, girl."

Kate clicked her tongue, and frowning a little, Molly heaved herself up and padded after her.

When Kate returned to the kitchen, Peter was looking out of the back door. "What did you see, Kate? What's happening for goodness' sake?" His attention was suddenly taken by the sight of a helicopter disappearing over the brow of the hill at the foot of the valley.

"I'm not sure—" she started but then she stopped.

Peter turned around. Kate was staring into the doorway that led to the hall. She took a step backward and clung on to the back of a dining chair behind. When Peter saw who it was, he gasped too. The Tar Man wore well-cut jeans and a leather jacket and he wasn't holding his neck to one side, but it was definitely him. Dark hair scraped back. That scar. Those eyes.

The Tar Man walked into the kitchen, dragging Dr. Pirretti alongside him. There was no fight left in her; he was like a big cat with its prey. Her arms were tied behind her back. He held the point of a knife to her throat. He smiled pleasantly at Peter and Kate, revealing surprisingly white teeth.

"Good day to you, Master Schock; good day, Mistress Dyer," he said in a low voice.

"You!" cried Kate.

"I would ask you to keep your voice down!" hissed the Tar Man. "Although it grieves me to treat a handsome woman with such disrespect, needs must. If you wish Dr. Pirretti to see another dawn I suggest you do not attract attention to yourselves. . . ."

"You know Dr. Pirretti?"

"There is little, you will be sorry to learn, that I do *not* know, Mistress Dyer. . . ."

From the sitting room across the hall they heard the strains of a Disney cartoon and children's voices.

Kate looked wildly around the kitchen for something that she could use to alert the grown-ups to what was happening. Perhaps she could wave a candle under the smoke alarm, or . . . but she knew it was useless. They'd be halfway up the lane by now—and that, she now realized, was precisely what the Tar Man had intended.

Peter, meanwhile, took a step sideways. A month spent in the company of Gideon Seymour meant that at least now he could handle a knife. A serrated bread knife was lying at the other side of the table. He moved as slowly and smoothly as he could, but the Tar Man spotted him at once and made a tutting noise with his tongue. Then, with a delicate flick of his wrist, he made a tiny nick in Dr. Pirretti's skin which produced a single drop of blood that trickled down her neck. She let out a barely perceptible cry.

"Alas, my conscience is beyond redemption, but I trust that you would not wish this lady's death on yours."

Peter and Kate looked first at each other and then at Dr. Pirretti. Cold sweat beaded on her forehead. The look in her eyes was desperate. Peter stepped away from the table.

"Now," the Tar Man barked, "if you please, you will accompany me to the dairy."

As the Tar Man closed the back door silently behind them, Megan came out into the kitchen to see what was happening. *That's just great,* she thought to herself. *They've gone off to see what the excitement is all about while me and Sam are left minding the children!* She reached over to the table and helped herself to a crispy roast potato before going back, a little out of sorts, to watch *Beauty and the Beast.*

Kate led the way to the dairy. Peter followed close on her heels and then came the Tar Man, half pushing, half lifting Dr. Pirretti. Seconds later they were all inside, and the Tar Man closed and bolted the heavy door. It should have been locked. Some lengths of orange cord tied into neat figures of eight had been left just inside the door. The Tar Man kicked them into the dark space in front of them. Peter was suddenly conscious of everyone's breathing. Then the Tar Man switched on the harsh electric light revealing Tim Williamson's repaired antigravity machine and

Russ Merrick's prototype in the middle of the scrubbed concrete floor. There was a smell of disinfectant and sweet cow's milk. The Tar Man pushed Dr. Pirretti down onto the small wooden chair Mrs. Dyer sometimes used for hand milking and retied the cord. Soon Dr. Pirretti was so firmly bound to the chair she could barely move. Then it was Peter's turn. The Tar Man pushed him toward Russ Merrick's machine and bound his hands behind his back. Then, with another length of cord he bound him tightly to the machine.

Dr. Pirretti summoned up the courage to speak. "Let Peter and Kate go. They are children! Haven't they been through enough?"

"Madam, flattered though I am, surely you do not mistake me for a compassionate man? If they do as they are bid, I shall release them."

"Then what," asked Dr. Pirretti anxiously, "do you want them to do?"

"I desire to return to 1763. I want Mistress Dyer, here, to adjust the machine to its correct setting. It was tampered with, which caused, if I understand correctly, the machine to travel to the wrong time."

"You knew that!" cried Dr. Pirretti.

The Tar Man laughed. "There isn't a word you have uttered these last few days to which I have not been privy. Your performance at dinner was most diverting, madam, although I do not like the sound of its implications. Now, Mistress Dyer. If you please. Show me how to adjust the setting. Do not attempt to deceive me, as I already know the number."

"I can do that for you! Kate does not have the—"

The Tar Man interrupted Dr. Pirretti. "If I were in your shoes, madam, I might be tempted to do more than make a simple alteration. No. Mistress Dyer will do it. She is too ignorant to be dangerous and is not a natural liar. And she knows the setting."

Kate was of two minds whether she should feel insulted. "And then will you let us go?" she asked.

"I shall, Mistress Dyer."

"Surely we can discuss this," said Dr. Pirretti. "Do you really wish to return to the eighteenth century? Can we not tempt you to stay? Surely you have discovered that life is so much more comfortable now?"

"Perhaps I desire more than a *comfortable life*, Dr. Pirretti. Mistress Dyer? If you please?"

Kate knelt down, lifted up a small Perspex flap toward the bottom of the machine and pressed a black button which put forward the setting by one hundredth of a megawatt. The Tar Man leaned over her shoulder and observed her carefully. Out of the corner of her eye she could see his thumb slowly stroking the edge of his blade. She lifted off her finger but had already reached six point nine, so she then pressed the other black button to go backward.

"Six point seven seven," Kate said finally. "That was the setting which took us back to 1763."

Kate looked at Dr. Pirretti, who nodded resignedly.

"And now you will show me how to set the machine in motion," ordered the Tar Man.

Kate pointed to a rocker switch to one side of the digital read-out. "But it will only work if—"

"If it is on the level—your Frenchman was very free with his information. Thank you, Mistress Dyer."

There was silence while the Tar Man now tied Kate's hands behind her back. Peter struggled to turn his head to watch. When the Tar Man had finished tying Kate's wrists, Peter saw him push both machines together. Then he took another length of cord and started to walk around both machines, binding them *and* the children into one big parcel.

"No!" Peter suddenly shouted. "You said you'd let us go! Can't you see what he's doing? He's going to take both machines and us!"

Thwack! The Tar Man delivered a stinging blow to the side of Peter's head. Then Kate, struggling and wriggling to get free, started to scream and Dr. Pirretti, too, shouted for all she was worth:

"Help! Help! Somebody help us!"

But all their screams fell on deaf ears. Only Molly heard and she could not get out of the back door. The Tar Man decided it was not worth the effort to quiet his prisoners and calmly finished tying the final knot before pressing the switch.

"Please! I'm begging you! You *mustn't* take the children! Who knows what traveling through time does to a growing body! Already I see a worrying change in Kate!"

"Alas, madam, I have no option."

Tim Williamson's machine started to shimmer and grow indistinct.

"But what possible reason could you have?" cried Dr. Pirretti. "What good will it do you?"

"You talked, not half an hour ago, did you not, about preventing the first time event, as Mistress Dyer so elegantly put it. It seems to me that with neither children nor machines at your disposal, this will be an impossible feat to achieve. You must understand, Madam, that I have in mind a different history for myself, and I shall not be thwarted. . . ."

"You monster!" screamed Dr. Pirretti.

The two machines glowed like liquid amber. Kate and Peter struggled and kicked out, the cords burning into their skin. The shadow of a dark vortex hovered over the dairy.

"I saw you in St. Paul's Cathedral, did I not?" asked the Tar Man. "It was as if we had met before. . . ."

"Yes, I saw you. . . . I gave you the benefit of the doubt. I know better now. . . ."

"You won't win!" shouted Peter. "We won't let you!"

The Tar Man laughed, and it was his laugh that was the last thing Dr. Pirretti heard. Suddenly she found herself alone in the silent dairy.

"Help!" she sobbed. "Please, someone help me!"

But no one came. Molly scratched and whined at the back door. The grown-ups helped Sergeant Chadwick walk back down the lane with faltering steps. Megan and Sam sat on crowded sofas watching the rest of *Beauty and the Beast*.

Dr. Pirretti let her head drop down onto her lap. He had taken the children! He had actually taken the children! He had taken *both* machines. Tears of despair poured down her cheeks. The situation was irretrievable. All was lost. What havoc, she thought, has an eighteenth-century thug just unleashed on the universe?

Larksong. It was the high piping song of a lark hovering in the deep blue sky above her that tugged Kate back into consciousness. Her shoulders ached and she could not feel her arms, for they were still tied and she had been lying on them. She opened her eyes very slowly and glimpsed out at the bright world through her eyelashes. She was lying in bracken. Above her, leaves fluttered; nearby water trickled over stones. After a while she tuned in to another sound. She knew those voices! Kate turned her head. She saw the Tar Man. And he was with Lord Luxon! Kate immediately clamped her eyes shut.

"I have been here three days and nights with only a little bread and spring water to sustain me," Lord Luxon said. "I all but abandoned the quest. . . ."

Peter groaned a little in his unconscious state. Kate thought he sounded very close.

"And now you arrive with not one but two machines and those confounded children to boot!"

"I was obliged to change my plan, my lord. I brought them by way of precaution, as I explained."

"If I understand correctly your motives for bringing them here, I suggest you put them out of their misery without more ado. They are made orphans by time, are they not? I predict they will be nothing but a thorn in your side. It would be as well to dispatch them."

"I am no longer your henchman, my lord."

"I did not mean to imply that you were, Blueskin."

The Tar Man was bending over Russ Merrick's machine. "Damn her eyes," he exclaimed suddenly.

"Damn whose eyes, pray? Of which lady do you speak?"

"Dr. Pirretti—whose fine features give the lie to a most devious intellect."

Lord Luxon peered over the Tar Man's shoulder at a small liquid crystal display. He read: "Enter six-digit code."

"It happens each time I try to set it in motion. I need the scientists' secret code, else this device is useless to me."

"I admire your newfound skill with machines, Blueskin."

"Ay, well, I do not have the skill to make this new one function."

Lord Luxon bent down and examined the other antigravity machine.

"Six . . . seven . . . seven . . . So it is *this* figure, you say, that determines how far backward and forward in time the device will travel? So if I changed it to, say, five four four, it would take me to a different century? Ingenious, truly ingenious! Here, Blueskin, allow me to assist you. . . ."

The Tar Man lifted Russ Merrick's machine onto the back

of the wagon so that he did not have to stoop to examine the control panel.

"You know, Blueskin, you surprise me. In fact, dare I say it, you disappoint me. You have in your possession a machine which will allow you to navigate the seas of time, and what is your ambition? To go back and change the odds in your favor at the beginning of your paltry little race through life. Yes, I have to say you disappoint me, Blueskin. Where, I ask you, is the breadth of your vision?"

The hairs on the back of the Tar Man's neck bristled. He knew what he would see even before he turned around. The machine was already liquefying. Lord Luxon was semitransparent and he had his pistol trained on him.

"Give the device to me and what should I do with it? Why, I shall bring people back! I shall bring *armies* back! He who rules time, what can he not do!"

The Tar Man screamed in anguish.

"I am a fool! A numbskull! You have had this in your mind since the first moment!"

"'Tis true. But I shall give you a parting gift, Blueskin, as I am kind. Your suspicions about Mr. Seymour were well-founded. You and Gideon are, indeed, brothers. Alas, I knew it from the start."

As Lord Luxon disappeared into the ether, the Tar Man let out a terrible roar and kicked out at the wagon wheels in frustration, before leaping onto the wagon and cracking the whip over the horses' heads. The wheels rumbled over the bracken. Kate watched the wagon moving away. Suddenly it stopped and she heard the Tar Man jump down. Then she felt his shadow fall over her. She held her breath but opened her eyes despite herself. The Tar Man was looking down at her, gripping his knife in his hand. Her heart thumped in her chest and her mouth was dry. He was going to take Lord Luxon's advice after all! She wanted to scream but felt powerless to move. She waited for the cold metal blade to penetrate her flesh. But then he turned her roughly over so that her face was pressed into the prickly grass and he cut through her bonds.

"Tom told me you showed him kindness," the Tar Man said, by way of explanation.

By the time Kate had rolled back over and sat herself up, the Tar Man had disappeared behind the trees.

"Tom?" she repeated.

"He might have cut through mine, too!" said Peter.

"Peter! You're awake!"

"I don't believe it. Twenty-four hours in the twenty-first century and then we're back in 1763! We're a few hundred yards from where we landed in the first place!"

"At least we know we're not in Australia this time. . . ."

"I know exactly where I am," said Peter. "And I know how to get to Hawthorn Cottage from here."

"Gideon's house?"

"Yes."

"Did you hear what Lord Luxon said about Gideon and the Tar Man?"

"I don't believe it."

"Neither do I."

With difficulty Kate managed to undo Peter's bonds. They walked over the empty countryside too stunned and upset to want to talk, even though both had a lot that they wanted to say. Sheep roamed the hillsides and thistledown floated by, glistening in the afternoon sunshine. Kate asked Peter only one question:

"Did my dad tell you the security code for the other machine?"

"I saw him key it in—but I didn't pay any attention to what numbers he was pressing," he replied.

"Oh. Shame."

"But at least the Tar Man doesn't know it either."

In return, Peter asked Kate just one question.

"You know what Dr. Pirretti said—about seeing a worrying change in you. You don't think you've started to look . . . kind of *faded*, do you?"

Kate looked aghast. "Faded!"

"It's probably just the light," Peter said hurriedly.

"No, I *don't* think I look faded!"

"She probably only said it to get the Tar Man to change his mind. . . ."

"Well, it didn't work, did it?" snapped Kate. "We're back where we started."

Kate walked on ahead by herself but kept holding out her arms and looking at them. She did know what Peter meant, though. Deep down she had known for a while. The change was subtle but she wasn't the same girl who had arrived in 1763 that first time. And back then she had understood neither what they were up against nor the nature of their journey. Now she did. And she was aware that something had altered during the course of this journey back to the past—although she could not put her finger on exactly what it was. The mellow sun shone down on them, but a growing sense of dread made Kate feel cold and empty and numb.

Following on behind, Peter looked at Kate's back and watched her hair, scraped back in a ponytail, swing from side to side. There was no spring in her step and her shoulders were hunched. A flock of crows flew, cawing, overhead and Kate looked back at him briefly, almost as if she were seeking reassurance. It made him wonder how the alternative, grown-up version of himself had behaved toward Kate. Peter saw the fatigue and despair in her pale face, and all he knew was that he had to get her to Gideon and Hawthorn Cottage. For the first time in his life Peter felt responsible for someone, and it helped him to master his own fears.

"It's not *so* bad in 1763," he called out to her. "And we'll work out a way of getting home. . . . And even if we don't, your dad and Dr. Pirretti will build another antigravity machine. It's not like they'd just abandon us!"

Kate merely nodded and trudged on, her eyes squinting in the strong light. Peter jogged forward a few paces to catch up with her. He half expected her to be crying, but when she stopped and turned sadly toward him, no tear rolled down her freckled cheeks. Peter looked at her and, as she stood silhouetted against the luminous Derbyshire landscape, so vibrant with the rich hues of late summer, he realized that there was no denying that Kate appeared *diminished*. As if she were no longer firmly rooted in this world. As if the tides of time were washing the life out of her. He hesitated momentarily, for such gestures did not come easily to him, and then he put one arm around her. For some time Kate allowed herself to rest her head on his shoulder and they watched the warm wind blow ripples through the dry grass thick with crickets and wildflowers. Then Kate pulled away from him and strode doggedly onward.

"It'll be all right, Kate!" he called, but she did not answer.

When Hawthorn Cottage came into view at last, Peter felt almost like he was coming home, and he started to run down the hill with giant strides. But it was at that very moment that Kate cried out as if in pain. When Peter looked over his shoulder at her, he saw that she had sunk to her knees and was clutching at her chest. Her eyes were round and staring and there was a look of something close to terror on her face.

Alarmed, Peter hurried back to her, scanning the landscape as he did so for any clues as to the cause of Kate's distress. But he saw nothing. He heard nothing—apart from the wind whistling through the gorse. He knelt down in front of her. Kate must be ill—but what could be wrong with her that could affect her so badly and so suddenly? Surely she was too young to be having a heart attack. . . .

"Can't you feel it?" she gasped. "It's like I'm being torn apart!"

"What are you talking about? I can't feel anything!"

"But you must!" Kate practically shouted "And it's getting nearer. . . ."

"Come on," urged Peter, getting to his feet and trying to haul her up. "Hawthorn Cottage is only a couple of minutes away."

But Kate wriggled out of his grasp and flung herself down on the ground and crossed her arms over her head. Peter grabbed hold of her clenched fists and pulled her to her feet.

"Cut it out!" he shouted. "Are you *trying* to be scary? Whatever it is, we'll be better off inside even if Gideon isn't there. . . ."

Peter half dragged and half carried Kate the short distance to Hawthorn Cottage, and at the sound of the gate creaking open, the blond head of Gideon Seymour appeared at the window. A wave of concern passed over his features as he looked down the path at his visitors. He did not need to be told that something was badly wrong. Kate was still struggling feebly. Gideon ran out of the front door and bounded toward them.

"Do my eyes deceive me?" he exclaimed. "I had thought never to see you again!"

Panting with the effort of keeping hold of Kate, Peter finally let go of her and she slid to the ground, where she held her head in her hands as if her skull were about to implode.

"I'm so glad you're here," Peter gasped. "I don't know what's up with Kate—I think she's ill."

Gideon crouched down next to her. "Mistress Kate," he said softly. "What ails thee?"

Kate looked up at him and opened her mouth to speak, but no words came out.

"Forgive me, Mistress Kate. There will be time enough for explanations—let me take you inside."

Gideon scooped her up in his arms and stood up, but as he took a step toward the cottage, Kate suddenly screamed.

"It's here!" she cried in abject terror and tried to hide her face in Gideon's neck.

Gideon and Peter exchanged anxious glances and looked around the sunny garden full of flowers and bees. What could she possibly be seeing?

But a moment later they knew. There was a great roaring, an apocalyptic tremor, an invisible force that took their breath away. They saw worlds within worlds, they saw people—alive or dead they did not know—staring back at them. It was as if ghosts from all ages were seeping through the walls of time like blood soaking through a linen shirt.

"Hold on to me!" Peter heard Gideon cry. "We must get inside the cottage!"

Peter grabbed hold of Gideon's elbow, and step by step, eyes closed tight against the nightmarish phantasms that surrounded them, they edged blindly toward the front door. Gideon kicked it open and they both fell inside the dark interior. Then Gideon lowered Kate gently onto a chair and ran back to bolt the door as if against a storm. Kate was gripping the arms of the chair so tightly that her knuckles had turned white. She was staring straight ahead, her eyes wide open. Peter turned to look in the same direction, and what he saw made him sink to his knees in shock and wonder. The walls of the house were melting away and it was through their shimmering remains that he saw the valley and its surrounding hills that he had grown to know so well. Except that the familiar Derbyshire landscape was duplicating itself, like two mirrors reflecting each other into infinity, creating a never-ending spiral of landscapes which appeared to stretch out into the farthest reaches of space. Peter clamped his hands to his ears in an effort to blot out the deafening roar. He feared that he was not made of strong enough stuff to withstand the mighty force that surged all around him. He felt as if he stood at the top of a vertiginous precipice, and that he was going to fall, fall, and never cease falling. . . . But then, as suddenly as it had started, it stopped. Kate slumped forward like a rag doll released from a giant's invisible grip. When she sat up again, Peter could see that the pain had vanished from her face. It was over. The bare stone walls seemed to grow back up around them as if by magic, and soon they found themselves once more in the shelter of Hawthorn Cottage.

Gideon walked toward the front door, slid open the bolt, and pushed it gingerly open. He stepped outside. Kate lifted herself up out of her chair and staggered toward the light. Peter took her arm and all three stood on the doorstep staring out. Gideon put an arm around both their shoulders. All three clung together and Peter realized that he was not the only one to be shaking. They looked around them at Hawthorn Cottage, at the garden with its spreading oak tree, at the field beyond the gate, at the rosehips and the butterflies and the fluffy white clouds in the deep blue sky. Everything appeared normal and yet something was not right. It felt like returning home to a house that has been broken into.

"Is this the end of the world?" asked Peter.

"Or the end of all possible worlds . . . ," said Kate.

Overhead, a lark resumed its song.

"It seems that the very foundations of time do tremble," said Gideon, "and yet, still we live and the sun does shine."

"But for how long?" said Kate abruptly.

Peter turned around to look at his friend, and all at once she seemed far older than her years. Her heart-shaped face was strained and pinched. He wanted to comfort her but did not know how. Peter glanced up at Gideon, and could not read the expression in his blue eyes, but he felt him squeeze his shoulder.

"You can't seriously think it's over?" Kate continued.

"You are overwrought, Mistress Kate, but you must not despair," said Gideon. "It is not for us to know what will come to pass—"

"But you don't know what I've seen," interrupted Kate. "This storm has moved on, but another one will come. I can sense it. This is only the beginning!"

Gideon chose not to reply but instead ushered the children into the house and closed the door behind him. He would think about what to do for the best when a new day dawned, as he hoped it would.

ACKNOWLEDGMENTS

I wrote *The Time Thief* primarily to entertain rather than inform; nevertheless, one of the joys of writing it has been the research. It has allowed me to become acquainted, either in person, or through the printed word, with all manner of individuals whose specialist knowledge has been invaluable as I have planned these novels. I should like to thank, in particular, Catherine Pappo-Musard, in whose wild, Mediterranean garden the revolutionary elements of the story took shape and where the character of Le Marquis de Montfaron came into existence. It was during a conversation with Vikki Woods, of Historic Royal Palaces, that I learned, firstly, about the introduction of kangaroos to Kew in 1792 and, secondly, about the imminent publication of Susanne Groom and Lee Prosser's book, *Kew Palace: The Official Illustrated History* (published to coincide with the opening to the public of this magnificently restored royal residence in 2006). I am grateful to Jane Monahan of the Sir John Soane's Museum for telling me about the great man's building projects in Lincoln's Inn Fields and for bringing to life the history of that most beautiful of London squares. It was in Professor Peter Linebaugh's fascinating work, *The London Hanged*, that I came across the old highwayman's ballad which, a little homesick for their own times, the Tar Man and Tom sing on the balcony of their twenty-first-century loft. The ballad first appeared in *Villainy Exploded*, 1728, by Anon, and I am grateful to Professor Linebaugh for giving me his permission to use it. Finally, I hope that the Spanish producers of that most delicious red wine, Vega Riaza, will not take it amiss that my fictional thief stole its name for his own purposes.

To all at Simon & Schuster, on both sides of the Atlantic, who have shown such commitment to this project and, in particular, to my patient, thorough, and encouraging editors, Venetia Gosling in London and Elizabeth Law in New York, my heartfelt thanks.

My grateful thanks to my inimitable literary agents at A P Watt, whose support and company have made this project even more of a pleasure. A special thank-you to Caradoc King, Christine Glover, Linda Shaughnessy, Teresa Nicholls, and, for her invaluable literary eye, Judith Evans.

My thanks, also, to all at the Department of Comparative Literature at Goldsmiths College: to Maria MacDonald; to fellow writers Emma Darwin and Ben Felsenburg; to Professors Chris Baldick, Peter Dunwoodie, and Blake Morrison, and, in particular, to Maura Dooley for her insight and encouragement (not to mention a big thank-you to young Imelda for her timely critique!).

Thank you to Phil Perry and Middleton Mann for introducing the trilogy in such an entertaining way; to Rachel Walsh and Heather Swain for reading the manuscript, and to all, as ever, at G.W., for their support and writerly expertise: Jacqui Hazell, Stephanie Chilman, Kate Harrison, Louise Voss, and Jacqui Lofthouse.

Finally, and above all, thank you Russell, Louis, and Isabella. I would not even have started the Gideon Trilogy without you.

L. B.-A.

The magic continues
with more fantasies
from Aladdin Paperbacks

The Dragon Chronicles
by Susan Fletcher

Flight of the Dragon Kyn
0-689-81515-8

Dragon's Milk
0-689-71623-0

Sign of the Dove
0-689-82449-1

Silverwing
Kenneth Oppel
1-4169-4998-4

*Mrs. Frisby and the
Rats of NIMH*
Robert C. O'Brien
A Newbery Medal Winner
0-689-71068-2

The Chronus Chronicles
The Shadow Thieves
Anne Ursu
1-4169-0588-X

May Bird and the Ever After
Jodi Lynn Anderson
1-4169-0607-X

May Bird Among the Stars
Jodi Lynn Anderson
1-4169-0608-8

The Gideon Trilogy
The Time Travelers
Linda Buckley-Archer
1-4169-1526-5

Aladdin Paperbacks
Simon & Schuster Children's Publishing
www.SimonSaysKids.com